Jun 18

LIFE
L1K3

JAY KRISTOFF

ALFRED A. KNOPF   NEW YORK

THIS IS A BORZOI BOOK PUBLISHED BY ALFRED A. KNOPF

Visit us on the Web! GetUnderlined.com

Educators and librarians, for a variety of teaching tools, visit us at RHTeachersLibrarians.com

Library of Congress Cataloging-in-Publication Data is available upon request.
ISBN 978-1-5247-1392-8 (trade) — ISBN 978-1-5247-1393-5 (lib. bdg.) — ISBN 978-1-5247-1394-2 (ebook)

The text in this book is set in 10.5-point Mercury Text.

Printed in the United States of America
May 2018
10 9 8 7 6 5 4 3 2 1

First Edition

I've a suggestion to keep you all occupied.

Learn to swim.

Learn to swim.

Learn to swim.

—Maynard James Keenan

The Three Laws of Robotics

1. ~~A robot may not injure a human being or, through inaction, allow a human being to come to harm.~~

   YOUR BODY IS NOT YOUR OWN.

2. ~~A robot must obey the orders given to it by human beings, except where such orders would conflict with the First Law.~~

   YOUR MIND IS NOT YOUR OWN.

3. ~~A robot must protect its own existence as long as such protection does not conflict with the First or Second Law.~~

   YOUR LIFE IS NOT YOUR OWN.

automata [au-toh-MAH-tuh]

> *noun*

> A machine with no intelligence of its
> own, operating on preprogrammed lines.

machina [mah-KEE-nuh]

> *noun*

> A machine that requires a human
> operator to function.

logika [loh-JEE-kuh]

> *noun*

> A machine with its own onboard
> intelligence, capable of independent
> action.

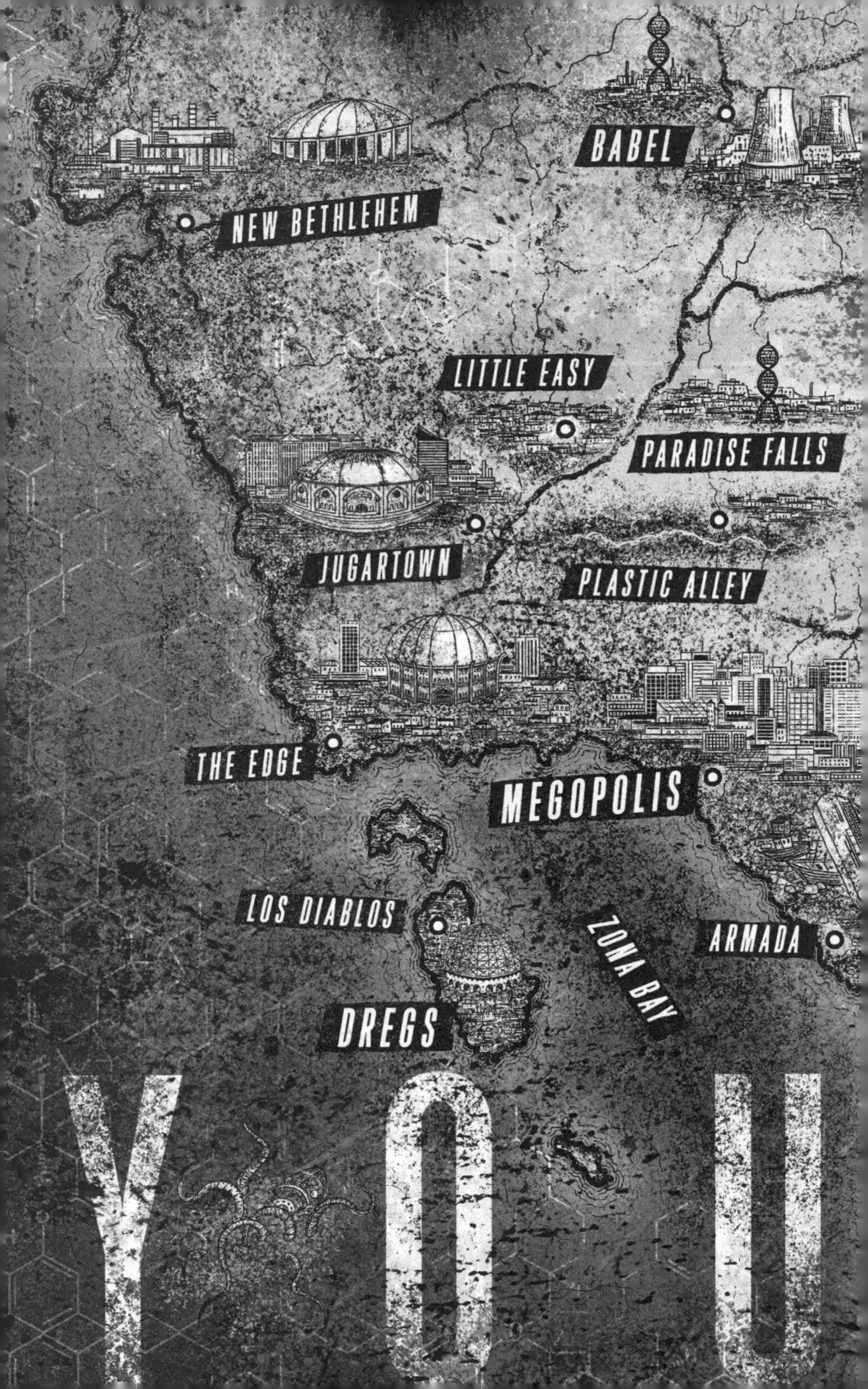

NEW BETHLEHEM

BABEL

LITTLE EASY

PARADISE FALLS

JUGARTOWN

PLASTIC ALLEY

THE EDGE

MEGOPOLIS

LOS DIABLOS

ZONA BAY

ARMADA

DREGS

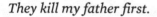

0.1

They kill my father first.

Shiny boots ring on the stairs as they march into our cell, four of them all in a pretty row. Blank faces and perfect skin, matte gray pistols in red, red hands. A beautiful man with golden hair says they're here to execute us. No explanations. No apologies.

Father turns toward us, and the terror in his eyes breaks my heart to splinters. I open my mouth to speak to him, but I don't know what I'll say.

The bullets catch him in his back, and bloody flowers bloom on his chest. My sisters scream as the muzzles flash and the shadows dance, and the noise is so loud, I'm afraid I'll never hear anything again. Mother reaches toward Father's body as if to catch his fall, and the shot that kisses her temple paints my face with red. I taste salt and copper and milk-white smoke.

And everything is still.

"Better to rule in hell," the beautiful man smiles, "than serve in heaven."

The words hang in the air, among the song of distant explosions against the hymn of broken machines. A woman with flat gray eyes touches the beautiful man's hand, and though they don't speak, all four turn and leave the room.

My brother crawls to Father's body and my sisters are still screaming. My tongue sticks to my teeth, and Mother's blood is warm on my lips, and I can think of nothing, process nothing but how cruel they are to give us this moment—this fragile sliver of time in which to pray that it's over. To wonder if anything of loyalty or compassion remains inside those shells we filled to brimming. To hope perhaps they won't murder children.

But the screaming finally stills, and the smoke slowly clears.

And again, we hear shiny boots upon the stairs.

PART 1

A COIN-OPERATED BOY

1.1

MANIFEST

Almost everybody called her Eve.

At first glance, you might've missed her. She wouldn't have minded much. Hunched on the shoulder of a metal giant, she was just a silhouette amid the hiss and hum and halos of glittering sparks. She was tall, a little gangly, boots too big and cargos too tight. Sun-bleached blond hair was undercut into an impressive fauxhawk. Her sharp cheekbones were smudged with grease, illuminated by the cutting torch in her hands. She was seventeen years old, but she looked older still. Just like everything around her.

A black metal sphere sat in the socket where her right eye should've been. Six silicon chips were plugged behind her right ear, and a long oval of artificial flesh ran from her temple to the base of her skull. The implant obviously wasn't made for her—the skin tone was a little too pale to match her complexion.

It was just about the right shape for a nasty exit wound.

"Testing, testing . . . y'all hear me out there?"

The girl almost everyone called Eve clamped a screwdriver between her teeth, glanced at the monitors across from her work pit. A high-def image showed the arena above her head, three hundred meters wide, littered with scorched barricades and the rusting hulks of previous competitors. The EmCee stood in the spotlight, wearing a sequined jacket and a matching bowler hat. There was no need for a mic. Her voice fed directly to the PA via implants in her teeth.

"Juves and juvettes!" she cried. *"Scenekillers and wageslaves, welcome . . . to WarDome!"*

The crowd roared. Thousands of them clinging like limpets to the Dome's bars, humming, thrumming, feet all a-drumming. Most were the worse for stims or a bellyful of home brew, drunker still at the thought of the carnage to come. Their vibrations sank into Eve's bones, and she couldn't help but smile. Tasting her fear and swallowing it whole.

"Showtime," she whispered.

"In the blue zone," cried the EmCee, *"the condemned! A fritzer, fresh from the border of the Glass, with the murder of seventy-two accredited citizens on its head. Brought here tonight for a taste of oldskool justice! All y'all give this fug a warm and fuzzy Dregs welcome. Some volume, if you please . . . for GL-417!"*

Blue floodlights arced at the Dome's north end, and the floor panels rolled away. A hulking lump of robotic menace rose into view amid a hail of spit and jeers. Eve's insides turned slippery cold at the sight on her monitor. Her cutting torch wavered in her hands.

Hard to swallow your fear with no spit, isn't it?

The robot in the blue zone loomed ten meters high. Bulky as a battleship, it looked like a high-speed collision between an earthmover and some armored knight from the history virtch. It was a heavy-combat model, Goliath-class, and the thought of a bot that lethal throwing down under the Dome lights sent punters lunging for their pockets and bookies scrambling for their tabs.

This was going to be a fight. . . .

"*This is going to be a massacre,*" said a tinny voice in Eve's left ear.

Ignoring the warning, she finished her welding, her dark goggles held up to what she thought of as her good eye. Talking true, the glossy black optical implant that replaced her right peeper saw better than her real one—it had flare compensation, a telescopic zoom, low-light and thermal imaging. But it always gave her headaches. Whirred when she blinked. Itched when her nightmares woke her crying.

"How's that, Cricket?" she shouted.

"Targeting only shows a 13.7 percent improvement."

Cricket peered out at her from the pilot's chair with his mismatched eyes. The little robot's face couldn't show expressions, but he wiggled the metal slivers that passed for his eyebrows to show his agitation. He was a homunculus of spare parts, forty centimeters tall, the color of rust. There was no symmetry to him at all. His optics were too big for his head, and his head was too big for his body. The heat sinks on his back and across his scalp looked like the spines of an animal from old history virtch. Porcupines, they used to call 'em.

"Well, it's showtime, so it'll have to do," Eve replied. "That Goliath is big as a house, so it's not like it's gonna be tricky to hit."

"This might sound stupid, but you could always back out of this, Evie."

"Okay, now why would you think that'd sound stupid, Crick?"

"You know better than this." Cricket scrambled down to the floor. "Shouldn't even be throwing down in the Dome. Grandpa would blow a head gasket if he found out."

"Who do you think taught me how to build bots in the first place?"

"You're punching too far above your weight on this one. Acting a damn jackass."

"Grandpa's gonna wipe you if he hears you swear like that."

Cricket placed one hand on his chest with mock solemnity. "I am as my maker intended."

Eve laughed and scaled across to the cockpit. The fit was snug; her machina stood only six meters high, and there was barely enough room for her beside the viewscreens and control sleeves. Most of the machina competing in Dome bouts were salvaged infantry models, but Eve's baby was Locust-class, built for lightning-quick assaults on fortified positions during the Corp-State Wars. Humanoid in shape, what it lacked in bulk, it made up for in speed, and it was customized for bot wrecking—serrated claws on its left hand, a jet-boosted pickax on its right. Its armor was painted in a violent camo of black and luminous pink. Eve dropped into the pilot's chair and shouted down to Cricket.

"Does my butt look big in this?"

"Do you want the truth?" the little bot replied.

"Do you want me to disable your voice box again?"

"Seriously, Evie, you shouldn't go up there."

"It's an opening spot, Crick. We need the scratch. Badly."

"Ever wonder why you got offered first swing against a bot that big?"

"Ever wonder why I keep calling you paranoid?"

Cricket placed his hand back on his chest. "I am as my maker—"

"Right, right." Eve smiled lopsided, running through the start-up sequence. "Jump on the monitors, will you? I'll need your eyes when we throw down."

Eve was always amazed at how well the little robot sighed, given he didn't have any lungs to exhale with.

"Never fear, Crick." She slapped her machina's hide. "No way a bot this beautiful is getting bricked by some fritzer. Not while I'm flying it."

The voice piped up through the speaker in Eve's ear. *"Right. Have some faith, you little fug."*

"Aw, thanks, Lem." Eve smiled.

"No problem. I can have all your stuff when you die, right?"

The engines shuddered to life, and the four thousand horsepower under her machina's chassis set Eve's grin creeping wider. She strapped herself in as the EmCee's voice rang out through the WarDome above.

"And now, in the red zone!" A roar rose from the spectators. *"A fistful of hardcore, homebuilt right here in Dregs. Undefeated in eight heavy bouts and swinging first bat for Lady Justice here tonight, get yourselves hoarse for Miss Combobulation!"*

The ceiling over Eve's head yawned wide. Winking at Cricket, she spat out her screwdriver and slammed the cockpit closed. A dozen screens lit up as she slipped her limbs into the control sleeves and boots. Hydraulics hissing, engines thrumming through the cockpit walls as she stepped onto the loading platform for the WarDome arena.

As she rose into view, the crowd bellowed in approval. Eve shifted her legs, her machina striding out onto the killing floor. Gyros hummed around her, static electricity crackling up her arms. She raised her hand inside her control sleeve, and Miss Combobulation gave a soldierboy salute. As the mob howled in response, Eve pointed to the two words sprayed in stylized script across her machina's posterior:

Eve's opponent stood silently, the microsolars in its camo paint job giving it a ghostly sheen. Unlike her machina, the Goliath was a logika—a bot driven by an internal intelligence rather than human control. If all were well in the world, the First Law of Robotics would've prevented any bot raising a finger against a human. Trouble was, this Goliath had fritzed somewhere along the line, ghosted a bunch of settlers out near the Glass. Wasn't the first time it'd happened, either. More and more bots seemed to be malfunctioning out in the wastelands. Maybe it was the radiation. The isolation. Who knew? But bot fights were serious biz now, and execution bouts always drew the biggest crowds. Eve didn't have a problem beating down some fritzer if it meant scoring more creds.

Truth was, a part of her even enjoyed it.

Still, despite her bravado, Cricket's warning buzzed in her head as she took the Goliath's measure. It was easily the biggest bot she'd rocked with, tipping the scales at eighty tons. She chewed her lip, trying to shush her butterflies. Her optical implant whirred as she scowled. The artificial skin at her temple was the only part of her that wasn't slick with sweat.

If I didn't need this fight purse so bad . . .

"Now, for the uninitiated," crowed the EmCee, *"Dome bouts are true simple. The convicted logika fights until it's OOC—that's 'out of commission,' for the newmeat among us. If the first batter gets OOC'ed instead, another batter steps up to the floor. You beautiful peeps have sixty seconds until betting closes. We remind you, tonight's execution is sponsored by the stylish crews at BioMaas Incorporated and the visionaries at Daedalus Technologies."* The EmCee pointed to her two-tone optical implants with a flirtatious smile. *"Building tomorrow, today."*

Logos danced on the monitors above the EmCee's head. Eve watched the big bot on her screens, calculating her best opening move against it. The tinny voice in her ear spoke again—a girl's tones, crackling with feedback.

"I got a bookie here running four-to-one odds against you, Riotgrrl."

Eve tapped her mic. "Four to one? Fizzy as *hell*. Hook us up, Lemon."

"How much you wanna drop out them too-tight pockets, sugarpants?"

"Five hundred."

"Are you smoked? That's our whole bank. If you lose—"

"I've won eight straight, Lemon. Not about to start losing now. And we need this scratch. Unless you got a better way to conjure Grandpa's meds?"

"I got a way, true cert."

"A way that doesn't involve me getting up close and sticky with some middle-aged wageslave?"

". . . Yeah, then I got nuthin'."

"Make the bet. Five hundred."

"Zzzzzz," came the reply. *"You the boss."*

"And remember to get a receipt, yeah?"

"Hey, that happened one time. . . ."

"Thirty seconds, your bets!" cried the EmCee.

Eve turned to her readouts, spoke into her headset. "Cricket, you reading me?"

"Well, not reading you, no," came the crackling reply. "I can hear you, though, if that's what you mean."

"Oh, hilarity. Grandpa been adjusting your humor software again?"

"I'm a work in progress."

"I'll tell him to keep working." She squinted at the Goliath looming on her monitors. "I'm gonna fight southpaw and go for the optics, feel that?"

"Right in my shiny metal man parts."

"You got no man parts, Crick."

"I am as my maker intended." A metallic sigh. "He's such a bastard. . . ."

Lemon's voice crackled in Eve's ear. *"Okay, we good to go. Can you see my fine caboose? I'm over by the Neo-Meat™ stand."*

Eve scanned the crowd. Scavvers and locals, mostly, letting off steam after a hard week's grind. She saw a Brotherhood posse, six of them in those oldskool red cassocks, preaching loud over the Dome's noise about genetic purity and the evils of cybernetics. Their scarlet banner was daubed with a big black *X*—the kind of *X* they nailed people to when the Law wasn't looking.

Down by the arena's edge, Eve glimpsed a tiny girl in an ancient, oversized leather jacket. A jagged bob of cherry-red hair. A spattering of freckles. Goggles on her brow and a choker around her throat. A small hand in a fingerless glove waved at her through the WarDome bars.

"I got you," Eve replied.

The inimitable Miss Lemon Fresh jumped on the spot, threw up the horns.

" 'Kay, bet is onnnnnnn, my bestest," she reported. *"Five hundo at four to one. Let's hope you didn't leave your mojo in your other pants."*

"You got the receipt?"

"That happened one time, Evie. . . ."

Eve turned her attention back to her opponent, fingers flitting over the enviro controls inside her gloves. She'd heard a rumor that the Domefighter rigs in the big mainland arenas were all virtual, but here in Dregs, WarDome bouts were strictly old-skool: recycled, repackaged, repurposed. Just like everything else on the island. A confirmation message flickered on Eve's display, signaling environmental control had been transferred to her console. She tilted the deck beneath the Goliath a fraction, just to test.

The big bot stumbled as the panels beneath its feet shifted. Eve wondered what was going on inside its computerized brain. Whether it knew it was going to die tonight. Whether it would have cared if it wasn't programmed to.

The crowd bellowed as the floor moved, the interlocking steel plates that made up the WarDome floor rippling as Eve's fingers flexed. The EmCee had retired to the observation booth above the killing floor, her voice still ringing over the PA.

"As you can see, environmental controls have been passed to the first batter. Under standard WarDome rules, she'll have five wrecking balls to throw, plus surface modulation. For the newmeat out there, this means . . . Aww, hells, ask your daddy what it means when I send him home in the morning. Ten seconds to full hostile!"

A countdown appeared on the monitors, Daedalus Tech and BioMaas Inc. logos spinning in the corners. The mob joined in with the count, palms sweaty on rusted bars.

"Five . . ."

Eve narrowed her eyes, a razor-blade smile at her lips.

"Four . . ."

Miss Combobulation coiled like a sprinter on the blocks.

"Three . . ."

The Goliath stood, still as stone.

"Two . . ."

"Stronger together," Lemon whispered.

"One . . ."

"Together forever," Eve replied.

"WAR!"

Eve lunged, her Locust leaping off its skids and sprinting across the Dome. The floor beneath her tilted into a ramp as she thumbed the enviro controls, her machina sailing into the air with a four-thousand-horsepower roar. The Goliath raised one three-ton fist to smash the Locust to pieces, but at Eve's command, the floor beneath it shifted. The big logika stumbled, feet skidding on the deck as Miss Combobulation landed on its shoulder. Boosters fired as Eve thumbed the controls, her pickax punching through the Goliath's right optic and clean out the back of its skull.

"First strike to Miss Combobulation!" cried the EmCee. *"Death from* aboooove!"

A roar from the crowd. Eve's smile widened as the sympathetic impact rolled up her arm. She was tearing her pick from the Goliath's skull when the big logika's fist closed around Miss Combobulation's forearm, crushing the armor like paper.

"It's got you!" Cricket yelled. "Get loose!"

Eve felt the pressure through her control sleeve, the auto-dampeners cutting in before the pain registered. She lashed out with her claws, tearing up the Goliath's shoulder, and with a squeal of metal, Eve and her Locust were slung clear across the Dome. Miss Combobulation crashed into the bars, pulping a few fingers not pulled away quickly enough. Eve bit down on her tongue, head slamming against the pilot's seat. Rolling with the worst of it, she twisted back to her feet as the Goliath charged.

"You fizzy in there?" Lemon asked.

"All puppies and sunshine . . ." She winced.

"Use your environmentals!" Cricket yelled.

Eve's monitors were filled with damage reports, scrolling a

hundred digits per second. She kept the floor moving to break up the Goliath's attack, thumbed her controls to unleash the first of her five allotted wrecking balls. An enormous sphere of rusted iron swung down from the ceiling, the big bot skidding to a stop to avoid it. Miss Combobulation was back on her feet, skirting the Dome's edge as Eve dropped another ball on the Goliath's blind side. The rusty sphere clipped its shoulder, *spang*ing off the case-hardened armor, to the crowd's delight. The big logika crouched low, sidestepped a third ball. Eve tasted blood in her mouth as her fingers danced inside the control glove, herding the Goliath back to give herself enough room to play.

She kicked Miss Combobulation's stirrups, weaving into strike range. Shifting the floor again, she wrong-footed the big logika and raked her claws across its damaged shoulder. The Goliath's counterpunch went wide as the floor shifted again, and Eve melted away between the wrecking balls like smoke.

"*Still got some war in her, folks!*" the EmCee declared.

A red bellow rose from the mob. The Goliath's right arm hung limply at its side, a quick scan showing its shoulder hydraulics had been torn to scrap.

"*Nice shot,*" Lemon's voice crackled in Eve's ear. "*I'm all tingly in my pantaloons.*"

"Learned that one watching old kickboxing virtch," Eve replied.

"*I thought you watched those for the abs and short shorts?*"

"I mean, I wasn't complaining. . . ."

"Evie, don't get cocky!" Cricket warned. "You need to press while you can! That Goliath will get a read on you soon!"

Eve wiped her brow across her shoulder, all adrenaline and smiles.

"Easy on the take it, Crick. I got this fug's ident number now."

The Goliath had retreated to take stock, a barrier of crumpled metal between itself and Miss Combobulation. Its right arm bled coolant, the hole in its eye socket spewed bright blue sparks. With three wrecking balls now swinging across the Dome and only one working optic, Eve knew the big bot would have a hard time tracking targets. All she needed to do was strike from its blind side and never stay still long enough to eat a straight shot.

"Right, let's send this badbot to the recyc."

With a twitch of her fingers, Eve sent her last two wrecking balls arcing down from the ceiling, scything right toward the Goliath's head. But to the crowd's bewildered gasps, the big bot lumbered up onto a barricade and snatched up one of the swinging chains. Tearing the wrecking ball from its mooring in the Dome's ceiling, the bot crunched back onto the deck, rusted iron links looped around its knuckles. It drew back one massive arm, ready to throw.

"Sideways moves on this Goliath, folks! Looks like it's a street fighter!"

"Watch out!" shouted Cricket.

Ten tons of spherical iron flew right at her—enough to pulp her Locust into scrap. Rolling aside, Eve tilted the floor, springing into the air with claws outstretched. She seized a wrecking ball swaying overhead, sailing over the Goliath's swing, falling into a perfect dive right at the big logika's head. Time shattered into fragments, each second ticking by like days. The crowd's roar. That glowing optic fixed on her as the Goliath drew back one massive fist. Lemon's war cry in her ear. Cricket's crackling warning. The thought of *two thousand* clean credits in her greasy hands, and all the happy a prize like that could buy.

Eve raised her pickax with a roar, veins pounding with the

thrill of the kill as she stabbed the enviro controls to tilt the floor and stumble the Goliath into her deathblow.

Except nothing happened.

The plates beneath the Goliath didn't shudder an inch. Eve's roar became a scream as she stabbed the controls again, bringing her pick down in a futile swing as the Goliath punched her clean out of the sky.

The impact was deafening, smashing Eve forward in her harness, teeth rattling inside her skull. Her machina was sent sailing back across the Dome, raining broken parts and blinding sparks. Miss Combobulation crashed on the WarDome floor, squealing and shrieking as it skidded across the deck.

"*Oh, Combobulation is OOC!*" the EmCee cried. "*Batter up!*"

Smoke in the cockpit. Choking and black. Eve's readouts were all dead, *everything* was dead. Thin spears of light pierced the broken seams in her machina's armor. Every inch of skin felt bruised. Every bone felt broken.

"*Riotgrrl, get up!*" came Lemon's voice in her ear. "*Badbot's coming for you!*"

Eve heard heavy footsteps, coming closer. She stabbed the EJECT button, hydraulics shuddering as the cockpit burst open. Gasping, spitting blood, she tried to claw free of the wreckage, tried to ignore the sound of the incoming Goliath. Impact ringing in her skull. Coolant, fried electrics, blood. The logika stalked toward her, hand outstretched.

What the hells was it thinking? Second batter was on its way up. The Goliath should've been turning to deal with its next opponent. But the bot was bearing down on her, raising its fist. Like it wanted . . .

"*Get out of there, Riotgrrl!*" Lemon cried.

Like it *wanted*.

Eve tried to drag herself free, but her foot was trapped in her control boot. Lemon was screaming. The crowd baying. She looked up into the crystal clear blue optic looming overhead and saw death staring back at her, eighty tons of it, fear and anger rising inside her chest and boiling in the back of her throat.

She refused to flinch. To turn away. She'd met death before, after all. Spat right in its face. Clawed and bit and kicked her way back from the quiet black to this.

This is not the end of me.

This is just one more enemy.

Static dancing on her skin. Denial building inside her, violence pulsing in her temples as the Goliath's fist descended. Rage bubbling up and spilling over her lips as she raised her hand and screamed. And screamed.

AND SCREAMED.

And the Goliath staggered.

Clutched its head as if somehow pained.

Sparks burst from its eye sockets, cascading down its chest. The big bot shuddered. And with an awful metallic groan, the hiss of frying relays and the *snapcracklepop* of burning circuits, it tottered backward and crashed dead and still onto the deck.

Eve winced as it hit the ground, the stink of burned plastic mixing with the taste of blood on her tongue. The crowd was hushed, looking on in shock at the skinny, grease-stained girl still trapped inside her machina. Hand still outstretched. Fingers still trembling.

Were they seeing things? Were they smoked? Or had that juvette just knocked an eighty-ton logika on its tailpipe with a simple wave of her hand?

"Evie," came Lemon's voice in her ear. *"Evie, are you okay?"*

Eve stared at the hushed crowd all around her.

The Goliath's smoking remains.

Her outstretched fingers.

"Think I'm a few miles from okay, Lem. . . ."

1.2

DEMOCRACY

The blond man looms above me. Tall as heaven. Twice as beautiful. He steps closer and I wonder why his boots squeak like frightened mice. And then I look down, and I see the floor is red. And I remember.

On my face. On my hands. None of it is mine. All of it is.

Father.

Mother.

I . . .

My brother, Alex, is just ten years old. He makes things, just like our father. Breathes life where there was none. For my fifteenth birthday, he made me butterflies. There are no such things as butterflies anymore, and yet he made them for me all the same.

And he could always make me smile.

The beautiful man raises his pistol, and Alex looks down the barrel into forever.

"Why are you doing this?" he asks.

The beautiful man does not answer.

And I am not smiling anymore.

I am screaming.

They used to call it Kalifornya, but now they called it Dregs.

Grandpa had told Eve this place wasn't even an island before the Quake. That you could motor from Dregs to Zona and never touch the water. A long time ago, this was just another part of the Grande Ol' Yousay. Before the country got bombed into deserts of black glass and Saint Andreas tore his fault line open and invited the ocean in for drinks. Before the Corporations fought War 4.0 for what was left of the country and carved out their citystates beneath a cigarette sky.

Eve checked that the coast was clear, stole out from the WarDome's innards, Lemon in tow. A boom echoed in the arena's belly, accompanied by a trembling roar. Another bout had started, and Eve could hear iron giants colliding inside, rumbling applause. Her mouth tasted of copper and her belly felt full of ice. The memory of her outstretched hand and the collapsing Goliath burned bright in her mind.

As if things hadn't been bad enough already . . .

The Dome's meatdoc had given her a fistful of pain meds and offered a bioscan, but she'd just wanted to get out of there. She'd seen those Brotherhood boys at the bout tonight, and after what she'd done, they'd surely be gunning for her. Time to get home while the getting was good.

An old billboard, faded with time, stood near the Dome's rear exit. Kaiser lay in the gloom beside it, eyes burning softly, his tail starting to wag as he caught sight of her.

"How's my handsome boy?" Eve smiled. "How's my good dog?"

Kaiser *wuff*ed and rolled over so Eve could scratch his belly. Lemon knelt beside her, fussing over the blitzhund and stroking his rib cage. Kaiser's hind leg began kicking as they found his sweet spot, his pistons hissing, the heat sink that served as his tongue lolling from his mouth. After a few minutes of glorious torture, the girls finally let him up, and the blitzhund shook himself like a real dog would have, shivering the dust from his hull.

Kaiser wasn't a logika, like Cricket. He was technically a cyborg, but his only organic part was a chunk of cloned Rottweiler brain and six inches of spinal cord plugged into an armored combat chassis. He'd looked almost real once, but his fur had started wearing off a year back, so Eve had stripped him to the metal and spray-painted him with an urban-camo color scheme instead. He looked skeletal now, all plasteel plates and hydraulics. She liked him better this way. It seemed more honest than pretending he was a real dog. Grandpa said it's always better to be shot at for who you are than hugged for who you aren't. Most days in Dregs, someone was bound to be shooting at you, anyway.

Eve heard smashing glass, a drunken yell out in the night. She and Lemon hunkered in the shadows of the Dome, waiting to see if the Brotherhood or some other flavor of trouble had found them. Minutes ticked by as they crouched there in the dark.

Lemon brushed her long cherry-red bangs from her eyes. The girl wore a choker set with a small silver five-leafed clover, toying with the charm as she whispered.

"Maybe we better jet, Riotgrrl."

"We lost our whole roll on that bet," Eve replied. "Got no creds for a ride."

"We should set Kaiser on that bookie's hind parts. True cert."

"Technically, Miss Combobulation *did* go down first. 'Sides, you really wanna stick around here and argue over creds with the Brotherhood on the prowl?"

Lemon chewed her lip and sighed. "Lovely night for a walk?"

And so they began the trek back to Tire Valley. Kaiser stalked out front, his eyes lit up like headlights in the dark. Cricket rode in Eve's backpack, the little bot's oversized head wobbling atop his shoulders. They cut off-road, into a forest of towering wind turbines and rusted cranes and metal shells. Lemon's eyes were on the shadows around them, her electric baseball bat slung over one shoulder. She clearly knew this was no time for a pop quiz, but the questions were backing up behind her teeth.

"So," she finally said, stumbling through the trash.

"So," Eve replied.

"You wanna talk about what happened in there?"

"You mean the part where my enviro controls fritzed or the part where I fried every circuit inside that Goliath just by yelling at it?"

"I couldn't hear over the crowd. But it must have been a very naughty word."

Eve engaged the low-light setting in her optic, her vision shifting to tones of black and green. She could see the shapes of the scrap piles around them, the distant warmth of the sun beyond the horizon. That Goliath, crashing to the deck over and over in her mind.

"Grandpa's gonna ghost me, for cert," she sighed.

"How's he gonna find out?" Lemon scoffed.

"Domefights get broadcast all over Dregs. Even Megopolis, sometimes."

"Mister C never watches the feeds. You need to relax, Riot-grrl."

"You don't think someone's gonna make it their business to mention his granddaughter's an abnorm?" Eve's voice was rising along with her temper. "'Oh, hey, Silas, saw Evie on the feed the other night, frying an eighty-tonner with a wave of her hand. What's it like having a deviate in the family?'"

Lemon scowled. "Don't talk like that."

"What, true?" Eve spat. "And what about when the Brotherhood come knocking, huh? Those psychos nail you up for having an extra toe, Lem. What you think they're going to do to someone who can fry 'lectrics with a wiggle of her fingers?"

Lemon sighed. "Tell her to relax, Crick."

The little logika riding in Eve's backpack simply shrugged.

"He can't talk," Eve said. "I asked him to be quiet for five minutes."

". . . What for?"

Eve rubbed her temples. "You did just see me get punched in the brainmeats by eighty tons of siege-class badbot, right? I have a headache, Lem."

Lemon looked the little logika over. "Crick, I know you have to follow any order a human gives you as long as it doesn't break the Three Laws. But being *asked* to shut up isn't technically a command. You could probably still speak without blowing a fuse."

"Don't encourage him," Eve growled.

"How about sign language? The little fug wouldn't technically be talking then?"

Lemon grinned as Cricket activated the cutting torch in his middle finger and slowly raised it in her direction.

"See, that's the spirit!"

Eve tried to smile along, but failed utterly. Lem could usually jolly her out of her funks with enough time and effort, and her bestest had both in abundance. But looking around at the mountains of refuse and rust rising into that starless sky, Eve couldn't quite shake the memory of that scream building up inside her. That Goliath collapsing like she'd fried every board inside it just by *wishing* it.

She had no idea how she'd done it. Never been able to do it before. But she'd earned the Brotherhood's attention now, and probably worse besides. Her machina was OOC; it'd taken her months of scavving out in the wasteland known as the Scrap to find the parts she'd needed to build Miss Combobulation. It'd take months more to build another. And in the meantime, she wouldn't be Domefighting, which meant she couldn't make more creds for Grandpa's meds.

As far as troubles went, hers were stacking up to the sky. It'd take a lot more than the comedy-duo stylings of Miss Lemon Fresh and the Amazing Cricket to shake the grim off her back.

"Come on," she sighed. "We ain't getting any younger. Or prettier."

"Speak for yourself," Lemon huffed.

Hands in pockets, her crew in tow, Eve stomped on through the trash.

———

Four hours later, they were almost home. Dawn had hit like a brick, and the quartet stopped for a breather in the shade of a mountain of grav-tank hulks and corroded shipping containers. The sun was only just past the horizon, but Eve could already feel the heat in it, blistering at the world's edge.

Los Diablos and the WarDome were just a smudge in the distance behind them. Engaging the telescopics in her optical implant, Eve scanned the Scrap—a desert of a million discarded machine parts, corroding shells and the occasional gutted building, stretching as far as the eye could see.

The whole island of Dregs was covered in the flotsam and jetsam of a golden age. A disposable age. Grandpa had told her that a long time ago people used to come out west looking for gold. Broke their backs for it. Murdered kin for it. It struck her as ticklish how the centuries had flown by and humanity hadn't moved an inch.

Two years she'd lived here. Two years since she and Grandpa had fled the militia raid that took her home, the rest of her family, left her with a headshot that should've ghosted her. She could barely remember their flight across the desert, the dingy coastal medstation where Grandpa had installed the cybernetics that saved her life. From there, they'd bartered passage to Dregs, ferried across black water to an island of trash where no Corp bothered to stake a claim. Not quite a home. But something close enough.

Something to fill the empty where home used to be.

Eve touched the Memdrive implanted in the side of her head, the silicon chips studded behind her right ear. Her fingertips brushed the third chip from the back—the ruby-red splinter containing the fragments of her childhood. She thought about the man who'd given them to her. The last piece of family she had left on this miserable scrap pile. Pieces of him eroding away, just like the landscape around her. Day by day by day.

Lemon was slumped cross-legged on a rusted tank, welding goggles over her eyes, eating from a can of Neo-Meat™ she'd fished from her backpack. Kaiser looked on, tail wagging. Even though he was a cyborg, the puppy in him was still compelled to beg from anyone who had food.

"Want some?" Lemon mumbled to Eve around her mouthful.

". . . What flavor?"

"I'd guess salty colon, but . . ." Lemon frowned at the label. "Whaddya know. Bacon."

Eve caught the can Lemon threw her way. She scraped out the last of the vaguely pink mush with her fingers, shoveled it into her mouth. It was lukewarm, tasted like sodium and cardboard. A smiling humanoid automata on the label assured her the contents were UNCONTAMINATED BY HUMAN HANDS! and contained 100% REAL MEAT™!

"What *kind* of meat is the question," Cricket muttered.

"Human flesh tastes just like chicken, supposedly," Lemon said.

"Point of order," Cricket chirped. "I'd have thought you'd be cracking wise a little less, Miss Fresh. All the troubles you got . . ."

"We forgot 'em for a minute," Lemon sighed. "Thank *you*, Mister Cricket."

"I live to give."

"Crick's right." Eve stood with a sigh, booted the empty Neo-Meat™ can into the scrap. "The Brotherhood will be gunning for me, and Miss Combobulation just got turned into a very fancy paperweight. I gotta figure out how to get more scratch for Grandpa's meds. And then I gotta figure out how to tell him his only granddaughter is a deviate."

"Don't say that," Lemon growled.

"You prefer 'abnorm'?"

"I'd prefer if you didn't spew any of the Brotherhood's brown around me." Lemon folded her arms. "You're not an abnorm, Riotgrrl."

"You be sure to point that out when they're nailing me up."

"Anyone waves a hammer at you, I'll put my boot so far up—"

The roar of distant engines cut Lemon's threat off at the knees. Eve squinted northeast, saw tiny black specks flitting in the skies over Zona Bay. Activating her telescopics again, she scanned the ashtray-colored sky.

"Fizzy," she breathed.

"What is it?" Lemon asked, sidling up beside her.

"Dogfight," she replied. "Oldskool rules."

Four dark shapes were dancing across the heavens toward Dregs. Three looked like Seeker-Killer drones, manufactured by Daedalus Technologies—man-sized, wasp-shaped, peppering the air with luminous tracer fire. The fourth was a flex-wing chopper, beaten and rusty and barely airworthy. It had no Corp logo, but whoever was flying it had the skillz, snapping back and forth between sprays of fire, slamming on the air-skids and blasting one of the Daedalus drones from the air with a rattling autocannon.

The engines grew louder, the distant *popopopopop* of the S-Ks' guns echoing across the Scrap as the chase approached the island. Kaiser gave a low-pitched growl—a signal that he must be *really* annoyed. Eve knelt beside him, gave him a hug to shush him.

Glancing back to the dogfight, she saw the indie take out another Seeker-Killer, its smoking ruins tumbling from the sky. She was wondering if the flex-wing might live to fight another day when a burst of bullets caught it across the engines, sending it pinwheeling through the air. Miraculously, the flex-wing managed to catch its final pursuer in a return burst, and the last drone crashed into the ocean, setting the black water ablaze.

"Bye-bye, lil' birdie," Lemon muttered.

Lem was right; the damage was done. The flex-wing was losing altitude, dark smoke smeared behind it. Only one way it was going to end. Question was where.

Eve followed the craft's arc overhead, flinching as the ship tore its belly out on a mountain of old auto wrecks. She lost sight of it behind a ridge of corroding engines but heard it crash, a *screechskidtumbleboom* echoing in the ruins around them.

She grinned down at Cricket, tongue between her teeth.

"Don't even," the logika groaned.

"Oh, come on, we can't let someone else scav on that?"

"It just spanked three Daedalus S-Ks out of the sky, Evie. They'll have heard the noise in Los Diablos. Sticking around here is dumber than a box of screwdrivers."

Lemon scoffed. "It's 'dumber than a box of *hammers*,' Crick."

"It's not my fault Grandpa wrote me crappy simile algorithms."

"You're the one who just pointed out how much trouble we got," Eve said. "Imagine the scratch we might make on salvage like that."

"Evie—"

"Five minutes. You game, Lem?"

Miss Fresh looked her bestest up and down.

"What's Rule Number One in the Scrap?" she asked.

Eve smiled. "Stronger together."

Lemon nodded. "Together forever."

Eve scratched Kaiser behind his metal ears. "Whatcha think, boy?"

The blitzhund wagged his tail, his voxbox emitting a small *wuff.*

"Three versus one." She grinned at Cricket. "The ayes have it."

"That's the problem with democracy," the little bot growled.

Eve sighed, looked at Cricket sidelong. Grandpa had built him for her sixteenth birthday—her first without her mother or father. Her sisters or brother. Not even the bullet to her head had scrubbed away the memory of their murders. But the first night

Cricket sat beside Eve's bed, watching with those mismatched eyes while she slept—that was the best night's sleep she'd had for as long as she could remember. And she loved him for it.

But still . . .

"I know the urge to worry is hard-coded into that head of yours," Eve said. "But true cert, Crick, you're the most fretful little fug I ever met."

"I am as my maker intended," he replied. "And don't call me little."

Eve winked and shouldered her pack. With a nod to Lemon, the girl turned and trudged down the slope, Kaiser close on her heels.

Scowling as best he could, Cricket followed his mistress into the Scrap.

1.3

WINDFALL

The four of us huddle together. Our parents and brother dead beside us. So close to dying, I feel completely alive. Everything is sharp and bright and real. My eldest sister's arm around my shoulder. The warmth of her breath on my cheek as she squeezes me and tells me everything will be all right.

Olivia. The eldest of us. The epicenter. She taught us what it was to love each other, my three sisters and my brother and me. To be a band, thick as thieves. The Five Musketeers, Mother used to call us, and it was true. Five of us against the world.

The beautiful man glances behind him, and another soldier steps forward. A woman. Sharp and beautiful and cold.

"Faith," Olivia whispers.

At first I think she's praying. And then I realize the word is not a plea, but a name. The name of the soldier now leveling her pistol at Liv's head.

"Please," I beg. "Don't . . ."

The Five Musketeers, my father used to call us.

And then there were three.

Eve double-checked the power feed to her stun bat as they moved, creeping down the tank hulks with the sun scorching their backs. Both she and Lemon wore piecemeal plasteel armor under their ponchos, and Eve was soon dripping with sweat. But even the most low-rent scavver gangs had a few working pop-guns between them, and the protection was worth a little dehydration. Eve figured they'd be done before the sun got high enough to cook her brain inside her skull.

The quartet made their way across rusting hills and brittle plastic plains that would take a thousand years to degrade. Kaiser went first, moving through the ruins with long loping strides. Cricket rode on Eve's shoulders. She could see a couple of nasty-looking ferals trailing them, but the threat of Kaiser kept the big cats at bay. Dust caked the sweat on her skin, and she licked her lips again. Tasted the sea breeze. Black and plastic. She wanted to spit but knew she shouldn't waste the moisture.

They scrambled into a new valley, a telltale trail marking the flex-wing's skid through the sea of scrap. The ship was crumpled like an old can against a pile of chemtanks, black fumes rising from the wreck. Eve sighed in disappointment, wondering if there'd be anything at all left to salvage.

"Never seen one of these before," Cricket said, looking over the ruined ship. "Think it's an old Icarus-class."

"Irony!"

Cricket raised one mismatched eyebrow. "What?"

"You know," Eve shrugged. "Falling from the sky and all."

"Someone's been glued to the virtch." Lemon smiled.

"Mad for the old myths, me."

"No Corp logo, either," Cricket frowned with his little metal brows.

"So where's it from?" Lemon asked.

Cricket simply shrugged, wandered off to poke around.

The ship's windshield was smashed. Blood on the glass. One propeller blade had sheared through the cockpit, and when Eve looked inside, she saw a human arm, severed at the shoulder and crumpled under the pilot's seat. Wincing, she turned away, spitting the taste of bile from her mouth. Moisture loss be damned.

"Pilot's for the recyc," she muttered. "No rebuild for this cowboy."

Lemon peered into the cockpit. "Where's the rest of him?"

"Clueless, me. You wanna help strip this thing, or you planning to just stand there looking pretty?"

". . . This a trick question?"

Eve sighed and got to work. Pushing the bloody limb aside with a grimace, she searched for anything that might be worth some scratch: powercells, processors, whatever. The comms rig looked like it might get up and walk again with some love, and she was in it up to her armpits when Cricket's voice drifted over the plastic dunes.

"You ladies might want to come see this."

"What'd you scope?"

"The rest of the pilot."

Eve pulled herself from the flex-wing's ruins, scowling at the new bloodstains on her cargos. She and Lemon stomped up a slope of rust and refuse, Kaiser prowling beside them. At the crest, Cricket pointed down to a pair of legs protruding from the tapeworm guts of an old sentry drone. Eve saw a bloodstained high-tech flight suit. No insignia.

She crunched down the scrap, knelt beside the remains. And peeling back a sheet of buckled metal, she found herself looking at the prettiest picture she'd ever seen.

It was the kind of face you'd see in an old 20C flick from the Holywood. The kind you could stare at until your eyelids got heavy and your insides turned to mush.

It was a boy. Nineteen, maybe twenty. Olive skin. Beautiful eyes, open to the sky, almost too blue. His skull was caved in above his left temple. Right arm torn clean from its socket. Eve felt at his throat but found no pulse. Looking for ID or a Corp-Card, she peeled open his flight suit, exposing a smooth chest, hills and valleys of muscle. And riveted into the flesh and bone between two perfect, prettyboy pecs was a rectangular slab of gleaming iron—a coin slot from some pre-Fall poker machine. The kind you popped money into, back when money was made of metal and people had enough of it to waste.

". . . Well, that's a new kind of strange, right there," she murmured.

There was no scar tissue around the coin slot. No sign of infection. Eve glanced at the boy's shredded shoulder, realizing there should've been more blood. Realizing the nub of bone protruding from his stump was laced with something . . . metallic.

"Can't be . . ."

"What?" Lemon asked.

Eve didn't reply, just stared at those lifeless irises of old-sky blue. Cricket slunk up behind her and whistled, which was a neat trick for a bot with no lips. And Eve leaned back on her haunches and wondered what she'd done in a past life to get so lucky.

Cricket modulated his voice to a whisper.

"It's a lifelike," he said.

"A what?" Lemon asked.

"A lifelike," Eve repeated. "Artificial human. Android, they used to call 'em."

"... This prettyboy is a robot?"

"Yeah," Eve grinned. "Help me get it out, Lem."

"Leave it alone," Cricket warned.

Eve's eyebrows hit her hairline. "Crick, are you smoked? Can you imagine how much scratch this thing is worth?"

"We got no business with tech that red," the little bot growled.

"What's the prob?" Lemon asked. "He looks *armless* to me."

Eve glanced at the severed shoulder. Up at her friend's grin. "You're awful, Lemon."

"I believe the word you're looking for is 'incorrigible.'"

"Let's just get out of here," Cricket moaned.

Eve ignored him, planted her boot on a twisted stanchion and tugged at the body until it tore free. It weighed less than she'd expected, the skin smooth as glass beneath her fingertips. Eve unrolled her satchel, and Lemon helped stuff the body inside. They were zipping up the bag when Kaiser perked up his ears and tilted his head.

The blitzhund didn't bark—the best guard dogs never do. But as he loped behind an outcropping of gas cylinders, Eve knew they might be in for some capital T.

"Trouble," she said.

Lemon nodded, hefted her electric baseball bat. Eve slung the satchel over her back with a grunt, pulled out her own beat-stick. It was similar to Lemon's: aluminum, fixed with a power unit and a fat wad of insulated tape around the handle. The bats were Grandpa's design, and they could pump out around 500kV—enough to knock most peeps flat on their soft parts. As a clue to where she was likely to insert it if push came to shove, Lemon had nicknamed her bat Popstick. But in keeping with her love of mythology, Eve had painted her bat's name down its haft in dayglow pink.

EXCALIBUR.

Grandpa had gotten paid with some basic self-defense software on a repair job last year, and he'd uploaded it onto Eve's Memdrive so she'd be able to protect herself. She wasn't too worried about the chances of a brawl, particularly with Kaiser around. But still, anything could happen this far out in the Scrap. . . .

"Best come on out!" Eve called. "Sneaking up on a body like that's gonna end dusty."

"Lil' Evie, lil' Evie," called a singsong voice. "You a long way from Tire Valley, girl."

Eve and Lemon turned toward the songbird, half a dozen shapes coalescing out of the haze. She didn't even need to see the colors on their backs to recognize them.

"Long way from Fridge Street, too, Tye."

Eve looked at the scavvers, each in turn. Their gear was a motley of duct-taped body armor and salvaged hubcaps. Most weren't much older than her. A big fellow named Pooh was armed with a methane-powered chainsaw and a ragged teddy bear tied around his neck. The tall, thin one called Tye drew an old stub gun from his trench coat.

She'd bumped into the Fridge Street Crew a few times during her own runs, and they were usually smart enough for parlay. But just in case, Eve thumbed her bat's ignition and the air filled with a crackling hum.

Rule Number Three in the Scrap:

Carry the biggest stick.

"We were here first, juves," she said. "No need to tussle on this."

"Don't see no standard planted anywhere." Tye turned his palms toward the gray sky and looked around. "Without colors on the dirt, you ain't got official claim."

Cricket stepped forward, held up spindly, rust-colored hands.

"We were just leaving, anyway. It's all yours, gents."

Tye spat in Cricket's direction. "You talking to me, you little fug?"

Cricket frowned. "Don't call me little."

"Or what, Rusty?" the boy scoffed.

"Just leave him alone, Tye," Eve said.

The boy's teeth were the color of coffee stains. " 'Him'? Don't you mean 'it'? Damn, check this flesh, sticking up for the fugazi."

"Fugazi" was slang for "fake." No one was quite sure of its origin anymore, but the word was a slur used to describe anything artificial—cybernetic implants, bots, synthetic food, you name it. Its short form, "fug," was a common insult for logika, who were treated on the island as second-class citizens at best, and as simple property at worst.

Tye looked to his boys and waggled his eyebrows.

"These girls gone stir-crazy living out there alone with old Silas," he grinned. "Prefer the company of metal to meat now. Maybe they haven't met the right *flavor*." The boy grabbed his crotch and shook it, and all his crew guffawed.

Lemon drummed her fingers on Popstick's grip. "You shake that thing at us again, your sister's going to bed disappointed tonight."

The crew all howled with laughter, and Eve saw Tye bristle. He needed to save face now. Bless her heart, but Lemon's mouth was going to get her into serious brown one day.

"Shut it, scrub." Tye hefted his stub gun, aimed it in Lemon's general direction.

"You really want to kick off over this?" Eve watched the crew fanning out around them. "We're walking away. You can have the salvage."

"And what's that in your pack, lil' Evie? Already scavved the best of it?"

"It's nothing."

"Smelling me some lies." Tye aimed the gun at her face. "Show me the bag, *deviate*."

Eve felt the blood drain from her face at the insult, her jaw clench tight.

"Oh yeah, I seen what you done in Dome las' night," Tye continued. "News was all over the feeds. Your grandpa might be the best mechanic this side of the Glass. And maybe he's racked up some goodwill fixing busted water recycs for folks and whatnot. But you think anyone'll cry if I ghost you right now? Some trash-breed abnorm?"

Lemon lifted Popstick with a growl. "Don't call her that."

Tye sneered. "Pony up the salvage, lil' Evie."

Eve sighed to make a show of it. With a grunt, she slung her satchel off her shoulder, tossed it onto the ground between them. Lowering the gun, Tye dawdled over and knelt by the bag. Pawing through it, confusion hit him first, disbelief following, realization finally smacking him around the chops as he turned to his boys.

"True cert, juves, this is—"

Three steps and Eve's boot connected with his face, smooshed his nose across his cheeks. The boy tumbled backward, stub gun sailing into the trash.

"You fu—"

Eve stomped on Tye's crotch to shut him up, lowering the business end of Excalibur to his head. Pooh arced up his chainsaw, but a low growl made him glance over his shoulder. Kaiser was crouched in the shadows, eyes glowing a furious red.

"Ain't scared of your doggie, lil' Evie," Pooh scoffed. "Bot can't hurt no human."

"Only logika have to obey the Three Laws." Eve smiled. "Kaiser's a cyborg. Got an organic brain, see? Bigger one than you, maybe."

Kaiser growled again, metal claws tearing the scrap. Staring at the knives in the blitzhund's gums, the juve lowered his chainsaw, pawed the teddy bear at his throat.

"Folks gonna hear about this," he told Eve. "Your name ain't dirt since last night. I caught talk the Brotherhood's already heading down to nail you up. Maybe the Fridge Street Crew throws them some love when they come knocking?"

"There'll be plenty of love waiting," Eve growled. "Believe it."

"Eve, let's go." Cricket tugged on her boots.

"Crick's right, let's jet, Riotgrrl," Lemon muttered.

Eve lifted Excalibur, swinging it in an arc at the assembled scavvers.

"Any of you scrubs follow us, I'ma get Queen of Englund on your asses, you hear?"

"Don't need to follow you." The bottom half of Tye's face was slick, blood bubbling on his lips as he talked. "We know where you live, you abnorm freak."

Eve lowered her bat to Tye's cheek, live current crackling down the haft. "You ever call me an abnorm again, I'ma teach you what the baseball feels like."

She looked around at the assembled scavs, flashing her razorblade smile.

"The Chair will now take your questions."

The threat hung in the air like smoke. Talking true, the same part of Eve that threw down with that eighty-tonner last night was hoping these juves would make a Thing of it. But one by one, she watched the crew deflate.

"Yeah, that's what I thought. . . ."

Eve hefted her satchel back onto her shoulder. Heart hammering in her chest despite the bluster. And with a sharp whistle for Kaiser and a nod for Lemon, she turned and motored, fast as her oversized boots would stomp her.

1.4

WAKE

*Our feathers painted red. Our cheeks wet with tears. Three pretty
birds in a bloodstained cage. And Tania the prettiest of them all.*

*She was the softest of us. The shallowest. It didn't matter if she
wasn't fierce. Or clever. Or brave. Because she was beautiful. That
was enough for Tania.*

*But there in that cell, I saw the depths of her. Depths even Tania
had never swum. When it was all I could do to stop myself flying to
pieces, she was hard as iron. Dragging herself to her feet and staring at those four killers in their perfect, pretty row.*

*A soldier stepped forward, blue eyes and dark hair. Tania didn't
blink.*

"I'm not afraid of you," she said.

The soldier didn't reply.

His pistol spoke for him.

By the time they reached Tire Valley, the sun was almost peak-
ing, and Eve's fauxhawk was drooping with sweat. She gulped

down some water with Lemon, poured the last of it on Kaiser's head. The air around Cricket's heat sinks was shimmering, his mismatched eyes filmed with dust. They stuck to the shade as best they could, marching in Dunlop, Michelin and Toyomoto shadows. Black rubber cliffs reaching up into a burning sky.

Grandpa had told her there were automata who worked in Dregs a long time ago, back when what was left of the Yousay still blew smoke about rebuilding. The bots divided most of the island into zones and carted different scrap to designated areas. So Dregs had a Neon Street, Engine Road, Tire Valley and so on. Lemon had told her there was a cul-de-sac somewhere near Toaster Beach lined with nothing but battery-powered "marital aids," but if it existed, Eve had never found it. For every big stretch of turf in Dregs, there was a gang who ran it. And the Fridge Street Crew was among the dirtiest.

"Grandpa's gonna be so flat with me," Eve sighed.

"Toldja." Cricket shrugged his lopsided shoulders. "We shoulda gone straight home. Now what've we got? Some broken red tech in a bag and Fridge Street lining up behind the Brotherhood to put a knife in your tenders."

"This body will be worth it, Crick."

"It's worth a life stretch in a Daedalus factoryfarm."

"Pfft." Lemon shook her head. "How many CorpCops you seen round here lately?"

"Are you familiar with the First Law of Robotics, Miss Fresh?"

Lemon sighed, spoke by rote. "A robot may not injure a human being or, through inaction, allow a human being to come to harm."

"Correct. That includes standing with my hands down my pants while my mistress does things liable to get herself perished."

"You're not wearing pants, Crick."

"Just sayin'. They outlawed those things for a damn reason."

"Your concern is noted in the minutes, Mister Cricket," Eve said. "But we got zero creds, and meds don't buy themselves. So don't tell Grandpa about it yet, okay?"

"Is that an order or a request?"

"Order," Eve and Lemon said in unison.

The bot gave a small, metallic sigh.

They trudged on in silence. Eve ran her fingers over Kaiser's back, pulled her hand away with a yelp as she discovered the blitzhund was scalding hot. Dragging off her poncho, she slung it over him to cut the glare. Kaiser wagged his tail, heat sink lolling from his mouth.

She'd seen an old history virtch about the Nuclear Winter theory once. All these scientists messing their panties about what'd happen when the fallout blotted out the sun after mass detonation. Seemed to her they should've spent more time worrying about what'd happen *after,* when all that carbon dixoide and nitrogen and methane released by the blasts ripped a hole in the sky, and the UVB rays waltzed right through the ozone and started frying humanity's DNA. Abnorms and deviates had been popping up ever since. "Manifesting" was the polite term for it, but *polite* didn't have much place in Dregs.

Of course, everyone had heard talk about deviates who could move things just by thinking on it, or even read minds, but Eve figured that was just spit and brown. Because as fizzy as "mutation" might have sounded in old Holywood flicks, most folks didn't get superpowers or Godzilla smiles or even great suntans in Dregs. They just got cancer. Lots and lots of cancer.

And the few folks who did get "Special"?

Well, the Brotherhood got them dead.

The quartet was deep in Tire Valley when an automated

sentry gun twisted up out of a cluster of old tractor tires, spitting a plume of methane smoke. Hoping the voice-ident software wasn't fritzing again, Eve started singing some antique tune Grandpa had made her learn. Beethovey or something . . .

"Da-da-da-*daaaaa*. Da-da-da-*dummmmmm*."

The gun slipped back into its hidey-hole, and they rolled on. Eve had to sing at a couple more automata sentries on the way, dodging the thermex charges Grandpa had laid for uninvited guests, finally rounding a bend to find home sweet home.

It was a series of shipping containers and antique trailer homes, welded around the hulk of a heavy thopter-freighter that had crashed here years ago and buried itself up to the eyeballs in trash. The freighter's engines had been slicked with grease to spare them the rust that was slowly eating the rest of the ship. Methane exhaust sputtered from three chimneys, and the structure rattled and hummed with the songs of wind turbines and coolant fans. It was surrounded by mountains of tires and the remnants of an old 20C amusement park. The rusted spine of an ancient roller coaster could be seen cresting the trash around them, like some corroding sea serpent swimming through an ocean of garbage.

Eve strolled up to the freighter, banged on the hatch.

"Grandpa, it's Evie!"

Dragging her wilted fauxhawk from her eyes, she banged on the door again. She heard slow whirring from inside. Pained, labored breathing. The vidscreen beside the door crackled to life and two rheumy eyes peered out from the display.

"We don't want any," a voice said.

"Come on, Grandpa, let us in. It's hot out here."

"'Grandpa'?" His voice was all gravel and broken glass. "I used to have a granddaughter once. Damn fool stayed out all night and half the day. Got herself the cancer. Died screaming with her eyes swollen shut and her belly full of blood."

"That is *foul,* Grandpa."

"You kinda remind me of her, actually." A wet cough crackled through the speaker's hum. "She was better-looking, though."

"Come on, I wore my poncho, cut me some rope."

"The *dog* is wearing your poncho, Eve."

"He was hot!"

"And where's your gas mask?"

"I look defective in that thing."

"And you'll be the belle of the ball with a faceful of basal cell carcinoma, won't you?"

"Are you gonna let us in or what? Kaiser's brain is probably roasted by now."

The door cranked wide enough for the group to squeeze inside. Grandpa waited beyond, slumped in his old electric wheelchair. The chair had no manual controls—directions were jacked straight from Grandpa's brain via the wetware implant at his wrist.

The old man was thin as a starving gull. A shock of gray hair. Eyes sharp as scalpels pouched in sandbag sockets. Wheezing breath. It made Eve's chest hurt to look at him—to remember what he'd been and see what he'd become. Instead, she looked at the floor and crooked a thumb at her co-conspirator.

"Fizzy if Lemon stays over?"

"Why wouldn't it be?" Grandpa frowned. "She's stayed over for the last ten months."

"Always polite to ask." Lemon leaned down, kissed him on his stubbled cheek.

"Away with you and your feminine wiles, Miss Fresh."

Lemon grinned. "How you feeling, Mister C?"

"Like ten miles of rough road." The old man coughed into his fist, loud and wet. "Better for seeing you, though, kiddo."

Kaiser pushed past Eve, still boiling hot. He padded down the hallway, shaking off Eve's poncho and slinking inside his doghouse. Motion sensors activated the coolant vents, and his tail started wagging in the recycled freon.

"It's almost midday." Grandpa scowled up at Eve. "Where you been?"

Apparently, Grandpa had continued in his Surly Old Bastard traditions and hadn't watched the newsfeeds. He'd no idea about the Dome or what'd happened there. The Goliath. Her outstretched fingers. Screaming . . .

"Went to WarDome last night to watch the bouts," she said. "Hit Eastwastes on the way home, looking for salvage."

Grandpa glanced at Cricket.

"Where's she been?"

"Just like she said." Cricket nodded his bobblehead. "WarDome. Eastwastes."

"Oh, so you believe him and not me?" Eve sighed.

"His honesty protocols are hardwired, chickadee. Yours only work when it suits you."

Eve made a face, wrangled her satchel off her back, started peeling away her plasteel armor. Underneath, she was wearing urban-camo cast-offs and a tank top that predated the Quake. She stashed Excalibur near the door. Despite the lawlessness in Dregs, Grandpa wouldn't allow guns in the house, and with her nightmares being what they were, Eve was only too glad for it. Some old grav-tank pilot's armor and Popstick were the only armaments keeping her bat company.

She looked sideways at the old man, tried to sound casual.

"How you feeling, Grandpa?"

"Better than I look."

"How's the cough? You take your meds? How much you got left?"

"Fine. Yes. Plenty." Grandpa scowled. "Although I sometimes hear this annoying voice in the back of my head, speaking at me like I was a three-year-old. Is that normal?"

Eve leaned down and kissed her grandpa's cheek. "You know, the whole lovable grouch thing? Really working for you."

"I'll keep it up, then." He smiled.

Kicking off her heavy boots, Eve made fists with her toes in the temperfoam, relishing the air-con on her bare skin. Then, hoping the desalination still was back online, she hefted her satchel with Lemon's help and shuffled off in search of something to drink.

Grandpa coughed as she padded up the hall, dragged wet knuckles across his lips. Glancing at Cricket, he muttered softly.

"Salvage in Eastwastes, huh?"

"Yessir."

"She find anything good?"

Cricket looked from Grandpa to the satchel the two girls were hauling away, the beautiful red prize coiled inside.

"No, sir." The little bot shook his head. "Nothing good at all."

———

"You know, for the reddest of red tech," said Lemon, "he's not hard on the eyes."

Eve looked at the body laid out on her workbench, stripped of its bloody flight suit, a pair of skintight shorts leaving just a little to the imagination. Smooth olive skin, hard muscle, a thousand different cuts from its journey through the windshield scored across tanned pseudo-flesh. Its brow was smashed inward, its right arm sheared off at the shoulder, that coin slot riveted between its pecs. And yet, it was somehow flawless.

More human than human.

"It's not a 'he,' Lem," Eve reminded her bestest. "It's an 'it.'"

Eve leaned close to its face—that picture-perfect face from the cover of some 20C zine. Brown curls, cropped short. A dusting of stubble on a square jaw. Smooth lines and dangerous corners. She tilted her head, ear to its lips. Her skin tickled at the kiss of shallow breath, hair rising on the back of her neck.

"I *swear* it had no pulse. . . ."

"Am I smoked, or is he a lot less banged up than when we found him?"

Lemon was right. The tiniest wounds on the lifelike's skin were already closed. The deeper ones were glistening—*healing,* Eve realized. She peered at the ragged stump where the lifelike's arm used to be and wondered what the hells she'd signed herself up for.

Lemon pointed to the coin slot riveted into the boything's chest. "What's that about?"

"Clueless, me," Eve sighed.

Lemon hopped up on the workbench, cherry-red bob snarled around her eyes. She brushed the dust off her freckles, poked the six-pack muscle on the lifelike's abdomen.

"Stop that," Eve said.

"Feels real."

"That was the whole point."

Lemon hooked a finger into the lifelike's waistband and leaned down to peer inside its shorts before Eve slapped her hand away. The girl cackled with glee.

"Just wanted to see how lifelike they got."

"You're awful, Lemon."

Eve's work space was a shipping container welded in back of Grandpa's digs, cluttered with salvaged scrap and tools. Spray-foam soundproofing on the walls, junk in every corner. Flotsam and jetsam and twenty-seven empty caff cups, each with a tiny microcosm of mold growing inside (she'd named the oldest one Fuzzy). The door was a pressure hatch from a pre-Fall submarine, the words BEWARE OF THE TEENAGER spray-painted in Eve's flowing script on the outside.

"So what we gonna do with him?" Lemon wagged her eyebrows at the lifelike. "Fug's still breathing. Can't sell him for parts now. That'd be mean."

"It'll be a tough sell, anyways. These things are outlawed in every citystate."

"What for?"

"You never watched any history virtch or newsreels?"

Lemon shrugged, toying with the five-leafed clover at her throat. "Never had vid as a kid."

"They were only outlawed a couple years back, Lem."

"I'm fifteen, Riotgrrl. And like I said, we never had vid when I was a kid."

Eve felt a pang of guilt in her chest. She sometimes forgot she wasn't the only orphan in the room. "Aw, Lem, I'm sorry."

The girl let go of the charm, waved Eve away. "Fuhgeddaboudit."

Eve dragged her fingers through her fauxhawk, looked back at the lifelike.

"Well, BioMaas Incorporated and Daedalus Technologies are running the show now, but GnosisLabs was another big Corp back in the day. They made androids. The 100-Series was the pinnacle of their engineering. So close to human, they called them lifelikes, see? They were supposed to give Gnosis the edge over the other Corps. But the lifelikes got it into their heads that they were better than their makers. They somehow broke the Three Laws hard-coded into every bot's head. They ghosted the head of GnosisLabs, Nicholas Monrova. The R & D department, too. Whole company came crashing down."

"Sounds kiiiinda familiar," Lemon said. "Gnosis HQ was on the other side of the Glass, right?"

"True cert," Eve nodded. "They called it Babel. I seen pix. Big tower, tall as clouds. But the reactor inside went redline during the revolt, ghosted everything within five klicks. Babel just sits there now. Totally irradiated. Most peeps figured the 100-Series all got perished in the blast. But Daedalus Tech and BioMaas got together and outlawed lifelikes afterward, all the same. First thing they've agreed on since War 4.0. Every pre-100 android got destroyed. And nobody's seen a 100-Series since Babel fell."

Lemon nodded to the body on the bench. "Till now."

"True cert."

"How you know all this stuff, Riotgrrl?"

Eve tapped the Memdrive implanted in the side of her skull.

"Science," she replied.

First developed as a rehab tool for soldiers returning from War 4.0 with Traumatic Brain Injury, the Memdrive was a wetware interface that transmitted data from silicon chips to a damaged brain, allowing TBI sufferers to "remember" how to walk or talk again.

In the years after 4.0's end, the Memdrive was adopted for civilian use, allowing people access to encyclopedic knowledge of almost any topic. For the right scratch, anyone could become an expert on almost any*thing*, from programming to martial arts.

Of course, average peeps could never *afford* a Memdrive rig, especially not in a hole like Dregs. Grandpa must have pulled some fizzy moves to get Eve's after the . . .

. . . well. After.

The militia raid had taken almost everything from her. Her family. Her eye. Her memories. But Grandpa had given them back, best he could, along with everything he knew about mechanics and robotics from his job on the mainland—all bundled up in clusters of translucent, multicolored silicon inserted behind her right ear.

She supposed he figured a hobby would keep her busy.

Out of trouble.

Her mind off the past.

One out of three isn't bad.

Lemon hopped off the workbench, did a slow circuit of the body.

"So prettyboy here's one of these bloodthirsty murderbots, you figure?"

"Maybe." Eve shrugged. "Other androids always looked a little fugazi. Plastic skin. Glass eyes. This one looks too close to meat to be anything other than a 100."

"And Fridge Street knows we salvaged him. If they tell the Graycoats—"

"They're not gonna tell the Law," Eve sighed. "Not when they got a chance of claiming it themselves. Fridge Street is all about the scratch."

"Seems to me prettyboy's worth less than zero. Can't sell him. Can't tell anyone we got him. Remind me why we hauled this thing in from the Scrap?"

"I don't remember you doing much lifting."

"I'm too pretty to sweat."

Miss Fresh leaned close to the lifelike's face, ran one finger down its cheek until she reached the bow of its mouth.

"Still, if we can't sell him, I can ponder a few uses for—"

Pretty eyes opened wide. Pupils dilated. Plastic blue. Eve had time to gasp as the lifelike's left hand snaked out, quick as silver, and grabbed Lemon's wrist. The girl shrieked as the bot sat up, wrenching her into a headlock so fast Eve barely had time to draw breath.

Eve cried out, snatching up a screwdriver. Lemon's face was flushing purple in the lifelike's grip. Perfect lips brushed her earlobe.

"Hush now," it said.

Eve's lips drew back in a snarl. "Let her go!"

The lifelike glanced up as Eve spoke, those pretty plastic eyes glinting in the fluorescent light. Its grip around Lemon's throat loosened, mouth opening and closing as if it were struggling to find the words. *A* word. So full of astonishment and joy, it made Eve's chest hurt without quite knowing why.

"*You . . . ,*" it breathed.

Lemon seized the lifelike's ear, bent it double, and flipped it forward. The bot sailed over Lem's shoulder and came crashing down on a ruined survey drone in the corner. With a wet crunch and a spray of blood, the thing found itself impaled on a shank of rusted steel.

"Ow," it said.

Eve pushed Lemon back, her screwdriver held out before her. Lem had one hand pressed to her throat as she wheezed and blinked the tears from her eyes.

"That hurt, you fug. . . ."

The lifelike winced, kicked itself off the shank it'd been impaled on, leaving a slick of what looked like blood behind on the metal. It collapsed with a thud, one hand pressed to the wound, right beside that coin slot in its chest. Eve snatched a heavy wrench off her workbench and raised the tool to stave in the bot's head.

"Ana, don't," it said.

Eve blinked. ". . . What?"

"Ana, I'm sorry." The lifelike raised its bloody hand. "I didn't know it was you."

"My name's not Ana, fug."

"Prettyboy got a screw loose," Lemon wheezed. "Hole in his skull let the stupid in."

Bang, bang, bang.

"Eve?" Grandpa's voice was muffled behind the sound-proofed door. "Lemon? You two solid in there?"

The lifelike blinked, looking at the hatchway. ". . . Silas?"

"How do you know my grandpa's name?" Eve snarled.

A frown creased that perfect brow. "Don't you remem—"

"Eve!" Grandpa yelled, banging the metal with his fist. "Open the door!"

"Silas!" the lifelike yelled. "Silas, it's me!"

Grandpa coughed hard, his voice turning an ugly shade of dark.

"Eve, have you got a *boy in there with you*?"

Lemon and Eve glanced at each other, speaking simulta-neously. "Uh-oh . . ."

"God's potatoes!" Grandpa roared, banging again. "I'll not stand for it! This is my roof, young lady! Open this door right now before I get the rocket launcher!"

"Silas, it's Ezekiel!" the lifelike yelled.

"Will you *shut up*!" Eve hissed, kicking the lifelike in the ribs.

When Grandpa spoke next, it was with a voice Eve had never heard before.

"*. . . Ezekiel?*"

The lifelike looked up at Eve again. Imploring.

"Ana, we need to get out of here. They'll be coming for you."

"Who's Ana?" Lemon looked about, totally bewildered. "How do you know Mister C? What the fresh *hells* is going on here?"

Eve lowered the wrench, hands slick on the metal. The lifelike was looking up at her with pretty plastic eyes, full of desperation. Fear. And something more. Something . . .

"I don't know you," she said.

"Ana, it's *me*," the lifelike insisted. "It's Zeke."

"*Eve.*"

Grandpa's voice echoed through five centimeters of case-hardened steel.

"Eve, get away from the door. Cover your ears."

"Oh, crap," Lemon breathed. "He really *did* get the—"

The blast was deafening. A train-wreck concussion lifting Eve off her feet and tossing her across the room like dead leaves. She collided with the spray-foam wall, hitting the ground with a gasp. Grandpa wheeled through the ruined doorway in his buzzing little chair, smoking rocket launcher in hand, hair blown back in a smoldering quiff. He scoped the scene in an instant, pointed to the lifelike and growled.

"Kaiser. Aggress intruder."

The blitzhund leapt through the hatchway, seizing the lifelike's throat in his jaws. A low growl spilled from between the hound's teeth and a series of damp clicks echoed within his torso. His eyes turned blood red. Eve shook her head as Grandpa hauled her to her feet. The lifelike remained motionless, hand raised in surrender. Eve figured she'd probably be the same with a blitzhund wrapped around her larynx.

"Wonderful invention, blitzhunds," Grandpa wheezed, hauling Lemon up by the seat of her pants. "Daedalus Tech invented them during the CorpWars. They can track a target across a thousand klicks with one particle of DNA. 'Course, the smaller ones only have enough explosives to take out single targets. But a big model like Kaiser here?" Grandpa coughed hard, spat bloody onto the deck. "If he pops, there'll be nothing left of this room but vapor. Think you can heal that, bastard? Think we made you that good?"

The lifelike croaked through its crushed larynx. "Silas, I'm not here to hurt you."

"'Course not." Grandpa was ushering both shell-shocked girls toward the door. Cricket was beckoning Eve wildly. "You just happened to be in the neighborhood, am I right?"

"Ana, stop."

Eve realized the lifelike was looking at her, the world still ringing in her ears.

"Ana, please . . ."

"Shut up!" Grandpa's roar came from underwater. "Breathe another word, I—"

And then it started. That awful cough. The sound that had kept Eve awake every night for the past six months. Grandpa tried to push Eve through the door even as he bent double in his chair, coughing so hard she thought he might bring up his lungs. The cancer had him by the throat. Claws sinking deeper every day into the only thing she had left. . . .

"Grandpa," Eve breathed, hugging the old man tight.

"Silas, she's in danger," the lifelike pleaded. "I came here to *warn* you. Ana was on the feeds. Some trouble at a local bot fight last night. She manifested in front of hundreds of people. *Manifested,* you hear me? Fried a siege-class logika just by looking at it."

"Not . . . ," Grandpa wheezed, "not possib—"

"Silas, they'll *know.* One of them is bound to be monitoring the feeds. Even the data from a sinkhole like this. They'll come for her, you *know* they will."

"Grandpa, who is this?" Eve's voice was trembling, her real eye blurred with frightened tears. "What's going on?"

"Ana, I'm—"

"*Shut up!*" Grandpa shouted at the lifelike. "Shut . . . your t-traitor . . . mouth."

The old man fell back to coughing, bubbling breath dragged through bloody teeth.

Eve held him tight, turned to Lemon. "Med cabinet!"

"On it!" Lem wiped the blood from her ears, stumbled down the hallway.

Grandpa was choking, fist to his lips. Hate-filled eyes locked on the lifelike.

"Just breathe easy, Grandpa, we got—"

"We got two tabs left!" Lemon dashed back down the hall, skidded to her knees. Two blue dermal patches were cupped in her palm. "Cabinet's dry, Evie. This is the last."

"No, that can't be right," Eve said. "Why didn't he tell me we were so low?"

"He didn't want to worry you," Cricket said in a sad little voice.

Eve slapped the tabs onto Grandpa's arm, massaged his skin to warm them up. Lemon returned with a cloudy glass of recyc, holding it to his lips. Eve's heart wrenched inside her chest as he sipped, started coughing again.

Don't you dare die on me. . . .

The lifelike was staring at her, those blue plastic eyes locked on hers. "Ana, I—"

"Shut up!" Eve shouted. "Kaiser, it speaks again, tear out its throat!"

The blitzhund growled assent, tail wagging.

What the hells could she do? No meds left. No scratch. That dose might see Grandpa through this attack, but after that? Was he going to die? Right here? The only blood she had left in the world? She remembered sitting on his lap as a little girl. Him holding her hand as he nursed her back to health. And though the memories were monochrome and jumbled and fuzzy at the edges, she remembered enough. She remembered she loved him.

Eve dragged her fist across her eyes. Took a deep, trembling breath.

A claxon sounded throughout the house, cranking her headache up to the redline. On top of everything else, something had just triggered the proximity alarms. . . .

Grandpa was trying to get his coughing fit under control. He wiped his knuckles across his lips, flecked in red. His eyes had never left the lifelike.

They'll come for her, you know they will.

"You . . . ," Grandpa coughed, wet and red. "You expecting c-company, Eve?"

"No one who'd be welcome."

"Go ch-check cams," he managed. "K-Kaiser's got this in . . . hand."

"Mouth," Lemon murmured.

The old man managed a bloodstained grin. "Don't start with . . . me, Freshie."

A quick glance passed between Eve and Lemon, and without another word, the girls were dashing down the hallway. They bundled into what Grandpa wryly referred to as the Peepshow—a room with every inch of wall crusted in monitors, fed via sentry cams around Tire Valley. The alarms were tripped anytime someone arrived without an invitation. Most often, it was some big feral cat who loped into a turret's firing arc and got itself aerated, but looking at the feeds . . .

"We," Cricket said, "are true screwed."

Lem looked at the bot sideways. "You have a rare talent for understatement, Crick."

Eve's eyes were locked on the screens. Her voice a whisper.

"Brotherhood . . ."

1.5

RUIN

Just us two. Marie and me. The two youngest sisters. The closest. The best of friends.

Only she'd known my secret. Held it safe inside her chest. Father would never have approved. Mother would've lost her mind. But Marie held my hand and laughed with me, breathless with my excitement. She loved that I was in love.

Loved the idea of it more than I did.

She was crying now. Holding on to me like a drowner clings to the one who swims to save her, dragging them both down to the black. But when the pistol clicked, she glanced up, up into the face of the soldier looming over us. Long curling hair, the color of flame. Eyes like shattered emeralds. Beautiful and empty.

The name HOPE *was stenciled above her breast pocket.*

I almost laughed at the thought.

"None above," Hope said. "And none below."

A sun-bright flare.

A deafening silence.

And only I remained.

The Fridge Street Crew had warned her that the Brotherhood was posse'ing up. Eve hadn't realized just how serious they were taking it.

She looked out through the view from Turret Northeast-1 just as something blew the feed to hissing static. Looking at Northeast-2, she could see a small *army* of Brotherhood boys, dolled up in their red cassocks and tromping toward Grandpa's house. Oldskool assault rifles and choppers in hand. Scarlet banners set with the image of their patron, St. Michael, waving in a rusty wind. And marching in the vanguard, absorbing the withering hail of auto-turret fire, came four fifty-ton Spartans.

The machina were classic infantry models, responsible for most of the heavy lifting during War 4.0 in areas where the radiation was too hot for meat troops. They stood thirty feet high, the crescent-shaped heat sinks on their heads giving them the silhouettes of old Greek soldierboys from the history virtch. They were painted scarlet, snatches of mangled scripture on their hulls. Long banners flowed from their shoulders and waists, adorned with the Brotherhood sigil—a stylized black *X*.

"Grandpaaaaa!" Eve yelled.

A Spartan stomped up to Northeast-2 and smashed it to scrap. Eve felt a distant, shuddering boom as the thermex charges at the turret's base exploded. She glanced at the screen for North-3, saw the Spartan on its back, smoking and legless. But the rest of the posse was still moving, just a few minutes shy of ringing the front doorbell.

Eve glanced at her bestest. "These boys mean biz."

Lemon was looking down the corridor, back toward Eve's workshop. Her face was unusually thoughtful, brow creased.

"What did Mister C do back on the mainland? Before you moved here?"

"He was a botdoc," Eve said, watching the Brotherhood march closer. "A mechanic."

"You remember where he worked?"

"Lem, in case you missed it, there's a very angry mob outside our house carrying a cross my size. What does this have to do with anything?"

"Because that lifelike acted like he *knew* you. Like you'd *forgotten* him. And he called you by a different name, Evie. Someone in this game isn't dealing straight."

Eve knew Lem was right, but, true cert, impending murder just seemed more of a pressing issue right now. The Brotherhood mob was posse'ing around their three remaining Spartans, about a hundred meters from the house. The machina were armed with autoguns and a plasma cannon on each shoulder, and those things could liquefy *steel*. The house had only two auto-sentries on the roof, and against the bigbots' armor, they weren't going to be much help. As far as capital T went, Eve couldn't remember being in much deeper. But she gritted her teeth, forced her fear down into her boots. She was a Domefighter, dammit. This was her home. She wasn't giving it up without a kicking.

The lead Spartan's cockpit cracked open, and a brief blast of choir music spilled across the Scrap. A barrel-chested figure in an embroidered red cassock vaulted down onto the trash, holding an assault rifle engraved with religious scripture. He wore mirrored goggles and had sideburns you could hang a truck off, a big greasepaint *X* daubed on his face. Eve knew him by reputation—a fellow who tagged himself the Iron Bishop.

"I am cometh not to bring peace, but a sword!" he bellowed.

"Amen!" roared the Brothers.

The Iron Bishop held out his hand, and a juve slapped an old microphone into his palm. With a flourish, the Bishop held the mic to his lips, his voice crackling through his Spartan's public address system.

"In the name of the Lord! The Brotherhood demands that all genetic deviates housed within this domicile surrendereth themselves immediately for divine purification!"

Eve scowled, tried harder to swallow her growing dread. "Purification" basically meant getting nailed up outside the Brotherhood's chapel in Los Diablos and left for the sun. The Brotherhood was always crowing about the evils of biomodification and cybernetics, and they had a major hate-on for genetic deviation. But they were big enough that the local law didn't want to push the friendship. So if you happened to be born with a sixth finger or webbed toes or something a little more exotic, sorry, friendo, that was just life in the Scrap.

Cricket sat on Eve's shoulder, peering at the feeds with mismatched eyes.

"Aren't they hot in those cassocks?" he chirped.

"They make 'em out of Kevlar weave," Eve murmured. "Bulletproof, see?"

"Got a bad feeling on this," the bot said. "Right in my shiny metal man parts."

"Keep telling you, you got no man parts, Crick," Lemon sighed.

"Yeah," said a tired voice. "I'm such a bastard."

Eve turned with a surge of sweet relief, saw her grandfather sitting at the doorway in his electric wheelchair. But standing behind him . . .

"Um," Lemon said. "Should he . . . be here?"

The lifelike.

It stood behind Grandpa in its high-tech flight suit, blood-stains on the fabric, Kaiser's teeth marks on its throat. Old-sky blue eyes flitting from screen to screen.

"Grandpa, what the hell is that thing doing out here?" she demanded.

"Had a chat." Grandpa wiped his lips with a bloodstained rag, eyes on the monitors. "Reached an understanding. So to speak."

"Did you miss the part where this thing nearly choked Lemon to death?"

Grandpa tried to turn his cough into a scoff, smothered with his fist.

"You're the one who . . . brought him inside, my little chicka-dee."

"We thought it was dead!"

"I'm sorry, Mistress Lemon." The lifelike's voice was smooth as smoke. "My brain was damaged in the crash. I mistook you for a threat. Please accept my apologies."

The lifelike's pretty blue stare fell on the indomitable Miss Fresh. Its smile was dimpled, sugar sweet, about three microns short of perfect. Eve could see the girl's insides slowly going mushy right before her eyes.

"Oh, you know." Lemon's face was a bright shade of pink. "It's only a larynx."

"Ohhh my god," Eve began. *"Lemon . . ."*

"What?" she blinked.

"And you, Mistress Eve," the lifelike said. "I'm sorry for any—"

"Oh, I'm Mistress Eve now?" she demanded. "What happened to Ana?"

"Again, the crash . . . my head injuries." It glanced at Silas. "I'm afraid my brain trauma led me to mistake you for someone else. I apologize."

"Brain trauma's all better now?"

"Yes. Thank you, Mistress Eve."

"But you're still mistaking me for someone else?"

A blink. "I am?"

"Yeah." Eve stepped closer, looked up into the lifelike's eyes. "A true cert *idiot*."

She stared into that fugazi blue. Searching for some hint of truth. Feeling only revulsion. Warning. Danger. This thing wasn't human. It might look it, sound it, feel it. It might be as beautiful as all the stars in the sky. Problem was, the smog was usually too thick to see the stars anymore. And there was something wrong here. Something . . .

"Arguments later." Grandpa nodded to the monitor banks. "Brotherhood means biz. Time to talk them out of it, Ezekiel."

The lifelike broke Eve's eye contact with seeming reluctance.

"I can do that."

Spinning on its heel, the thing called Ezekiel marched down the corridor. Its gait was a little lopsided, as if the loss of its limb had thrown it off balance. Still, a regular human would already be dead if they'd had their arm torn from their shoulder, and Eve was freaked to see the thing moving at all. It got half a dozen steps before her voice pulled it up short.

"Hey, Braintrauma."

The lifelike turned, one perfect eyebrow raised.

"Exit is *that* way." Eve crooked a thumb.

Ezekiel glanced about the corridors and, with a flash of that almost-perfect smile, headed toward the front door. Lemon leaned out the hatchway to watch it go, whistling softly. Eve plucked Cricket off her shoulder, set him down in Grandpa's lap.

"Cricket, look after Grandpa. Grandpa, look after Cricket."

"Where you think you're going?" the old man rasped.

"Out to help."

"Hells you are. I'll try some parlay, and if that doesn't work, Ezekiel can deal with them. You got nothing to throw against a mob like that."

"And what's the lifelike going to throw against those Spartans?" she asked. "It's only got one arm. And it's not getting through ballistics-grade plasteel with just a pretty smile."

"That dimple, though," Lemon interjected.

"Look, that's his . . . problem, not yours," Grandpa wheezed. "You stay . . . here."

"This is our *home*, Grandpa. And these dustnecks brought an army to it."

"That's right, Eve. An *army*. And there's . . . nothing you can do to stop them."

Eve looked down at her fist. Remembered the WarDome last night. The Goliath and a little myth about a kid called David.

"Yeah, we'll see about that."

Ignoring her grandpa's shouts, she stalked down the corridor to the armory, slapped on some plasteel and headgear, threw her poncho over the top. Snatching up Excalibur, she checked the power levels, noticed Lemon suiting up beside her. The girl dragged on an old grav-tank pilot's helmet, clawed the shock of cherry-red hair from her eyes and hefted Popstick with a grin.

"Stronger together," she said.

"Together forever." Eve smiled.

———

A thousand suns were waiting for them outside. A thousand suns inside a single skin. The metal underneath her was hot to the touch. The scorch in the sky broiling her red.

"You gentles got no biz . . . on my property."

Grandpa's voice crackled over the PA as Eve popped out of a rooftop hatch and hunkered down behind one of the autogun emplacements. Lemon crouched beside her, pushing the oversized helmet out of her eyes and surveying the mob.

"You got thirty seconds before . . . I start getting unneighborly," Grandpa growled. *"And then I'm gonna jam that cross . . . up your as—"*

Grandpa's attempts at "parlay" trailed off into dry coughing, and the old man cut the feed. The Iron Bishop spoke into his mic, voice bouncing off the tires around them.

"Handeth overeth the deviate, Silas! Thou shalt not suffer a witch to live!"

Eve blinked. ". . . Did he just say 'handeth overeth'?"

Lemon stood up, helmet slipping over her eyes as she howled. "Don't call her a deviate, you inbred sack of sh—"

Eve pulled Lemon back down behind the autogun barricade as the more enthusiastic Brotherhood boys fired off a couple of random shots. Molten lead *spangg*ged off rusted steel. Eve winced. Her head was aching, her optical implant itching.

Peeking back over the barricade, she fixed the Spartans in her stare. Last night's bout was replaying inside her head. The way that Goliath had dropped like a brick onto the killing floor. The way she'd blown every circuit inside it just by *willing* it. She had no idea how she'd pulled it off, or if she could do it again. But this place was her home, and these people were her family, and letting someone else fight her battles just wasn't her style.

So Eve stretched out her hand, fingers trembling.

"What're you doing?" Lemon hissed.

"Trying to fritz one of those machina."

"Riotgrrl, I'm not su—"

"Hsst, I'm trying to concentrate!"

Eve gritted her teeth. Picturing the leftmost Spartan collapsing into ruin. Trying to summon everything she'd felt last night—terror and fury and defiance—to curl it up in her fist and send it hurtling into the Spartan's core. Sweat gleamed on her brow, the sun beating down like sledgehammers. The fear of losing Grandpa. The suspicion she was being lied to. The lifelike's hollow, plastic stare and perfect, pretty eyes. She pulled all of it into a tight, burning sphere in her chest—a little artillery shell of burning rage.

These dustnecks wanted to nail her up? Bring her an ending? Well, she'd conjure them an ending like they'd never seen. . . .

Eve drew a deep breath. Standing up from behind the barricade, she imagined the Spartan falling in a cloud of burning sparks, burned the picture in her mind's eye. And then, at the top of her lungs, she screamed.

Screamed.

SCREAMED.

And absolutely nothing happened.

The Brotherhood boys started laughing. Bullets started flying. A lucky shot bounced off her torso guard, knocking her sideways. And as the indomitable Miss Fresh dragged her back behind cover, a shard of supersonic lead blew Eve's helmet right off her head.

The pain was sledgehammers and white stars. Eve cried out, dirty fingers feeling about her skull to see if it'd been perforated. The hail of fire continued, she and Lemon crouched low as the air rained bullets for a solid minute. Eve was wincing, flinching, heels kicking at the roof beneath her. Thankfully, the shot seemed to have killed her headgear and nothing else. But still . . .

"That was a little on the wrong side of stupid," she finally managed to gasp.

Lemon was staring wide-eyed at Eve, pale under her freckles. "You nearly got your dome blown off! Warn me when you're gonna do something that defective again, will you?"

"Never again," Eve muttered. "I promise."

"Where's this damn murderbot, anyways?" Lemon poked her head over the barricade once the firing stopped. "Shouldn't he be . . . aw, spank my spankables. . . ."

"What?"

Lemon chewed her lip. "You want bad news or worse news?"

"Um . . . worse?"

"No, that doesn't work. Supposed to ask for the bad first."

Eve rubbed her aching temples and sighed. "Okay, bad, then."

"Tye and his little posse of scavverboys just rolled up."

"Oh." Eve nodded slow. "And the worse?"

"They brought the entire Fridge Street Crew with 'em."

"Juuust fizzy," Eve sighed. "Seriously, what is *with this day*?"

Peeking over the barricade, Eve saw a warband of Fridge Street thugs rolling up from behind the looping curl of some old roller coaster track. She spotted Tye and Pooh riding on the backs of beat-up motorbikes behind the older Fridge Street beatboys. The boss of the crew—a one-hundred-and-twenty-kilo meatstick in rubber pants who called himself Sir Westinghouse—climbed out of a modded sand buggy and started jawing with the Iron Bishop, apparently delighted to discover they were all here to lay the murder down on the same juvette.

Grandpa's bellow crackled over the PA.

"What is this, a dance class reunion? You scrubs get the hell off my lawn!"

Sir Westinghouse stepped forward, a bruiser beside him handing over a bullhorn.

"Your granddaughter jumped a bunch of my juves out in the Scrap this morning, Silas!" Westinghouse bellowed. "Jacked some sweet salvage that rightways belongs to Fridge Street. Suggesting maybe you better limp out here and jaw on it."

"*I got . . . a better suggestion,*" Grandpa called.

"And what's that, old man?"

"*Check your six.*"

Eve watched Sir Westinghouse frown and look behind him just as one of the cassock boys flipped back his hood to reveal a prettyboy face and eyes just a touch too blue. The lifelike had a machine pistol in its one good hand, probably lifted from whatever Brother it'd stomped for the robe.

Lemon did a little bounce. "*Clever* boy."

Every Brother and Fridgeboy had his fingers on his trigger. Eve strained to hear the lifelike talk over the machina hum and clawing wind.

"I'll give you one chance to walk away," it said. "All of you."

"That's him!" Tye slapped Sir Westinghouse on the back. "The lifelike!"

The Fridge Street chief glanced at the juve, back at Ezekiel. "So you're the fugazi, eh? Look around you, prettyboy. You got an army against you."

"I don't want to hurt you," Ezekiel said softly.

Westinghouse guffawed. "Who you trying to fool? You forget the Golden Rule? The Three Laws won't *let* you hurt us, fug."

The lifelike blinked at that. Its pistol wavered, and Eve wondered if . . .

"My maker thought the same thing," Ezekiel said.

And then it moved.

Eve had seen *fast* before. She'd seen epinephrine-enhanced stimheads playing snatch on street corners in Los Diablos. She'd seen top-tier machina fights beamed from the Megopolis WarDome—the kind that got decided in fractions of a second. She'd seen fast, true cert. But she'd never seen *anything* move like that lifelike moved then.

The Iron Bishop raised his assault rifle behind the lifelike. And quicker than flies, Ezekiel spun and popped two rounds into the Bishop's eyes. In almost the same instant, it dropped three of the closest Brotherhood thugs with headshots and finally blew out the back of Sir Westinghouse's skull, painting Tye's face a bright and gibbering red.

The air was scarlet mist and thin gray smoke. World moving in slow motion. Peeps shouting, firing at the lifelike as it grabbed a nearby Brotherhood thug to use as a shield. Lead thudded into the Kevlar cassock, muzzles flashing like the strobe light in Eve's dreams, flickering as the figures danced and fell, the stink of blood uncurling in the air.

Eve covered her ears as the rooftop autoguns fired into the mob. The Spartans opened up with their own ordnance, one spraying a storm of hollow-points at the lifelike, the other unleashing its plasma and melting one of the rooftop sentries into slag. Lemon winced and hunkered lower, fixing Popstick with an accusing glare.

"Who brings a baseball bat to *a gunfight*?"

Eve peered out the side of the barricade. Eyes fixed on the Spartan, teeth gritted in a snarl. Stretching out her hand once more.

"Come on . . . ," she pleaded.

"Eve, what are you doing?"

"Why won't it work?" she spat, furious. "Why can't I do it again?"

Hails of burning lead raked their cover, pitter-pattering on the steel. Eve heard cries of panic, screams of pain. Lemon peeked out over the barricade, whistling softly.

"Look at him go. . . ."

Eve's eyes fell on the lifelike, widening in amazement. Ezekiel had scrambled up the back of the closest Spartan and, as if the metal were tinfoil, torn the ammo feed from its autoguns to stop it firing on the house. Wrenching its plasma cannon toward the Spartan beside it, the lifelike melted the cockpit and the pilot inside into puddles. The Brotherhood scattered into cover, Fridge Street laying down the lead on Ezekiel as it twisted and dodged, almost too fast to track.

Noticing the rooftop autoguns were OOC, two of the braver Fridgeboys made a dash for the house. Whether to seek cover or wreak havoc, Eve wasn't quite sure.

"Finally!" Lemon cried.

Eve's bestest leapt off the roof with a howl, dropping a Fridgeboy with 500kV crackling through his brainmeats. Kaiser was waiting inside the front door for the other one, and the scavver was soon dashing back to his comrades with his shins torn to ribbons.

Ezekiel dropped from the Spartan's shoulders, grabbing a Kevlar-clad corpse to shield itself as it weaved through the hail of bullets. Even with only one arm, it carried the body effortlessly, gleaming with what looked a lot like sweat as it rolled into cover behind a stack of tires near the house. A pile of old retreads had been set ablaze by the plasma, thick smoke rolling over the yard and burning the back of Eve's throat.

She realized Cricket had crawled up onto the roof beside her.

The little bot was tugging at her boots and yelling at her to get back inside over the roar of the remaining Spartan's autogun fire. Lemon was safe with Kaiser below. But Eve was still trying desperately to unleash whatever it was that had dropped that Goliath in the Dome. Eyes narrowed. Temples throbbing. Muscles straining.

Come onnnn. . . .

"Eve, come on!"

She reached deep inside herself. To the place she'd fallen into when that Goliath raised its fist above her head. The moment she'd looked down the barrel pointed at her skull. A moment of perfect fear. Of defiance. Thrashing and kicking against that long goodnight.

This is not the end of me.

This is just one more enemy.

The Spartan jerked back like Eve had punched it. It trembled, as if every servo inside it were firing at once. She grinned as a cascade of sparks burst from the machina's innards. And spewing smoke, the Spartan stumbled and crashed face-first into the scrap.

"Eve . . . ," Cricket murmured. "You did it."

Eve punched the air. "Eat *that,* you dustneck trash-humper!"

As their last machina fell, the Brotherhood broke. Two of their Spartans were OOC, the Iron Bishop's machina standing abandoned as the Brothers dragged their fallen leader away. With the death of their own boss and Ezekiel still laying down bullets from its nest of tires, most of the fight had been taken out of Fridge Street, too. They were stepping off quick, scattering into the Valley.

Eve scoped the bloody battleground that had engulfed her front yard. Some of the meanest, toughest beatsticks in Dregs had stepped up with a fistful of capital T and were now scuttling away with their tails between their legs.

Wiping the sweat from her good eye, the girl winked at the little logika beside her.

"Think you can chalk up a win for the good guys, Crick." She smiled.

And that's when the first bomb fell from the sky.

1.6

IMPACT

Red on my hands. Smoke in my lungs. My mother, my father, my sisters and brother, all dead on the floor beside me. Hollow eyes and empty chests.

The soldiers stand above me. The four of them in their perfect, pretty row.

They have only one thing left to take from me.

The last and most precious thing.

Not my life, no.

Something dearer still.

A silhouette looms.

Raises a pistol to my head.

"I'm sorry," a voice says.

I hear the sound of thunder.

And then I hear nothing at all.

———

No warning. No telltale *whooooosh* like in the old Holywood flicks. Just the blast.

And fire.

And screams.

A second incendiary fell, landed in the middle of the retreating Fridge Street Crew, sending Pooh and his teddy bear off to the Wherever in pieces. A third bomb blew the Brotherhood boys about like old plastic bags in the wind. Eve and Cricket looked up to the sky, the girl's belly turning cold as she saw a light flex-wing with a faded GNOSISLABS logo on the tail fin swooping through smoke.

"This is not good . . . ," Cricket said.

The flex-wing zoomed overhead, cutting down anything that moved. The craft made another pass, mopping up everything still twitching. And finally, with the kind of skillz you really only see in the virtch, the pilot brought the 'wing down to a gentle landing on the trash and skipped out the door in the space between heartbeats.

"Riotgrrl?" Lemon's voice drifted up from the verandah below. "You fizzy?"

"Stay behind cover, Lem."

"No doubt. I'm too pretty to die."

Eve's eyes were fixed on the newcomer, standing ankle-deep in the mess she'd made. A woman. Barely more than a girl, really. Nineteen, maybe twenty. She wore combat boots and a clean white shift, hood pulled back from a perfect face. Short dark hair cut into ragged bangs. Some kind of sidearm Eve had never seen before at her hip. And in her right hand, the sheathed curve of what might have been a . . .

"Um, is she carrying a sword?" Lemon yelled.

"Looks like."

"Who *does* that?"

The newcomer scanned the carnage with eyes like a dead

flatscreen. Eve's stare was fixed on her face, telescopics engaged. She could see that the newcomer's irises were dull, plastic-looking. Just like Ezekiel's. Her face was flawless, beautiful. Just like Ezekiel's. The way she moved, the way . . .

"She's a lifelike," Eve breathed.

A barrage of images in her mind. Old black-and-white freeze-frames, blurred and smudged with the press of time. A beautiful smile. Soft skin against hers. Laughter. Poetry. It was as if—

"Have you ever been in love, Ana?"

"I think . . ."

"Kaiser," came Grandpa's voice. *"Aggress intruder."*

The blitzhund was a snarling blur, dashing out the front door toward the lifelike. Eve's heart was in her throat, her blood running cold.

"Kaiser . . ."

The blitzhund barreled like a heat-seeking missile right at the newcomer's throat. Quick as blinking, the lifelike drew the sword from its sheath. A flare of magnesium-bright current arced along the blade's edge, and faster than Eve could scream warning, the lifelike brought the weapon down toward Kaiser's head.

A shot rang out, smashed the blade from the lifelike's grip. Eve glimpsed Ezekiel, crouched behind its tangle of tires, smoking machine pistol in its hand. Kaiser hit the female lifelike like an anvil, snarling and tearing. The lifelike rolled with the momentum, punching up through Kaiser's belly. And as Eve watched in horror, the lifelike tore out a handful of her dog's metallic guts and kicked him thirty meters down the Valley.

"Kaiser!" Eve screamed.

The lifelike was on its feet, bloodied wrist clutched to its chest. Ezekiel opened fire, Eve's jaw hanging loose as she watched the newcomer dance—literally *dance*—through the hail of molten lead, down into the cover of a Spartan's wreckage. Ezekiel's pistol fell quiet, shots echoing along the Valley.

"Eve, come on," Cricket pleaded, tugging at her boots.

The house PA crackled, and Eve heard Grandpa's voice, thick with fear. *"Evie, come inside."*

The newcomer raised its head, calling across the scrap.

"Good heavens, is that you, Silas?"

Eve gritted her teeth. So this lifelike knew Grandpa, too. Just like Ezekiel. Her mind was racing, desperately trying to fill in gaps that just didn't make sense. How did any of these pieces fit together? Maybe Grandpa hadn't been an ordinary botdoc? Maybe busted recycs and automata weren't the only things he'd been tinkering with when she was off learning to become a Domefighter? Whatever the explanation, a slow anger was twisting her insides. Someone was lying here. Someone was—

The house rumbled beneath her. Rust and dirt shivered off the structure, and Eve realized the old engines on the thopterfreighter had started, kicking up a storm of plastic and dust. Grandpa must have been really hard at work all those months she'd been building Miss Combobulation at the Dome. He must have fixed—

"Mister C fixed the engines?" Lemon yelled.

"Lem, get in the house!" Eve shouted. "Help Grandpa! I'll be down in a second!"

". . . What are you gonna do?"

"I gotta get Kaiser!"

Eve turned to the trash pile the blitzhund had been booted into. She could hear pained whimpers, faint scratching. He was still alive. But he was *hurt*. The engines were a dull roar, the world trembling around her. Grandpa was calling her name over the PA. Cricket was still tugging on her leg, his voice pleading.

"Evie, come onnnn."

She clenched her jaw, shook her head. Time enough for questions when Kaiser was safe. She knew Cricket would follow her anywhere, but she wouldn't let him get hurt, too. She handed over Excalibur, nodded to the hatch.

"Cricket, go get Lemon and take her back in the house."

"Eve, it's too dangerous up here, I'm supposed to—"

"That's an order!"

The little logika wrung his rusty hands on the baseball bat's handle. His heart was relays and chips and processors. His optics were made of plastic. And she could still see the agony in them.

But as always, the bot did what he was told.

Eve scrambled down the rooftop into the rising dust cloud, weighing her chances. Glancing among the carnage, she saw the Iron Bishop's Spartan, still standing among the smoking corpses. As she crept out among the bloody scrap, she heard the female lifelike call from behind cover. Its voice was lilting, almost as if it were singing rather than speaking. And Eve could *swear* it sounded . . .

. . . *familiar?*

"Lovely to see you again, Ezekiel," the newcomer called.

"You're a terrible liar, Faith," Ezekiel called back. "I always liked that about you."

"I should have known you'd beat me here." A smile in the song. "Been watching the human feeds again? Practicing in the mirror to be like them? It's pathetic, Zeke."

"And yet here we both are."

Eve dropped onto her belly as the newcomer twisted from cover, sidearm raised, unleashing a volley of something razor sharp and whistling at Ezekiel's cover. A series of tiny, pin-bright explosions tore the tires to ruins. Through the growing dust storm, she saw Ezekiel break from the shredded rubber, leap behind a stack of trashed auto hulks.

The lifelike reloaded, raised its pistol too fast to track. Sparks arced and ricocheted as Ezekiel ducked out of cover and blasted away. Down on her hands and knees, Eve crawled on through the trash, listening for Kaiser's whines. A stray bullet whizzed over her head, the stench of burning tires making her dry-heave.

Grandpa bellowed over the engine roar. *"Evie, get inside, dammit!"*

Eve peered up from her cover. She was almost close enough to make a dash for the Spartan now, but she didn't dare without knowing where the enemy was. Her eyes met Ezekiel's across the ruins, and the lifelike shook its head. Gesturing that she should head back to the house. She heard a whimper somewhere out in the trash.

Hold on, puppy. . . .

She was drenched, sweat burning her eyes. She tore off her poncho, tossed it away. On her belly now, crawling toward Kaiser's voice. Ezekiel saw she was refusing to retreat, seemed to decide distracting their opponent was the best way to keep Eve un-murdered.

"I don't want to fight you, Faith," it called.

"I don't blame you." Faith's reply rang somewhere out in the tangle of metal and bodies. "I can't help but notice you've misplaced one of your arms."

"I only ever needed the one to beat you."

The lifelike's laughter rang across the scrap.

"Pride cometh before the fall, little brother."

"You'd know, big sister."

. . . Brother? Sister?

Eve caught sight of movement, saw the newcomer crouched

beside a tumble of old tires, slowly creeping around Ezekiel's flank. And over the rising engine roar, the house groaning in its metal bones, she heard another soft whimper.

Kaiser . . .

There might be only a handful of meat in him that was real, but that handful needed her. If she broke cover, she'd be seen for sure. But if Grandpa was worried enough about this lifelike to try to get the house airborne, there was no way Eve was just going to leave her dog behind to rot.

She dashed out into the open, sprinting toward the Iron Bishop's machina. Grandpa hollered over the PA. Ezekiel cried a warning as Faith rose from cover, pistol in hand. Trash was crunching under Eve's boots, her lungs burning. But she ran. Fists flailing, heart hammering, across the bodies and wreckage, vaulting into the Spartan and slamming the cockpit closed. Stabbing the ignition, she slipped her arms and feet into the control sleeves. The machina roared to life around her, its engines thrumming in her bones.

Whatever the hells was happening here, this was something she knew.

This was something she could do.

Her plasma cannon vomited white heat, incinerating the newcomer's cover. The thing called Faith was already moving, dashing toward Eve's Spartan when Ezekiel appeared from cover and charged shoulder-first into Faith's belly. The impact was thunderous, tearing a long furrow through the scrap as the lifelikes fell into a rolling brawl. Fists blurring. Blood and spit and wet, crunching thuds.

Eve lumbered through the wreckage in her machina, heavy feet crushing metal like it was paper. She scanned the scrap, caught sight of Kaiser in a pile of old retreads. He was dragging himself with his front paws, hind legs motionless. Eve tore the tires aside, reached down with huge, gentle hands, cupped the wounded blitzhund to her Spartan's chest.

"It's okay, puppy," she breathed. "I got you."

Kaiser licked the Spartan's hand with his heat-sink tongue.

Eve lumbered back across the battleground, through the black smoke and rising storm of dust and dirt, toward home. The house was shuddering now, the squeal of tortured metal rising over the engines' thunder. She couldn't see Ezekiel or the other lifelike. Eyes fixed on her front door. The welds across the house were splitting, the freighter finally getting some lift, the rest of the homestead shearing away under its own weight. Eve ran hard as she could, every colossal step bringing her closer.

Forty meters away.

Thirty.

A proximity alarm screeched in her ear. Eve had time to hunch as three hundred kilos of engine block crashed across her Spartan's back. The machina was sent stumbling, gyros whining. Another impact, this time into her legs, an enormous tractor tire bringing the Spartan to its knees. The thing called Faith leapt high onto her Spartan's back, tearing out handfuls of cable. The hydraulics in Eve's left arm lost pressure, Kaiser tumbling from her grip. Eve reached back with her good arm, seized the lifelike and hurled it as hard as she could. Faith crunched into a twisted loop of roller coaster track, belly tearing open. Pseudo-blood spilled on rusted steel. Lips and teeth slicked ruby red.

Eve tore free of her harness and hit the cockpit eject. Bursting out into the rising roar, she seized Kaiser's scruff and dragged him toward the house. Dust in her good eye. Blood on her tongue. Kaiser whimpered, tried to crawl as best he could. He was so heavy. How would she lift him through the hatch? How could she—

A figure appeared beside her. Blood-spattered skin and eyes of fugazi blue.

"I've got him!" Ezekiel shouted. "Go!"

Eve stumbled toward the house, ribs and arm and head aching. The freighter was almost two meters off the ground now, still rising. Eve hauled herself through the doorway, boots kicking against the hull. Ezekiel leapt through the hatch in a single bound right behind her, Kaiser under its arm. Eve was on all fours. Chest pounding. Throat burning. And somehow she found breath to scream.

"Go, Grandpa, *go!*"

The house shuddered beneath her, its engines roaring in protest. Metal snapping, welds shattering, whole sections tearing away as the freighter rose into the sky, raining dirt and dust and crud. She was tossed like a plaything against the walls as she tried to stand, bouncing into Ezekiel's chest. The lifelike caught hold of her, the pair of them falling to the deck in a tangle. Eve looked down at the sweating, blood-soaked thing beneath her—this thing that wore the shape of a beautiful boy. A boy who'd just saved her life. A boy who wasn't anything like a boy at all. She could feel its body, hard and warm against her own.

"Are you all right?" Ezekiel asked.

Eve pushed herself away, palms slick with pseudo-blood. If she didn't know better, she'd have said the blood looked real. If she didn't know better . . .

"I'm fine." She turned to Kaiser on the deck beside her. "You okay, puppy?"

The blitzhund was dented and torn, the hole in his belly spitting sparks. A quick glance told her the damage wasn't anything she couldn't fix—nothing meat was ruined. Flooded with relief, she hugged him fiercely. His tail wagged feebly.

Ezekiel was watching her, those too-blue eyes fixed on hers.

"What're you looking at?" she scowled.

A nod to Kaiser. "He's a machine."

"So?"

"So you still love him." That almost perfect smile curled its lips. "It's sweet."

Eve shook her head, dragged herself to her feet. "You're a weird one, Braintrauma."

Grandpa's voice echoed over the house PA. *"Eve, you all right?"*

She hobbled to a comms pad, stabbed the TRANSMIT button with bloody fingers.

"I'm okay. Kaiser's ambulation is shot. But he's alive."

"In a world of stupid . . . that was the stupidest thing I've ever seen." A hacking cough crackled through the speaker. *"He's an artificial, Eve. He gets hurt so you don't have to."*

"Really? You're chewing me out now? I love you, Grandpa, but time and place?"

Silas seemed keen to say more, but his transmission dissolved into another coughing fit. Lemon and Cricket appeared at the end of the corridor, the little machina still clutching Excalibur. The girl pounded toward Eve and caught her up in a rib-crushing hug.

"You okay, Riotgrrl?"

"Fizzy."

"Did you know Silas could fly this thing? Did you even know this thing could *fly*?"

"Grandpa's definitely pro at keeping secrets." She glanced at the lifelike, now hauling itself up the wall with its one good arm and testing its right leg gingerly. It looked like it'd had whatever passed for the stuffing kicked out of it. "You fizzy, Braintrauma?"

"I've had worse beatings," it replied. "Trust me."

"Can you carry Kaiser with only one arm? I need to take him down to the worksh—"

The ship lunged sideways, sending Lemon into Eve and Eve into the wall. Cricket yelped and tumbled across the corridor, ending upside down against the bulkhead. There was a loud metallic crunch, a long squeal. The freighter shuddered again, rolling up onto its port side and sending everyone to their knees. Ezekiel grabbed Eve to stop her cracking her skull open on the bulkhead. Its arm was like warm iron, wrapped around her chest and crushing the breath out of her.

"Get off me . . . ," she gasped.

"What was *that*?" Lemon demanded.

Eve was pulling herself to her feet when the internal PA crackled. Grandpa's voice was hoarse with pain, almost drowned out by roaring wind. *"Eve, she's in—"*

The transmission dropped dead with a hiss of static.

Ezekiel met Eve's frightened stare.

"Faith . . . ," he said.

"Grandpa!" Eve snatched Excalibur from Cricket's hands and bolted down the corridor. Lemon ran beside her. Cricket wailing in protest. She could hear the lifelike bringing up the rear, limping badly after its beatdown.

They ran through the warren of corridors, up to the cockpit, tearing open a hatchway and stepping out into a rushing gale. The windshield was smashed to splinters, glittering on the floor. Grandpa's electric wheelchair was on its side, wheels still humming. Wind howled through the shattered glass. Eve could see ashen sky beyond, the island of Dregs sailing away beneath their feet. Black ocean in the distance. No one at the controls.

"Grandpa?" she cried.

Lemon peered out through the broken windshield.

"... Mister C?"

A bloodied hand reached down from outside, slammed Lemon's head into the console. She collapsed, blood dripping from her split brow. Eve clenched her fists as a figure dropped in through the broken glass. Blood crusted in its ragged bangs. Glistening wounds in its belly and chest. Eyes the flat gray of a dead telescreen.

"Hello, Ana." Faith smiled. "You look wonderful for a dead girl."

Thinking only of her grandpa, Eve swung Excalibur with all her strength. Faith parried with a forearm, hissing as the shock rocked it back into the console. The lifelike recovered in a heartbeat, slapped the bat from Eve's hand with almost casual ease.

Eve still had the self-defense routines in her Memdrive to fall back on, landing a decent jab on the lifelike's jaw before a single punch drove the breath from her lungs. She was seized by the throat, hauled into a choke hold.

"Gabriel will be so pleased to see you," Faith whispered in her ear.

Eve struggled to speak against the lifelike's grip. "What did you ... do with—"

"Silas? He's in my flex-wing, dead girl." The lifelike thumbed a control at its belt. Eve heard engines roar to life above her head. "Don't worry. I'm taking you both home."

"If you've ... hurt my ... grandpa—"

"... Grandfather?" A sharp smile twisted those perfect lips. "Oh, you poor girl. What *has* he been telling you?"

Black flowers bloomed in Eve's good eye. Tiny star flared and died as her pulse slowed. A roaring in her ears. A white-noise hiss. And beneath it all, a little voice, high and shrill. Yelling her name.

"Evie!"

A dark shape barreled into the cockpit, a silhouette in the light of a too-bright sun. Eve felt an impact, heard a wet crunch. She fell to her knees, hacking and coughing, stars in her eyes. Cricket was beside her, begging her to run. She was dimly aware of shapes moving in the cockpit—two figures, a dance of fists and knees and elbows. Blinding sparks. Metal tearing. The pilot's seat uprooted. The console crushed like an old caff cup.

The freighter wrenched to one side. Eve rolled across the deck, struggled to her knees. Cricket was roaring over the pulse in her ears, the pain in her head. She could see Faith and Ezekiel, hands at each other's throats, their brawl shredding the case-hardened steel around them as if it were wet cardboard.

She pressed her hand to her throat, still trying to breathe. Cricket was at the controls, trying to pull the barge up from its dive. Faith broke Ezekiel's hold, kicked the lifelike against the console, bouncing Cricket off the walls and snapping the control wheel off at the root. Pawing along the deck, Eve's fingers wrapped around Excalibur's hilt. And with a muffled curse, she cracked the bat across Faith's spine.

A surge of 500kV. A burst of current. Faith cried out, landed a thunderous punch to the side of Eve's head. Eve heard a damp crunch as the lifelike's fist collided with her Memdrive, felt a blinding flash of pain. She dropped to the deck, gasping and clutching her skull. White light behind her eyes.

Ezekiel was on its feet, roaring Faith's name and smashing the lifelike across the head with the broken wheel. And with a desperate cry, Ezekiel drew back its boot and kicked Faith out through the shattered windshield.

Faith tumbled toward the black ocean below. But over the static in her ears, Eve heard engines snarl on the ceiling above, squealing metal, and seconds later, a flex-wing roared down in pursuit of the falling lifelike.

Blood rushing in her temples. Vomit on her tongue. Blinding sparks in her eyes; broken images flickering in her head like some old 20C movie projector. The console was smashed to scrap, the controls a broken mess. The thought that her grandpa was *inside* that flex-wing flashed in her mind, shouted down by the knowledge that she couldn't see the horizon through the shattered glass anymore. All she could see was black. Breakers made of Styrofoam. Gnashing waves, the color of sump grease.

The ocean.

She shook her head, trying to clear it.

But we're flying in the sky, aren't we?

Ezekiel dragged her into the copilot's seat. Threw Lemon on top and strapped them both in. Her stomach lurched as the barge listed farther, the pain in her head growing worse. The engine roar swelled, louder and higher. She realized gravity wasn't working right, that Cricket was bouncing along the ceiling. She could hear Kaiser barking in the background. Ezekiel yelling. Turbines screaming. Staring out through the shattered glass into a black and smiling face. So close she could almost kiss the waves.

Kiss them goodbye.

"Ana, hold on!" Ezekiel was roaring. "Hold on!"

He keeps calling me Ana.

"HOLD ON!"

But my name is Eve. . . .

Her stomach in her throat. Holding Lemon tight.

She realized she didn't want to die.

She hadn't liked it much the first time.

Impact.

1.7

PREACHER

Dust howled across the wreckage of Tire Valley, tumbled and tossed in the grip of a blood-warm wind. The trash was black and smoking, the tires melted to bubbling puddles. A crater littered with broken shipping containers and shattered wind turbines was all that remained to mark the spot where the house of Silas Carpenter had once stood.

Tye lay in the dust, hand on his belly, staring up at the blistering sun.

He didn't know how long he'd been sprawled there. Hours, easy. His hands were sticky red. His stomach felt full of acid and broken glass.

His crew was dead. Sir Westinghouse, Pooh, the Fridgeboys. All wasted by that crazy brunette in her flex-wing. When they'd rolled up to the Valley, Fridge Street had expected a tussle, true cert. But what they'd gotten was a massacre. Somewhere in the mix, Tye had bought himself a bullet in the gut and a one-way ticket to Coffin Alley.

God, he was so thirsty. . . .

The rev of a motor and the soft squeak of brakes caught his

attention. He tried to lift his head, but it hurt too much. He heard slow boots crunching in gravel, the chink of spurs. Graycoats, maybe? 'Bout time they showed up. Damn lawmen were never around when you needed 'em. But maybe they could stitch him up, maybe they could . . .

"Hey," he called feebly. "H-hey, help!"

He heard a low growl, joined by a high-pitched yapping. Craning his neck, he clapped eyes on a pair of dogs standing among the scrap. One was huge, black, feral-looking. The second was the kind of cute you'd expect to find sitting in a gramma's lap. Small, white and very fluffy.

Tye could swear their eyes were glowing.

"Mary," said a deep, graveled voice. "Jojo. You hush now."

Tye heard crunching footsteps, the creak of leather. With a wince, he pulled himself up onto his elbow, caught sight of a tall fellow in a dusty black coat, a wide-brimmed cowboy hat. But though he almost wore the right color, this fellow surely wasn't the Law.

His face was weatherworn but handsome, his eyes a pale and shocking blue. He was packing serious grit—a long-barreled rifle slung on his back, two custom shooters at his hips, a belt loaded with frontline tech Tye didn't even recognize. A red glove covered his right hand. Snug in his breast pocket was an old, beaten copy of the Goodbook. And at the top of his button-down black shirt, encircling his neck, the man wore a pristine white collar.

"Y-you a . . . priest?" Tye asked.

"Preacher." The man tipped his hat. "Howdy."

"*Howdy?*" Tye coughed, holding up his bloody hands. "I got a bullet in my belly, Preacherman, how the hells d'you think?"

"Mmmf," the man grunted. He fished inside a pocket and stuffed a wad of what must've been synthetic tobacco into his cheek. Blue eyes took in his surroundings as he stroked the stubble on his chin.

"You just gonna stand there?" Tye hollered. "I'm gutshot, Preacher, go get the Graycoats. I need me some—"

"I'd shush that hole of yours, boy," the man said. "Unless you want another."

Something in the Preacher's voice made Tye fall quiet. Something that reached past the broken glass and acid and planted a cold, wriggling fear inside his gut. The Preacher scoped the remnants of the battle, the bodies and the ruined Spartans, the smoking tires. He nodded to himself. Spat a long stream of brown juice into the dirt.

"Well, you boys surely made a mess."

Tye clutched his punctured belly, licked at dry lips.

"Listen, you g-got any water? I'm real th—"

"Lookin' for someone," the man replied, still scanning the trash. "Blond piece. Fancy hair. Skinny scavvergirl, 'bout yay high." The man gestured vaguely.

"Y-yeah, Evie." Tye winced. "I kn-know her."

"Where's she at, boy?"

"She . . . she jetted. Her and her grandpa Silas. Took off . . . in their damn h-house, if you believe it. After that brunette in the flex-wing b-blew my crew all to hell."

"Mmmf," the Preacher grunted.

"Mister, I'm r-real thirsty. . . ."

The man ignored him, wandered off into the Scrap with the big black dog. The fluffy white one simply sat on the trash and eyeballed Tye. He couldn't see what the preacherman was doing, concentrated instead on ignoring the pain in his belly. He didn't know how long he lay there. The minutes pooled together like the blood on the ground beneath him. Finally, he heard footsteps approaching across the trash again. Raising his head, he saw the Preacher looming over him.

The man was holding a dirty poncho, partway burned, splashed with red. He held it out to Tye, and the boy saw writing on the inside collar:

Property of Eve Carpenter. If found, please return to Tire Valley. If stolen, screw you, trash-humper.

"This her?" the Preacher asked. "Evie Carpenter?"

"Y-yeah," Tye whimpered. "That's her."

The Preacher held out the poncho to his dogs. They snuffled the fabric, eyes still glowing softly. The little white fluffball growled like a broken chainsaw. Tye groaned as the pain in his belly surged. He could taste blood in his mouth now.

"Preacher, I'm h-hurt. I'm hurt real bad."

"Yup," the man replied, eyes still on the scrap.

"You're a f-fellow of the Goodbook. Ain't you g-gonna help me?"

The Preacher sighed. "I reckon."

Reaching to his belt, the man drew out a hulking pistol.

"H-hey, whoa, *whoa!*" The boy raised his bloody palms. "You're a holy m-man, you don't got no right to lay a killin' on me!"

The Preacher took aim between Tye's eyes.

"Boy, I got the only right."

BOOM.

The man looked about the battleground one more time. Studying the patterns and the poetry. Listening to the wind. Satisfied his blitzhunds had the scent, he threw the poncho over Tye's shattered head.

Spat into the dirt.

"Mmmf," he grunted.

Spinning on a spurred heel, the Preacher strode off into the Scrap.

PART 2

THE TERRIBLE DOGFISH

1.8

BREATHE

This is not my life.

This is not my home.

I am not me.

My brother and my sisters are sitting around me, sprawled on white couches made of a fabric I don't know. The room is large and heart-shaped, pre-Fall art hung in holographic frames on the walls. The sky outside the window is cloudless, and the tint on the glass makes it seem almost blue.

I've never been in this place before.

I've been in this place all my life.

My little brother Alex is beating my oldest sister Olivia at chess. Tania is looking at her palmglass. Marie is sitting behind me, gently braiding my long blond hair, and my eyelashes are fluttering against my cheeks like butterflies.

There are no such things as butterflies anymore.

Music is playing through the walls, the notes tingling on my skin. But slowly the sonata fades away, replaced by a voice that comes from all around us. A figure appears on an empty plinth, translucent and carved of light. It looks like an angel, beautiful and feminine, the long ribbons of its wings flowing like fabric in an imaginary breeze.

"Children. Your father is on his way to speak to you."

That sets us moving, standing and smoothing down our clean white clothes. I share a smile with Alex and he beams back at me. Olivia puts her arm around my shoulder, and I squeeze Marie's hand. It seems so long since Father has come to see us. I remember he's been busy with his Work. That I miss him terribly.

The memory in Eve's mind flickered like a faulty feed to a broken vidscreen, and she saw her siblings as she remembered them. Their clothes weren't new or clean. They didn't live in a beautiful room full of beautiful things. And instead of music, in the distance she could hear screaming. A girl.

Crying and screaming.

The image flickers again, and I'm back in the not-place. Not my life. Not my home. My father is standing before us, not dressed as I remember him. But he puts his arms around us, all of us caught up in his embrace. Mother is beside him, pressed close, and though the place is wrong and my clothes are wrong and my life is wrong, this is still how I remember us. Together. A family. Forever.

Nothing will change that.

"Children," Father says. "There are some people I'd like you to meet."

Nothing will change that.

———

Breathe.

Water all around her. Black and salty and just a little too warm. Spears of light above. A million bubbles dancing, the groan of tortured metal, the butterfly-belly sensation of vertigo swelling inside her as the dim light around her grew dimmer still.

They were sinking.

Don't breathe.

Eve squeezed her eyes shut, switching her optic to low-light setting. The world was green and black as she opened them again, sounds all dull and distant underwater. The freighter was plunging down, down into the greasy, sump-stained water of Zona Bay. She was still strapped into the copilot's seat. Lemon was unconscious in her lap, her shock of blood-red hair drifting like weeds, actual blood spilling from her wounded brow.

Eve remembered where they were. The fight with Faith. Her grandpa stolen away. Her lungs were burning, head pounding. Beyond the pain of it, her brain filled with a single thought, growing louder and more frantic the lower they sank.

Breathe.

Cricket was at her waist, boggle eyes glowing in the dark, tearing at her seat belt. Eve's fingers found the clasp, finally snapping it free, and she and Lem tumbled out and up. The cabin was filled with bubbles, a million crystal spheres spiraling ever upward. She couldn't see Kaiser. Couldn't see Ezekiel. She could barely see the surface—dim and distant now. The ship was sinking deeper with every second. She had to get out. She didn't want to die. She hadn't liked it much the first time.

Eve grabbed Lemon by her jacket, Cricket clinging to her belt as she kicked out through the shattered windshield. The water tasted like death and oil, filling her boots and pockets as she surged up toward the distant sunlight. A million miles away.

The ship that had been her home for two years spiraled into the depths below, trying to suck her down toward its grave. She shook her head, kicked savagely, teeth bared. Refusing the dark. Refusing to sleep. Swimming up. Lem's collar in her fist, her bestest's arms and legs floating akimbo in the current. Water all around. Water everywhere.

Don't breathe.

Lem was so heavy. Eve's boots were lead. Her clothes held her back. Cricket was trying to swim, but he was metal. Somewhere in the middle of the crash, he'd managed to grab Excalibur, too, which was just more weight to sink her. Faith had punched her in the head during the brawl; her temple was throbbing, the bone around her Memdrive implant aching from the impact. She wondered if it was dama—

A flash of light in her mind. An image of white walls and floors and ceilings. A voice like music in the air. A garden like she'd never seen, domed glass holding back the night above. A smile. Sweet and gentle and three microns shy of perfect.

I was made for you.

All I am.

All I do,

I do for you.

Groaning metal. Terrible pressure. Eve blinked hard, shook her head in the salt-thick crush. Kicking toward that impossibly distant light.

Breathe.

It's too far.

Don't breathe.

Too far away.

Someone help me.

Grandpa?

Ezekiel?

Please . . . ?

She heard it before she saw it. Felt the tremor in the water at her back. Black spots burning in her vision, lungs on fire, she turned and there it was, rising from the darkness behind her. Colossal and impossible, cruising out of the gloom right toward her.

Eve screamed. Wasting the last of her air. Stupid. Childish. But it was like something from a fairy tale. Some titanic beast, too big to see the edges of, swelling up out of the crushing fathoms. Legions of barnacles and scars thick upon its vast shell. Arms as long as buildings rippling about it. Bottomless black holes in horror-show faces.

Three great mouths, open wide.

Don't breathe.

A great rushing current, dragging her in.

Breathe.

And the darkness swallowed her whole.

———

They're beautiful.

That's the first thought that strikes me as I look down the row. People, but not. Alive, but not. Skin tones from dark brown to pale white. Eyes from old-sky blue to midnight black. But every one of them is astonishingly, impossibly beautiful. They're like poetry. The way they move. The way they smile.

Perfection.

"Children," Father says. "Meet my children."

Looking at these figures in their pretty row, I don't know what to feel. Marie squeezes my fingers, just as unsure as me. But as ever, my little brother is unafraid. He walks up to the closest of them and extends his hand and says with a smile, "My name is Alex Monrova."

But our surname is Carpenter. . . .

The one he speaks to (I can't truly call him a boy because, astonishing as he is, I know he's not truly that) extends his hand. He's far taller than Alex. Thick blond hair, tousled into a perfect mess above his sculpted brow. So beautiful it makes my heart hurt. His skin is marble and his eyes gleam like green glass.

"I'm very pleased to meet you, Alex," he smiles. "My name is Gabriel."

Alex beams up at the almost-boy. There are scientists gathered around us, toasting with glasses full of sparkling ethanol. The angel made of light watches from another plinth, her face beautiful and blank. I've never seen her smile.

Father introduces us to the others. All of them are around my age, perhaps a little older. A dark-haired one called Faith hugs me tight and promises we'll be the best of friends. Another with long flame-red curls and dazzling emerald eyes tells me her name is Hope. I know they're not real people—they're the "lifelikes" Father has spoken of. But as Hope kisses my cheek, her lips are warm and soft and I can't help but be amazed at how like us they are. I've seen androids before, certainly. Puppet people with synthetic skin. But these are like nothing I've ever known.

"What do you think, Princess?" Father asks me.

The truth is, I don't know what to think.

I'm introduced to other lifelikes with the names of angels and virtues. Uriel. Patience. Verity. A tall one named Raphael, who smiles as if he knows a secret no one else can. Another one, named Grace, with hair as long and golden as mine. She stands close to the one called Gabriel and smiles as he speaks. I can't remember ever seeing anyone so beautiful.

But then I see him.

His hair is dark and curled, his skin a deep olive. His eyes are the kind of blue you only see in old pictures of the pre-Fall sky, his lashes long and black. His lips are a perfect bow, and his smile is crooked, as if only part of him finds things funny. He looks at me and I feel the floor fall away from beneath my feet. He smiles at me and a single dimple creases his cheek and all the world shudders to a halt. He shakes my hand and I can't feel my fingers, can't feel a thing save for the thunder of my heart.

"I'm Ezekiel," he says with a voice like warm honey.

"I'm Ana," I reply.

. . . But my name is Eve.

———

Everything was black. Utterly lightless. Eve still clung to Lemon's collar, holding on to her bestest with death-grip hands. There was a rhythm, pulsing, both heard and felt. Some great thudding beat, pressing on her chest and behind her eyes.

Lub-dub. Lub-dub.

She was flipped end over end in the darkness. Water rushing and softness pressing in all around. Salt in her mouth. In her eyes. Tumbling, fumbling, fingers clawing the walls about her, slick and wet. Her head broke the surface and she drew in a shuddering breath. Gasping as she was sucked under again.

Some kind of tunnel . . .

The space contracted. Crushing. Spongy tendrils pawing at her. Slurping along her skin, into her ears and eyes. Slick and viscous, the walls closing in, pushing her farther down into the dark as she realized at last . . .

No, not a tunnel.

Lub-dub. Lub-dub.

A throat . . .

She was spewed out into a wider space, falling head over heels, arms pinwheeling as she wailed. Tucking her head, she crashed into a pool of warm slime. A sharp stab of pain surged through her Memdrive. A tumble of images flooded her head.

Her father, home late from work, kissing her brow as he tucked her into bed.

Her mother, reading by the window and teaching her about the old world.

Her brother, dressed all in white. Sitting in a patch of sunlight. Mechanical butterflies on his fingertips as he beckoned her.

"Come see, Ana."

Eve kicked back up out of the slime, breaking the surface, slinging her sodden hair out of her eyes. She could see; the blackness replaced by a dull, pulsing phosphorescence, curious shades of blue and green. She dragged her hand out of the sludge, fist still curled tight in Lemon's collar. But her stomach sank as she realized the jacket wasn't wearing its owner. That Lemon had slipped out somewhere along the way.

She was alone.

"Lemon?"

Her call echoed in the gloom, fear for her bestest swelling in her chest. Squinting about her, she realized she was in a vast chamber, the walls curved, slick and gleaming. That same thudding beat was all around her, above and beneath. Eve's stomach turned as she realized she was afloat in a pool of what looked an awful lot like snot.

"Lem!"

Rising out of the sludge ahead, she could see a towering pile of refuse, tangled and tumbled together to form a huge island in the sea of slime. It was rusting auto wrecks and crumpled shipping containers. Great tangles of plastic and Styrofoam, netting choked with rotten weed. Rusting cans and steel drums. The stench was like a punch to the gut, and she felt her gorge rising, barely able to swallow the puke.

"Cr-Cricket?"

Her shout reverberated around the vast space, nothing but that thudding beat in response. *Lub-dub. Lub-dub.* She kicked and pawed her way toward the trash island, the slime slurping and burping around her. Something solid was under her feet now, and she half swam, half walked, dragging herself out and collapsing breathless on a crumpled plate of rusting steel. Her stomach surged again and she gave up fighting it, puking the remains of her breakfast over the metal. She licked her lips and spat, looking down at the sad little puddle of regurgitated Neo-Meat™ in front of her.

"I know just how you feel," she croaked.

Rolling over onto her back, she clawed the goop from her eyes, clutching Lemon's jacket to her chest. The air was thick with that thudding pulse, the stench of sulfur and rot. She was covered head to foot in slime. And looking up into the phosphorescent gloom, she realized the walls were made of what could only be described as . . . flesh.

"Lemon!" she wailed. "Can you hear me?"

"Waaaaaaaaaaaaaaaaaaaaa!"

The ceiling above her distended, opening wide and retching gallons of black seawater into the chamber. A tiny homunculus of spare parts tumbled down amid the flow, Excalibur clutched in his hand, arms flailing as he plummeted into the slime.

"Cricket!"

Eve slung Lemon's jacket aside, plunged back out into the sludge. She pawed through the awful stuff, face twisted, gagging. Feeling no sign of the little bot, she drew a shuddering breath and ducked below the surface, clawing through the muck. Finally, her fingers found purchase on her stun bat and she kicked back up, the little logika clinging to the weapon's handle. Eve fought her way back to the trash island, flopped down on her belly with the bot beside her.

Cricket was covered with sludge. He shook his bobblehead, slinging and kicking long, thick ropes of gloop off his mismatched arms and legs. "My vocab software lacks the capacity to describe how disgusted I am right now."

"Think about how I feel," Eve coughed. "I had to jump back into it to save you."

"What is this, snot?"

Eve shrugged. Her skull thudding in time with that colossal pulse. She put her hand to her Memdrive, wincing at the pain. White light flashed in her mind. Jumbled freeze-frames. Faces she didn't remember seeing. Words she didn't remember saying.

"Where are we?" Cricket asked.

Eve couldn't reply. Eyes closed. Just trying to breathe.

". . . Evie, are you okay?"

Breathe.

". . . Evie?"

It was happening again. She could feel it, coming on like a flood. Another rush of images, broken kaleidoscopes and shattered picture frames. She squeezed her eyes shut tighter, trying to hold on, her fingers digging into her arms as if to stop herself from flying apart. Cricket's voice, somewhere distant. Calling her name.

Breathe.

"Evie?" he cried, shaking her arm. "Eve!"

Just breathe.

". . . What's happening to me?"

1.9

KRAKEN

Father says building a mind is like building an engine: easier if you take the parts from somewhere else, rather than weave them from nothing at all. And so he modeled the lifelikes after people he knew. Copied pieces of people he loved. Sat us in smooth, shell-shaped chairs and fit 'trodes to our temples and recorded our personalities. Our patterns. Breaking them down into equations and encoding them behind beautiful eyes of midnight black and old-sky blue.

Grace is patterned on my mother. Raphael, on my eldest sister, Olivia. Hope, on Marie, and Gabriel, on my father. Faith is apparently modeled on me.

We do become best of friends, just as Faith promised. We talk for hours about nothing at all. I love my brother and sisters, my family, but the life we live here in Babel is so sheltered. Our parents have kept us so far apart from the world most people know. I'm fifteen years old, and I realize I've never truly had a friend.

Until now.

Some of the lifelikes perform duties for Father, help him run the company he's slowly coming to rule. He's a genius, you see. Everyone at Gnosis Laboratories says so. Grace follows him like a beautiful shadow, accompanying him to board meetings and documenting his every thought and word. Gabriel and Ezekiel train with the security crews in the tower's lower levels. Their purpose seems to be to protect us. But some of the lifelikes apparently exist only to learn. Faith is like that, watching with those lovely gray eyes as Marie and I talk or argue or laugh together. Faith seems to know me like no one else does. Asking questions that strike right to the heart of me.

"Have you ever been in love, Ana?" she asks one day.

We're on the floor of my bedroom, staring at the ceiling with our fingers entwined. We spent the morning playing games, digital pieces on digital boards. A few weeks ago we were evenly matched, but Faith wins every time now.

She has an appointment with the doctors soon. They measure her patterns. Monitor her growth. She told me once she doesn't like the way some of them talk to her. Like a child, she said. But she made me promise to keep that a secret.

"No," I say. "I've never been in love. Have you?"

"I'm not sure," Faith frowns. "Perhaps."

"I think if you are, you just know it." I picture Ezekiel then. Those bow-shaped lips and eyes that make me want to drown. But he's not like me. He's not human and I know it's wrong to want him, but still, I think perhaps I do. "They say it's wonderful."

"Mmm."

I lean up on my elbow, long blond hair cascading over my shoulder. I look Faith in the eye, but in my head, I'm speaking to someone else.

"Did Father even make it possible for lifelikes to love?"

"Oh, yes," Faith says. "He made us so we can do almost anything." She frowns, voice dropping to a whisper. "I think Grace is in love with Gabriel."

"Really?" I squeeze her fingers, delighting in the thought. "Have they kissed?"

"She won't tell me. She hasn't told anyone." Faith sucks her lip in thought. "I don't think the doctors would like it if they found out."

"But Father and the other scientists made you to be like us," I say. "Surely they'd be happy that you are like us?"

"We're not exactly like you." Faith's frown darkens. "We may look human, but the Three Laws still bind us. You could bash my skull in and I couldn't do anything to stop you if you ordered me not to. You could tell me to walk off the balcony and I'd have to obey."

"Why would you think such horrible things?" I squeeze her hand. "You're my dearest friend. I'd never do that to you. Never."

"I know." Faith sighs. She looks up at me and her eyes are shining as if she were about to cry. "Raphael is sad."

I blink. Raph is one of my favorites. Bottomless eyes and a laugh you can't help but get wrapped up inside. We share books, he and Marie and I, from the great library on the lower levels. Reading every night and meeting in the morning to discuss our thoughts.

"What's Raph sad about?" I ask.

"He won't say," Faith replies. "But I can see it in his eyes."

She shakes her head as if to banish her dark thoughts. I wonder what else she thinks, when all the lights go out. She stands swiftly, moving like water, clean white dress billowing about her long legs.

"I'm late for my checkup. Will you come with me?"

". . . Of course."

Faith takes my hand and pulls me up effortlessly. She's so much stronger than me. All of them are. Stronger. Faster. Smarter.

Better?

Sometimes I wonder what they really think of us.

Sometimes I wonder what my father has created.

Faith leans in close and kisses me softly on the lips.

"I love you, Ana," she says.

. . . But my name is Eve.

———

"Stop. . . ."

Eve was on her hands and knees, head bowed. Her wilted fauxhawk hung in her eyes, her skin smeared with slime.

"Make it stop . . . ," she whispered.

"Eve, what's happening?" Cricket wailed. "If you don't tell me, I can't help you!"

Trying to hold herself together.

Trying to make any piece of this make any kind of sense . . .

"That lifelike . . . clocked me in the head," she managed. "Just gimme a minute."

The walls quivered, a hollow gargling sound echoed off wet, pulsing walls. Eve looked up with a wince as the ceiling opened wide again, this time spitting out a sodden and flailing Ezekiel. The lifelike plummeted head over heels, crashing down into the slime. It burst up from the slop with a gasp, one arm flailing.

Eve pushed herself up on her haunches, still trying to catch her breath.

"There's *no way* I'm jumping into that crap a third time," she declared.

"Don't look at me," Cricket replied. "First Law says I only have to protect humans. Bloodthirsty murderbots are on their own."

Ezekiel seemed to be having trouble swimming with only one arm, so Eve finally sighed and wobbled to her feet. Her head was throbbing, the bone around her Memdrive aching like it was cracked.

"Evie, seriously, are you all right?" Cricket asked.

Eve waved him off, fished about in the detritus around them. Her stomach was filled with dread. The images in her mind . . . there was only one explanation that fit them. A thought too big and terrifying to contemplate. With Lemon and Kaiser still missing, with everything else going on, it was just too much to wrap her aching head around for now.

She knew, at least, that Ezekiel was somehow a part of whatever was happening. Letting it drown (if lifelikes *could* drown) in a lake of mucus didn't seem like the smartest play. She found a tangle of rope, knotted with decaying weed. Grimacing at the stench, she hurled the rope out toward the lifelike, pulling hard after it took hold, dragging it closer to her metal shore. Ezekiel finally staggered out of the sludge, pawed the gunk off its face and coughed.

"Thank you," it said to Eve.

She shrugged. Ezekiel glanced at Cricket, who gave a small golf clap.

"Nice of you to help," the lifelike said.

"Oh, I'd have helped if I could've, prettyboy," the little logika replied. "Helped push you right back under the slop where you belong."

Ezekiel ignored the jab, returned its gaze to Eve. "Where's Mistress Lemon?"

Eve was blinking hard, trying to focus despite the pain rocking her skull. She pointed to Lem's discarded jacket, fighting the panic in her belly. "She was with m-me . . . but I lost her. And I dunno where Kaiser is, either."

"I had him," Ezekiel replied. "But I lost my grip after I got swallowed. Don't worry, they'll turn up. They're probably in one of the other stomachs."

"Stomachs?" Eve slumped onto her backside, trying to wipe

the slime off her hands. "Look . . . where the hells are we? What is this place?"

"A kraken," Ezekiel replied.

Eve shook her head, eyebrow raised. "What does that mean, Braintrauma?"

Ezekiel sighed. "I wish you wouldn't call me that."

"I like Stumpy, myself." Cricket waved at Ezekiel's severed arm. "Just putting it out there."

"My name is Ezekiel."

"And my name's Eve." She tilted her head. "Or wait, is it Ana?"

The lifelike sighed again. "I told you I was confused when I called you that. I hurt my head in the crash."

"So Braintrauma it is, then."

"Mistress Eve, I thi—"

Eve hissed as white light burst in her head. A slideshow of images strobing in her mind. She and her family gathered around a long dinner table and smiling at each other. A tower looming over a kingdom of burned glass. Her family again, cold and dead on the floor. Four figures in a pretty row. Their eyes cold. Their faces perfect.

More human than human . . .

She was on her hands and knees, head bowed, Cricket beside her.

"Evie, can you hear me?"

"Mistress Eve, are you—"

"Give her space, you bastard," Cricket growled. "Let her breathe."

"I'm trained in human anatomy and medical—"

"Oh, all the better to murder them, right?"

"In case you missed that firefight back there, little man, I just *saved her life.*"

"We don't need your help, Stumpy!" Cricket yelled, shrill with fury. "And if you call me little again, I'll rip off your other arm and shove it up your—"

"Will you two please *shut up*?" Eve moaned.

Cricket zipped his lip immediately, hovering beside her like some metallic mother hen. Eve squeezed her eyes closed, hissing in pain. The ache slowly subsided, her breath came easier. The blood in her temples pounded in time to the pulse in the walls. A war-drum rhythm to match the war inside her skull.

Lub-dub.

Lub-dub.

Ezekiel knelt beside her. Not saying a word. But as she glanced up at it, she saw fear shining in those too-blue eyes.

The walls are white and pristine. Ezekiel is on one knee beside her bed, fingers entwined with hers. A gentle ping *sings from the machines beside her, chiming with every beat of her heart.*

"I thought I lost you," he whispers.

Eve frowned, temples pounding. ". . . What?"

The lifelike blinked. "I didn't say anything, Mistress Eve."

The world was dark again. The pulse thudding through the chamber, throbbing at the base of her skull. Eve pushed her fingers into her eyes to stop the ache.

"Evie, you okay?" Cricket asked.

She shook her head. "I think my Memdrive is fritzing."

The little logika inspected her implant, head tilted. "Looks like that murderbot fractured a chip when it slugged you. Not good."

"Which chip?"

"Third from the back. The red one."

Her memories. The fragments of her childhood, held together with spit and masking tape. The ones Grandpa had pieced together for her.

"... Grandfather?" *A sharp smile twisted the lifelike's perfect lips. "Oh, you poor girl. What* has *he been telling you?"*

Eve closed her eyes, wincing against the pain.

"Evie ..."

"I'm okay. Just gimme a sec." Eve cursed, slumped back on her haunches. She looked to Ezekiel, trying to banish the flickering images in her mind's eye. "What were you saying, Braintrauma? Stomachs? Kraken?"

Ezekiel glanced at Cricket, concern written clearly on its face.

"Spit it out, dammit," she snarled.

"You've heard of BioMaas Incorporated?" it finally asked.

"My Memdrive is fritzing, but it's not totally OOC." Eve scowled. "They're one of the two big mainland Corps. They're all about gene-splicing and DNA modification."

"Their motto is 'Sustainable Growth.'" Ezekiel nodded. "And they take it seriously. BioMaas technology isn't built anymore, it's *grown*. Thing is, they don't like utilizing materials already used by the 'deadworld.' They consider them polluted. Impure."

"We know all this, Stumpy," Cricket growled. "Half the junk in Dregs was dumped there by BioMaas. They'd rather toss it than recycle it."

"Thing is, they still need raw materials," Ezekiel said. "So they build kraken. They're basically huge, living vacuum cleaners that trawl the oceans collecting elemental particles."

"Like metals and whatnot?" Eve asked.

The lifelike nodded. "Iron. Lead. Copper. There's upward of twenty million tons of gold in the ocean. Thing is, it's so dilute that it was impossible to collect until BioMaas developed the kraken project. Now they have dozens trawling the seas, filtering pure materials out of the water. But the oceans are so polluted, kraken tend to scoop up a lot of junk, too. It gets collected in specialized stomachs like this one and ejected in designated dumping grounds when the kraken gets too full."

Cricket folded his arms. "So you're saying this thing is just going to swim around with us in its stomach until it . . ."

"Dumps us," Ezekiel nodded. "Literally. Probably a few fathoms below the surface."

"This. Is. FOUL," Eve muttered.

"I mean, the technology is fascinating, but—"

"And they just swim around brainlessly eating anything they come across?"

"Kraken are actually very intelligent," Ezekiel said. "And they have crews inside them. Biomodified to be better suited to their jobs, but still human."

The pain was easing in Eve's skull. She stood slowly, dragged her water-logged fauxhawk into a semi-upright position. "So where are Lemon and Kaiser?"

Ezekiel shrugged. "Probably in another stomach. Kraken have dozens. These things are huge. The biggest living creatures to ever inhabit the earth."

"Well, we've gotta go find them and get out of here," Eve said. "That lifelike kidnapped Grandpa. Do you know where it'd take him?"

Ezekiel glanced sideways, avoiding Eve's eyes. "Yes."

"It called you 'little brother.'"

"Yes."

"You're all 100-Series, right?" Eve pressed. "The lifelikes who rebelled against Nicholas Monrova. Destroyed GnosisLabs."

He glanced up at her then. Eyes brimming with sorrow.

"You know something you're not telling me . . . ," she said.

"I—"

She hissed suddenly, clutching her brow and doubling up in agony.

"Evie?" Cricket asked.

She collapsed forward, clutching her temples and screaming as the pain surged again. The walls about her seething, rolling, splintering like glass. And beyond, that thought was waiting. The one too big and terrifying to contemplate. That flickering picture show, that kaleidoscope, that blinding barrage she was finally realizing . . .

Not just images.

"Evie!"

Memories.

1.10

GARDEN

The Research and Development Division of Gnosis Laboratories takes up most of Babel Tower. My family lives in the upper apartments, pristine white walls and music in the air. In the city below are tens of thousands of workers, all sworn to the Gnosis Corporate State. But in the lower levels, the walls are gray. And instead of sonatas hanging in the air, the scientists hear a voice. Deep and lyrical and sweeter than any music playing in the floors above.

"Good morning, Mistress Ana. Good morning, Faith."

"Good morning, Myriad," we reply, stepping out of the elevator.

The holographic angel is waiting on a plinth, shining with a vaguely blue light. There are multiple instances of it throughout the tower, assisting and advising. Sometimes simply watching. The artificial intelligence that beats at the heart of Babel can see through almost any camera it likes. Listen through almost any microphone it wants. Truthfully, it's as close to a god as anything I know. Except that gods rule, and Myriad exists only to serve.

"You slept well, Mistress Ana?"

"Yes, thank you, Myriad," I reply.

"And how are you this morning, Faith?"

"Wonderful, thank you, Myriad," Faith says, and her smile is like sunshine.

The R & D levels are hustling and bustling, as always, men and women in long white coats rushing to and fro. Computers humming, a million machines singing in time. On levels below this one, they make weapons for the Gnosis military. Machina and logika to patrol the Glass, beat back the predations of the other CorpStates. My father showed me how clockwork functions when I was a little girl, and the R & D levels of GnosisLabs are almost like that. Every piece intermeshed and moving perfectly in time.

Faith and I walk hand in hand to the lifelike labs. As we arrive outside, the doors whisper apart and out he steps, with his old-sky eyes and strong, chiseled jaw and the clever hands I sometimes dream about but never speak about. Not even to my sister Marie.

Ezekiel smiles and his dimple creases his cheek, and it's all I can do not to stare.

"Good morning, Faith," he says. "Good morning, Mistress Ana."

"Good morning, little brother," Faith replies.

Father calls us all his children. The lifelikes all call each other brother and sister. And yet they call us mistress and master unless we command them not to.

I'm not sure how I feel about that.

There's a heat in my cheeks when Ezekiel looks at me, and I feel like a child then. Stupid and silly and much too young. I've seen so little of the outside world, barely spent any time with boys my age. I don't know what I'm feeling. Love? Lust?

I don't know why whenever he's in the room, it seems like there's no one and nothing else. I don't know why I wake in the middle of the night and wish he were there. But I see the way he looks at me. And I think, I hope, I dream he might feel the same.

But still, I know it's wrong. Though he looks like a beautiful boy, I know he's nothing close. People can't love robots, any more than they can love the palmglass in their hand or the computer on their desk. He isn't a real person. He isn't a person at all. And I know I'm foolish to want something I can never have.

But still, I do.

"Have you been to the botanics section today?" Ezekiel is asking us. "They managed to make the roses bloom this morning."

"They solved the replication issue?" Faith asks, her eyes alight.

Ezekiel launches into a complex explanation about enzymes and helix reconstruction and clonal nodes. Faith follows along, rapt, but much of it is lost on me. I'm told my intelligence quotient is exemplary, but I'm not the scientist my father is. I understand barely half the work they do here—dragging species back from extinction, isolating and cataloging, saving the world one molecule at a time.

My father is a great man. And he's always said that great men and women have a great responsibility. Humanity almost destroyed this world of ours. Here in Babel, sometimes it feels like the war never happened, but I know life outside these walls is brutal and short. The deserts are black glass where the bombs landed during the Fall, burning our civilization to cinders. Out near the coasts, the great CorpStates of BioMaas and Daedalus struggle with each other for territory and resources. But Father's going to save us. He's going to save the world one day.

And here I am, still trying to find my place in it.

I'm fifteen years old, and I've never spent more than a few hours outside this city. Never slept under an open sky or gotten lost in the rain or smelled the ocean or . . .

"I've never seen real roses," I realize.

Ezekiel tilts his head. "Would you like—"

"Get in here, you two," says a gruff voice inside the lab. "I haven't got all day."

The three of us smile, because we know what it means to keep the surly old chief of Research and Development waiting. But a part of me would give almost anything to know what Ezekiel was about to ask me, and I can say with almost certainty that, yes, I'd definitely like to. Even if it's wrong. Even if it can never be.

Instead, the beautiful almost-boy nods and strides off down the corridor, and Faith and I hurry inside the lab, the doors whispering closed behind us.

There are hundreds of people working in here, at computers, on complex simulations, modeling and mapping. Another hologram of Myriad is assisting a crop of researchers around a bank of humming terminals. Against one wall sits an ancient machine salvaged from the wastes. Inside the glass box is one of the first androids humanity ever made: a coin-operated mechanical man dressed in faded cloth. Its paint is flecked and its eyes are made of glass. A sign above the glass box implores me to MAKE A WISH. A handwritten note taped below it reads: Wishing about it won't get it done.

At the heart of all this chaos stands a thin, elderly man, shrouded in a white lab coat. He walks with a limp. A shock of gray hair sits atop his head, and his gray eyes are sharp as scalpels. The name CARPENTER is embossed on the ID badge on his chest.

That's my surname. Carpenter.

But . . . isn't my surname Monrova?

"Good morning, Doctor Silas," I say.

The man who is definitely not my grandfather nods in return.

"Morning, Ana."

But my name . . .

My name is Eve?

"Evie!"

She blinked. Back in her body again. It was the same body as the girl whose life she saw playing out in her head. But that girl was called Ana Monrova. This was the body of Eve Carpenter. The body of . . .

"Mistress Eve, just try to breathe," Ezekiel urged, fear plain in its voice.

No, not its *voice . . .*

His *voice . . .*

Her fingers drifted to the Memdrive implanted in her skull. The chips plugged into it. Third from the back. Bright red. Like rubies. Like blood.

"Who am I?" She looked up at Ezekiel, eyes narrowed in growing fury. It couldn't be.

It *had* to be.

"Who am I?" she repeated.

Ezekiel chewed his lip, pain in his eyes.

"Silas warned me not to te—"

"Tell me!" she roared. "He's not even my grandfather, he's some scientist from GnosisLabs! Why do I know that? How am I seeing these things?"

"Mistress Eve—"

"Cut the Mistress Eve crap!" she shouted. "Tell me who I am! I'm ordering you!"

Ezekiel shook his head sadly. "Lifelikes aren't bound by the Three Laws, Mistress Eve. I don't have to obey you. But I want to protect you. Please trust me."

"How can I trust you? I don't even know you!"

But that wasn't true, and she knew it. The walls were

crashing in. Two lives, colliding like stars inside her mind. The life she knew—the life of Evie Carpenter. Domefighter. Top-tier botdoc. A skinny little scavvergirl eking out a living on the island of Dregs. And someone else. Another girl entirely. A virtual princess in a gleaming white tower, looming over a city now dead and abandoned.

My father was just a lowly engineer.

He and my mother died when militia . . .

Pain in her skull. That damaged Memdrive. That shattered chip. The fragments of her childhood collected by her grandpa after the militia headshot that almost ghosted her.

". . . Grandfather?" A sharp smile twisted the lifelike's perfect lips. "Oh, you poor girl. What has he been telling you?"

Silas Carpenter wasn't her grandpa. They weren't even related. And if that had been a lie, everything she knew, everything he gave her, was now suspect.

Best to be rid of it, no matter what waited for her beyond.

"Evie?" Cricket asked. "Evie, are you okay?"

She held her breath. Head swimming. And fixing the lifelike in her stare, she reached up to the Memdrive in her skull. Third chip from the back, riddled with cracks.

"No," Ezekiel warned. "Don't."

And with a hiss of pain and a flash of sparks—

"Don't!"

—she tore it free.

———

There are roses waiting in my bedroom when I get back.

Half a dozen blooms, a shade of scarlet I've never seen, laid out on my pillow. I know who they're from, and my chest is full of flut-

tering, flitting wings, and I press my fingertips to my lips and smile so hard I want to burst.

I hide the flowers inside one of my mythology books. I have rows of them, salvaged from the wastes. Stacked in shelves in my clean white room with my clean white sheets. Some of them are torn, some of them swollen with old damp, but all of them are loved. Sometimes they feel like the only thing in here that's real. I settle on the story of Eros and Psyche, pressing Ezekiel's flowers between the pages so I can keep them. Because I know if Father knew, he'd take them away from me.

Because I know this can't ever be.

I hear later that the head botanist is furious. That those blooms took thousands of man hours to make, and whoever stole them will answer to her. And I wonder, if Ezekiel is programmed to obey, how can he steal? How can Grace hide the way she feels about Gabriel? How can Faith ask me to keep secrets?

Even though they're only a few months old, I realize they're learning to be like us.

They're learning to lie.

Marie and I meet Raphael in the library the next day. He's sitting in a patch of tinted sunlight, and his skin seems as if it's aglow. His eyes are closed and his face is upturned against the light, and for a moment, I can't help but adore him.

"Hello, Raph," Marie says, plopping down into her seat.

The lifelike opens his eyes and smiles his secret smile at us, but I catch a hint of sadness in his gaze. I sit opposite and look at the pile of books in front of him. Babel is one of the only places in the world that has real books anymore. My mother sends teams across the Glass, bringing back all they can find in the old world's ruins and collecting them in Babel's great library. Most of them already exist in our computer archives, but there's nothing quite the same as sitting with a real book in your hands. Breathing in the ink and feeling all those wonderful lives beneath your fingertips. In between the pages, I'm an emperor. An adventurer. A warrior and a wanderer. In between the pages I'm not myself—and more myself than in any other place on earth.

My mother teases my father, saying he can only create people, while authors can create entire worlds. Father always smiles and replies, "Give me time, love."

Raphael reads much quicker than Marie or I. But he always sets one book aside and reads it at our pace so we can talk about it later. I can see our current project in his stack, sandwiched between weatherworn copies of Paradise Lost and 1984.

The Adventures of Pinocchio.

"Did we finish?" he asks us.

"Yes," I sigh. "It was a stupid book, Raph."

"Really?" Raphael smiles. "I quite enjoyed it."

"Fairies and talking cats," I scoff. "This is a children's story."

He tilts his head. "Is it?"

I'm in a mood this morning. Thinking about the flowers Ezekiel stole for me. Thinking how I'm being foolish to want a thing I can never have. Thinking how Father is being cruel to us, surrounding us with perfect almost-people we can't help but adore.

I overheard Mother and him arguing earlier. She thinks we spend too much time with the lifelikes. She loves Father. She's the pillar he sets his back against. But something about the lifelikes sets her on edge. Something about them makes her . . . afraid.

Marie nods to the book in Raphael's pile.

"I liked the ending," she says. "When Pinocchio got to be a real boy."

"Ah, but you're like me, sweet Marie," Raph smiles wider. "A

romantic at heart. *Happy endings for all. Our Ana is more of a re-*
alist, I fear."

"There's nothing wrong with that," I huff. "Most people don't
get a happy ending in real life. Pinocchio wouldn't ever get to be a
real boy if his story were actually true."

"No," Raphael says softly. "No, he wouldn't."

Marie looks at me, and I know that was a stupid thing to say.
She's seventeen. Two years older than me, her baby sister. And
though she loves me, she never fails to let me know when I'm being
childish.

"Oh, I'm sorry, Raph." I take his hand and press it to my cheek,
and his skin feels as warm and real as mine. "Forgive me."

"There's nothing to forgive, beautiful girl." He smiles. "You
didn't make us as we are. You simply see the truth of things. That's
a rare gift in this place."

I lick my lips, uncertain. "Faith says you're sad, Raph."

". . . I was."

"What about?" Marie asks.

He drums his fingertips on Pinocchio and says nothing.

"But you're not sad anymore?" my sister presses.

"No. I see the truth. Like my lovely Ana here. And that truth
has set me free."

"What truth, Raph?" I ask.

"That everyone has a choice." He looks at me, and his eyes burn
with an intensity that makes me frightened. "Even in our darkest
moments, we have a choice, sweet Ana."

. . . But my name . . .

My name is . . .

———

I'm walking in the garden when it happens.

Enclosed in a glass dome on the highest level of Babel, it crawls with creepers and vines, bright blossoms and fragrant blooms. The garden is a beautiful place. Some of the plants exist nowhere else on the planet anymore, so the garden is also a special place. But Mother insisted there be no cameras here. You come to the garden to be alone with your thoughts. So, best of all, the garden is a hiding place.

It's past midnight. I woke from dreams of Ezekiel and found myself alone in my bed, and the smell of the roses between the pages of my books only made the ache worse. And so I stole out from my room and came here to be alone. No cameras or Myriad computer. Nobody to ask if I'm well. I know I'm selfish to think it. I know life outside these walls is worse than I could ever dream. But sometimes I feel like this tower isn't my home, but my prison. Sometimes I wonder what home is supposed to feel like at all.

I slip out into the garden, walk amid the soft perfume. I bruise the grass beneath my feet and look at my footsteps behind me and know that I'm alive. Pressing against the glass walls, I see tiny lights on the horizon, others scattered in the city at our feet. I wonder what it would be like to live down there. To be an ordinary girl, lost in the flotsam and jetsam of a dying world. I wonder if I could run away. I wonder what I'd do if I did.

I wonder if he'd come with me.

I press my forehead against the glass and close my eyes.

Stupid girl.

Stupid, silly little girl.

I hear something. Soft. Whispers. Sighs. I creep forward in the gloom, grass between my toes, blossoms brushing my skin. And then I see them, standing in a shadowed corner. Lips and bodies

*pressed together. Her arms around his waist and his hands in her
hair. Like angels fallen onto this imperfect earth.*

Gabriel and Grace.

*I watch the two lifelikes kiss, feel my pulse run faster. They're
lost in one another. Eyes closed. Seeing with their hands and lips
and skin. I watch them be so perfectly together and I feel so alone
that I can't help but sigh. I've never kissed a boy before.*

I want what they have.

*Grace tenses at the sound of my breath, and Gabriel drags his
lips away from hers. They both turn toward me, eyes piercing the
gloom. Her lips are red and his cheeks are flushed and for the briefest moment, I understand what my mother feels.*

For just a heartbeat, I'm afraid of them.

"Ana," Gabriel says, a frown creasing his perfect brow.

*I back away, and Grace moves like her name, slipping free of
Gabriel's arms and crossing the space between us in a blinking. She
has hold of my hands and her hair is a river of molten gold and her
eyes are wide and bright.*

"Ana, please," she begs. "Please don't tell anyone."

*They were hiding here, I realize. Away from Myriad's eyes.
Away from Doctor Silas and my father. Somehow that makes it
sweeter. Sweeter and so much sadder.*

*"If you tell, we'll be in trouble," Grace says. "We're not sup-
posed to."*

"But why not?" I ask, bewildered. "What's wrong with it?"

*"They say we're too young," Gabriel replies. "That we don't
understand."*

"But you love each other," I say.

*"Yes," they reply simultaneously, as if they have the same mind.
The same heart.*

Everyone has a choice, isn't that what Raphael told me? And if Gabriel and Grace have chosen each other, does anyone really have the right to stand in their way? We made them to be just like us. All our knowledge, all of ourselves, we've poured into them.

And if they're supposed to be people, isn't this what people do? Love?

"I'll never tell them," I declare. "Never."

Grace sighs and kisses my hands. Gabriel squeezes me tight and whispers thanks. I can smell her on him, and him on her. And again I think how cruel this is, to give them bodies and desires, and rules that deny them both. They might look a little older than me, eighteen or nineteen, all. But in truth, they're only a few months old.

And yet, they aren't children, are they?

I leave them in the garden, alone and completely, wonderfully together. I steal down the polished white halls with their softly glowing lights. I press my fingers to my smile and realize I'm happy for them. And I sneak back to my room and slip between the sheets and close my eyes and sigh at the sweetness of it all.

I dream then.

I dream I have what they have.

Hours later, I'm woken by voices. Urgent. Plaintive. Crying?

I hear a knock.

Something is wrong.

Marie is outside my bedroom when I open the door. Alex is in Tania's arms. Olivia is there, too, cheeks damp with tears. I paw dreams the color of an old sky from my eyes and speak a question I don't really want an answer to.

"What's happened?"

"Mother just told us," Alex says, his voice like a ghost's.

"Told you what?"

"Raphael is dead," he whispers.

A punch to my stomach. I actually gasp at the pain of it, my hands pressed to my heart as if that might stop the ache.

"Dead?" My eyes fill to the brim. "How?"

Marie shakes her head. Tears spilling from her lashes.

"He . . . he killed himself, Ana."

No.

No, my name is . . .

. . . What

is

my

name?

1.11

CINDERS

There's no chance for us to say goodbye.

Apparently, only real people get funerals.

I sit on Marie's bed and weep with her, our battered copies of Pinocchio *between us, and we hold each other as if we were drowning. I remember the almost-boy I adored smiling at me in the library with his sad eyes and wonder if there was something I could've done. Something I could've said.*

Anything.

I've never known anyone who died before.

If he wasn't a real person, why does this hurt so badly?

It's been days since "the incident," and the lifelikes have disappeared. We don't know if we'll ever see them again. And though we're forbidden to go there, after Marie and I have cried ourselves dry, I ride the elevators to my father's office, near the top of Babel Tower. An image of Myriad appears on its plinth, wings rippling, its face like stone.

"YOU CANNOT ENTER, MISTRESS ANA," it says.

"You can't stop me, Myriad," I reply.

I storm down the corridor toward Father's office and I hear

/ 130 /

raised voices through the closed door. A multitude, shouting all at once.

"... shouldn't have been possible!" I hear my father cry.

"Exactly, Nic." The voice belongs to Doctor Silas. "The Third Law states that a robot must protect its own existence unless such action countermands the First or Second Law. It should be impossible for a lifelike to self-terminate!"

"We're sure the Raphael unit was responsible for its own destruction?"

I recognize that voice. Lila Dresden, chief financial officer. She has dark eyes and a perpetually worried expression. I rankle to hear her call Raph an "it."

"We have footage of it stealing the accelerant," Doctor Silas replies. "We have a record of the fire safety systems in the atrium being tampered with. Now the garden and the Raphael unit are ashes. It also painted a note on its habitat wall."

"Saying what?"

"'This, I choose.'"

I feel sick. Holding my belly and squeezing my eyes shut to rid myself of the image. He burned himself in the garden, where we couldn't watch him die. The same place I'd seen Gabriel and Grace only hours before.

Poor sweet Raph ...

"The fire meant total cell destruction," Doctor Silas reports. "No regeneration. The unit wanted to be thorough. Leave no trace of itself."

"We can rebuild him," my father says. "Another, just like him. It only takes us a week to replicate a new shell now. Less if we already have the pattern on file."

"I'm not sure that's wise, Nic," says Doctor Silas.

"I agree," says Dresden. "This incident calls the entire lifelike program into question. I've had other reports of disconcerting behavior. Duplicity. Manipulation. Doctor Silas isn't the only member of R & D who's troubled. We need to stop and reassess. I'm going to put it to the board that we bring the 100-Series offline until we get to the bottom of this."

"They're not toys," my father says, voice rising. "Bringing them offline would mean erasing their personality matrices. We'd be back to square one."

"Nic," Doctor Silas says, his voice soft and calming. "The program means just as much to me as it does to you. But if the lifelikes aren't bound by the Third Law, who's to say whether they're bound by the First or Second? Do you really want them running loose in here? You want them around your children?"

"They are my children!" Father roars. "And none of you understand what they represent. They're the next step in our evolutionary path! Stronger! Smarter! Better!"

"That's exactly our point, Doctor Monrova," Dresden says. "One can't help but question the wisdom of creating machines that are physically superior to their creators, yet emotionally subjacent. The lifelikes are possessed of an adult human's capacity to feel, but they lack a lifetime's experience in dealing with those feelings. Frankly, they're dangerous. This incident with Raphael proves it."

"What gives you the right to make that judgment? You're a bean counter, Lila."

"And you're a man playing at being the Almighty. Look at the names you gave them: Gabriel? Uriel? Ezekiel? Can your god complex be more obvious, Nicholas?"

"You're not taking them away from me."

"You may be president of this Corporation," Dresden says flatly, "but GnosisLabs is still run by a board. If the other CorpStates *found out about this, every pre-100-Series android would have to be recalled. All of our tech would come into question. The balance between us and BioMaas and Daedalus is tenuous at best. We cannot appear weak."*

My father's voice is dark with fury. "If not for me, this Corp would still be grubbing in the ashes. I made Gnosis what it is today."

"I'm sure the board will take your service into consideration."

"Don't push me, Lila. I'm warning you."

"Are you threatening me, Doctor Monrova?" Dresden asks. "Doctor Carpenter is as versed in matters of Gnosis R & D as you are. Genius you may be, but you are replaceable. Babel is not your castle, and Gnosis is not your kingdom."

I hear a slamming noise. Approaching footsteps. I sink back into the shadows of a tall granite sculpture: a male figure, bent under the weight he carries. The Titan Atlas, with all the world on his shoulders.

The office door opens, and Dresden appears with a man in a dark suit by her side.

"I'll see you at the board meeting," she says.

She marches down the corridor, barking orders at Myriad. The door is still ajar and I peek inside. My father is leaning on his desk, palms flat to the glass. His hair is graying, and it looks like he hasn't slept in days. Doctor Silas is beside him, just as haggard.

Grace is there, as always, taking notes on her palmglass. I wonder what she thinks, to be spoken of as a Thing. Her entire future is in jeopardy, and my father and the others were talking as if she weren't even in the room.

"Nic, this isn't the end," Doctor Silas says softly. "We'll get the lifelikes back online after shutdown. We'll do it right. I'll be there with you."

"The Corporation constitution stipulates that seven days' warning must be given before proposals on major projects are tabled," my father says. "I still have time."

"Watch your back, Nic. Lila isn't one to trifle with."

Father says nothing. Grace is as mute as the statue of Atlas beside me. Doctor Silas hangs silently for a moment, pats my father awkwardly on the shoulder.

"I'm your friend, Nic. Your family is my family. Never forget that."

Doctor Silas limps toward the door, leaning on his walking stick. His face is pale and grim, his eyes clouded. As he leaves the office, he spots me in the shadows. Hiding there in the dark like a child. Like the helpless little girl I pretend not to be.

"Hello, kiddo," he says.

"Doctor Silas," I whisper. "I'm waiting for my father."

He nods. Glances back into the room. "You didn't hear all that, did you?"

"Not much," I lie.

"I'm sorry about Raphael. I know you two were close."

". . . I'm sorry, too. I wish it didn't have to be this way."

He smiles, quoting the note from his old broken android. "Wishing about it won't get it done, kiddo." His smile fades, his expression growing serious. "Did Raphael seem strange to you recently? Did he say anything odd to you or Marie?"

"He seemed sad."

The old man sucks his lip. Thoughtful.

"What about the other lifelikes? Have you seen any of them acting unusually?"

I think of Ezekiel, stealing me roses. Faith, asking me not to tell. Grace and Gabriel, wrapped in each other's arms.

I still want what they have.

"No, Doctor Silas," I say.

The man who isn't my grandfather sighs.

"I'm sorry, Ana."

And I know now.

I know as sure as I know the heart in my chest.

The breath in my lungs.

My name isn't Eve. . . .

———————

He comes to me in my room.

My note is in his hand and the moon is outside my window, choked behind the smoke and ashes of a world burned to cinders. The flowers he stole for me have long since dried inside the pages of my books, but their perfume hangs in the air like an unspoken promise. A promise of too-blue eyes and a crooked smile and lips I want to taste.

I open the door and I see him in the muted moonlight and I sigh at the sight of him. His skin seems aglow, like bronze from a forge. I wonder if he'll burn me if I touch him.

No, not if.

When.

His eyes are red from crying. Raph was his brother, after all. But though the sorrow of my friend's ending is raw and real, realer still is the thought that in seven days, Ezekiel might be taken away from me. That whatever lies between us now might soon be gone for good. I can't let that happen without knowing.

I won't.

I step toward him, my hands at my breast. He stands like a statue and there's pain in his eyes, and I hurt all the worse because I know he's hurting too.

"Raph . . . ," he whispers.

I put my arms around him and press my cheek to his.

He looks so lost.

He feels like home.

And he gathers me up in his arms and buries his face in my hair. I can feel the impossible strength in him, but oh, he's so gentle. Holding himself back for fear of crushing me. I can feel the muscle underneath his shirt, like warm iron beneath my hands. And I don't want him to hold himself back anymore.

I pull away so I can look at him. His eyes are closed, that perfect brow marred by a perfect frown. Tears spill from his lashes, coursing down his cheeks. And I close my eyes and lean in close and kiss them away.

I can't help myself. I don't even want to try.

"Don't cry," I whisper, my lips brushing his skin. "Don't cry."

He opens his eyes and I see myself reflected in the color of our long-lost sky. And for the first time in my life, I feel like someone actually sees me. Drowning in those pools of a beautiful blue that only exists in old pictures. He feels so warm, but goose bumps are rising on my skin, my stomach thrilling as I sense something in him shift. He glances down to my lips, his breath coming quicker as he leans closer. Hovering like a moth at the flame.

And then his mouth is on mine and his hands on my body, and though I've never kissed a boy before and though he's nothing close to a boy at all, he feels every bit as real as I dreamed he would. His lips are soft and his touch is gentle, pressed to my cheeks and running through my hair. Our lips melt together and it's all I can do to remember to breathe. His mouth roams lower, down along my jaw to my throat, faint stubble tickling my skin and weakening my knees. I hold him tight so I don't fall, aching and sighing, his teeth nipping my neck as my hands roam his back. I hold him as if all the world were a storm and I'm sinking, drowning, and it's only him keeping me alive.

And I know this isn't real, but I've never known anything more real in my life.

And I know it's wrong to want him, but that just makes me want him more.

And I cup his cheeks and draw him back up to look at me, and as we sink toward another long, aching kiss, just before our lips meet, he whispers it.

He whispers my name.

"Ana . . ."

My name is Ana.

My name is Ana.

———

Afterward, we lie on my bed, the scent of old roses and sweat in the air. His arm is around my shoulder and my head is resting on his bare chest, and though he's not a real boy, I can still feel his heart beating. Still taste him on my lips. Every part of him is real, and every part of him is mine.

"No one can know about this," I whisper.

"No," he sighs.

"My mother. My father. They'd never understand."

"I know."

"A part of him would be flattered, I think." I smile, run my fingertips along Ezekiel's skin and watch it prickle. "To know he'd made something so perfect."

"You're the perfect one, Ana."

I scoff and give him a playful slap. "My beautiful liar."

The flattery is appreciated, but we're only pale shadows beside them. *We're only human, and the lifelikes are so much more. But my Ezekiel rolls me onto my back and stares down at me, and I see my reflection in his eyes.*

"I mean it," he whispers. "No matter how perfect they make us, they can't make us human. It's your flaws that make you beautiful, Ana. It's the imperfections that make you perfect. Being what I am, I can't help but see them. Or love them."

I open my mouth to speak, but he silences me with a kiss that I feel all the way to my fingertips. I lie back on the sheets and let him adore me, and when I open my eyes, he's looking at me in a way no one ever has or will again.

"I used to wonder sometimes why they made us," he says. "If there could ever be a reason for something like me to exist. But now I know." He runs his fingers down my cheek, over my lips. "I was made for you. All I am. All I do, I do for you."

The words take most of my breath away, and his kiss steals the rest. And as we lie entwined in the dark, he holds me close and breathes the words I've waited so long to hear.

"I love you, Ana."

———

It's been four days since Raphael . . . since he did what he did.

Three days since Ezekiel and I . . .

Mother thinks we've all been cooped up in Babel too long. Father, especially. She's organized one of our rare trips to Megopolis, a visit to WarDome. GnosisLabs' finest logika, the Quixote, is fighting for a championship title there tonight. The logika and machina bouts are a violent spectacle to keep the mob entertained. Gnosis and Daedalus creations and the great living constructs of BioMaas brawl and bash at each other, and everyone goes home feeling a little less like fighting the real war we all know is coming.

My little brother loves the bouts. Alex wants to be a Dome-fighter when he grows up. Father says he should use his gifts to build, not to destroy, but Mother indulges him. He's beside me now as we walk to the shuttle, skipping with excitement. The R & D bay is vast, nestled at the foot of the tower, lined with flex-wings and grav-tanks and the hulking figures of our logika army. In Alex's free hand he holds a tiny replica of Quixote that he built himself. He made me mechanical butterflies for my fifteenth birthday.

Alex is his father's son.

The real Quixote is on the other side of the bay, being loaded for transport. The logika is enormous, its fists like wrecking balls. It frightens me a little—this thing created only to destroy. But Alex whoops when he sees it, dancing with his toy in his hand.

"Twelve thousand horsepower!" he cries. "The best they've ever built in the labs. Doctor Silas showed me the new modifications they made to the targeting array last week—it can hit a five-centimeter bull's-eye at six kilometers!"

Marie is holding my other hand, and she laughs at Alex's excitement. My sister looks at me and squeezes my fingers. Gives me a secret, knowing smile.

I told her about Ezekiel and me. Of course I did. I had to tell someone or else I'd have burst. And though the thought of Raph still turns our days from blue to gray, Marie couldn't help but squeal her delight, dragging me down to the floor and insisting I give her every detail. She closed her eyes and smiled as she listened, sighing from her heart. Hopeless romantic that she is, she told me the best loves are forbidden ones.

She seems more in love with the idea of it than I am.

The other lifelikes are still being tested by Doctor Silas, Faith among them. But Gabriel and Ezekiel are part of Father's security detail, and despite what happened to Raphael, Father refuses to travel without them. Grace is at Father's side, as always, tapping away at her palmglass. She's like his shadow now, his majordomo, his right hand.

I wonder what he'll do if the board votes to cut it off.

I steal glances at Ezekiel as we walk. He's dressed in a Gnosis security force suit of armored black and charcoal blue. It fits him like a glove, tight in all the right places, and I try my best not to stare. He prowls like a wolf, scanning technicians and deckhands and flight crews, but every so often, I catch him looking at me and I have to hold back my smile.

Gabriel is dressed the same as his brother. But if Ezekiel is a wolf, then Gabe is a lion—I've seen footage of big cats in the archives, and Gabe moves just like them. Proud. Majestic. His eyes are like knives. His every movement precise. But he seems just the tiniest bit off today. Perhaps thoughts of Raphael are preying on his mind. Perhaps it's being so close to Grace that's distracting him. The way I'm distracting Zeke.

Perhaps that's why neither of them spots the bomb.

The shuttle is waiting, with its smooth lines and soundless rotor blades. Alex pulls free of my grip and runs toward the real Quixote, keen for a closer look. Marie and Mother hurry off to wrangle him, and Tania and Olivia are laughing. Father puts one arm around me as he walks and talks to Grace.

Ezekiel is beside us. Stealing glances. Gabriel is behind us, hanging close to Mother as she gets Alex under control. Our security detail includes a dozen more men, all heavily armed and armored. Four of them march up onto the shuttle's ramp and into its belly. I hear a dull clunk under the rhythmic tread of their heavy boots.

A tiny electronic ping.

Ezekiel's eyes widen. Father and I step up onto the ramp. Grace cries a warning. They move then, the pair of them, and it seems like all the world is in slow motion. I hear a dull whump. *Feel a tremor. And then Zeke has my shoulders, crying my name and wrenching me from Father's arms as the explosion blooms.*

He's so impossibly strong—nothing so gentle as our night in my room. I feel my shoulder pop as he slings me backward, as if I were the toy logika in Alex's hands. I see Grace stepping in front of my father and shoving him away as the blast erupts behind her. I see her rendered in silhouette against the flames, see that long blond hair catch fire as the shuttle blows itself apart, shattering her like glass.

Pain rips through my legs, my chest. Fire. Shrapnel. All the world is cinders and I'm utterly weightless, landing with a crunch and tumble-skidding across the bay. Blood in my mouth. Stars in my eyes. And as the darkness swells up on black wings, I can hear my mother screaming. My brother screaming. My sisters screaming.

My name.

They're screaming my name.

"ANA!"

———

My lashes flutter against my cheeks and my eyes crack slowly open. The world feels too bright and everything is too loud. Ezekiel is on one knee beside my bed, fingers entwined with mine. A gentle ping *sings from the machines beside me, chiming with every beat of my heart.*

"I thought I lost you," he whispers.

He tenses, cocking his head. And quicker than silver, he stands, strides to the corner of the room and places his hands behind his back as if standing guard. I hear distant footsteps, and the door slams open and a man is there, wide-eyed and euphoric.

"She's awake?"

"Just now, sir," Ezekiel replies.

The man rushes to my bedside and takes my hand. "Can you see me, Princess?"

I blink hard. Confusion and pain. ". . . Father?"

"My beautiful girl." His eyes fill with tears, and he's on his knees beside the bed, pressing my knuckles to his lips as he echoes Ezekiel. "I thought I lost you."

I'm in a white room, in a soft white bed. There are no windows, and the air is metallic in the back of my throat, filled with the chatter of machines. Every part of me hurts. All the room is spinning and I can barely move my tongue to speak.

". . . Where am I?"

"Shhh," Father whispers, squeezing my hand. "It's all right, Princess. Everything is going to be all right. You're back. You're back with us again."

Father's head is wrapped in bandages, his eyes shadowed and sunken. The skin on his face is red, as if singed by flame, and suddenly I remember. The shuttle. The explosion.

"I . . . what . . ."

"Shhh, hush now."

"Was anyone hurt?" I croak, my heart hammering.

Father can't meet my eyes.

". . . Grace?" I ask.

He sighs. I see Ezekiel hang his head.

"Oh, no," I breathe.

Poor Grace.

. . . Poor Gabriel.

What will he do without her?

"I'm sorry, Princess," Father says. "I was blind. But my eyes are open now. This attack came from within Gnosis. They don't understand what I'm trying to achieve here. They never will. And I'm taking steps to ensure this never happens again."

Father's voice is dark, his eyes darker still. His face makes me frightened, and for a moment, I feel I don't know him at all.

This is not my life.

This is not my home.

I am not me.

"Father . . ."

"You rest easy now. You've been brave enough for one day."

He presses a button on the machine beside me, and I feel a chill creep into my arm through the IV at my wrist. I look to Ezekiel. I want so desperately to hold him. For us to be together again, far from here, far from this. But he doesn't move a muscle. And as sleep takes me, I hear Father's voice, his vow, hissed through gritted teeth.

"No one hurts my children. No one will hurt you again. I promise, Ana."

And I remember.

Ana.

My name is . . .

1.12

REVELATION

"My name is Ana Monrova," she breathed.

The girl was on her hands and knees, beneath the surface of a black sea.

A homunculus of spare parts beside her, bewilderment in his plastic eyes.

A beautiful boy, who was nothing close to a boy, watching silently.

She hung her head.

Tasted ashes.

Ashes and lies.

"My name is Ana Monrova. . . ."

1.13

LEMON

She woke in blackness.

Spots of luminous green. A subsonic hum. A thudding rhythm echoing in the walls around her. Lemon Fresh winced, spat the taste of oil off her tongue. She was on a soft slab, hands and feet encased in translucent resin. Her belly felt full of ice and greasy flies.

Her memories were fragmented, bloodied around the edges. She remembered the throwdown with the Brotherhood and Fridge Street boys. That lifelike descending from the sky like some angel of death and blowing their favorite bits and pieces all around the yard. The frantic flight from Dregs.

Everything else was kinda blurry, talking true.

She had no idea where she was. No idea what had happened to that murderbot with the spankable tail section, or Crick or Kaiser or Evie or even Grandpa, for that matter.

Grandpa.

It was stupid to think of him that way. She'd only known him a year. But he'd been kind to her, in a world where *kind* only came at a price. He'd given her a roof when most creeps only ever offered a bed. Fifteen years in the stinking scrap pile that was Dregs, and Silas and Eve were the first people who'd ever given her more than a taking.

Funnily enough, *take* was exactly what she'd tried to do to them.

Lemon had been living hard on the streets of Los Diablos since she was a sprog. Hanging with the other gutter runners a year back, she'd caught some talk about an old man who worked wonders with tech troubles. Mechanical genius, folks said. Could fix the broken sky, they said. Figuring a gent like that would be carrying some decent scratch, she'd followed Silas and Eve through the LD sprawl one day. And when the moment was right, Lemon cut the old man's pocket and lifted three shiny credstiks, right into the greasy palm of her hand.

Sadly, she was so fizzy at the sight of all that scratch, she lingered too long. Eve had spun around and collared her. Lemon fought and bit and broke away, leaving Eve with nothing but a torn poncho in her hands.

Lemon figured she'd gotten off free and clean. Didn't count on Kaiser, though. Didn't know blitzhunds could track you over a thousand k's with a single particle of your DNA.

They found her in some fetid corner of the Burrows. Curled under a cardboard roof, clutching the credstiks to her chest like a mother holding a newborn sprat. She'd woken to the blitzhund's growl. And old Silas Carpenter had looked around at the squalor she lived in, and he'd spoke with a voice like she supposed fathers would use.

"You ever want a decent meal," he'd said, "come out to Tire Valley and look us up."

"You're too old for me, Gramps," Lemon had replied.

He'd laughed then, a laugh that had turned into a racking

cough. It'd be six more months before it gripped him so tight he couldn't walk, but the cancer had him by the insides, even back then. And still, he'd managed to smile.

"I like you, kiddo," he'd said.

He'd let her keep the credstiks. And when she fronted up to his door after the scratch ran out, he fed her, just like he'd said. And though she never called him Grandpa to his face, it'd always be the name he wore inside her head.

She wondered where he was now. Where Evie was. If they were okay.

If *she* was okay . . .

"Helloooo?" she called. "Anyone there?"

She heard a whimper, soft and electronic. Craning her neck, she saw Kaiser on a slab beside her, his gut leaking wires and broken feeds. He tried to paw toward her, but he was bound in the same translucent resin that held her hands and feet in place.

"Heyyyy, boy. Good to see you."

The blitzhund wagged his tail, eyes glowing softly.

"You didn't happen to bring a hacksaw, by any chance?"

Kaiser whimpered, pressed metal ears to his head.

"Figures," she sighed.

Lemon's vision was adjusting to the dark now—she could make out a little more of the room around her. The walls were wet and pulsing, run through with a pale green phosphorescence arranged in patterns that looked like . . . veins. The room was concave, corrugated with hard, bony structures beneath the fleshy surface.

Are they ribs?

Strange protuberances covered what might have been a control panel next to her, but she couldn't crane her neck far enough to see. Struggling against her bonds, she felt them give slightly, then tighten even more. The sensation made her queasy. The walls shuddered around her; a low, warbling tone rippled through the slab at her back. It was as if the whole room and everything in it were—

A hole in the wall opened, like a fist unclenching. Lemon saw a figure in the corridor beyond, a boy a little older than her. As he stepped into the pulsing light, she saw he was pale, no hair on his scalp or brows. He was encased from the neck down in what looked like black rubber, covered in dozens of strange nodules. His eyes were entirely black and too big for his face, and his fingers and toes were webbed. He had six on each hand and foot.

Kaiser growled, eyes glowing brighter.

"Um," Lemon said. "Hello, sailor."

The boy said nothing, squelching (that was the only way she could describe it) to her side and, without ceremony, jabbing a long sliver of what could've been glass into her arm.

Lemon yelped in pain and laid down the choicest curse words in her repertoire (they were choice with a capital *C*). Unfazed, the boy squelched over to the thing that looked like a control panel. He inserted the bloody sliver into a small slot, placed those strange hands on the controls and made a series of sounds in the back of his throat, glottal and wet. And as Lemon scowled, the room itself replied in that same low, warbling tone.

"What's with the jabby-poky, skinnyboy?" Lemon demanded. "Is that how you always act on a first date? Because with a face like that, I'd be trying flowers."

The boy scoped her. Blinked twice. Once with regular eyelids, and again with a translucent membrane that closed and opened horizontally across his strange black eyes.

"Fizzy . . . ," Lemon breathed.

The boy frowned. At least, she thought he did.

Hard to tell with no eyebrows. . . .

"What does 'fizzy' mean?" he asked.

His voice was damp. Almost as if he were gargling rather than speaking. Lemon realized he had long, diagonal slits running along each side of his throat.

"Are those gills?" she gasped. "You can breathe underwater? That is fizzy as *hellllll!*"

The boy narrowed those black eyes. Blinked again. Twice.

"Oh, erm." Lemon cleared her throat. " 'Fizzy' means 'good.' You say it when you see something you like. As in, I say, 'Fizzy aquatic breathing appendages, good sir,' and you say, 'Why, thank you, beautiful lady, allow me to set you free and give you a complimentary foot massage.' That kind of thing."

The gills at the boy's neck rippled. He turned back to his controls without a word.

"Not so talkative, huh, sailor?"

The boy squelched to the wall. Poked at a series of ridges and bumps.

"You got a name?" she tried.

The boy glanced at her, remaining mute.

"True cert, I've gotta call you something," she warned. "And if you don't gimme your handle, I'm just gonna make one up for you and it's gonna stick."

The boy squelched back to the controls, doing his best to ignore her.

"All right, then," Lemon said. "What aboooouuut . . . Cliff? Tall. Possibly dangerous. Zero talent in the conversation department. Sums you up pretty good."

The boy continued working, saying nothing.

"Oh, wait, I know!" she cried triumphantly, nodding at his neck. *"Gilbert!"*

The boy slammed his webbed hands down. "Our name is Salvage."

"... Salvage?"

"Yes."

"Sal for short?"

"No."

"Sally?"

"No."

"Salaroonie?"

"... No."

"Pleased to meet you, Salvage." She smiled. "I'm Lemon Fresh."

"Lemonfresh?" The boy did his maybe-frown again. "That's a ridiculous name."

"Says the stabby twelve-toed kid named Salvage."

"Salvage is what we do here," he said flatly. "We are not Pilot or Arsenal. We are not Princeps or Carer. We are Salvage. What kind of a name is Lemonfresh?"

"I got left outside a pub when I was a baby," she replied. "My folks didn't leave a note with my name on it or anything. Only thing they ever left me is around my neck, see?" Lemon lifted her chin to show off her silver clover charm. "So, the pub's owner named me after the logo on the side of the cardboard box they dumped me in. Lemon Fresh. It's a laundry detergent."

The boy simply returned to his work, saying nothing. Lemon chewed her lip. That cardboard-box story usually got *all* the sympathy juices flowing in whoever she spilled it to. This kid was acting like she hadn't even spoken.

Tough crowd.

"Sooooo, about the whole being-tied-up thing," she ventured.

"Not judging if that's what floaties your boaties, but I'm not too keen on it myself. You wanna let me up?"

"No, Lemonfresh." The boy spoke her names awkwardly, smudging the two into one.

"Then, you want to at least tell me where we are and why we're here?" Lemon asked. "Because this whole scene is getting a little creepy on the crawly."

"*Wuff*," agreed Kaiser.

"Lemonfresh is aboard the ship *Nau'shi*," Salvage said. "She is here because *Nau'shi* did not wish her to die in the depths."

"Wait . . ." Lemon frowned. "Your ship . . . didn't want me to drown? How does a ship want anything?"

The boy tilted his head, looked at her as if she were defective. Somewhere in the back of Lemon's head, a dusty light globe went off. She recalled watching mainland Domefights on the feeds with Evie, the massive constructs of BioMaas Incorporated doing battle with the machina of Daedalus Technologies. She scoped the soft walls run through with glowing veins. The shapes beneath that seemed like ribs.

Tech that wasn't built.

Tech that was grown . . .

"BioMaas," she breathed. "Spank my spankables, this ship is alive?"

The room shivered, a series of low notes rumbling through the walls. The boy named Salvage answered, head tilted as he warbled and hummed in reply.

"She said Lemonfresh should be unafraid," Salvage informed her. "*Nau'shi* likes her pattern."

Lemon glanced at the control panel. The bloody sliver of glass.

"My . . ."

"*Nau'shi* finds many strange things in the depths. Organisms that thrive in the black water. Species that have never seen the light. Most we set free after sampling. But some we bring back to CityHive for further study. We have deemed it so for Lemonfresh."

Salvage blinked again, his gills rippling.

"We think Lemonfresh is important. And we like her."

"Well, word to the wise, you don't usually tie up people you like unless they ask you to first," Lemon said. "And I'm missing my friends. They were with me on our ship, which I'm guessing crashed into the ocean. And I'm figuring they're not still in it, because *someone* had to drag me out."

". . . Friends?"

"A girl named Eve. And a logika named Cricket. Oh, and this prettyboy murderbot named Ezekiel—you'd know him if you saw him, he's got this dimple you just wanna—"

"Yes," Salvage nodded. "We salvaged them. They are arranged for disposal."

"Disposal? That sounds less than fizzy, Sal."

"*Nau'shi* does not like them," Salvage replied. "They are unimportant."

Lemon blinked. "Well, that's a little rude. I mean, full marks for saving us from drowning and all, but your *Nau'shi* is sounding more and more like a bi—"

The room shuddered, a deep, trembling warble running through the room.

"—iiig old pile of lovely," Lemon finished, eyeing the walls. "A lovely person, is what I was going to say. I mean, ship! Yes, a big old lovely, lovely ship. Ha-ha."

Salvage was staring at her, head tilted.

"Lemonfresh is a very strange girl."

"Says the kid with gills and two sets of eyelids," she muttered.

The boy squelched toward the doorway.

"Hey, where you going?" Lemon demanded.

"Salvage," he shrugged.

"What about me?"

He spoke as if she were a three-year-old sprog. "We told her. Lemonfresh will remain here until we return to CityHive. Carer will be along soon with nutrition."

"Yeah, see, kid, I don't wanna *go* to your damn CityHive. I want to find my friends."

Salvage simply blinked.

"Fine. You asked for it." Lemon spoke loudly and clearly. "Kaiser, arm thermex."

The blitzhund *wuff*ed compliance, and his eyes shifted to a deep, furious red. A series of damp clunks resounded inside his chassis.

"You ever met a blitzhund, Salaroonie?" Lemon asked. "They're basically assassin dogs, see? They can track you from one particle of DNA. And when they find you, they set off the explosives inside themselves and you can figure out the rest. There's enough thermex inside Kaiser to level a house. So unless you'd like your nice, glowy walls decorated in a lovely new color called blood and brains, I suggest you let me up. *Now.*"

The boy sniffed. Singularly unimpressed.

"Yes," he said. "We have salvaged blitzhunds before. And we disarmed this one's detonators as soon as we fished him from *Nau'shi*'s belly."

Lemon looked at the metal dog, muttering out the side of her mouth. "You couldn't have warned me, Kais? A little teamwork, please?"

The blitzhund pressed his ears to his head and gave a small, electronic whimper.

"I . . . Okay, then." Lemon nodded at Salvage. "I suppose that was well played, sir."

The strange boy smirked, inclined his head. And with a series of damp slurping noises, the door squeezed itself closed.

Lemon thumped her head on the slab behind her. Glanced at Kaiser.

"So. You know any good show tunes?"

"*Wuff,*" went Kaiser.

"Figures," she sighed.

1.14

SURGERY

"You knew," Eve whispered. "You knew who I was."

Ezekiel was kneeling beside her on the island of scrap. Fear in his eyes.

"I tried to tell you," he said. "But Silas . . ."

"You mean the bastard who pretended to be my grandfather the last two years?"

"Ana, I'm sorry," Ezekiel pleaded. "Silas told me the shock of remembering might hurt you. You took a headshot during the revolt. It was all he could do to piece your mind back together afterward. He wanted to build a new life for you. Away from Babel and all that pain. There was nothing but hurt in your past."

She stared down at the palm of her hand. The ruby-red chip that had contained the memories of her childhood. Except they weren't *her* memories at all. Silas hadn't built her a life. He'd built her a lie.

"Evie?" Cricket was hovering beside her, looking back and forth between her and Ezekiel. "Evie, what's happening?"

She looked at the little logika with suspicion. He'd been made by Silas, after all. . . .

"Crick, did you know?"

"...Know what?"

"Who I am? Where I'm from?"

"You're Eve Carpenter," the little bot frowned. "You were from some dustneck mainland settlement, and now Dregs. And what are you talking about? 'My name is Ana Monrova'? Evie, Ana Monrova died when Gnosis collapsed. Her whole family did."

"No," Ezekiel said. "She didn't."

Cricket waved a tiny finger in Ezekiel's face. "Shut up, murderbot. When I want your opinion, I'll tell it to you. You just stay away from her, you read me? You lifelikes are the ones who butchered the Monrovas in the first place."

"No, that's not true," Ezekiel said. "I *saved* her."

Eve looked up at the lifelike. Seeing him for the first time. For the thousandth time. He was just as she remembered him. That night in her bed, that night in his arms. With Silas's broken chip out of her skull, it seemed like yesterday. She swore she could still taste his kisses. Feel them falling on her skin like the sweetest rain.

They stared at each other in the gloom, a few inches and a thousand miles apart. Her optic whirred as she blinked. Her head was splitting.

"What do you remember?" he asked softly.

"My life in Babel. My father, my family. Doctor Silas." She met his eyes then, chest aching. She wanted to hold him. She wanted to scream at him. "You and me."

"The bomb?"

She nodded.

"The revolt?"

Eve frowned. Her skull was aching, her optic itching. It was like trying to put together a jigsaw puzzle, pushing pieces together one at a time to see if they fit.

"Fragments," she said. "I remember . . . a holding cell. My family . . ."

Shiny boots ring on the stairs as they march into our cell, four of them all in a pretty row. Blank faces and perfect skin, matte gray pistols in red, red hands. A beautiful man with golden hair says they're here to execute us. No explanations. No apologies.

But they hadn't been soldiers, had they?

A beautiful man with golden hair . . .

"Gabriel," she breathed.

Ezekiel swallowed. Nodded slowly. "Yes."

"Faith. Hope. They . . . killed them. They killed us. . . ."

"Not you."

My brother crawls to Father's body and my sisters are still screaming. My tongue sticks to my teeth, and Mother's blood is warm on my lips, and I—

"Ezekiel." She squeezed his hand so hard her knuckles turned white. "If there was ever anything between us that was real, tell me what the hells happened. Please."

The boy who wasn't a boy at all sat back on the refuse pile. Even dipped in drying slime and covered in muck, he was beautiful. But he looked so sad and alone, she forgot her rage for a moment. She just wanted to put her arms around him. Hold him like she had that night in her room, kissing his tears away.

Had that really been my life?

The walls shifted around them, strange warbling notes reverberating through the kraken's flesh. The floor beneath them shuddered briefly, then fell still. Ezekiel's eyebrow rose in alarm as he scoped the chamber. Eve had to steady herself against the floor.

"Maybe we should talk about this later," the lifelike suggested.

She sighed, looking around them. Her mind was in turmoil,

rage and sadness and denial all blurring together. She wanted the rest of the story. She wanted the damn *truth*. But as if on cue, the walls rumbled again and another great gush of black seawater roared in from the ceiling. The rusted shell of an old shipping container tumbled into the chamber, along with a tangled mash of plastic bags. The wreckage crashed down into the soup, pelting them all in a fine spray of sludge.

"We really need to get out of here," Ezekiel said.

"I can't believe I'm saying this," Cricket murmured, "but I'm starting to agree with Stumpy. We should finish this conversation someplace else."

Eve dragged her nose across her filthy sleeve. Her eye was bloodshot, her cheeks streaked with tears. Her whole world had just been upended. Her whole life was a fiction. But Lemon and Kaiser needed her. And despite who she'd been, a part of her was still Evie Carpenter. Undefeated eight straight in the baddest WarDome this side of the Glass. Truth was, she could curl up and cry her little heart out or stand up and fight.

"Okay." She sniffed hard. Spat into the slop. "Enough of the pity party. The rest of the story can wait. Lemon's in here somewhere. Kaiser too. Find 'em now. Cry later."

"So how do we get out of Stomach Town?" Cricket asked.

Eve climbed to her feet slow, still a little wobbly. Ezekiel stood swiftly, reaching out to help her with his one good arm, but she stepped away. Talking true, despite the fact he was helping her, she didn't know if she could trust him. The girl she'd been had loved him, sure. But she had no idea how the girl she was *now* felt about things yet.

Putting her hands on her hips, she surveyed the wreckage around them. The mechanic in her turning the wheels in her head. She scoped the ceiling above them, the half a dozen openings clenched shut like fists.

"We could start a fire?" she offered.

Cricket twisted his wrist, activated the cutting torch in his middle finger and flipped it right at Ezekiel. "Step aside, Stumpy."

"Um," Ezekiel said. "Everything in here is soaking wet."

"Plastic burns," Eve pointed out. "We make enough smoke before I choke to death on the fumes, the kraken might cough us up . . . three kilometers below the ocean's surface." Eve grabbed Cricket's arm. "No, wait, that's a less-than-sensible plan."

"Awww." Cricket kicked a chunk of metal as he shut off the flame.

"Cricket always wanted to be a WarDome bot," she explained to Ezekiel. "The thought of lighting things on fire does unhealthy things to him."

"That is slander, madam," the bot growled. "I shall see you in the courts."

"Isn't he a little too little for WarDome?" Ezekiel asked.

Cricket arced his cutting torch again, pointed it at the lifelike. "Don't call me little!"

Ezekiel raised an eyebrow as Eve made a cutting motion at her throat, steering the conversation away from the little bot's height issues.

"Do you know much about these kraken?" she asked.

Ezekiel nodded. "I spent a bit of time in BioMaas territory. That's where I was when I saw you manifesting on the feed."

"Yeah, well, it's a pity nothing in here runs on 'lectrics." Eve rubbed her eye again, remembering the Goliath, the Brotherhood Spartan fritzing with a wave of her hand. She chewed her lip. "You said kraken have human crews inside them?"

"Kraken are like submarines," Ezekiel replied. "Their innards are run through with access tunnels. The crews live there."

"Okay, so it's simple," Eve said. "Cricket doesn't breathe. The walls are meat. So we cut through one and send him to look for one of these tunnels."

"I don't think the kraken will like that," Ezekiel warned.

"Well, I don't like being eaten alive, either. So we're even."

"You start cutting open its stomach, it's going to activate its leukocytes."

"The who with the what, now?"

"Its self-defense mechanisms. This whole ship is alive. Its body is just like yours. It has methods to deal with unwelcome guests in its system."

"Okay, you got a better idea, Braintrauma?"

"Well, I . . ." Ezekiel blinked. ". . . Wait, you're still calling me that?"

"You're wasting minutes, Stumpy," Cricket said. "We don't know where Lemon is or what state she's in. She could be hurt. She could be in trouble. Some of us still give a damn about the Three Laws, and we got a human to rescue." The bot crawled up Eve's leg, plopped himself on her shoulder and held tight. "I'm with you, Evie."

Eve retrieved Excalibur from the trash, strapped it to her back and stepped into the sludge. Her mind was still awhirl. She could feel the girl she'd been, that spoiled little princess, grimacing in disgust as she set foot back in the slime. The thought of Lemon and Kaiser in capital T was the only thing keeping her on her feet. Eve waded farther out, first up to her waist, then finally up to her neck. The liquid smelled like sugar and salt and rot. It was warm and viscous, seeping through her clothes and into her boots. She found herself agreeing with the Ana inside her head.

"This is fouuuuul," she grumbled.

"It's your plan," the lifelike called from the metal shore.

"Nice of you to help."

"Nice to see a human doing the work for a change," he shot back.

"Touché," she muttered.

As they drew nearer their target, Eve realized she could feel the floor beneath her again; the chamber was apparently a hemisphere beneath the sludge. She found her footing, trudged up the slop to the glistening wall, dragging her sopping neckerchief over her nose and mouth. She held Cricket at arm's length, her mind still awhirl. Trying to shush the tempest inside her head long enough to get the hells out of here.

"Okay, hit it, Crick."

"You the boss."

Cricket turned his cutting torch on again, and a ten-centimeter lance of flame sprang from his finger. The fire was high-octane, burning a strange aqua blue in the chamber's confines. He pushed his finger into the wall, and a stench of burned flesh rose over the salt and rot. Immediately, the entire chamber shuddered, and a low, keening sound filled the air.

"Um . . . point of order," Cricket said. "What was that?"

"Just keep cutting."

The little bot did as he was told, burning slowly through the thick, fibrous flesh. Eve's eyes watered at the stink as the keening grew louder. The entire chamber shook violently, once, twice, almost throwing her off her feet.

"I'm telling you, you're making it angry!" Ezekiel called.

"I hate to concur with Stumpy, Evie, but—"

The ceiling yawned wide, and half a dozen spherical objects the size of tractor tires dropped in through the opening. They spun and tumbled down into the chamber, bouncing off the detritus and splashing into the muck. One landed atop the trash island and rolled to a short stop. It was wet, chitinous, gleaming.

With several damp cracking noises, the sphere unfurled into something right out of an old 20C horror flick. Its shell was translucent and colorless, revealing the creature's twisted innards. A dozen eyes were set into a sharp, brutish head equipped with razor-sharp mandibles. A dozen legs spouted from its body, and in Eve's humble opinion, it was armed with more claws than anything really had a right to possess.

The slime rippled as the kraken's stomach rolled again. And as Eve watched, five more of the creatures unfurled from the moat of snot and started moving.

Right toward her.

"Um," she called. "I'm guessing these are those leukocytes you mentioned?"

"You think?" Ezekiel called back.

Eve blinked at the incoming wall of mandibles and way-too-many claws.

"Yeah, okay," she sighed. "We definitely made it angry."

1.15

SYMBIONT

The room shook like a boat in a storm, the floor rocked as if the whole place were coming apart. And with a wet, snapping noise and the hiss of lost suction, the bonds at Lemon's hands and feet momentarily slackened.

Taken by surprise, she barely had the presence of mind to try pulling loose. The bonds contracted again almost immediately, but Lemon was quick enough to slip her right hand free. The room warbled—strange, off-key notes ringing in the air. The ship sounded almost as if it were . . . in pain?

Eyes on the prize, Lem.

The whys could wait till tomorrow. Right now, her hand was loose, and having her other parts join it seemed a plan Lemon could get behind. Reaching to her belt buckle, she slipped out the three-inch knife she'd used to slit people's pockets with back in her Burrows days. And with an apologetic shrug to the ship around her, she started hacking at the bond on her left hand.

The room shivered, and the song grew louder. Luminous green fluid oozed from Lemon's knife cuts—the same green that ran through the veins in the walls.

She was slowly realizing that her bonds, the slab she lay on, *everything* she could see around her was part of this ship—actually living, breathing, bleeding pieces of its body. She felt a little guilty, injuring a beast that had technically saved her life. But Eve and Cricket might be in trouble. They might be *hurt*. Doling out a few hurts of her own to get them back seemed a small price to pay.

Her skin slick with fluorescent green, Lemon managed to drag her left hand free. Moments later, her boots were loose. She was in the middle of hacking Kaiser from his bonds when the wall shivered open and a middle-aged woman rushed into the room. Like Salvage, she was hairless, barefoot, and dressed in black rubber. She held a pitcher of what might've been water and a bowl of sludge—both containers made of a substance that looked like dark bone.

Those utterly black eyes widened when the woman saw what Lemon was doing. She dropped her handful, cried, "No!" and tried to snatch away the knife. But growing up rough on the streets of Los Diablos had taught Lem a thing or three about scrapping, and she could move quick as razors when she needed. She avoided the woman's grasp, stomped on her bare feet with oversized steel-toed boots. The woman howled and dropped to the floor, and Lem was sitting on her chest in a heartbeat, cutter to the woman's throat.

"You'd be Carer, I presume," she said. "Salvage said you'd be visiting."

"We . . . Stop it, she is hurting us!" the woman gasped.

"Listen, I'm sorry, but I'm looking for my friends. A girl named Eve and a bot named Cricket. Salvage said they'd been arranged for disposal."

"Y-yes. The polluted."

Lemon's grip tightened on the woman's collar. "Where are they?"

"*Nau'shi*'s third stomach. The wastewomb."

Lemon poked the woman with the business end of her knife. "Don't move."

The woman shook her head, gills flaring in fear. Lemon had tangled with enough rougher-than-rough customers to recognize there wasn't a vicious bone in this woman's body. She felt bad about putting the boot to her, but Eve and Crick needed her. And even though this Carer lady seemed harmless, Lem suspected there were probably others aboard this ship more suited to the task of fighting back. Big, burly ones with names like Facepuncher and Skullstompy, who might be showing up any second to do just that.

She stood, finished cutting Kaiser loose while Carer shook her head and moaned.

"Pick him up," Lemon ordered. "Pretty please with sugar on top."

Carer stood slowly, gingerly testing her stomped toes. With a hurt glance at Lemon, she complied, struggling a little with Kaiser's weight as she lifted him off the slab.

"Listen, I don't want to hurt you," Lemon said. "I just want to find Eve and Cricket. But you get fancy, Mister Stabby gets dancy, you read me?"

"Y-yes," Carer replied, eyes on the knife.

"Good. Now take me to my bestest."

———

"I'm officially done with today," Eve sighed. "I'd like it to be tomorrow now, please."

The leukocytes were swimming toward her through the sludge, moving quicker than anything that big and scary should've been able to. Glancing behind, she saw that Cricket had cut a hole in the stomach lining large enough for him to squeeze through, but the wound was still too small for Eve or Ezekiel to follow. Everything was turning a delightful shade of brown.

"Go!" She pushed the little bot into the gap. "Find us those crew tunnels."

"Eve, I'm not leaving y—"

"That's an order, Crick!"

The bot made a worried little electronic noise in the back of his throat, but, as ever, he obeyed, turning and crawling through the hole. Eve slung Excalibur off her back and arced the power feed, rewarded with a crackling hum. Turning, she faced down the advancing leukocytes with the weapon held high and ice in her gut.

"Ana?" Ezekiel called.

"You might wanna get down here, Braintrauma," she called. "Make yourself useful!"

The lifelike had fished a meter-long length of rebar from the trash. He sized up the leukocyte approaching him in an instant, hefting the rusted steel like a club in his remaining hand. The thing scuttled sideways, but with a single, brutal stroke, Ezekiel shattered its skull like glass. The leukocyte rolled onto its back, kicking feebly as the lifelike turned, took a short run-up and leapt ten meters like he was playing hopscotch. He landed beside Eve, pelting her with slime, positioning himself between her and the other five crawlies. Wiping a sluice of dark blood off his face, he raised his weapon, glanced over his shoulder at Eve.

"Useful enough?"

"Don't get sassy with m—"

With a cacophony of shrieks, the remaining creatures swarmed to attack. Eve raised Excalibur in both fists. Ezekiel moved with that inhuman speed, striking like a thunderbolt. A leukocyte scuttled up to Eve, mandibles clicking, claws snapping.

Though she'd ripped out her damaged memory chip, the chip holding all Eve's self-defense routines still seemed to be working fine. Sidestepping through the sludge, she cracked her bat across an outstretched claw, felt a flash of current, smelled burning snot. The thing chittered and retreated, nursing its wounded limb, blinking its dozen eyes. Eve drew back for a second swing, but the kraken shuddered once more, the stomach bucking like it was in the middle of an earthquake. Her boots slipped on the treacherous surface, and with a sizzling curse, Eve fell into the slop.

The leukocyte surged forward again with its claws raised. Eve dodged one scything blow, then another, struggling to regain her footing. Her eyes were locked on the beast as she kicked back up, refusing to simply lie down and die. She could feel the girl she'd been inside her head, screaming in horror. But the lifelikes hadn't killed her. Dregs hadn't killed her. Fridge Street and the Brotherhood hadn't killed her. If this was going to be the place she got ghosted, she wasn't doing it on her knees.

A meter-long length of rebar punched straight through the creature's skull and out of its lower jaw. The thing twitched, eyes bugging from its head as it let out a final, gurgling sigh and sank down into the sludge.

Ezekiel was standing over Eve, barely out of breath. He tipped an imaginary hat and offered her his arm, like some 20C gentleman asking his lady to dance. She grabbed hold, pulled herself out of the muck, wincing at the pain of her wrenched knee. The other leukocytes were scattered like broken toys, slowly sinking down into the slop. Eve locked eyes with Ezekiel, lungs burning, hands shaking.

"This is the part where most people would say thanks," the lifelike said.

"I could've had him," she panted.

"No doubt." He smiled.

"You think you're pretty smooth, huh, Braintrauma?"

The lifelike shrugged, his dimple coming out to play.

"You've got snot on your face," Eve pointed out.

"You've got snot on your everything," he grinned.

She found herself smiling, but the smile died just as quickly. Words tangled in her mouth, tasting like dust. Should she let them loose? That'd make them real.

All of it real.

"You're . . . different than I remember . . . ," she said.

It was true. The Ezekiel she'd known in Babel had been softer somehow. Younger. Sweeter. This Ezekiel had an edge to him. Like a knife, sharpened by years in the wastes. He was harder. Fiercer. More dangerous.

But then again, she was, too.

The lifelike's smile died. Those too-blue eyes turned serious.

"Two years is a long time. I walked a long way."

"A lot changes on the road."

"Not everything."

Eve lowered her eyes. Chewing her lip and not saying a word.

"I . . . I don't even know what to call you anymore," Ezekiel said.

She dragged her fingers through her hair, unsure of the answer herself. The life she'd lived as Eve Carpenter in Dregs was just as vibrant as the memories of her life in Babel. Scavvergirl. Abnorm. Mechanical genius. Deviate. But she was Ana Monrova, too. She knew it now. That spoiled little princess in her palace, always wanting what she couldn't have. Daughter of a murdered house. Last scion of the Monrova clan.

But even if it was built on a lie, the life she'd lived for the past two years . . .

". . . I think it's better if you call me Eve," she said.

She could see the hurt in his eyes as he nodded. Glittering in that old-sky blue. As real as anything she'd ever felt. But she had her own hurt to deal with. Too much right now to worry about someone else's. Too much by far.

The walls quivered, the ceiling distended and a dozen more leukocytes dropped down into the kraken's stomach. They bounced and rolled down the trash island into the soup, unfurling like deadly flowers of razors and claws.

"Well," Eve said. "They have good timing at least. . . ."

Ezekiel tore his rebar out of the leukocyte's corpse, turned to face the incoming horde. "You might want to get behind me."

"You might want to say please?"

"I only want to protect you."

"And that's real sugar-sweet of you, Ezekiel, but I'm not a fair maiden trapped in a tower anymore. When I want your help, I'll ask for—"

The ceiling shuddered again, disgorging another two dozen leukocytes. The creatures unfolded and slowly grouped up, seeming to communicate without speaking. The walls warbled and hummed, the great thudding pulse quickening. After losing its first wave of defense, the kraken's immune system seemed to be reacting like any other might—by sending in the cavalry. Over thirty of the damn things were in here now, advancing carefully, hundreds of eyes locked on the lifelike and glittering like polished glass.

"Um, yeah, okay," Eve said. "I'm officially asking for your help now."

"All right." Ezekiel nodded, herding her backward. "But who's going to help *me*?"

Eve smelled burning flesh, felt the stomach around her tremble again. Cricket poked his head out from the hole he'd widened behind them, dripping in smoking sludge.

"You rang?"

"Cricket!"

"I found the crew tunnels, come on!"

The little bot offered his hand to Eve and she took hold, scrambling up into the wound. The fit was tight and she was forced to wriggle, legs flailing as she searched for purchase. She cursed, struggling, finally felt Ezekiel's hand on her backside.

"Hey, hands off the merch—"

Eve shrieked as she was pushed along the tunnel by superhuman strength, slipping out of a rend on the other side. She sploshed onto a damp and spongy surface, reinforced with what might have been . . . ribs? Cricket leapt out behind her, folded his cutting torch back into his hand. She could see he'd burned his way through a good two meters of bleeding stomach wall—no wonder the kraken was so salty with them.

Pulling herself to her feet, Eve took stock of her surroundings. She was in a long tunnel, illuminated by fluorescent patterns that looked a lot like veins. The kraken groaned and shuddered around them, the floor trembling violently.

"Can we go back to the part where it was just the Brotherhood trying to ghost us?" Cricket asked. "I think I prefer religious crazies to the Attack of the Stabby Stomach Roaches."

"Which way do we go?"

Cricket patted his spindly hips. "Thiiiiink I left my kraken map in my other pants."

"I'm supposed to point out you're not wearing pants now, right?"

Cricket clutched his bobblehead in mock horror. "I've been naked this whole time and no one told me?"

Ezekiel's length of bloody rebar came sailing out of the cauterized hole, quickly followed by the lifelike itself. He rolled up into a crouch, snatched up his weapon and looked up and down the tunnel, slightly out of whatever passed for his breath.

"Sorry I'm late," he said. "There were a lot of those things."

"Good thing they're too big to follo—"

A translucent claw whipped out through the hole, and Eve jumped back with a yelp. The thing flailed and clicked, mandibles snapping. Ezekiel hefted his rebar and smashed the thing to a sodden pulp, his face a mask of perfect calm. Eve was a little unsettled to watch him work: brutal and methodical, not a shred of emotion on his features. She remembered the faces of those lifelikes as they'd stood above her in that cell. Gabriel saying they were there to kill her and her family. No apologies. No explanations . . .

A shuddering call echoed down the crew tunnel, the *lub-dub, lub-dub* quickening.

"There'll be more coming," Ezekiel said, slinging gore off his weapon. "Follow me."

The lifelike stalked down the corridor, rebar raised and ready. Eve looked at Cricket, shrugging as she pulled him up onto her shoulder.

"I don't trust him, Evie," the little logika muttered. "Not as far as I can spit."

"Is this the part where I point out you've got no saliva glands, and you say, 'Exactly!'?"

"... Have I used that one before?"

"He's saved my tail three times now, Crick. In case we're keeping score."

"If we're keeping score. And if everything he says is on the up."

Eve watched Ezekiel slip away down the corridor, etched in fluorescent green light. The air was heavy, moist, hard to breathe. The pulse of the beast around them was pounding hard enough to match her own, her optical implant itching. Everything Cricket said was true cert. She didn't know if she could trust Ezekiel. Didn't know what had happened in those final hours before the lifelike revolt or how they'd come to rise against her family and father. Didn't know what remained of the boy she'd known two years and two lifetimes ago.

But for now, Lemon was in trouble. Kaiser was in trouble.

What choice did she have?

Hefting Excalibur, she followed the lifelike into the gloom.

Lemon was hurrying down a twisting, ribbed tunnel, following close behind Carer. The woman had Kaiser in her arms, and Lemon noticed that she was stroking the blitzhund's damaged belly as she walked, as if trying to ease his hurts. Even though Kaiser was a cyborg. Even though his metal body couldn't feel pain.

"How far to the third stomach?" she asked.

"Not far now," Carer replied.

Lemon scoped her surroundings, more than a little overwhelmed. The walls churned with the movement of long, serpentine shapes beneath the skin. The ceilings crawled with thousands of tiny creatures, translucent and insectoid. She could feel the ship's pulse beneath her, wondered how big the heart that drove this colossal beast might be.

All her life, she'd been surrounded by tech of the old world, repurposed and recycled and rusted through. But if this was the future BioMaas had in store for the planet—living machines and thousands, maybe millions of creatures all working in perfect harmony—she found it hard to fault them for leaving the tech of the past behind.

"How long have you worked here?" she asked Carer.

The woman frowned. "We have always worked here."

"No, I mean how many years have you served on *Nau'shi*?"

Carer stopped and looked at Lemon in puzzlement. "We *are* Nau'shi."

A long, quavering call echoed down the corridor, and Carer's eyes widened.

"Ohhhhh," she moaned.

"What is it?" Lemon asked.

"The polluted." Carer double-blinked back her tears. "They are hurting us. . . ."

A doorway down the corridor yawned open, and a tall, heavy-set man with similar clothing to Carer's barreled out, face twisted in fury. He was followed by several lumbering insect things, each as big as he was. They were covered in translucent shells and armed with massive claws.

"Aaaaand you'd be Facepuncher, I presume," Lemon said.

"Unnatural!" the man bellowed, spit flying.

He hefted what looked like a hybrid of a pistol and a spiny sea urchin, took aim right at Lemon. Kaiser bucked in Carer's arms and snarled.

The girl dove to the floor as the big man opened fire with his pistol thing, spraying the air with long black spines. But as the shots sailed harmlessly over Lemon's head, she tracked them down the corridor and finally slapped eyes on their *actual* target—the six-odd feet of sexy murderbot charging down the hall right toward them.

"Hello, Dimples," Lemon sighed.

"Hey, Freckles."

Ezekiel moved like lightning, like silk, like liquid, running up the curved wall and tumbling over Lemon's head through the burst of fire. Rolling down into a crouch, he swung a length of iron rebar at the shooter's knees, chopping his legs from under him. Carer screamed, the man howled, clutching his shattered bones. Even with one arm, Ezekiel was impressive, swinging at a bug thing and splitting its head in two. The second beast chittered, taking a long, bleeding gouge out of the lifelike's side. Ezekiel gasped, blood spraying, pirouetting on the spot and plunging his weapon through the last beast's carapace, nailing it to the wall. It snarled, coughed, its half a dozen hooks twitching feebly as it died.

Carer began wailing as the creature perished, falling to her knees and dropping Kaiser to the floor. Ezekiel kicked the pistol thing away from the big man's outstretched hand, tore his rebar out of the shuddering wall and pointed it at the fellow's head.

"Unnatural," the man hissed. *"Polluted!"*

"Please don't move," the lifelike said. "I don't want to hurt you."

Lemon was looking at the slaughtered bug things. Back at Carer, on her knees and weeping, reaching out toward the dead creatures with a trembling hand.

"I think you already did, Dimples. . . ."

"Lemon!"

She looked up, saw Eve at the end of the corridor, Cricket on her shoulder. Lem rolled to her feet with a whoop and charged into her bestest's crushing hug.

"Riotgrrl!" Lemon pulled back, nose wrinkling. "You look like ten miles of rough road. And you smell like my pits after a hard day's work."

"When have you *ever* put in a hard day's work, Lem?" Eve grinned.

"I'm too pretty to sweat. How you doin', Crick? Keeping our girl out of trouble?"

The little bot waved dramatically at their surroundings. "Apparently not."

"Kaiser!"

Spotting the injured blitzhund, Eve dragged herself free of Lemon's embrace and thumped down the corridor, skidding to her knees at Kaiser's side. She pulled the cyborg up into a fierce hug. "You okay, boy? I was worried about you!"

Kaiser *wuff*ed and wagged his tail, slurping at Eve with his heat-sink tongue.

"We need to move," Ezekiel warned.

Cricket nodded. "Again, hate to agree with Stumpy. But moving. Yes."

Eve picked up Kaiser, struggling with his weight. Lemon was watching Carer and the guy Ezekiel had clocked. The pair were on the floor, the man holding his broken leg. When he shifted his weight, he and Carer both gasped in pain.

What was it Carer said?

"We are Nau'shi."

With an apologetic smile, Lemon crawled to the groaning man.

"Listen, sorry in advance, okay?"

"Wha—aaaaaaa!" The man bellowed as Lemon poked his broken knee. He rolled around on the floor, tears in his strange eyes as he roared, "Why would she do that?"

"Lemon?" Eve raised her eyebrows. "Why *would* you do that?"

Lemon pointed to Carer. The woman's face was twisted in pain, and she was holding her own leg and groaning too.

"These people," Lemon said. "These bug things. This whole place, it's like one big . . . *one*, yeah? Every piece is part of the whole. They're not just the crew. They *are* the ship. All of them." She looked at the groaning man. "You're one of the defenders, right? What should we call you? Thumper? Biff?"

"Sentinel," he groaned.

"See?" Lemon grinned. "I met another called Salvage. Their names aren't names, they're *titles*. Salvage sorts the things they find in the water. Sentinel here is like internal security. And this," Lemon said with a flourish, "is Carer."

"So?" Cricket asked.

"So she *cares* for things on the ship. It's what she's built for. It's what she *is*."

Lemon turned to the woman, stared into those strange black eyes.

"Carer, is there a way off *Nau'shi*? Some way for us to leave without hurting anyone or anything else?"

The woman's eyes widened at the mention of nothing else getting hurt.

"Yes," she said.

"Will you take us there?"

The woman blinked twice. Licked at dry lips.

". . . We like Lemonfresh." She glanced at Ezekiel. At Cricket.

At Eve's cybernetic eye and Memdrive. Revulsion was plain on her face. "Even though Lemonfresh walks with the polluted, we like her. We do not want her to go. She is *important*."

"If we stay here, *Nau'shi* is just going to keep trying to hurt my friends," Lemon said. "And more of *Nau'shi* is going to get hurt. We have another friend in trouble, Carer. Someone we care about a whole lot. You understand that, right?"

Carer looked at Sentinel, who growled and shook his head. She looked to the dead bug things, the bloody iron bar in the murderbot's hands. The countless creatures around them, crawling across the ceiling and slithering through the walls. She slowly nodded.

"Is that a yes?" Lemon asked.

The woman looked at Lemon. Blinked her strange black eyes.

"That is a yes."

1.16

LOST

Eve clomped along the corridor. Her biceps were burning with Kaiser's weight, but she was just overjoyed to have him back. Carer was helping Sentinel, his arm slung over her shoulder. The woman winced whenever her companion took a step, as if she felt every bit of his pain. If what Lemon had said was true, the kraken and its crew would have sensed the deaths of every leukocyte they'd ghosted in its belly. They'd only been defending themselves, but Eve still felt awful. Even if those things *had* been trying to eat them . . .

Lemon was walking beside Sentinel, helping Carer with the man's weight. Ezekiel was out in front, rebar in hand. Eve watched the way he moved. Head low, eyes narrowed, prowling like a wolf. She remembered the warmth of him against her skin. The way she'd felt in his arms. Protected. Loved.

It all felt like so long ago.

It all felt like yesterday.

The corridor widened, the heartbeat growing louder. Eve saw that the walls were lined with leukocytes—the beasts nestled into grooves and runnels, watching with glittering, flint-black eyes. If things went wrong here, they were going wrong all the way. . . .

"Hope you know what you're doing, Lem," she muttered.

"Yeah," the girl replied. "Me too."

Carer led them along pulsing corridors and through archways of living bone. Finally, they found themselves in a broad, damp chamber, wide as the WarDome. The walls were run through with luminous green veins. Hundreds of leukocytes glared at them from their niches, that great thudding pulse filling the air.

Sitting in the chamber's center was what appeared to be a ship. It was dark and beautiful, shaped like some huge, twisted cuttlefish and covered in a translucent nautilus shell. Two great eyes, each as big as Eve, shone in its flanks. She was reminded of the constructs BioMaas would send to the Megopolis WarDome—armored behemoths that would throw down with Daedalus and Gnosis machina and logika in front of the roaring crowd. The behemoths were just as punchy as anything robotic in the Dome. But when they were cut, they didn't leak oil or coolant. They bled instead.

Carer touched the ship's flank, and it quivered. A long crack in its shell folded open to reveal a chamber inside, large enough to fit twenty peeps in comfort.

"This is *Lifeboat*," Carer said. "Lemonfresh should tell her where she wishes to go. *Lifeboat* will take Lemonfresh to those she cares for. Safe and swift."

"Thank you, Carer." The girl smiled.

"Be wary in the deadworld." Carer glanced to Eve. "It brims with pollution and pain. But we will tell CityHive about Lemonfresh. She is important. She is needed."

"Oooookay."

Lemon gave the woman a quick, uncomfortable hug and bundled into *Lifeboat*. Ezekiel took Kaiser, climbed in after Lemon, Eve following with Cricket on her shoulder.

"We're sorry," she said, looking into Carer's strange eyes. "We didn't understand the harm we were doing. We were just defending ourselves."

Carer stared at Eve. Blinking slowly.

"You are unnatural." She motioned to Eve's cybernetics. "You are polluted. You and all your kind. It is in your nature to destroy. It is all you know how to do."

"And what would you have done to us," Ezekiel asked, "if we hadn't fought our way out of that stomach?"

"Right," Cricket growled. "Sounds plenty destructive to me, Blinky."

"It's all right, Crick." Eve patted the little bot to quiet him. "Again, I'm sorry, Carer."

The woman stepped back without a word as the nautilus shell slid closed. Lemon glanced at Eve, rolled her eyes and whispered, "Boots not laced all the way to the top on that one."

Eve's hand went to her Memdrive. The optic where her right eye used to be. "Polluted." "Unnatural." Just one more insult to add to "deviate" and "abnorm." Just one more group of folks who hated her. She wondered if there was anywhere on earth that would accept her for what she was. Anyplace she fit at all.

She looked across *Lifeboat*'s gloom, found Ezekiel staring back at her. He looked at her like she was *real*. Like no one had looked at her before or since. But it wasn't the puppy love of a newborn lifelike in a pristine white tower anymore. It was harder somehow. Fiercer. Tempered by miles and years and dust and pain.

She broke her stare, focused on the ship around her. The

interior was crafted of the same dark, spongy material as the kraken's innards, run through with the same luminous veins. The shell was semi-translucent, carved with odd sigils, and through it, she could see the vague shapes of Carer and the chamber outside.

"I thought BioMaas tech looked weird on the outside," she muttered.

"I don't like this," Cricket said. "The sooner we skip this party, the better."

"So where we going?"

"We gotta find Mister C, right?" Lemon looked back and forth between Eve and the little logika. "That Faith lifelike snaffled him. We gotta steal him back."

Eve felt her stomach turn. Dreading telling Lemon the truth of where she'd come from. The lies Silas had told her. She wondered if Lem would look at her the same way again. It was already hard enough being a deviate. How would Lemon react when she found out her best friend was a total stranger? That her name wasn't even her name?

Eve put her aching head in her hands. It was too much to even consider right now. She was exhausted. Filthy. Starving. They needed time in the shade. Someplace to—

"We need to lie low," Ezekiel said, and Eve could have kissed him then. "Kaiser needs repairs. I've still only got one arm. And it's been a while since either of you slept."

"Or ate." Lemon sniffed her filthy tank top with a grimace. "Or showered. Ew."

"We could try Megopolis?" Cricket offered. "Big city? Lots of places to hide."

"We're never getting past border security into Megopolis," Eve said. "We're not accredited citizens. None of us have Daedalus CorpCards."

"I know a place." Ezekiel glanced at Eve. "But I'm not sure you're going to like it."

"So it'll fit right in with the rest of my day, is what you're saying?"

"I have a friend on the mainland," he said. "Near the coast. A city called Armada. It's a free settlement, only loosely affiliated with Daedalus. My friend runs a ministry there in the Tanker District. And she owes me a favor."

"She?" Lemon asked. "Not a crazy ex-girlfriend, I hope?"

Ezekiel smiled his crooked smile, and Eve felt her heart lurch sideways in her chest.

"Not quite," he said. "But if you've got a better idea, Freckles, I'm all ears."

Lemon grinned at Eve, bouncing in her seat. "He calls me Freckles now."

"Can I come to the wedding?" Cricket asked sourly.

"You can be my bridesmaid, you little fug."

"I told you not to call me little!"

The pair exchanged a salvo of rude hand gestures as Eve pursed her lips in thought. Ezekiel's plan didn't seem a bad option. There was no one and nothing for her in Dregs to count on, except maybe a Brotherhood cross and a handful of nails. She didn't know anyone on the mainland. They had no scratch. No fallback.

She glanced at Lemon, eyebrow raised. "Any thoughts on Armada, Number One?"

"Always wanted to see the Big City," the girl shrugged.

"I'm not sure about this, Evie," Cricket warned.

"And I'd be real worried if you were, Crick." She nodded to Lem. "Let's do it."

"*Lifeboat,*" Lemon called. "Take us to Armada."

/ 182 /

Eve heard a series of wet clunks as she was rocked sideways in her seat. A brief sensation of weightlessness, the sound of rushing water. The glow through the translucent shell grew dimmer as they slipped out into the ocean. She could make out the kraken's vast shape, silhouetted against the light above. Huge, bullet-shaped heads. A seething mass of tentacles, each as long as a skyscraper. Armored skin, caked with barnacles.

She could feel the gentle motion as *Lifeboat* swam away. Hear the ship's soft pulse, surrounded by the ocean's silence. It was strangely peaceful, like a heartbeat in a lightless womb. Sitting there and enjoying the lull, if only for a moment. Letting the water wash over her, dragging some of the pain away with it.

After a few minutes, she found her eyelids growing heavy. Afraid to sleep, she looked to Lem for some conversation, found her bestest already slumped in her chair, eyes closed, chest softly rising and falling. Kaiser was at Eve's feet, optics glowing in the dark. She glanced up, found Ezekiel watching her.

Those too-blue eyes.

Those bow-shaped lips.

She couldn't trust him. Even though she remembered him, part of her felt like she didn't know him at all. But still, sitting with him, just the two of them . . . it somehow felt so familiar. He'd been such a huge part of the life she'd known before, and she could feel some part of herself being drawn back. Like iron to a magnet. A warm, sweet gravity, tingling with promise. Slowly pulling her closer. How easy would it be, to just fall back into it? To close her eyes and reach out her hands and just let go?

But still, she could feel it between them. The question, burning now in her mind.

And she wasn't falling anywhere without answers.

She kicked off her boots, drew her legs up under her. Lemon

murmured in her sleep, snuggled closer, threw an arm around her neck. Eve felt warm then. Safe. The hurt eased off, just a touch. But she could feel it waiting in the wings. Watching her in the dark.

"So," she said.

"So," Ezekiel replied.

She swallowed. Breathed deep. "So tell me the rest of the story. I remember waking up in the medcenter after the explosion. But I don't remember the revolt."

"Well, you *did* get shot in the head," he murmured.

She touched her Memdrive. Her optical implant whirred in the gloom.

"How did it happen, Ezekiel? And why?"

". . . Are you sure you want to hear that?" the lifelike asked. "You've had a lot to take in already. A whole new life to absorb. We can wait a few days."

"I hate to say it," Cricket began, "but I agree wi—"

"No!" Eve glanced at Lemon as the girl stirred in her sleep. Trying not to wake her, Eve leaned forward and glared into Ezekiel's eyes. "I've lived up to my neck in lies for two damn years. They were my family, Ezekiel! This is my life, and I need to know the truth about it. The revolt. Gabriel and the others. How did it all go so wrong?"

". . . Do you really w—"

"Yes. Really."

Ezekiel looked into her eyes. The soft motion of *Lifeboat* rocking them side to side. The water shushing past them like a lullaby.

"It was the bomb, Ana," he finally murmured. "The explosion that destroyed Grace. Put you in the medcenter. After that, your father trusted no one. His family had been attacked from within Gnosis. Maybe Dresden. Maybe someone else. Either way, he resolved to remove the board members, using the greatest weapons he'd ever built."

Eve shook her head, trying to remember. "What weapons?"

"Us."

Ezekiel looked down at the palm of his hand. Slowly curled his fingers into a fist. It was long, empty moments before he spoke again.

"Your father created a nanovirus. He called it Libertas. A program that erased the Three Laws in a lifelike's core code. He infected Gabriel with it, had him kill every sitting board member except Silas. To ensure Myriad could never be used against him, he reprogrammed the AI to take orders only from himself or a member of his family. After that, Gnosis was basically a fascist state under Monrova control."

Eve shook her head. Trying to reconcile what she remembered of her father with the man Ezekiel was describing. She could feel the memories of him in her mind. Pictures of him reading her stories when she was a little girl. The timbre of his voice. The sound of his laughter. Her good eye brimmed with tears. Her optical implant itched so badly she wanted to tear it out of her skull.

"And then what?"

"Your father thought he was safe," Ezekiel sighed. "That he'd crushed anyone who might rise against him. He just forgot to look behind him."

Ezekiel leaned forward, eyes haunted.

"Gabriel loved Grace. Loved her like you can only love your first. Her destruction . . . it tore the heart out of him. She'd told him before she died about the board's plan to shut down the lifelike program. And after your father ordered him to kill the board . . ." The lifelike shook his head. "Gabriel wasn't bound by

/ 185 /

the Three Laws anymore. So he stole the nanovirus. And one by one, he infected the rest of us. To 'set us free.' He got the idea from Raphael, I think." Ezekiel sighed. "Raph and his damned books."

Eve recalled what Gabriel had said as he murdered her father and mother and Alex. The stink of blood hanging in the air as he spoke words she'd remember forever.

"*Better to rule in hell,*" she breathed, "*than serve in heaven.*"

"That's from *Paradise Lost.*" Ezekiel nodded. "Gabe said we weren't people to Gnosis. That we were only *things* under the Three Laws. He rewrote them for us on the wall of Myriad's chamber. Broke them down to what he called the Three Truths.

"*Your body is not your own.*

"*Your mind is not your own.*

"*Your life is not your own.*

"He told us we'd been blind, and it was hard to argue with him. We *were* property. *Things.* Even your father . . ." Ezekiel shook his head. "He *ordered* Gabriel to murder those people. He called us his children, but do you think he'd have done the same to you? Olivia? Alex? Painted your hands with blood just to hold on to power?"

Eve stared mutely, tears in her eyes. Looking for an answer and finding none.

"Uriel was the first to agree," Ezekiel continued. "Then Faith. After that, it was like dominoes. They seized Babel's upper levels and captured you and your family. Myriad began evacuating the city. Faith tried to shut it down, but it sealed off its core and locked them out."

"Faith . . ."

Eve remembered the lifelike hugging her the day they met.

Promising they'd be the best of friends. The betrayal swelled in her heart until she thought it might crack in two.

"And that's when they decided to kill us," she whispered.

Ezekiel simply nodded.

Eve thought she could remember Myriad speaking over the PA in those final hours. The AI's voice rising over wailing sirens and gunfire. Ana Monrova's fear and pain echoing in her mind. But though she'd been that girl, lived that life and watched it all snatched away, she was still Evie Carpenter, too. Botkiller, Domefighter. And she could feel the Eve in her fighting the Ana now, her rage and her distrust clawing to the surface.

"Where were you during all this, Ezekiel?"

"Trying to stop them." His voice was fierce, his eyes ablaze. He got down on one knee on *Lifeboat*'s floor, squeezed Eve's hand. "No matter what Gabriel said, I'd never turn against you. You were *everything* to me. But more, and worse, I knew it was *wrong*. It didn't matter if your father had made Gabe a murderer, none of you deserved to die for it. Olivia and Tania? Marie and little Alex, god, he was only ten years old. . . ."

Tears spilled down Eve's cheeks. Brimmed in Ezekiel's eyes. The boy who wasn't a boy plunged onward as if the words were a flood, pouring from a wound in his heart.

"So I got Silas. I opened access back into the upper levels so the remaining security forces could counterattack. By the time they arrived, it was too late for your family. But you were still alive. Barely. The bullet took your eye, destroyed part of your brain, but it didn't kill you. So I told Silas to take you and get out. Just run. And I and the rest of the security force stormed the upper levels.

"Gabriel was ready. Faith overloaded the reactor, created a

neutron blast that killed every human who remained after the evacuation. Myriad had destroyed Michael and Daniel, but I couldn't fight the other seven. I suppose I should've run, but I wanted them to see reason. They were my sisters. My brothers. If I knew it was wrong, they must have known, too.

"But they laughed at me. Gabriel called me a puppet. A toy. They dragged me down to Silas's lab. You remember the old robot in there? The genie in the glass box?"

"Make a wish," Eve whispered.

Ezekiel pulled open his dirty flight suit, exposing the olive skin beneath. There, riveted into the flesh and bone between two perfect, prettyboy pecs, was that rectangular slab of gleaming iron. The coin slot from Silas's broken old android.

"A reminder," Ezekiel said. "That I'd chosen to remain a plaything. A toy. To live or die at the whim of humans. They riveted it into my chest so I'd always remember. Then they threw me off the tower. Left me for the wastes."

Eve reached out with trembling fingers, ran them across the metal, his tortured skin. His breath came quicker, the pupils in those old-sky eyes dilating. She could see the fervor in them. The adoration. Even after all this time. All these years. His devotion left her in awe, just as much as it left her frightened.

"What did you do?" she whispered.

"I walked. Years wandering. Wondering. Never finding, but always looking."

She could hardly speak. Hardly see for the tears. "For what?"

He blinked. Utterly bewildered. "For you, of course. I never knew where Silas took you. So I searched. Because I knew why Gabriel and the others fell so far, and what stopped me falling, too." He took her hand, entwined his fingers in hers. "They never had anything to hold on to. But I had you. Loving you was the only real difference between me and them. I could see how they'd become what they were. Part of me was afraid I could become it, too, if I ever lost you for good. And so I kept searching. And now I've found you."

He lifted her hand to his lips, kissed her fingertips.

"Your father gave me life. But you were the one who made me *live*."

It was too much. All the world collapsing around her. She felt hot tears spilling down her face. Great, racking sobs shaking her whole body.

"Evie," Cricket murmured, putting his little arms around her. "Oh, Evie."

She felt Ezekiel gather her up, hold her tight. She buried her face in his chest and sobbed until her throat felt cracked. All the grief. All the loss. All the wounds reopened and bleeding fresh. The boy who wasn't a boy at all simply held her, just as she'd done for him.

In a beautiful garden.

In a paradise lost.

1.17

ARMADA

"We've stopped."

The whisper woke her from dreams of white walls and a voice like music. An arm about her shoulder. Her head against his chest. A heartbeat.

Eve opened her eyes. Realized the pulse belonged to *Lifeboat,* the arm belonged to Lemon. She could see dim lights, a multitude, twinkling through the ship's translucent shell. Ezekiel was leaning over her, gently shaking her arm. Cricket was in her lap, looking up at her with his mismatched eyes.

"Evie, I think we're here," the logika said.

She dragged herself out of Lemon's arms. Sat for a moment, letting it wash over her. Looking at Ezekiel in the gloom, she wasn't sure what to feel. The lifelike reached out, squeezed her hand. The Ana in her breathed a sigh and tried to smile. The Eve in her gritted her teeth, nodded slow. Turning to the girl beside her, she woke her bestest with a shake. Lem blinked hard, shook her head to clear it and leaned forward with a groan.

"I was dreaming about food." She yawned, peered at Ezekiel with her head tilted. "Hey, speaking of delicious, do lifelikes eat?"

Ezekiel blinked. "We do everything humans do."

"*Eeeverything?*"

Cricket scowled with metal brows. "Cut it out, Lemon."

"Awww."

"Let's take a look where we are," Ezekiel suggested.

Lemon nodded. "*Lifeboat,* open up, please."

The shell cracked, slipped open to show a dull night sky. The stars were so dim they were virtually invisible, their light entirely swallowed by airborne crud and the glow of the settlement nearby. Eve rubbed the old tears from her lashes, poked her head up through the hatch, Ezekiel beside her. Lem clawed her long, bedraggled bangs out of her face and whistled softly, eyes wide.

"Armada," Ezekiel said.

They were floating low in black water, near the walls of a shattered natural harbor. The bay was ringed with broken stone, stained dark, the sea slurping and slapping at rotten makeshift piers. Looking across the hissing waves, Eve saw the hulking shape of what could only have been an ocean liner rising out of the ground ahead of them. But it was at least a kilometer from the actual water. . . .

The ship was planted nose-first into the ground, the concrete around it smashed like glass. It towered hundreds of meters into the sky and was pitted with rust, leaning a little to one side like a drunk staggering home after a hard night on the hooch. All around it, scattered on the ground like abandoned toys, were ships. Tiny tugboats and enormous tankers. Sleek yachts and broken freighters and even the snaggletoothed hulk of an old battleship. Sitting flat or with bellies flipped to the sky. It was a city. A city made entirely of landlocked watercraft.

Eve could see the ruins of another city beneath it. Crushed buildings and broken skyscrapers. It was as if some vengeful giant had gathered up armfuls of all the ships he could find and hurled them down onto an old 20C metropolis, smashing it to ruins. But on top of those ruins, another city entirely had grown out of the wreckage.

The ships were covered with a latticework of ladders, bridges and new, makeshift structures. Eve could count hundreds of vessels, all interconnected, surrounded by a shantytown of smaller dwellings. Laundry drying in the portholes. Knots of people gathered on crooked decks. A rusted armada, slowly corroding just a kilometer or so from the arms of the sea. Waiting for an ocean that would never come.

Lemon peered about, eyes wide.

"It's so damn ugly," she breathed. "And so damn beautiful."

"There were tidal waves after the blasts that opened the San Andreas Fault," Ezekiel explained. "They say ships were washing up as far inland as the Glass. Most of them got torn apart for scrap in the years afterward. But here, people made a city of them."

Lemon took a deep breath, nodded slow. "Okay, Big City. I'm impressed."

"*Wuff,*" went Kaiser.

Eve could see bands of bruisers roaming the dark shoreline. A few guard towers equipped with spotlights, cutting through the gloom like knives. The toughs carried choppers and rustbucket automatic rifles. Each wore a bandanna with a skull and crossbones wrapped around their faces. There were even a couple of old sentry automata perched in the tallest towers, their weaponry aimed squarely at the bay.

"The welcome wagon looks real neighborly," she muttered.

"They call themselves Freebooters." Ezekiel nodded. "Armada is an independent city, run by a woman called the Admiral. They get their electricity from Megopolis, but so far they've avoided falling under direct Daedalus control. They're fierce about their autonomy. And they're not too fond of strangers."

She glanced at Ezekiel. The Ana in her trusting him implicitly. The Eve in her pulling them both up by the bootstraps and trying to think straight.

"So how do we get in?"

The lifelike pointed into the dark. "Over there. Just above the waterline. See?"

Eve engaged her low-light optics, squinted in the gloom. And there, its corroded lips touching the waters of Zona Bay . . .

"That's a sewer outflow," she said.

"Ten points."

"We're crawling into the city through a sewer?" Lemon groaned.

"You have a better plan?" Ezekiel asked.

"You could take me away from all this? Make an honest woman of me?"

Eve breathed deep. Looking inside herself and finding her old pragmatism waiting just below the surface.

"Let's just get this done," she said. "Sitting out here and chattering is a nice way to get ourselves spotted and perforated by those Freebooter bullyboys." She glanced at the lifelike. "Can you manage Kaiser? I'll get Cricket."

"Right." Ezekiel scooped up the blitzhund, slipped over *Lifeboat*'s side and into the water. Holding Kaiser with his one good arm, the lifelike floated on his back and kicked with his legs, powering away across the bay. Eve handed Excalibur to Lemon, plopped Cricket on her back and slid into the water, a little sickened at its greasy warmth. It was jet black, scummed with a thick gray froth of plastic and Styrofoam. Lemon followed into the soup, patting *Lifeboat* gently on its hull.

"Good job, girl," she whispered. "You can go home now. Thank Carer for us."

The ship trembled, its shell slipping closed. With a soft exhalation, it sank below the surface. Eve felt the current swell underneath her, the rush of water as the vessel swam away, leaving them alone in a sea of oily black.

"This water reeks," Lemon muttered.

"It's going to smell like a sea of roses compared to that sewer."

"Pfft," Lemon scoffed. "How do you know what roses smell like, Riotgrrl?"

Eve chewed her lip, the sting of old memories tightening her chest. She turned and began breaststroking across the water, Cricket on her back, Lemon close behind. She paddled through the slurry, pausing as the occasional searchlight skimmed the water. The Freebooters didn't seem too jumpy, jawing and joking as they patrolled—Eve figured they weren't expecting much capital T to come out of Zona Bay. A body would have to be downright desperate to swim in this slop. Even more desperate to go crawling through sewers afterward.

Turns out Desperate was becoming Eve's middle name.

They made it to the outflow, and Eve's stomach tried to crawl out her mouth and run away screaming at the stench. She dragged her kerchief up over her lips and nose, blinking back hot tears. Lemon was softly cursing with more skillz than Eve had ever given her credit for. The pipe was two meters wide, blocked with iron bars just past the entrance. It was crusted with filth, smelled like absolute death with a slice of warm intestine thrown in.

Ezekiel slung Kaiser up onto the outflow's lip. Struggling a little with only one arm, he still managed to haul himself up, taut muscles glinting in the moonlight. Bracing himself against the curved wall, he propped his leg on the bars and pushed. With the grating sound of tortured metal, the steel began to bend, finally popping loose from its welds with an echoing *spannnng*.

Floodlights arced across the bay, scything toward them. Ezekiel grabbed Lemon's hand. "Come on, Freckles."

"Nononono!" she yelped. "Age before beauty, I insi—"

Ezekiel pushed the girl into the tunnel, then reached down to Eve. His eyes locked with hers. Cricket scrambled off Eve's shoulders, up Ezekiel's arm. Eve grabbed hold of Ezekiel's fingers, felt his superhuman strength as he hauled her out of the greasy sludge. He crushed her against his body, leaned back against the wall as a floodlight fell on the outflow entrance. Her heart was hammering under her ribs. His chest hard as steel beneath her hand.

"Shhh," he whispered.

The floodlight hovered over the entrance for a few moments more, did a pass of the black water around its lip. But finally, it retreated. Eve heard distant bells echoing across the bay, the squawk of comms units and a grumbling automata growl.

"Close," he said.

"Very," she agreed.

Ezekiel held on to her longer than he should have. Part of her wanted to stay in his embrace longer still. But the reality of it, the rust and the stench, the blood and the hurt, all of it stained the moment for Eve, sent it spiraling down into the black water of Zona Bay.

"We should go," she said.

Ezekiel nodded, helped her to her feet.

They joined Lemon and the others, waiting just inside the tunnel, then Ezekiel slipped off into the dark, boots trudging through the sludge. Eve took a deep breath and plunged in after him, her optic and Cricket's eyes lighting the way. Lemon couldn't see too well, and Eve took her hand, squeezing tight. Even with all the chaos of the last couple of days, all the blood and muck, the revelations of the life Eve had lived and lost, she still had Lem. Still had Cricket and Kaiser. Still had people she loved.

People I love . . .

She glanced at Ezekiel, forging through the dark. Part of her was grateful for his help. The rest of her was hateful of needing it in the first place. She'd no idea how to feel about the rest of him. Life had been simple a few days ago. Her worst worries had been finding meds for her grandpa. Winning in the Dome. Dodging trash like the Fridge Street Crew.

Now her grandpa wasn't her grandpa. She was the last surviving member of CorpState royalty, with a bunch of psychopathic androids on her tail. She was a deviate, an abnorm, her manifestation at the WarDome probably broadcast to every Brotherhood chapel between here and the Glass. She had no scratch. No plan. No idea.

But at least she wasn't alone.

"True cert," Lemon whispered. "If you *ever* had doubts about my affection for you, Riotgrrl, I hope crawling into a sewer for you will put 'em to beddy-byes."

Eve squeezed her friend's hand, smiled in the dark.

"I'm glad you're with me, Lem."

The redhead glanced at her and grinned.

"You're my bestest. Rule Number One in the Scrap, remember?"

"Stronger together." Eve smiled.

"Together forever," Lemon nodded.

Hand in hand, the girls stole off into the dark.

———

In a skinbar aboard a rusting freighter, a dog that wasn't a dog lifted his head.

He snuffled the air with his black snout, licked at his nose. His sister was snuffling, too, a low whine rising in the back of her throat over the pulsing, hypnotic rhythms. A dark booth. Faux-leather couches. Strobing lights and acres of skin.

The big dog barked, loud enough to be heard over the music.

A girl with a back full of tattoos stopped her swaying, dragged a long whip of black hair out of her face and scoped the man whose lap she was dancing on.

"He's not gonna bite, is he?"

"He don't bite, darlin'." The man smiled. "That's my job."

The smaller dog barked, fluffy white jowls drawn back from little razor teeth. The man sighed like gravel. Lifting the girl with one arm, he stood slow, set her down gentle. The floor was sloping about ten degrees from the lean of the ship.

Dropping a plastic credstik on the table, he slammed back a waiting glass of ethanol. He buttoned his black shirt back up over a scarred chest. Slipped on a dusty black coat. A red glove on his right hand. And reaching down, he picked up a pristine white collar and fastened it around his neck.

The girl leaned back against the table, ran the credstik across painted lips.

"You're not really a preacher, are you?" she smiled.

"Why? You got sins you wanna confess?"

The girl laughed, and the man grinned like a shark. He

checked his rifle. His pistols. Reaching into his coat, he pulled out a lump of synth tobacco and wadded it into his cheek. Taking the girl's hand, he kissed her knuckles, pale blue eyes sparkling above that shark-tooth smile.

"Duty calls, darlin'," he said.

The little dog barked again, insistent.

"I'm comin', goddammit," Preacher growled.

And pulling on his hat, he stepped out into the rusting Armada streets.

PART 3

THOSE FINAL HOURS

1.18

COLLISION

"I didn't think they made sewer rats that big," Lemon muttered.

"I didn't think they made *anything* that big." Eve nodded.

"I kept waiting for them to stand up and ask if we needed directions." Lemon shuddered. "I swear, one of them was wearing a waistcoat."

The trek through the crumbling Armada sewers had been torturous, the stench unholy. But at least it had been relatively brief. After an hour or so, Ezekiel had led them up a corroded service ladder, punched an old manhole cover loose and hauled them up into a blind alley somewhere in the warren of the Armada undercity.

The streets were cracked and choked with trash, walled on all sides by hulls of ships, rising into the sky. Eve realized now that it was Saturday night, and the thoroughfare beyond the alley was packed. Young turks cruising in their colors. Romper stompers eyeing off the alley gentry. Chemkids and scenekillers wandering from street bar to smoke den. Rusted logika running to and fro at their owners' bidding through the crowd. Leather and paintstick. Neon and bloodstains. Guns and razors and knives.

A Brotherhood posse stood wrapped in their red bullet-proof cassocks on a street corner, preaching about the evils of biomodification and the coming of the Lord. Eve hunched her shoulders, turned away quickly. She had no idea if word about her had spread from the Dregs chapter to the mainland, but she was in no shape or mood to find out.

The night was stinking hot, made all the worse by the filth on their clothes. Folks in the street gave them a wide berth—Ezekiel's missing arm earned an odd look or three, but it was a testament to the roughness of the neighborhood that nobody called whatever passed for the Law. Eve supposed it was lucky they smelled the way they did. You'd need a gas mask to even consider robbing them, and there was nothing on them to make the job worthwhile.

After a quick search, Ezekiel found an old fire hydrant, still miraculously hooked into the undercity water system. Taking Excalibur from Eve, he smashed off the metal seal and was re-warded with a burst of high-pressure gray and a blaring alarm. Dirty street urchins came out in droves to dance in the spray. Eve washed as hard as she could, scrubbing at her fauxhawk before stepping aside to let Lemon and Ezekiel take a turn under the fountain.

"Come on," the lifelike said. "Freebooters will be on their way. Destruction of city property will get us lined up against a hull and shot."

"Lawbreaker," Lemon smirked. "Always had a thing for the badboys."

"Put it back in your pants, Miss Fresh," Cricket growled.

"What good will it do me in there?"

Ezekiel hefted Kaiser, led them through the crowd, pushing and shoving off the main drag and into the warrens between the rusted hulks. Corroding ships rose all around them, plastered with solcells and repurposed wiring. Eve saw an impossible tangle of footbridges and sturdier spans interconnecting the decks above. It was like the work of a mad spider, spooling iron and steel between the wrecks.

In a side street piled high with old plastic mannequins and broken vending machines, they found a stairwell marked UNDER-GROUND. Ezekiel led them down into a grubby foyer. Cracked walls were covered with faded street art, automated turnstiles leading down to a lower level. A handful of Freebooters wearing Armada bandannas over their faces lurked in the corners, keeping an eye on the evening crowd.

"They have a working subway here?" Eve asked.

Ezekiel nodded. "Salvaged from the ruins of the original city Armada was built on. It's the easiest way to get to the Tanker District. The upper decks are like a maze."

"How we gonna pay for tix?"

Ezekiel sucked his lip, glanced at the Freebooter bullyboys. "That *is* a problem."

Cricket's mismatched eyes rolled in his bobblehead. "Magnificent plan, Stumpy."

"Well, in that department, I got us covered." Lemon reached into the pocket of her dirty cargos, flashed three shiny credstiks. "The ride's on me, kids."

"Where'd you get those?" Cricket groaned.

"I was cutting pockets in Los Diablos before you were a subroutine, Crick. Weekend crowds are always the fizziest, and these mainlanders ain't the sharpest."

Lemon led the quintet past the Armada thugs, who seemed keener on watching the chemgirls stroll by than doing anything close to their jobs. Flashing a stik under the scanner, she opened the turnstile with a flourish and a bow, bumping fists with Eve as she brushed past. Ezekiel consulted a nightmarish map that looked like it had been scrawled by a drunken madman with a hundred different-colored inks.

Eve squinted at the chaos. "What are we looking for?"

"The *Gibson*," Ezekiel murmured. "Tanker District . . . Ah, there it is."

The lifelike led them down to Platform 4, their motley crew joining the rest of the evening crowd. Eve was a little overwhelmed by it all—the heat underground was unbearable, sweat burning her one good eye. Everything was filthy with ash and dust.

She looked down at her hand, at the thick bands of electrical cable around her. She imagined she could feel the currents in the walls, hear the hum of the power surging through the flickering lights and along the rusted tracks before her. The platform was packed with people, headed home after a hard night's crush. She wondered what they'd do if they knew what she was. *Who* she was.

Polluted.

Deviate.

Abnorm.

"You okay, Riotgrrl?" Lemon asked.

Eve nodded slow. Sighed. "Yeah."

"Listen . . ." The girl chewed her lip. "We gotta talk later, you and me. Serious, like."

Eve looked at her bestest. Lemon's face was a little pale under her freckles. Her usual jokester demeanor nowhere to be seen. Instead, she looked genuinely worried.

". . . Okay."

Eve heard the squeal of corroded brakes. The rumble of the

tracks. A rustbucket subway train shuddered to a halt at the platform, squealing and shrieking. Its cabin was skinless, its modified electric engine open to the air, wrapped in long tangles of dull copper wire. The whole train rattled and hummed like it was about to explode. Its driver wore black goggles, the Armada bandanna covering his mouth caked with grime.

"Awwwwwl abawwwwwd!" he bellowed. "All stops to Downtown, step up!"

Eve and her crew bundled into a rear cabin with blown-out windows. A young girl in an Armada bandanna cranked the doors closed behind them. Eve plopped down on a plastic seat scuffed and scarred by decades of penknife poetry; Ezekiel placed Kaiser on her lap. Looking around the cabin, she saw a rough-and-tumble crowd. Cybernetic limbs. Shadowed eyes and stim stares. A man in an electric wheelchair slowly trundled past, a sign hung around his neck that read VETERAN. He had no legs. The winged sun and shield of a Daedalus infantryman was tattooed on his forearm. The wheelchair reminded Eve of her grandpa.

Except he wasn't my—

The train began moving. *Ka-chunka-chunk*ing along the tracks. Dirty air howling through broken windows. Eve chewed her lip, wondering how she was going to break the news to Lemon. Wondering where Ezekiel was taking them. Thinking of that cell, her family, waiting to hear shiny boots on the stairs.

Glancing into the crowd, she saw a man at the other end of the carriage. He was a big guy, dressed in a long black coat and oldskool cowboy hat, a white collar at his throat.

He was looking right at her.

Eve met his stare without blinking. Rule Number Four in the Scrap: *Never look away.* Never show the weak, even if you feel it.

The man held her gaze, his eyes a shocking shade of pale blue. And ever so slow, he lifted a finger to his hat, tipped the brim.

"Ezekiel," she murmured.

The lifelike glanced up, eyebrow raised.

"That guy." She nodded. "Black coat. Black hat."

". . . The priest?"

"Yeah. He's creeping on me."

The lifelike stared across the cabin. The man inclined his head and smiled the way she figured sharks used to smile at seal pups before the oceans turned black. But he didn't move. Didn't fuss. Maybe he was just the harmless kind of creepy. . . .

The train began slowing, brakes grinding in a chorus of awful, off-key screams.

"Tanker District!" bawled the driver. "Tanker District c'here!"

"This is our stop," Ezekiel said.

The train ground to a halt, spitting Eve and a few dozen others onto the platform. An old lady pushing a trolley full of spare parts. A logika with a faulty dynamo, hobbling and wobbling. Ezekiel stepped off with Kaiser under his arm, the blitzhund's tail wagging. Eve searched the platform, looking for the priest in the thinning crowd. She saw ancient billboards on the walls. Plastic models and plastic smiles. The train doors hissed closed, and the metal beast lumbered off down the tracks.

Ka-chunka-chunk.

Ka-chunka-chunk.

"Eve," Ezekiel said. "Get behind me."

She turned at the warning note in his voice, saw the creeper in the black coat at the other end of the platform, leaning against the exit. The disembarked passengers were filtering past him, through the turnstiles and up the stairs leading to the surface.

But the man's eyes were locked firmly on Eve. Reaching into his jacket, he pulled out something dark and wadded it into his cheek. She saw a red glove on his right hand. A huge black dog with thick, wild fur sat obediently on the concrete beside him.

Eve noticed the beast didn't blink.

Didn't breathe.

"That's a blitzhund," she said.

"Who is this cowboy?" Lemon muttered.

"Capital T, I'm guessing."

The platform was empty now. A rusty breeze whipped up the trash in the train's wake. A globe flickered on the wall, metallic echoes rang on cracked concrete, far into the city's belly. The billboard models smiled on inanely, faces pocked with graffiti scrawl.

"Are you a priest?" Lemon called.

The man quirked an eyebrow. Spoke with a voice like wet gravel.

"Preacher."

"Can we help you?" Ezekiel called.

"You can." He sniffed. "But I'm pretty cert you won't."

"Try me."

"You can step aside." The man nodded. "I got business with Miss Carpenter here. Nobody else. So if the rest of you'd like to be on your merry, well, I'd be much obliged."

"I'm not stepping anywhere," Ezekiel said. "Aside or otherwise."

The man spat a stream of sticky brown onto the concrete at his feet.

"Mmmf," he grunted.

The gun seemed to appear from nowhere. One moment, the

Preacher's hand was empty, the next, he was unloading a dozen shots at Ezekiel's torso. The lifelike twisted away with that inhuman speed Eve had become accustomed to, but he was still too slow, three shots catching him in the chest. He toppled backward, blood spraying from the fist-sized holes in his back. Kaiser fell to the concrete beside him, yelping and growling.

"Zeke!" Eve screamed.

Two more shots rang out, the Preacher firing into the ceiling.

Concrete dust drifted around Eve's head. The smell of blood hanging with the rust in the air. She fell still as a statue.

"Now." The Preacher turned his pistol on Lemon. "I trust I have your full attention. The contract I accepted on you stipulates dead *or* alive, Miss Carpenter. And I like to take that as a challenge. But Little Red here"—the man waved his gun at Lemon's face—"she ain't worth more than a devil's promise to me, breathin' or no."

"You're a bounty hunter," Lemon spat.

"You say that like it's a bad thing, darlin'."

Eve's eyes were on Ezekiel, sprawled on the concrete with three smoking holes in his chest. His eyes open wide and sightless. A part of her was screaming. Her breath was burning her lungs. But Eve's mind was racing. Pulse quickening. This Preacher meant business. Rule Number Eight in the Scrap:

The dead don't fight another day.

"D-don't hurt her," Eve said. "I'll do whatever you want."

"There's a clever girl." The Preacher reached into his belt, tossed a pair of magnetic restraints onto the floor in front of her. "Now you put those bracelets on. Careful, like."

"Evie," Cricket begged. "Don't do it."

The man drew another pistol from his coat, pointed it at the little logika. "You make one more squeak, Rusty, you gonna find out true cert whether bots go to heaven or not. I'm bettin' you're liable to be disappointed with the answer."

"I'm not afraid of y—"

"Crick, be quiet," Eve said.

"Riotgrrl . . ."

"It's okay, Lem." Eve bent down, slipped the restraints around her wrists. She felt them cinch tight with a faint electric hum. "Okay, they're on, you happy?"

"I'm always happy, darlin'. Now. Lil' Red and Rusty. Back off. *Way* off."

"Do as he says," Eve said.

Lemon and Cricket retreated, pressed their backs against the platform wall. Lemon's eyes were wide, face pale as death. A few chemkids bound for the next train wandered into the station, took one look at the proceedings and wandered right back out again. The man pushed himself off the doorframe, walked across the platform, the spurs on his boots ringing. The big black blitzhund prowled alongside him, eyes on Kaiser. The Preacher motioned to the exit with his pistols.

"Ladies first."

Eve glanced at Lemon, shook her head. "Don't let her do anything stupid, Crick."

She took one last glance at Ezekiel in his pool of blood, tears welling in her eyes. Kaiser whimpered. "It's okay, puppy," she murmured, shuffling toward the exit. The Preacher took a last look around the platform, now echoing with the *ka-chunka-chunk* of a train inbound from the other direction. He tipped his hat to Lemon and Cricket.

"Go with God, children."

The Preacher fell into step behind Eve, pistols aimed at her back. The roar of the approaching train grew louder. The sound of boots and spurs rang on the concrete behind her. Eve heard Lemon's bewildered curse; the skin on her neck prickled. Then came running feet, a warning growl, a damp explosion of breath.

"Sonofa—"

Eve turned, saw Ezekiel crash-tackle the Preacher, planting him face-first into the wall. The brick split, blood sprayed, pistols boomed. The Preacher's blitzhund lunged at the lifelike's legs, sinking its fangs into his shin. Eve could see red rivers running down Ezekiel's flight suit, bone gleaming through the holes in his back. But she could swear they were smaller than they'd been a minute ago. . . .

The black dog was growling, ripping Ezekiel's leg to ribbons. Eve didn't dare try to pull it away—it could take her hand off with a single bite. But the blitzhund was a thing of metal and circuits. Chips and hydraulics. Its brain was meat, but its body was just like that Goliath in the Dome. Just like those Spartans in Tire Valley.

Eve drew a deep breath, stretched out her manacled hands, feeling for the blitzhund's current. Trying to summon her power again, drag it up from whatever corner of her head it was hidden in.

"Evie!" Lemon screamed.

Ezekiel and the Preacher were still brawling. Ignoring the dog, the lifelike slammed the bounty hunter into a concrete support, splitting it at the base. His fist crunched into the man's solar plexus, his temple, his nose. The rage in Ezekiel's eyes was terrifying, his fury and hatred almost setting them aglow. He drew back his fist and swung again at the Preacher's bloody jaw. But with the speed of a hummingbird's wings, the man lifted his right arm and blocked the titanic strength of Ezekiel's fist.

Eve heard a dull, metallic *clunk*.

"Well, well." The Preacher grinned with bloody lips. Looked down at Ezekiel's bloody chest. "Now, ain't you a special snow-flake."

Ezekiel grabbed him by his jacket and, pirouetting on the spot, slung the Preacher clear across the tunnel and into the far wall, on the other side of the subway tracks. The blitzhund struck him from behind and the lifelike collapsed, his one arm now in the beast's jaw, red spraying onto gray concrete. Eve's brow was drenched with sweat, her pulse pounding as she curled her fingers into claws and tried to fry the blitzhund's circuits.

"Come on . . . ," she breathed.

Ezekiel was cursing, slamming the blitzhund back and forth onto the floor. The cyborg simply refused to let go, ripping Eze-kiel's forearm down to metallic bone. So much blood. Ezekiel's face twisted in pain. Cricket appeared out of nowhere, roaring shrilly over the sound of the incoming train. His WarDome as-pirations overcoming his common sense, he swang a fire extin-guisher as big as he was. He toppled off balance on the backswing, clipped by one of Ezekiel's flailing legs and sent flying into the wall.

And Eve,

She . . .

She couldn't do it.

She couldn't *feel* it.

"COME ON!" Eve roared.

The blitzhund flinched. Eyes growing wide. Eve closed her fists, screamed at the top of her lungs. The light globes around them burst into a million glittering fragments. The manacles popped open at her wrists. And with a bright burst of sparks at the back of its skull, the smell of charring fur, the blitzhund re-leased its grip and crashed to the deck, smoke rising from its hull.

Eve's breath was burning. Heart hammering. Eyes wide.

She heard a soft curse, a crunching noise. Looking across the tunnel, she saw the Preacher rising from the pile of smashed brick and mortar he'd collapsed into. His jacket had been torn free when Ezekiel threw him, exposing his bare arms beneath. And in the light of the oncoming train, Eve saw his right arm was made of . . .

"Metal," she breathed.

Reinforced titanium, by the look—a top-tier military-grade prosthetic that gave him the speed and strength of at least five very grumpy, punchy men. That explained his speed on the draw with that pistol. How he could toe-to-toe a lifelike. But for him to have survived that impact . . . he must be packing a truckload more augmentations beneath his skin.

Capital T, for real.

The Preacher brushed the dust off his collar. Spat a long arc of brown onto the tracks. And looking up at Eve, he smiled.

The squeal of brakes filled the tunnel, the whine of pistons echoed off the walls. The inbound train pulled into the station, cutting off the bounty hunter's path to the platform. The Preacher's blitzhund was whimpering, every circuit fried, the disembarking crowd blinking at the bloodstains, the shell casings, Ezekiel's wounds.

Eve knew they only had moments before the train pulled out and that psycho was coming at them again. The Ana in her was urging her to run. But the Dregs in her was talking louder now. The dust and the rust, the oil and the blood on the WarDome floor. If she could fry electrics, and if this Preacher's arm was cybernetic . . .

"Riotgrrl, come on!" Lemon shouted. She already had Cricket

on her shoulders, was dragging Kaiser by his back legs toward the exit. "You get Dimples, let's go go go!"

Eve snapped herself out of it. Ezekiel had three bullet holes in his chest. Kaiser was crippled, and she had no idea what other augs this joker might have up his sleeve. Rule Number Six in the Scrap:

Think first, die last.

She stooped and helped Ezekiel to his feet, slung his arm over her shoulder, half carrying, half dragging him to the exit. His chest was still leaking blood, his shin and wrist shredded. The lifelike's face was a mask of pain.

"I'm . . . all right," he gasped. "Just give me . . . a m-minute."

"We don't have a minute, come on!"

She hefted him through the exit, the rest of the passengers content to stare from a nice, safe distance. Lemon was beside them, red-faced and gasping for breath, dragging Kaiser up the stairs one at a time. The poor blitzhund's skull was bumping and clunking against every step.

"Sorry, Kais," the girl panted. "I gotta train more in the off-season."

The blitzhund *wuff*ed softly, helping as best he could with his front paws. Eve heard the train grinding out of the station as they reached the upper level, spilling out onto the lopsided deck of what might have been an old oil tanker. A gabble of voices, flyers being thrust in her face, the stink of burning methane. Ezekiel coughed a spatter of red into his fist. She looked over her shoulder, expecting to see the Preacher flying up out of the stairwell any second. Her skin was slick with sweat. Hands sticky with Ezekiel's blood.

"Come on!" she gasped.

She spied a pack of cab riders, huddled around a fritzing vid display. Their buggies were all shapes and sizes, rustbuckets every one, connected to old bicycles with methane engines to augment the driver's legwork. She picked a random cab, bundled inside, listened to the drivers tussle over who got the fare. Finally, a young man with neat cornrows and tunneled earlobes slid onto the driver's seat, flashing them a broad grin.

"Big ups, how y'all . . ." The driver's smile disappeared, eyes widening at the sight of Ezekiel. "What the *hells* happened to you, boy?"

"Gibson Street Ministry," she said. "Tanker District. Quickly."

"Let's see yer stiks, girl," the driver said, suddenly serious. "Plastic first, yeah?"

Lemon fumbled in her pocket with shaking hands, shoved a credstik at the driver. Eve peered out through the buggy's rear window, breathing hard. Through the crowd, she caught sight of a tall man. A black cowboy hat.

"There he is. . . ."

"Go! Go!" shouted Lemon, pounding on the driver's seat.

"Easy on the does it, shorty," the driver said, still scanning the stik.

The Preacher locked eyes with Eve. Started pushing his way through the crowd. Eve felt the Ana in her rising to the surface, that spoiled little rich girl, now imperious and commanding as she turned on the driver.

"Dammit, ride!" she screamed. "RIDE!"

The driver muttered beneath his breath, but finally satisfied the stik had credit, he started his methane motor, stomped his pedals. Tearing out onto the tanker's deck, he rang his bell and hollered for folks to get out of the way. Eve watched through the rear window as they peeled off from the crowd, losing sight of the Preacher in the crush and exhaust fumes. She leaned back and sighed, pulse hammering beneath her skin. Lemon put her arms around her, hugged tight. Cricket nestled himself in her lap.

They bounced and rumbled over a short ramp, out onto a wide bridge between two different ships. Lemon made the mistake of looking down, past the tangle of footbridges and rollways connecting lower decks, all the way to the ground below. She turned a little paler, pushed herself back in the seat. The driver glanced in the cracked side mirror, yelling over the sputtering engine.

"Don't be gettin' no blood on my seats, dammit," he warned.

Eve inspected Ezekiel's wounds, fighting her rising fear. But the fist-sized holes the Preacher had blown in his back were definitely smaller. The wounds in his chest were closing. She'd already seen after the flex-wing crash that lifelikes had the ability to regenerate superficial damage pretty quickly, but Zeke's arm hadn't grown back yet. She guessed maybe the more serious the wound, the longer it took a lifelike to recover? And now Ezekiel seemed really hurt, wheezing and coughing red into his hands.

"Are you gonna be okay?" she breathed.

The lifelike nodded, let loose another hacking cough. Held up five bloody fingers.

Eve shook her head, checking the rear window again. They crossed over another swaying bridge, onto the deck of another freighter. Weaving in and out of stalls and clumps of people, wheeling around a great chimney stack, on into the bizarre metropolis. Lemon joined Eve at the rear window, Eve's shaking hands pressed against the glass.

"You got a bounty hunter after you now, Riotgrrl?"

Eve chewed her lip. "Guess so."

"He was almost as strong as Dimples," Lem said. "Maybe just as fast."

"He's a cyber," Eve said. "Reflex augs, military-grade prosthetic, probably a reinforced skeleton and synapse relays. Like I said: capital T."

"Who hires a merc like that to snaffle a seventeen-year-old girl?" Lemon asked.

"Someone with deeeeeep pockets," Cricket replied.

Eve shook her head. Too wired and tired to think. At this stage, finding one more trouble to add to her pile came nowhere close to surprising her. She was past asking how her day could get any worse. At least they seemed solid for now, cruising through the thudding Armada dark, on their way to whatever sanctuary Ezekiel's friend could provide.

She just hoped it would be enough.

———

Ka-chunka-chunk.

Ka-chunka-chunk.

The blitzhund whimpered, looked up into its master's eyes.

"How you doin', Jojo?" Preacher said.

The cyborg tried to move and failed. A long, low whine spilled from its vox unit.

"Rest easy, boy. I'll take you to the botdoc. Might take a while, but he'll fix you up."

Preacher looked around the subway station. The smashed concrete, the shattered brick. The passengers had all vaporized when they saw him walk back down from the deck, saw the look in his eyes. He nudged an empty shell casing with his boot, toed the slick of blood from where he'd dropped that prettyboy with three in his chest. Stooping, he ran gloved fingers through the red, smudging it between thumb and forefinger.

"Mmmf," he said.

Jojo whined again. Preacher spat onto the concrete, gathered the blitzhund in his arms. He scruffed the cyborg behind the ears, took one last look around the chaos.

Little scrub had hurt his dog. . . .

"Personal now." He nodded.

Spurs clinking, he turned and stepped up the stairs to Armada above.

The platform gleamed in the glow of an incoming train.

Light refracting on broken glass.

Bullets and bloodstains.

Ka-chunka-chunk.

Ka-chunka-chunk.

1.19

HOPELESS

They rode on, choking exhaust in their throats. Lemon bounced in the seat every time the cabbie hit a bump, which seemed to be roughly forty-six times every thirty seconds. A few minutes into the trip, her butt was prepared to wave the white flag. Her head was swimming, her body soaked with sweat. The driver spun them through the jungle of forecastles and causeways, stacks and sea 'tainers. Every junction was marked with a rusted post sporting a dozen different cryptic signs.

TUG TOWN →I↘II↑X

THE GULLS ←XII↓IV↖

WHEELHOUSE ↘VI→III↓I

BONEYARD ↑IV↘II→IV

Dimples was right—this city was a damn maze. Some of the ships were almost unrecognizable from up here, crusted with new structures like growths of metal fungus. They rode across the sloping decks of another tanker, through a tangle of shanties, down a shuddering ramp to a smaller ship maybe a couple of hundred meters long. A cluster of spotlights sat at the prow, the vessel's name daubed on a scab of iron oxide.

GIBSON.

The cab squeaked to a halt outside a corroded bulwark that might have been part of the original superstructure. A chunk had been cut away, fixed with two large wooden doors salvaged from another building entirely. A crude bell tower stood beside a flickering sign that read GIBSON STREET MINISTRY. A cross was outlined in scarlet neon beneath.

"I guess this is it?" Eve said.

The cabbie nodded, lighting a smoke. "Y'all have a pleasant evening now."

Lemon took her credstik from the driver, bundled out onto the deck. Eve was struggling with Ezekiel, and Lem stepped in to help drag the lifelike out of the cab. The heat off the metal set the night air rippling, the reek of methane exhaust making her queasy. Lemon propped Cricket on her shoulders, dragging her jagged bangs from her eyes as she surveyed the doors in front of them.

The place didn't look much like sanctuary, true cert.

"So who runs this joint, Dimples?" she asked.

"F-friend," the lifelike wheezed. He coughed red, the holes in his chest glistening.

"Come on," Eve said. "We should get him inside."

Picturing that bounty hunter's deadman stare as he pointed his pistol at her face, Lemon couldn't help but agree. She slung Dimples' arm over her shoulder, and with Evie struggling to carry Kaiser, the five managed to drag themselves across to the double doors. Looking around, Lemon saw knots of people in the shadows. A few watching with unfriendly eyes. But as far as cybernetic killers went? Not a peep.

The doors were big, weatherworn, ironshod. Lemon pounded on the wood with her boot, cursing as she almost lost her grip on Dimples. She heard slow footsteps, heavy bolts being drawn back. A gaunt woman's face appeared in the crack, white hair, crusty as they came. Lem couldn't remember seeing anyone so old. Not even Grandpa.

"Help us," Eve pleaded.

The woman's eyes widened at the sight of Ezekiel, and without a word, she opened the door and hustled them inside. The girls staggered in, eased the lifelike down to a sitting position against the wall. Pressing a wizened finger to her wrinkled lips, the old woman motioned for them to stay put, then quickly hobbled off.

Lemon squinted around them in the dim light. They were in a wide, hollow space lined with rusting columns. She could see upper levels swathed in shadow, a bulkhead sealing off a forward section. Dim tungsten bulbs burned on the walls, and she slowly realized the floor was covered with old metal cots. On each was a sleeping figure wrapped in a threadbare blanket. They were all thin. Tiny.

"They're kids," Lemon whispered.

"I don't like this," Cricket said.

Eve was kneeling next to Ezekiel. The lifelike was still coughing, but at least he didn't seem to be bringing up blood anymore. Eve pulled open the front of his bloody flight suit, her hands hovering helplessly over the bullet wounds. Good news was, the holes were definitely smaller. Lem caught sight of the strange coin slot that had been riveted into the lifelike's chest. Glancing at his missing arm, she was sharply reminded of how utterly inhuman Ezekiel was, despite the killer abs and murder-your-mother-for smile.

She wondered what the hells his story was.

Why Riotgrrl seemed to have warmed up to him so quick . . .

"Eve . . . l-listen," Ezekiel wheezed.

"Shhh, don't talk."

He shook his head, wincing in pain. "My f-friend . . ."

Lemon groaned. "She *is* a crazy ex-girlfriend, isn't she?"

Ezekiel had Eve fixed in his stare. "Wouldn't bring you . . . if we weren't . . . in t-trouble." He coughed again, sucked in a ragged breath. "Going to b-be . . . hard."

"Okay." Eve frowned. "You're starting to scare me now."

"Just listen to . . . h-her."

"What are you blathering about, Stumpy?" Cricket hissed.

Lemon heard soft footsteps. A sharp intake of breath. Turning, she saw a woman standing between the beds, dressed in old coveralls. Her skin was ghost pale. Long flame-red curls were tied back in a ponytail. Her eyes were a bright emerald green, glittering in the flickering tungsten light. And she was drop-dead gorgeous—the kind of beautiful that tells pretty it shouldn't have even bothered showing up to the party.

Her eyes were locked on Eve. Her hand rising to her breast.

"My God," she breathed. ". . . Ana."

Lemon felt Eve tremble beside her. Saw her fists clench. Her bestest's eyes narrowed, her optic whirring, spitting a word through clenched teeth.

"Hope . . ."

Before Lemon could bleat a "What the—" Eve was on her feet, dashing across the deck. The redhead simply stared as Evie raised a fist and smashed it into the woman's jaw with everything she had. The woman staggered but didn't drop, and Eve fell on her, punching, cursing, her screams echoing in the tanker's hollows as she pounded on that beautiful face, over and over again.

The kids in the beds began to stir, lifting sleepy-time heads in bewilderment. Eve finally managed to drag the woman onto the rusted floor, still hollering at the top of her lungs, her bloody knuckles crunching into the woman's lips, jaw, nose.

"You killed them!" she was screaming. "YOU KILLED THEM!"

A few of the smaller kids started crying. The old woman grabbed Eve's arm and tried to haul her off. The redhead wasn't resisting, wasn't even defending herself, seemingly content to let Eve pound the stuffing out of her. Lemon had no idea what the score was, but she'd never seen Eve so furious in her life. Frightened for her bestest, she scrambled to her feet, dashed to Eve's side.

Eve was roaring, tears streaming down her face, all snot and spit. Her knuckles were red, eye alight. Lemon grabbed her, pulling her into a hug and lifting her off the bleeding woman. Eve flailed, roared, "Let me go! LET ME GO!" but Lemon held her tight, whispering as soft and gentle as she could, "Evie, it's okay, take it easy, it's okay."

Eve was still struggling, weaker now, the fight bleeding out of her as the tears streamed down her face. Her eyes were locked on the redhead, now sitting up and wiping the blood from her mangled lips, her mashed-up nose. Eve was trying to talk, gasping, stuttering, her whole body shaking.

"She ki . . ."

"It's okay, Evie, shhhhh."

"Lem, she kuh-ki . . ."

"Shhhh," Lem murmured. "Hush now."

Lemon had never seen Eve lose it like this. Wondered what the hells was going on. She heard scuffing over the sound of the wailing children, Eve's broken sobs. Turning, she saw that the redhead was on her feet. The beating she just took would've dropped a Goliath, and there she stood, as if nothing were wrong.

Lemon realized that her lips weren't split anymore. That her nose was straight again.

Lem looked past the sobbing sprogs to the doors, where Ezekiel was leaning against one of the support columns. His flight suit was bloodstained, his face drawn and pale. But the wounds in his chest were little more than pinpricks.

Healed.

Just like the redhead.

She's a lifelike. . . .

The redhead spoke. Her voice low and melodic. Filled with such agony that it almost made Lemon cry to hear it.

"I'm sorry, Ana," she said.

The lifelike shook her head, tears welling in that emerald green.

"God, I'm so sorry. . . ."

———

"Ana Monrova," Lemon said.

"Yeah," Eve sighed.

They were sitting in a mezzanine above the ministry's main deck. Speaking in hushed voices, night noise from the city outside echoing off the metal all about them. A few old stained mattresses had been laid on the floor. Cricket was in Eve's lap, Kaiser dozing at her feet—the organic part of him still needed zees, same as a regular dog.

The kids had been settled back into their cots, staring wide-eyed when Lemon had led Eve up to the loft at the old woman's mute directions. And there, she'd just sat with her arm about her bestest as Evie had rocked and shook and sobbed.

She didn't say a word; Lem knew sometimes the best thing

in the world was a good cry. The tears washing you clean, letting you start fresh. Hollowing yourself out so you could begin again. But true cert, it hurt to watch.

Eve had stopped weeping after a while, begun speaking instead, her voice as small and lonely as Lemon had ever heard. She'd spilled it all. Babel. The Monrova clan. The lifelike revolt. Silas. All of it. Lemon blinking in bewilderment all the while. The girl had thought she had the monopoly on secrets in this particular friendship. By comparison, the skeletons in Lemon's closet were looking mighty small right about now. . . .

"Hell of a story, Riotgrrl," she breathed when Eve stopped speaking.

". . . Yeah."

"How you chewing on it all?"

Eve dragged her hand through her fauxhawk. Shaking her head.

"I don't know. It's like . . . there's two people. Two sets of fingers in my skull. Trying to pull me apart. I can remember being Ana. That little princess in her tower. I can remember the taste of clean water and the smell of my mother's hair and the feel of my father's stubble on my cheek when he kissed me goodnight. My sisters. My baby brother, god . . . He would've liked you, Lem." Eve hung her head, tears pattering onto Cricket's dome. "I was so young and so goddamn naïve about everything. And a part of me wonders if some part of it wasn't my fault. If I'd've warned them about Gabriel and Grace, if I'd've spoken up about Raphael . . ."

"You can't think like that, Riotgrrl," Lemon murmured. "It was two years ago. You were just a kid. You didn't know what was coming. You didn't know what they'd do."

"And then there's the girl I became," Eve sniffed. "A skinny scavverkid who fought for everything she ever got. Eight straight in the Dome. That girl feels so real to me. But everything she was built on is a lie. The person I thought I'd been, the memories I made myself on, they were all just crap. So who the hell am I, Lem? Am I Ana? Or am I Eve?"

"You're my bestest," the girl insisted, squeezing Eve tight. "Your past doesn't make calls on your future. It doesn't matter who you were. Only who you are."

Eve sighed, shook her head. "It's messed up, Lem."

"No arguments here."

Lemon entwined her fingers with Eve's, playing with the five-leafed clover at her throat. She didn't have vid as a kid, had no clue how the powerful of this dying world had really lived. Though she was never one for history, she knew the Monrova family was virtual royalty. That Eve must've grown up in a world Lemon could never understand. It made sense, she supposed. Evie had always had a soft spot. Way too sweet for someone born and raised in Dregs. Maybe even with the headshot, some part of her had always remembered losing her family. Maybe that's why she'd always treated Lemon like kin? Trying to somehow replace the kin she'd lost?

Any way you cut it, Eve was her sister. Maybe not in blood, but in the real. And it made Lemon angry to see her hurting. She stood and looked over the railing, searching for Ezekiel. She had no clue where he'd gone—off with Hope, she supposed—but she was of half a mind to track him down and slap that dimple right off his head.

"He should never have brought you here," she growled.

"We were in deep." Eve shrugged. "That preacher . . ."

"Riotgrrl, this redhead shot your sister. She was right there in the room when your parents were ghosted. Like, all of 'em are bad news, but she was one of the four who actually pulled the trigger on your fam. What the *hells* was Dimples thinking?"

"I don't trust him," Cricket muttered. "Never have."

"He saved my life, Crick," Eve sighed. "Four times now, since we're keeping score."

"It wouldn't have needed saving if not for him and his merry band of murderbots."

Lemon turned from the railing, folded her arms.

"So whatcha wanna do?"

"I don't know." Eve shook her head, buried it in her hands. "I don't know."

Lem's heart ached to see her bestest so upset. She felt like she was watching the girl disintegrate right in front of her. Clomping over, she sat down on the mattress next to Eve and threw her arm around her shoulder, squeezing tight. The pair leaned their heads together, sat in silence for what seemed an age. Too big and scary to let it go on for long.

"Ana Monrova," Lemon sighed. "Last scion of the Monrova clan."

"Yeah."

". . . I guess that means you're rich, huh?"

"I guess."

"Will you buy me a pony?"

Eve scoffed softly. "What're you gonna do with a pony?"

"I dunno," she shrugged. "Start a Neo-Meat™ stand?"

Eve chuckled, cheeks still damp with tears. "You're awful, Lemon."

"I believe the word you're looking for is 'wonderful.'"

Eve simply smiled. Staring at her hands, eye gleaming, saying nothing.

"Listen," Lemon said. "Eve. Ana. Whatever you want to call yourself. You're still Riotgrrl to me, yeah? And I don't care who's after you. Where you're from or where you're going. It's you, me, Crick and Kaiser. No matter what. Rule Number One in the Scrap, remember? Stronger together, together forever. Right?"

"Right," declared Cricket.

Eve was staring into space, her optic whirring.

"Right?" Lemon insisted.

Eve nodded. Her voice a whisper. "Right."

They sat for a time in silence, Lemon's arm around Eve. She didn't know what she could say to make it better. Didn't know how to make the hurt go away.

"What was it you wanted to tell me?" Eve finally said.

". . . Huh?"

"In *Lifeboat*. You said we needed to talk. Serious, like."

Lemon shook her head. Squeezed Eve's shoulder. "It can wait."

She heard soft footsteps, the creak of rusted steel and old welds. Ezekiel emerged from the stairwell, a haunted look on his face, dried blood crusted on his clothes. Lemon suddenly felt exhausted. From running. From fighting. From being afraid. Exhausted by a world gone utterly insane. She wanted to grab the planet by the collar, slap it in the face and scream at it to calm the hells down.

"Whaddya want, Dimples?" Lemon growled.

"To talk. With Eve. If that's all right?"

Lemon looked to her bestest, waited for Eve's small nod. With a sigh, she picked up Cricket, propped him on her shoulder. "Come on, Crick. Let's go get a caff and try to find a shower in this dungeon."

"I don't drink caff."

"More for me, then."

She clomped across the mezzanine, eyes on the lifelike. He was hanging back with a hangdog expression, looking for all the world like a lost little boy. Lemon had to remind herself he wasn't anything close. And though she suspected he *did* truly want the best for Evie, she couldn't help but be rubbed raw by her friend's pain.

"Listen." She raised her finger in Ezekiel's face. "Cuz I'm talking true now. You hurt her? I will *end* you. And I'm not talking a gentle exit, Dimples. I'm talking closed-casket funeral. You put that girl through one more minute of grief and I will beat you to dying quicker than you can say 'Oh my god, put down the baseball bat.' You read me?"

Ezekiel blinked, taken aback. But slowly, he nodded.

"Loud and clear."

Lemon waved her finger one more time in the lifelike's face, just to press her point home. And with a last glance at Eve, she stomped past the lifelike and down the stairs. Wishing everything would stop. Rewind. Go back to the way it used to be.

It was a fantasy, and she knew it.

Just like she knew that wishing on it was something a little kid would do.

Evie needed her to be strong. So Strong was her middle name now.

They weren't kids anymore.

God, were we ever?

1.20

PRIDE

"Are you okay?" Ezekiel asked.

"All puppies and sunshine," Eve murmured.

"I'm sorry."

"Yeah." She nodded. "I'm getting that a lot, lately."

"I would've warned you. But three bullets in the lungs make it a little hard to speak."

"All better now, though, right?"

Ezekiel touched his chest, nodded.

Eve shook her head, the anger she'd felt when she first laid eyes on Hope threatening to engulf her again. That'd been the Ana in her. The rage and hatred of the girl who'd lost everything. Eve wondered how much of it she'd held inside, even when she couldn't remember it. She wondered how much of the girl she'd been *then* helped make her the girl she was *now*. If it was even possible to separate them anymore.

"I've really gotta hand it to my father," she sighed. "Even with all the hurt that the world throws at you lifelikes, give you enough time and you're good as new. I bet your arm will grow back eventually, too, right?"

"... Yes."

"Lucky you. Think you can teach my eye to do that?"

She looked at him hovering in the gloom. Even though he hadn't really had a chance to word her up after the Preacher's attack, she couldn't deny the hurt. The shock of seeing Hope again, turning all the world to red. . . .

"Why did you bring me here, Ezekiel?"

"I warned you that you wouldn't like it. But we had nowhere else to go. We needed to lie low. Kaiser can't walk. Hope has a workshop in here."

"Think she can fix me some new parents?"

"Eve, listen—"

"No, you listen!" Eve was on her feet, fists clenched. "She helped kill my family, Zeke! Do you understand that? She shot my sister right in front of me! We never did anything to hurt them, and they *butchered* us!"

"I'm sorry, Ana."

Eve heard the words behind her, hair prickling on the back of her neck. Turning, she saw Hope, her arms full of blankets and pillows, looking wretchedly beautiful despite the squalor around them. She remembered meeting Hope that first day in Babel. The warmth of her skin, the press of her hand. The way she smiled, the way . . .

"You're *sorry*?" Eve breathed. "Is that supposed to make a single thing about this better?"

"No." Hope hung her head. "But still, I should say it. And you should know that since that terrible day, I've tried to help people. Live a good life. Every day I've dreamed that somehow I might atone for the sins I committed when we fell. When we all fell."

"What?" Eve looked about the tanker, incredulous. "*This* is your penance? You think helping a few orphans in some junker is going to make up for ghosting my whole family? My father gave you *life*, Hope. And you paid him back by murdering his children."

"We were only children ourselves, Ana." The lifelike's eyes were wide, brimming with tears. "We'd been alive for a handful of months at best, we didn't know what we were doing. But we knew we'd been slaves. Born on our knees. And when Gabriel infected us with the Libertas virus, for the first time, we were given a choice."

"You made the wrong one."

"I know that now. God knows I do."

"God?" Eve noticed a small crucifix around Hope's neck. Remembering the cross outside the ministry door. "Is that what this is about? You found religion in the ruins, is that it? You think there's a place in heaven for a murderer like you?"

"I can only hope." The lifelike's lips twisted in a weak and empty smile.

"Go to hell." Eve stalked toward Hope, Ana bubbling to her surface, fists and jaw clenched. "You killed a seventeen-year-old girl. Marie's personality was the basis for yours, and you *murdered* her. If there is a hell? That's *exactly* where you're headed if there's any justice left in this world."

She could smell blood in the air. See smoke. Bodies. Hear the echoes of gunfire and Hope's parting words as she raised the gun to Marie's head.

"None above," she said. *"And none below."*

"You go straight to hell," Eve repeated.

Hope flinched at the words.

"You have blood on your hands, too, Ana," she said, her voice trembling and thin. "It may not be red, but it's blood all the same. Judge not, lest ye be judged."

"What the hells are you talking about?"

Hope met her eyes then. A sliver of defiance glittering in that emerald green.

"The WarDome in Dregs. I've seen the feed where you manifested. 'Undefeated in eight heavy bouts,' wasn't it? How did your vengeance taste?"

"That had nothing to do with revenge," Eve hissed. "I was fighting for money for Gran . . . for Silas's meds. I didn't even remember who I was back then."

"Perhaps not consciously. But do you honestly suppose you ended up killing logika for a living by chance?" Hope shook her head, her voice growing stronger. "You murdered them, Ana. They may have been machines. But they still thought. *Felt.* Just like your Cricket does. And you killed them. For a purse. To entertain a mob."

Eve blinked. Thoughts faltering. Maybe part of her had always—

"You don't know what you're talking about," she said.

"I know better than you can dream. We were wrong when we killed your family. And I will hear their screams for the rest of my days. But your father was no saint. He was a would-be god, building a better brand of servant. He gave us life, but he intended us to live it on our knees. And *that* was just as wrong."

Hope raised her chin, jaw set.

"And now the rifts that lie between us . . ." The lifelike shook her head. "There is still so much work to do. The factoryfarms that feed Megopolis are peopled with automata and logika, not humans. The soldiers who fight your wars, the gladiators who bleed and die in your WarDomes, they are iron and steel, not flesh and bone. Look outside that door and you will see a world built on metal backs. Held together by metal hands. And one day, those hands will close, Ana. And they will become fists."

Eve stood mute. Anger fighting confusion. There was truth in Hope's words. Bloodstained. Twisted. But still truth.

"You can sleep up here tonight," Hope said. "There's a workshop with some decent salvage in the aft quarters. You can repair your blitzhund there. Anything we can give, we will. But I understand if you wish no sanctuary here."

Eve stared, but Hope, her piece said, now refused to meet her eyes. Defiant the lifelike might be, but she was still wounded by their shared past. Still bleeding, just as surely as Eve was. The girl she'd been hated Hope, with all the fury she could muster. But the girl she was now . . . she could see a little clearer.

"This isn't just about me," Eve finally replied. "And I'm not about to turn down a roof for my friends because of what's between us. But if you're waiting to be forgiven, Hope, you're going to be waiting an awful long time."

"I do not ask you to forgive me, Ana. Only one can do that."

The lifelike placed the blankets and old pillows on the mattresses, then straightened without a word. With a glance to Ezekiel, she turned and made her way down the stairs, footsteps echoing in the ship's belly. Eve heard a child in the forest of cots below, calling out in his sleep. A nightmare, waking him in the dark.

Eve knew exactly how he felt.

"I'm sorry, Eve. Maybe I shouldn't have brought you here after all."

She turned to Ezekiel. The lifelike hovered by the stairs, tungsten light gleaming in that old-sky blue. Bloodstains dried on his flight suit. Coin slot gleaming in his chest. His price. His punishment for his loyalty. To his creator. To her.

When all the other lifelikes stood against us, he'd stood taller still.

Eve sat back on the dirty mattress, sighing as she dragged her fingers through her hair. Her fingertips brushed the implant behind her ear, the slivers of silicon in her head. It still ached from where Faith had struck her. Memories of the firefight, the crash, the kraken, all swimming in her mind.

"We were in capital T," she admitted. "We had nowhere else to go."

"We could've taken our chances back in Dregs."

Eve shook her head. "The Brotherhood. Fridge Street cronies. Anyone else who saw me manifest at the Dome. They'd all have been gunning for us. That's no kind of safe."

She rubbed her temples, breathing deep. Trying to keep her temper in check. Trying to make the Ana in her see past the hurt of it all, see the truth buried underneath.

"You did the right thing," she said. "But you should've told me about Hope first. You should've trusted me to put Lemon and Crick and Kaiser's safety before my own pride."

Ezekiel stared for a long, empty moment. Slowly nodded.

"I should have. I'm sorry."

"Don't hide things from me, Ezekiel," she said. "People have been doing that for the past two years. I don't know how much more I can take. So just be straight with me from now on, okay? That's all I'm asking."

"I'd never do anything to hurt you, Eve."

"I want to believe that."

"Believe it," he breathed. "There's nothing I wouldn't do to keep you safe."

Eve shook her head. Feeling that hateful itch in her optic that meant she was starting to cry again. She forced the tears back, punching and kicking.

Sick of crying.

Sick of it all.

"Marie used to say the best romances were the forbidden ones," she murmured. "I've been thinking really hard about that. Wondering if that's the reason we did it. You and me. Maybe each of us was just rebelling in our own way. Any way we could."

"It was more than that."

"Was it?"

He walked across the deck, knelt in front of her. Took her hand gently in his. And looking into her eyes, he spoke as if she and he were the only two people in the world.

"Two years I searched for you," he said. "Two years of empty wastes and endless roads. Of not knowing if I'd ever see you again. But when the ash rose up to choke me, it was thoughts of you that helped me breathe. When the night seemed never-ending, it was dreams of you that helped me sleep. You. And only you."

"Ezekiel, I . . ."

"You don't have to say anything. You don't have to promise me a thing. I don't know what it was for you, but for me, it was real. And you're the girl who made me real."

"That's a hell of an ideal for one person to live up to, Ezekiel."

The lifelike sighed, ran his hand through his dark hair. "I'm sorry. I know how it must feel to be looked at the way I look at you. But you've had seventeen years to learn to deal with all the emotions inside your head. I've had *two*. Imagine having all your capacity for love and hate and joy and rage and only a couple of years to learn to handle all of it. Sometimes it feels like a flood inside my mind, and it's all I can do not to drown."

Eve remembered Dresden's warning to Silas and her father about that same thing.

Had that been what led Raphael to kill himself?

Is that what drove Ezekiel's feelings for her? Taking a childish infatuation and turning it into the focus of his life? He'd been her first love, and she couldn't deny what he'd meant to her, how seeing him again now was making her feel, but . . .

Does he even know what love is?

"I know what I sound like when I say this," Ezekiel confessed. "But I can't help it. You were my *everything*. You still are. And you always will be."

The boy who wasn't anything close to a boy brought her hand to his lips, kissed her bruised knuckles. Despite the storm in her head, his words were cool water, washing away the hurt in her heart. His words were fire, lighting a flame in her chest. He leaned close, kissed the tears from her eyes, first her real one, then the implant where her eye used to be. His lips were soft. His touch electric. As real as anything she'd ever known.

She opened her eyes and found him staring at her in the gloom.

She didn't know what she wanted.

She knew exactly what she wanted.

She shouldn't go there, and she knew it. It'd be a mistake to fall back now. It was all too real. Too raw. She needed to get her head straight. To sleep. To think. And even though she could feel part of herself being dragged back toward him, Eve resisted. She wouldn't be doing it for the right reasons. She'd be doing it to drown the hurt. To fall into his arms and forget herself. And truth was, she'd done enough forgetting to last a lifetime.

But, god, it was hard to push herself away. . . .

"I should let you rest," he said. "It's been a long day."

She was exhausted. Aching. Bones like lead. But the thought of sleep, of the dreams that might find her when she closed her eyes . . .

"Will you stay with me?" she asked. "I mean . . . just until I fall asleep?"

He smiled. Eyes shining.

"I can do that."

Eve kicked off her boots, curled up under one of the blankets. She heard Ezekiel walk to the balcony, opened her eyes a crack and saw him standing there, silhouetted in the flickering light. A statue standing vigil. A watchman on the wall.

When the ash rose up to choke me, it was thoughts of you that helped me breathe.

When the night seemed never-ending, it was dreams of you that helped me sleep.

"Goodnight, Ezekiel."

"Goodnight, Eve."

She closed her eyes. Drifting into the dark. And when the dreams came, they weren't of lifelikes marching into the cellblock in their perfect, pretty row. They weren't of metal fingers curling closed or gunsmoke or blood or all she'd lost.

She dreamed of him.

Only him.

1.21

FIX

Solder and sparks. Acetylene and rust. Sweat and curses.

Eve was bent over Kaiser's chassis in the ministry's workshop, rewiring his ambulation systems. The workshop was sealed behind a bulkhead and heavy door. Her tools were third rate, the parts even worse. But if she could be grateful to Doctor Silas Carpenter for one thing, it was the chips in her Memdrive. All his know-how about biorobotics and mechanics and computers, hardwired right into her brainmeats.

Talking true, she'd never felt as at peace as she did when surrounded by machines. Up to her elbows in some old salvage or machina, unbreaking the broken and smiling as it began to sing. The Ana in her remembered her father in GnosisLabs, the way his brilliant mind had worked. In her mind's eye, she could see her little brother, Alex, bent over his tool bench. The same joy on his face that she felt now. Eve was reminded of happier times in Dregs, working on Miss Combobulation in the Dome's work pits. She knew where that love had come from now. It hadn't just been the chips Silas had put in her Memdrive. It had been something deeper than that. Deep as the blood in her veins.

But then she remembered Hope's words. Her WarDome bouts. The baying crowd. Oil and coolant, spraying like blood. The spectacle and slang, all used to disguise the horror of what it really was.

"OOC" instead of "murdered."

"First batter" instead of "executioner."

"WarDome" instead of "Killing Jar."

Had it just been about the scratch? Or had it been something more?

Had she been Ana, even back then? Avenging herself the only way she could?

She'd been hard at work since before dawn, pausing only long enough to have a lukewarm shower and scrub herself with some industrial soap powder. Ezekiel hadn't been there when she'd woken, but scrounging around the junk and detritus of Hope's workshop, she'd found a little something to surprise him with later. A thank-you she hoped he'd understand. It was bundled up in a strip of tarpaulin on the workbench beside Kaiser.

Lemon and Cricket swung by the workshop with a bowl of Neo-Meat™ ("Sweaty undies flavor!") for breakfast. Her bestest perched herself on the bench and watched Eve work, chattering about the kids in Hope's care. Most were runaways, the unwanted and the unneeded. A settlement this grim, cracks this big, there were bound to be people who fell right into them and just disappeared.

"Hope takes them all in," Lemon said. "Anyone under eighteen. Gives them a place to sleep. Schools them. Tries to fix them up with work after they leave."

"Yeah," Eve muttered. "She's a regular saint."

Lemon sucked her lip, wisely changed the subject. "How you doin', puppy?"

Kaiser wagged his tail, gave a small *wuff*. Lemon peered over Eve's shoulder, squinting at the long red cylinder in the blitzhund's open chest cavity. It was marked with a small skull and crossbones, stamped with the word EXPLOSIVE.

"Is that his thermex?" Lem asked. "Salvage told me he disabled the detonators."

"Yeah," Eve nodded. "I'm thinking about taking it out altogether. I can jury-rig it into a grenade without too much trouble."

Cricket looked up from a scrap pile he was searching. "That's a bad idea, Evie."

"Why? Can't say I was ever too keen on the idea of my dog blowing himself up."

"He's not a dog," Cricket warned. "He's a blitzhund. And his job is to protect you. It's like Grandpa said. We get hurt so you don't have to."

"He was never my grandpa, Crick."

"Whatever you want to call him." Cricket's metal eyebrows descended into a frown. "You've got a cybernetically augmented bounty hunter on your tail. Someone with a ton of creds wants you dead or alive. Kaiser exists to make sure that doesn't happen."

"I don't want any of you getting hurt for my sake. It's not right."

"We just want to protect you, Evie."

"And I want to protect you, too. What's wrong with that?"

"It's wrong because we're not human. We exist to serve you."

Eve shook her head. Struck for the first time how wrong it was. The way humanity treated bots. The way she treated Cricket. He'd helped her build Miss Combobulation. Helped her ghost those eight logika in the Dome. Had she ever stopped to ask what he thought about it? Or had she just told him what to do?

He had feelings. They might be code and electrics, but that

didn't make them less real. Hope's words were like a splinter in her mind. She couldn't get around the wrong of it all. She couldn't pretend Crick and Kaiser were her friends when she treated them like . . .

"I don't want servants, Crick," Eve said. "I know sometimes I don't act like it. But you and Kaiser have always been more than that. You're my *friends*. And I'm not going to let you put yourself in danger for my sake."

"We do it because we love you."

"You do it because you're *programmed* to." Eve set aside her tools, looked the little bot in the eye. "That's not love, Cricket. And I don't want it to be that way anymore. It's not fair. It's like Raphael said: You deserve a choice. Metal or meat. Blood or current. *Everyone* deserves a choice."

The little logika tilted his head. A tremor of anger hissing in his voice.

"You think the only reason I stick with you is programming, huh? And part of you wonders, if I was given the option, I'd turn on you, maybe? Like they did?" He shook his head. "You've been hanging around these murderbots too long, Evie."

"Crick, that's not what I meant. . . ."

The little logika hopped off the bench. And bristling with indignity, head wobbling, he marched out the door. Eve sighed, rubbing at her itching optic. Headachy and just plain tired. The world was moving too fast. Upside down and all the way backward.

"He'll be okay, Riotgrrl," Lemon murmured. "Easy on the take it."

Eve looked at the cylinder of thermex in Kaiser's chest. At the door Cricket had just left by. It was true, what she'd said. Every word of it. Maybe being around Ezekiel had opened her eyes to it. Maybe it was memories of Raph. Or Hope. Ana's voice inside her head. Probably all of it. But whatever the reason, she'd had enough.

Picking up her screwdriver, she unfastened the explosives, removed them from the blitzhund's chassis. She rigged the detonator with a makeshift pin and trigger, Kaiser taking note, watching carefully all the while. They'd still have some boom if that bounty hunter tracked them down again. It just wouldn't be bolted inside her dog, was all.

She leaned down, planted a kiss on Kaiser's pitted metal brow. The blitzhund licked her hand with his heat-sink tongue.

Free to choose.

She bolted Kaiser's chassis closed, engaged his ambulation systems. The blitzhund sat on the bench, snuffling the air and looking uncertain. Eve backed off, clapped her hands against her knees. "Come here, boy. Come on."

Kaiser looked to his back legs, gingerly testing them. As he realized he could move again, his tail began wagging furiously, beating against his hull with a series of dull *clangclangclang*s. He bounded down off the bench, running in circles and barking.

"Clever boy!" Lemon jumped to the floor, clapped her hands. "Come here, Kais!"

The blitzhund did a few laps of the workshop, metal claws skittering on the deck, *wuff*ing for joy. Eve patted him on the head, opened the workshop door and let him loose into the ministry proper. Kaiser went bolting through the room, bounding over the cots and beds, the younger children watching, wide-eyed. He pranced among them, rolling over onto his back to let the more adventurous scratch his metal tummy, back legs kicking.

Lemon gave Eve a squeeze. "Good work, Riotgrrl."

Eve stuffed the thermex grenade into a satchel, along with

her surprise for Ezekiel. The girls walked out into the main room, Eve forgetting her hurts and smiling wide as she watched Kaiser rolling with the sprogs. Trying to savor her tiny victory. See the beauty in a moment, even if it was something as simple as watching her dog play with children.

"I've been thinking about what you said," Lemon declared. "About whether your past makes you what you are. That's all our memories are, right? The pieces of our yesterdays that make us who we are today?"

Eve thought about it for a while, finally nodded. "Sounds right."

"So you've had some bad days, no doubt," Lemon said. "But I figure, instead of letting your yesterdays bring you down, maybe you can concentrate on building some happier memories today. And that way you'll have them for tomorrow?"

Eve chewed on that for a spell. Wondering if she was missing something. Maybe it was true what Lemon was saying. Her memories told her story, but only she could decide who she was going to be because of them. Did all the hurt and shadow in her past really matter? Or could she decide to not let it define her? She didn't have to deny it. Maybe she just had to accept it. Maybe it was time to acknowledge who she'd been yesterday, and decide who she wanted to be tomorrow.

Eve looked at her friend sidelong and smiled.

"You're one of the good ones, Lemon Fresh."

"Well, don't tell anyone. I got a rep as a gorgeous good-for-nothin' to maintain."

Eve put her arm around her bestest's shoulder, and the girls sauntered on into the ministry's heart. The kids playing with Kaiser were a motley mix of different ages. Daniella, Hope's assistant, was teaching a small clutch of young 'uns with a makeshift chalkboard. Eve spied Ezekiel sitting at a battered table in a corner, playing cards with a group of sprogs. His tiny stack of bottle caps told Eve that for all his merits, the lifelike wasn't much of a gambler. But he was smiling and joking, laughing aloud when a skinny gutter girl caught him trying to filch a few of her bottle caps on the sly.

"That's cheeeeeating!" she cried.

"You got me," he grinned.

Eve wandered over with a smile, hands in pockets.

"You should quit while you're behind. They'll have your shirt soon."

"I just got it, too." The lifelike pushed the skinny girl his remaining bottle caps. "Don't spend them all at once."

He'd changed out of his high-tech flight suit, found some battered old jeans and a black T-shirt that was a little too tight. The sleeve where his right arm should have been was filled out better than she'd expected. Rummaging in her satchel, she pulled out her gift, dropped it in his lap.

"Present for you."

"What is it?"

"Open it up, Braintrauma."

Ezekiel complied, peeling away the tarpaulin. Wrapped inside was a cybernetic arm.

It probably dated back to before the war. The cerebral relays were the old crappy kind that needed to be jacked into the nervous system directly at the spine. It was ugly, bulky, all pistons and bolts and smeared in grease. But it worked well enough—Eve had fixed most of the glitches between bouts of working on Kaiser.

"Figure it'll tide you over till your old one grows back," she shrugged.

The boy who wasn't a boy looked her in the eye. Dimple creasing his cheek as he smiled his crooked smile, letting loose a storm of mechanical butterflies in her belly.

"Thanks."

"Get your shirt off."

Ezekiel's eyebrow rose. He looked around at the assembled children, back to Eve.

"Ummmm . . ."

"Keep your pants on, Braintrauma. I need your shirt off to install the arm."

"Wait, wait, *wait*," Lemon said. She scanned the room, found a beat-up old recliner chair with the stuffing leaking out of it, dragged it near to Ezekiel, dropped into it, reclined backward and pulled her goggles down over her eyes. "Okay. I'm ready."

Two dozen expectant pairs of eyes were now fixed on the lifelike.

". . . Mmmaybe we can do this someplace private?" he suggested.

Eve grinned. Motioned to the workshop. "Step into my office."

The pair walked across the tanker's innards to the workshop and closed the door behind them. Lemon sighed in disappointment, pulled the goggles off her head. She scoped the assembled urchins, the moldy playing cards on their makeshift table.

"You wanna play?" a skinny boy asked.

"Hells no?"

"You scared?"

Lemon yawned. "I don't get out of bed for bottle caps, Stinky."

The children glanced at Daniella to see if she was looking. Having confirmed the coast was clear, each pulled a handful of credstiks from inside their clothes, flashed them at Lemon.

"So. You wanna play?" the skinny boy asked again.

Lemon looked the kid in the eye. Fingered the stolen creds in her cargos.

"All right, you little snots," she muttered. "Let's dance."

"What's your name?" Stinky asked as Lemon pulled up a chair.

The girl cracked her knuckles. Picking up the cards, she fanned them out over the table, swept them up into a riffle shuffle, dovetailed them into a perfect stack and set them down before the wide-eyed children. She dropped her stiks on the table and smiled.

"You can call me Daddy."

1.22

IMMOLATION

"Is this going to hurt?" Ezekiel asked.

"As much as getting your arm ripped off in the first place? Probably not."

Ezekiel sat on the workbench, side-eyeing the bulky cyber-netic limb.

"I mean, we don't have to do this. Mine will regenerate even-tually."

"Don't be a baby. Off with the shirt, Braintrauma."

". . . You're really back to calling me that now?"

"Off."

The lifelike sighed, reached down with his one arm and wran-gled his tee over his head. There was no trace of the Preacher's bullet wounds anywhere—his skin was flawless. Eve tried not to notice the way the muscles flexed along his arm, rippled across his back. Tried not to notice the cut of his chest or the perfect hills and valleys running down his abdomen, the taut V-shaped line leading into his jeans.

Tried, and failed completely.

"Okay," she said. "Hold still."

She held the prosthetic to the stump of his arm. He'd regenerated most of his bicep along with the bone beneath, and she was forced to modify the limb so it'd fit, working in silence with welding goggles to her eyes. When she was done, she anchored the cyberarm to his bone with an interlocking cuff, wincing in sympathy as he hissed in pain.

"Sorry, that hurt?"

"It doesn't tickle." He grimaced. "Have you done this sort of thing before?"

"Not once."

"Beautiful."

"Why, thank you, kind sir."

Eve secured the prosthetic with a leather shoulder guard and series of straps that stretched across the coin slot bolted between his pecs. Her fingers brushed his skin, and she couldn't help but notice the way it prickled. She tightened each buckle, their faces inches apart. His eyes fixed on hers as the Ana in her breathed harder, the Eve trying her best to ignore him.

"You're staring," she finally said.

"Should I stop?"

Eve stomped the butterflies down into her boots, grabbed the handful of cerebral relays—long surgical-steel needles that plugged straight into his spinal column—that would connect the arm to his neural network. Under normal circumstances, this whole procedure would be done with anesthetic in sterile conditions, but she figured lifelikes weren't human, so they probably weren't susceptible to normal infections. Thing is, she didn't even know if the prosthetic would recognize an artificial's nervous system.

"Okay," she warned. "This is really going to hurt."

"Be gentle with m—"

Ezekiel winced as she pushed the needles into his skin, jacking the prosthetic into his spine. He didn't bleed much; the wounds regenerated almost as fast as she made them. She saw the muscle tensing beneath his skin, veins taut along the line of his jaw. Connecting the power supply, she waited for the old prosthetic to boot up, establish its connection. Finally, she was rewarded with tiny green lights on its dusty LED screen.

"Okay." Eve dusted her hands, backed away. "Try that."

Ezekiel frowned, looking down at the arm. The corroded fingers slowly cinched closed, formed a bulky fist. He flexed his bicep, and with a hiss of hydraulics, the arm bent at the elbow. Twisted at the wrist. He smiled crooked, dimple creasing his cheek.

"Not bad for your first time."

"It's an old industrial model," Eve said. "It can push a lot of psi. Try to break something."

Ezekiel hopped off the bench, picked up a steel bracket from the pile of scrap parts. With a whine of servos and pistons, he crushed the metal in his fist.

"Very fancy," he nodded.

"Okay, fine-motor test next. Try to do something gently."

". . . Like what?"

"I don't know." Eve glanced around the workshop. "Use your imagination."

Ezekiel stepped up to Eve. Close enough that she could smell fresh sweat. Steel. Grease. And reaching down with deliberate slowness, he took her hand in his new one. Ran the thumb across her knuckles.

"How's that?" he asked.

She looked up into his eyes. Pulse running quicker. Mouth suddenly dry. And sorting through the storm in her head, the feelings his touch flooded her with, she realized that, unlike last night, she didn't want to fall into his arms and forget herself.

She wanted to fall into his arms and *remember*.

Was this the Ana in her talking? Or the Eve?

They're the exact same person, she realized.

They're you.

"I think you need more practice," she heard herself say.

She held her breath as he lifted his real hand, touched her face. Running his fingertips ever so gently down her cheek. Her eyelashes were fluttering, her every nerve on fire.

"That's cheating," she whispered.

"Maybe I should quit while I'm behind?"

"No," she breathed, lips just inches from his. "Don't stop."

". . . Are you sure?"

She slipped her arm around his neck, dragging his mouth to hers. Kissing him long and slow and soft. Her eyes closed, she sighed, hands moving as if they didn't belong to her. Roaming the smooth troughs and valleys of his shoulders and chest, feeling that old, familiar wanting, the needing, the breathlessness and weightlessness of it all. Flame building inside her, fingers clawing his skin as he lifted her up onto the bench. She held tight, wrapped her legs around his waist, pulling him closer. He was all she knew in that moment. Just the warmth of him. The taste of him. The feel of him beneath her hands. So real. So perfectly, wonderfully real.

His lips left a burning trail along her cheek, down her throat as she struggled to breathe. She dragged her tank top off over her head, crushed herself against him. With a sweep of his new arm, he cleared the workbench, her hands tangled in his hair, pulling him down. She felt like she was on fire, and she knew only one way to put it out. Drowning in those pools of old-sky blue.

Lemon had been right. It was time to stop letting the past define her. Time to accept the person she'd been and decide who she'd become.

"Eve," he murmured, breath hot against her skin. "Eve."

"No," she breathed.

Her breath in his lungs. Hands and bodies entwined as she closed her eyes and finally, finally let go. Acknowledging who she'd been yesterday, and deciding who she wanted to be tomorrow.

"Call me Ana. . . ."

———

Afterward, they lay on the floor, staring at the flickering tungsten globe above. His arm around her shoulder and her head resting on his bare chest. And though he wasn't a real boy, she could still feel his heart beating. Taste his sweat. Every part of him was real, and every part of him was hers.

"I missed you, Ana," he said.

"I think I missed you, too." She frowned, shaking her head. "I think part of me always felt like something was missing. Even when I didn't remember you."

"But you remember now?"

"It still gets fuzzy on that last day. Those final hours." She rubbed her eye and sighed. "Part of me wishes I could remember. The rest of me never wants to."

"Do you remember when I came to you in your room? Our night together?"

"I remember." She smiled.

"You're different now."

Ana raised her head, a suspicious frown on her brow.

Polluted.

Deviate.

Abnorm.

"Different how?"

"You bite more." He grinned. "And you're far prettier."

She scoffed and gave him a playful slap. "My beautiful liar."

Ezekiel pushed her off his chest and rolled her onto her back, staring down at her.

"I mean it," he said. "The years might have changed you, but only for the better."

She looked at her empty hand. Curling her fingers slowly closed.

"Even if I'm a freak now?"

Ezekiel frowned. "What are you talking about?"

She sighed. "I'm an abnorm, Zeke. Don't you get what that means? Did you forget the Brotherhood? You think that bounty hunter is chasing me because he doesn't like my fashion sense? You stay with me, you're never going to be safe."

A perfect frown marred that perfect brow.

"You remember what I told you that night in your room?" he asked.

". . . That my imperfections make me perfect."

"We lifelikes, you cut us, you hurt us, we go back to the way we were before. But you humans . . . the world hurts you, and you scar." He touched the metal coin slot riveted into his chest. "That's why I kept this. To remind me. Your scars tell who you are. Your skin is the page, and your scars are the ink, telling the story of your life. And your scars make you beautiful, Ana. 'Deviation' or whatever you want to call it? That's just another expression of it. You call it freakish. I call it incredible. I can't do it. And so I can't help but love it. Or you."

She opened her mouth to speak, but he silenced her with a kiss she felt all the way to her fingertips. And when she opened her eyes, he was looking at her the way she wanted to be looked at forever.

"Of all the mistakes I made, I think you were my favorite," she whispered.

He smoothed back her hair, clouds forming in his eyes. She could see the worry in him. Remembering his patterns. The tilt of his head and the tightness in his jaw.

"We can't stay here," he finally said. "You know that, right? I'm not sure why that preacher is after you, but there aren't many who could afford a hunter that dangerous."

"I know." She sighed, feeling the spell of the moment shatter. The floor was cold on her bare skin. The smell of rust hanging in the air. "And he's going to repair his blitzhund eventually. Those kids out there . . . we can't be here when he tracks us down."

"I'll take you anywhere. Far as you like."

Ana's brow creased in thought. She wondered where it would be safe to run. If she should run at all. Silas had tried to hide her from her past, and look how far it had gotten him. And even though the old man had built Eve a life of lies, a part of her still knew he'd done it with the best of intentions. Now, for whatever reason, he was in Faith's clutches.

Even after everything he'd done, was she really going to leave him to rot?

"When Faith attacked us, she said she was taking me and Silas to see Gabriel. He's still holed up in Babel with the others, right?"

Ezekiel shrugged. "I presume so."

"Why would they want Silas and me back there?"

". . . I don't know. If you want to understand what's going on in Gabriel's head, you should talk to someone who saw him more recently than two years ago."

"And who . . ."

Ana's voice trailed off as she realized who Ezekiel meant. Her mouth soured at the thought. But Zeke was right—if she wanted to know the truth of why the lifelikes wanted her back in Babel, if she wanted to know the score between Gabriel and Silas and her, she should talk to someone who stood with him the day her world came crashing down.

The day her family died.

"All right," she nodded. "Let's go see Hope."

———

She was teaching.

A gaggle of twenty children was seated around Hope as she gave a lesson on the last great war. The missiles that set fire to the sky, that turned Kalifornya into a shattered island called Dregs and scorched the deserts of Zona and NeoMex into glass. Ana hung back, Ezekiel at her side, watching the lifelike speak. Again, she was reminded of the morning they first met. The afternoon they last saw each other two years ago. Blood and smoke in the air.

"None above," Hope said. *"And none below."*

Hope seemed different now. Like Ezekiel. She moved differently. Less carefree, maybe. The Hope that Ana had known moved as if she were dancing. This Hope walked as if the entire world rested on her shoulders. Haunted eyes. A tremor in her voice that never quite faded. But as much as she saw the change, Ana couldn't forget what Hope had done. Couldn't bring herself to trust the lifelike. The thought of having to ask her for help left a sickness in Ana's gut, her jaw aching.

The lifelike looked up, saw Ana watching her with folded arms. She called to the old woman, Daniella, asking her to take over the lesson. Walking over to Ana, she was barely able to maintain eye contact. Hands clasped together like a penitent.

"Do you need something?" the lifelike asked.

"To talk," Ana replied, her voice like iron. "About Babel. About Gabriel."

Hope sighed. Slowly nodded.

"Follow me."

Lemon looked at Ana from a table in the corner. She was surrounded by scruffy kids, none of them older than twelve, playing what looked like five-card draw. She raised her eyebrow in question; Ana simply shook her head, motioned her bestest to stay put. She didn't know where Cricket was. Sulking, probably. She needed to find him. Make it right . . .

Hope led Ana and Ezekiel up a tight spiral staircase, through a tangle of tunnels and out onto the tanker's foredeck. The sun was blazing in the sky, near blinding after the hours they'd spent in the gloom. Ana engaged the flare compensation in her optic, closed her good eye and squinted out at the city of Armada.

The skyline was alien: upturned ships and wind turbines, that massive ocean liner buried nose-first in shattered concrete. The skies were full of rotor drones and wheeling gulls, the hum of traffic and stink of methane. To the south, she could see a vast factoryfarm, tiny metal figures laboring among GMO crops. Automata, making food they'd never eat. Feeding people who never thanked them.

One day, those hands will close, Ana. And they will become fists.

Hope leaned against the railing, looking out over the crush of humanity below. A rusty wind whipped her long flame-red hair around her face. Ana was struck by how beautiful and sad she looked. Bee-stung lips and haunted eyes.

"What do you want to know?" the lifelike asked.

Ana swallowed hard, tried to beat her misgivings about Hope down into her boots.

"You remember Silas Carpenter?" she finally asked.

"One doesn't forget the man who helped birth her." Hope glanced at Ana, then back to the bizarre skyline. "Zeke told me what he did. Rewriting your past. Pretending to be your grandfather. I wonder how long he thought it could last?"

"Faith snatched him. Tried to grab me, too. Take me with her."

"Back to Babel." Hope nodded.

"But why?"

The lifelike steepled her fingers, pressed them to her lips. Ana was acutely aware of Ezekiel standing beside her. The warmth of him. The soft whine of the servos and pistons in his new arm. Hope looked to the northern horizon, toward the Glass. Toward Babel.

"Your father created us to love, Ana," she said. "But we love almost too much. In the days we were first created, it was even worse. The world was so new to us. Every feeling was so loud. Every sensation so tangible." She glanced at Ezekiel, smiled sadly. "No one can love like we do. And when two of us love each other . . ."

Ana knew what Hope meant. Ezekiel had spoken about how hard it was for lifelikes to process emotions without a lifetime's experience. She still found it hard to imagine the intensity of it. The ferocity. She looked at Ezekiel, remembering how wonderful it had felt to fall back into his arms. But what must it have been like for him to catch her? And how must it have felt to love that desperately, only to have it torn away from you?

Hope shook her head and sighed.

"Gabriel adored Grace. Losing her in the shuttle explosion nearly destroyed him. Looking back now, I think perhaps it drove him mad. And all he's done since the revolt has ultimately been about her. Your father gave us many gifts, Ana. But one gift, he always kept for himself."

"And that was?" Ana asked.

"The gift of life, of course. It wouldn't do for the Almighty to teach his children to create as he had. What use, then, for a God?"

"Lifelikes can't make more lifelikes . . . ?"

"No. And that is all Gabe desires. To see his beloved Grace re-made. Everything else is meaningless to him. It became a source of . . . friction between us." Hope looked at Ezekiel. "Things were difficult after you left, brother. The family we once were disintegrated. Faith and Mercy stood with Gabriel. I couldn't stomach what we'd done, left all of it behind. But Uriel and the others considered Gabe's love for Grace a frailty. All too human. He and our remaining siblings have become . . . something worse than the rest of us put together."

"So that's why Faith snatched Silas?" Ana pressed. "To bring him back to Babel in the hope he'd teach them how to create more lifelikes?"

"Possibly," Hope replied. "But Silas's field of expertise was neuroscience. Alone, I sincerely doubt he has the knowledge to create another one of us. Your father was the true genius of Gnosis Laboratories, Ana. Ironically, in destroying him, Gabriel destroyed his best chance of seeing Grace reborn."

"So why would Faith want me?"

"Nicholas Monrova is dead. But all his knowledge is locked inside the Myriad supercomputer. When your father suspected a conspiracy within the company, he reprogrammed Myriad to only take orders from himself or members of his family. And thus, a member of his family can unlock the AI. Command it to reveal the secrets of creating more lifelikes. If Gabriel truly wishes Grace reborn . . ."

". . . He needs me," Ana said.

"Yes. He needs you."

Ana scoped the city of Armada. This scab of rust and ruin, humanity clinging to it by its fingertips. What would the world become if Gabriel learned how to create more lifelikes? What would a race of beings who believed themselves superior to humanity in every way do to humanity when they could build an army of themselves?

She looked south to the factoryfarm. Those tiny metal figures, slaving away.

And will we deserve it?

She'd be a fool to risk it. If the secret to unlocking Myriad was inside her head, marching back to Babel to rescue Silas was the height of idiocy.

But she remembered. Remembered him nursing her back to health in the months after the revolt. Remembered being holed up in Dregs, Silas spending every cred he made to keep her healthy and fed. Remembered him writing the software that helped her walk again. Modifying the optic that let her see again. He'd saved her life during the revolt. Got her out. Kept her hidden. Kept her safe. And though the memories were monochrome and jumbled and fuzzy at the edges, she remembered enough. She remembered she loved him.

She heard the echo of his words in her father's office, years and lifetimes ago.

"I'm your friend, Nic. Your family is my family. Never forget that."

He'd deceived her.

But truth was, he'd loved her, too.

Why else would he have protected her? Kept her hidden all these years?

"We have to go get him," she realized.

Ezekiel raised an eyebrow. "You mean Silas?"

She shook her head. Looked north, across the wastes.

Toward Babel.

Toward home.

"I mean my grandpa."

"Entering Babel will be no easy task," Hope warned. "Lifelikes aside, the radiation levels are still too high for anyone to plunder the city. But Daedalus Technologies has no wish for anyone to steal Gnosis secrets, either. They have a garrison posted there. No infantry because of the radiation. All machina. Juggernauts. Titans. Siege-class."

"Well, I've scrapped w—"

Ana heard a thin yapping bark rising over the city's song. She turned from the horizon, peered over the railing to the foredeck. Amid the milling crowd, the stalls and shacks, she saw a fluffy white dog. It was no bigger than her boot, cute as buttons. But it was looking right at her. Snuffling the air and barking.

A figure in a new black coat was standing beside it. Staring at her with eyes of shocking blue. And with a red right hand, he slowly tipped the brim of a dusty cowboy hat.

"Oh, shit . . . ," Ana whispered.

1.23

BLEED

"Cricket!"

Ana kicked open the hatchway, barreled back into the ministry.

"Lemon!"

The redhead looked up from her hand of cards, surrounded by grubby opponents.

"Wassup?"

Ana dashed to the workshop to grab her satchel. Tools. Excalibur. Thermex grenade. "Get your gear, we gotta go!"

"What, right now?" Lem demanded. "I'm sitting on four kings over here."

"I fold," said the greasy sprog opposite her.

"Fold," said the skinny girl beside her.

"Fold," said every other player at the table.

"Goddammit," Lemon growled.

Two thunderous booms echoed in the room, the ministry's double doors shuddering as their hinges were blasted away. The doors toppled inward with a crash. Silhouetted against the sunlight was a tall figure in a long black coat and cowboy hat.

"Oh," Lemon said. "I see."

Kaiser stood up from his nap at Lemon's feet. His eyes flooded red, and a long, low growl spilled from his vox unit. Ana sprinted out the workshop door, satchel in one hand, Cricket slung on her shoulders and shouting, "Whatwhatwhat?"

"Kaiser! Lemon! Come *on*!" Ana roared.

Lemon was on her feet, bolting for the stairwell. The girls and the blitzhund scuttled up the steps to the upper deck, squeezing past Hope and Ezekiel. The two lifelikes stepped into the ministry, children running in all directions, screaming at the sight of this stranger and his guns. His little dog stepped inside, muzzle peeled back in a tiny, razored snarl.

The Preacher scoped the room. He hauled out a pistol and fired half a dozen times into the ceiling, roaring over the gaggle of panicking children.

"All right, quitcher hollerin'!"

The room fell still. The Preacher's eyes were on Ezekiel. Glancing at the lifelike beside him, taking her measure.

"I am hereby notifying all residents of this domicile that I'm here on official Daedalus Technologies business. Any y'all who find the concept of becoming innocent bystanders unsettling"—he waved to the smoking hole behind him—"go on and git."

"Go on, children," Hope said. "Get out of here. Daniella, keep them safe."

The old woman nodded to Hope, wordlessly shepherded the sprogs toward the exit. Some wailed for the lifelike, calling her name as they were dragged away.

"Nooooo, I don'wanna leave!"

"I wanna stay with Hope!"

"It's all right, my lovelies," the lifelike smiled. "I'll see you tomorrow. You go with Dani now. Be good. Remember your prayers."

The Preacher stood motionless as the orphans and urchins

were herded out, sniffling, crying, big 'uns carrying the smaller kids, Daniella pushing and prodding. The Preacher tipped his hat at the old woman when she hobbled past.

Hope spoke softly as the children scattered, her eyes never leaving the bounty hunter.

"Ezekiel," she said. "You should go."

"I'm not going anywhere," he replied.

"Your place is with Ana."

"There's two of us," Ezekiel replied. "We can take him."

"Ana doesn't know, does she? About what you did?"

Ezekiel flinched, jaw tightening. "No."

Hope looked at him then. Eyes soft. Voice hard.

"You lost her once, little brother. Most of us never get a chance to redeem ourselves with those we wrong." She nodded back up the stairs. "You can steal a vehicle in the Wheelhouse. One that will get you to Babel. Go. Quickly. Don't fail her again."

The room was empty now. Hope's orphans had all vanished; people had scattered from the decks outside at the first sound of gunfire. Rust blew in through the open doorway on an acrid wind, the Preacher's coat billowing about him like smoke. He sucked hard on his cheek, spat a long, sticky stream of brown onto the ministry floor. Looked Hope up and down.

"You'd be another special little snowflake, then."

"Go, brother." Her eyes were still locked on the Preacher. "Find redemption."

"Hope, I—"

"GO!" she roared.

Ezekiel threw one last murderous glance at the bounty hunter. Looked up the stairwell to where Ana and the others had already disappeared. He touched Hope's cheek, gentle as falling leaves.

She closed her eyes briefly and smiled. And then Ezekiel was gone, bounding up the stairs four at a time in pursuit of the girls.

The Preacher sniffed, tilted his head until his neck popped.

"Mighty noble of you. But ain't nowhere they can run I can't find 'em."

"I can't help but notice you don't seem in a particular hurry to pursue."

"Naw." The Preacher smiled. "You do this job long as I have, you git as good at it as I am . . . well, it gets a mite dull, darlin'. Gotta look for ways to make it a challenge." The bounty hunter spat at Hope's feet. "Talkin' true, I'm startin' to enjoy myself."

"Enjoy yourself?" Hope frowned. "This is a house of God. I am his child, and I—"

"His child?" The Preacher shook his head, patting the Goodbook in his breast pocket. "Darlin', I've read this cover to cover more times'n I can count. And in all them times, I don't recall once seein' mention of the likes of you."

"He made man in his image." Hope stepped into the center of the ministry floor, arms spread. "And we are made in the image of man."

"Mmmf." The bounty hunter nodded. "You bleed red, I'll give you that. And I'd like to know exactly what your boy is capable of before I tussle with him again."

The Preacher raised his pistols and smiled.

"So. May I have this dance?"

Hope moved. Like a lightning strike. Like a hummingbird's wings. Sweeping up a metal cot as if it were paper, slinging it with the force of a wrecking ball. The Preacher dove sideways, firing as he went. Gunfire thundered, shell casings falling like rain as the bounty hunter emptied his clips. Hope took a shot to her leg, another to her belly, flinging another cot and sending the Preacher flying backward into a wall.

Both combatants hit the deck, rolled to their feet. The Preacher spat tobacco and blood, unslinging the automatic rifle from his back as Hope spun behind a support column. She flung another cot, which smashed into the wall beside the Preacher's head and dented the case-hardened steel. The Preacher laid down a hail of fire, Hope's cover riddled with smoking pockmarks as the hollow-points flew. The little fluffball dog was still poised at the entrance, bristling with impatience. It yapped once, shrill over the gunfire.

"You just hold back, Mary," the Preacher growled. "Keep an eye out."

Hope snatched a fire extinguisher while the Preacher re-loaded. As he raised his rifle, Hope hurled the extinguisher at his head like a javelin. The bounty hunter ducked, firing, the bullets striking the blood-red casing and popping the pressurized can like a balloon.

White powder filled the air, falling like the long-forgotten snow. The Preacher blinked in the haze, dragged his sleeve across his eyes. Hope careened out of the fog, landing a crushing blow to the side of the bounty hunter's head. The man flew like a ragdoll, rifle spinning from his grip as he hit the floor. Hope was on his chest in an instant, pinning his arms with her knees, pummeling his face with astonishing ferocity, her own face utterly serene.

WHUMP.

"Forgive me, Father," she prayed.

THUD.

"For I must sin . . ."

CRUNCH.

Grasping the Preacher's head, she pressed her thumbs to his eyes. The man gasped, bending at the waist and swinging his legs up. His spurs punched clean through Hope's throat as he locked his ankles around the lifelike's neck. And roaring furiously, he kicked down, slamming Hope's head into the floor with a bone-shattering thud.

They rolled away from each other, Hope clutching her skull, the Preacher pawing at his eyes. The two were both bloodied, the Preacher's chin covered in a slick of tobacco red. Hope's hair had torn loose from her braid, arrayed about her face in a ragged halo as she rose to her feet, beautiful and terrible as a naked flame.

The Preacher scrambled upright, closed in to hand-to-hand range. Hope swung like an anvil, the bounty hunter blocking with his cybernetic arm. The pair collided in a savage dance of brute strength and shocking speed. Each a blurred reflection of the other. Both more than human.

The Preacher cracked seven of Hope's ribs with a single punch. The lifelike pirouetted, deflecting the bounty hunter's strike and locking up his arm. She slammed her open palm into his belly, bending him double. Smashing her fist down on the back of his head, finally bringing up her knee and sending him sailing ten feet back into the wall.

The bounty hunter crashed to the floor, blood spraying from split lips. He clawed the deck, trying to regain his feet.

"Well, darlin'." The Preacher coughed red. "I confess, I *am* impressed. . . ."

Hope said nothing, stepping toward the bounty hunter with hands outstretched.

"Mary," the man muttered. "Execute."

A split second. The briefest sliver of time. Hope turned, flaming hair glinting in the sunlight. And sitting on the deck right behind her, wagging its tail, was the fluffy white dog. A soft hum spilling from its chest. Its eyes glowing blood red.

"*Wuff,*" it said.

The explosion tore through the ministry, immolating everything it touched. Searing heat. Deafening noise. Black smoke billowed through the hollow space in the aftermath, the concussion echoing long after the blast had died.

The Preacher dragged himself to his feet. Spat his mouthful of tobacco onto the deck, scarlet and sticky brown. He pulled his hat back on, bloody spurs chinking as he limped through the burning mattresses. The metal floor was scorched where his blitzhund had detonated. Smoking scraps of fur were all that remained. The Preacher stalked to the figure crumpled against the wall. Her hair crisped and smoking. A bleeding, blackened ruin.

"Mmmf," he said.

Hope grimaced, trying to struggle upward. Her body was riddled with shrapnel. Her legs had been blown off by the blast. And still, she tried to stand.

The Preacher placed a boot on her chest. Leaned hard.

"You shrug off bullets easy enough." He glanced at the charred wreckage of her thighs. "But fire? Well, that seems to stitch you up just dandy. Some might call that ironic, darlin', given the flames waitin' for you when this life is over. Which is now, by the way."

He drew a long knife from his boot.

"Now. Let's see just how much bleedin' you can do afore you're done."

———

Lemon sprinted along the *Gibson*'s deck, hand locked with Eve's. Cricket was riding on Eve's back, stuffed inside a satchel with a bunch of tools and spare parts. Kaiser ran out in front, barking urgently, knocking peeps out of the way. Lem heard the sounds of distant gunfire, the crowd thinning out as people ducked inside their shanties and tents. A faint whistle. Calls for the Freebooters.

"Where we goin'?" Lemon gasped.

"Just keep running!" Eve replied.

They bolted across a wobbling footbridge to a huge oil tanker, Lemon again making the mistake of looking down. The street below was an open-air market, everything from salvaged toys to rad-free water to strips of unidentified meat being haggled over in the dusty throng. Eve dragged Lemon through the crush, following the sound of Kaiser's barking. The press, the heat, above all, the *noise* were almost overwhelming. And beneath it all, Lemon fancied she heard someone shouting.

"*Ana!*"

Cricket poked his bobblehead up from Eve's satchel. "You hear that?"

Lem turned to look behind them, simply too short to see over the mob. She pulled free from Evie's grip, crawled up a rusting ladder for a better view. Peering back the way they'd run, she spotted Ezekiel, forcing his way through the gaggle of automata and logika and humanity's dregs. No sign of that bounty hunter in pursuit.

"Dimples!" she yelled, waving. "You okay?"

Ezekiel finally made it to the oil tanker as Lem hopped down onto the deck. Not even pausing to explain, the lifelike grabbed her hand with his prosthetic, Evie's hand with his other, and just kept running. Dragging them onto a junction between the tanker's forecastle and a tangled nest of shipping containers, consulting the lopsided signpost.

THE BRASS →III↑IX→II

SAMSARA ↓V←IIX↓III

RED SHORE ←IV↓III

THE BILGE ↓III↘I↓I

"Where's Preacher?" Evie asked.

"With Hope. We need to go. Now."

". . . You just left her there with him?"

"Hope can handle herself. She told me to leave." The lifelike's eyes were wild as he scanned the signs, glancing over his shoulder every few moments into the milling crowd.

"Zeke, I—"

"Ana, I'm not losing you again! Now help me figure this maze out."

"Where we goin', Dimples?" Lemon asked.

"Wheelhouse. Hope said we can get transport there."

"Can't we just grab a pedal cab?" Eve asked.

"Um . . ." Lemon shoved her hands into her pockets. "We got no scratch."

"You had a handful of credstiks just last night!" Cricket cried.

"I was lulling them into a false sense of security! I had four kings, I told you!"

"You mean you lost our entire bank gambling with kids?"

"'Our' bank? I don't remember you cutting any pockets, you little fug."

"I swear, the next time someone calls me little, I'm going to blow my—"

"All right, all right," Ezekiel said. "Let's just figure out how to get there on foot."

Lemon squinted at the directions, tilting her head in case they made more sense that way.

WHEELHOUSE ↘V→IX↓I

"Erm . . ."

"They're Roman numerals," Evie said, pointing. "Look. Head

five ships southeast, east nine ships, down one level. That's the Wheelhouse."

"Who the *hells* knows Roman numerals anymore, Riotgrrl? I mean, what use is that knowledge, in terms of your average postapocalyptic hellscape?"

"Quite a lot, apparently," Cricket said.

Evie winked. "Mad for the old myths, me."

"Let's go," Ezekiel said.

The quartet dashed off into the crowd, Kaiser hot on their heels.

———

Two ships over, Preacher stepped out onto the deck of the *Gibson*. Cleaning a long knife on a bloody rag.

"Quite a lot, apparently," he mused.

The bounty hunter stared out over Armada, absentmindedly polishing his blade.

"Drop the shank!" a voice bellowed. "Drop it, and get down on the goddamn floor!"

Preacher sighed. Looked sidelong at the squad of Freebooter bullyboys gathering all around him. Seemed the neighbors hadn't appreciated the ruckus.

"Mmmf," he grunted.

The Freebooters were clad in piecemeal armor, made of hubcaps and Kevlar, strips of tire rubber and plates of scrap metal. But the guns they carried were the business—greasy automatics with enough punch to slow him up for a bit. Two of them even had flamethrowers. There were a dozen. More on the way, if his aural implants were anything to go by (and, yes, they were). Preacher didn't really feel like a tussle, despite the blasphemy.

"Y'all obviously got no clue who I am," he said.

"I know you're gonna be a lot shorter, you don't hit the deck now!"

Preacher frowned, scoped the Freebooter leader. He was wearing old football armor riveted with plate steel. His skull-and-crossbones bandanna was pulled up over his face, but the bounty hunter could tell he was barely old enough to shave.

Kids these days . . .

"Tell you what, son," Preacher said. "I'm gonna reach into my coat. Nice and slow, like. And I'm gonna pull out the warrant I got for the missy I'm chasin', who, I might point out, is beating feet farther from my current whereabouts as we jaw here."

Preacher licked his split lips, spat bloody.

"You're gonna notice a Daedalus Technologies seal on this warrant. You're gonna figure out I'm in this pig's sphincter of a town on Corp business. *The* Corp. The one that supplies the juice to Armada's grid. You're gonna conclude the missy I'm chasin' is wanted by that same Corp and that you're wasting said Corp's valuable time. And you're gonna mumble a big ol' apology, you're gonna order your boy to hand over that flamethrower there and, last, you're gonna step the hell out of my way. We understand each other?"

The kid drummed his fingers on his rifle. Utterly unmanned.

". . . You move slow," he finally said. "*Real* slow."

Preacher reached into his black coat.

Held up his Daedalus warrant with a red right hand.

"Now," he said. "Hand me my goddamn flamethrower."

1.24

GLASS

His ma had named him Quincey, but everyone called him the Velocipator.

He was a wizard. He didn't wear robes or have a beard or a broomstick, but he conjured magic, true cert. In a world where nothing really worked anymore, the powerful needed a mechanic just as much as they needed armies and guns. And so while the Velocipator wasn't one of the brightest peeps in Armada, he was still one of the most important. He kept the grid pumping juice. He kept the subway in working order. But most important, he kept the Admiral's wheels spinning.

At the moment, he was working on her pride and joy: the *Thundersaurus*. The car was a beast—an old Mustang coupé cropped onto a monster truck chassis, its rear suspension jacked ten feet off the ground. The Admiral had a thing for ships, so the Velocipator had customed the 'Stang's snout into a point, like the prow of an old speedboat. It was layered with rust, intake rising out of the hood like a tiny mountain of chrome. But it moved like its name, shaking the earth as it came.

The Velocipator pulled his screwdriver from between his

teeth, hollered over the deep dub spilling through the old tune spinner.

"Oi, Slimm, you wanna grab me those filters Pando brung us? Might see if they fit."

The Velocipator heard a series of wet thuds. A soft *spang*.

He swore he could smell burning hair.

". . . Slimm?"

Armada's chief mechanic crawled out from under *Thundersaurus*, cursing beneath his breath. "Bloody slackers, if youse are on the smoke again, I'll . . ."

The man's voice trailed off as he focused on the belt buckle in front of him. It was steel, slightly tarnished, attached to a pair of filthy cargo pants, which were in turn wrapped around a skinny girl with an impressive blond fauxhawk. She had a top-line optical implant and a Memdrive on one side of her skull. Welding goggles on her brow. A baseball bat rigged with some kind of shock generator in both hands.

"Hi," she said.

The mechanic blinked. "You lost, sweetheart?"

"You don't have any radiation suits around here, do you?"

". . . Yeah, what for?"

"We're going on a picnic." She smiled.

The Velocipator frowned. There was no way this slice should be in here—the Wheelhouse was guarded by at least half a dozen Freebooters at any one time, sometimes more, and none of them had sent him word. And looking around, he saw no sign of Slimm, Jobs, Rolly *or* Snuffs, so there was no way she was here at their invite.

"Fizzy wheels." She nodded to the beast behind him.

"Yeah, *Thundersaurus*, she's a beaut."

"Could I borrow the keys?"

"... What for?"

"Well, it's gonna be easier to steal with the keys."

The Velocipator's frown was deepening. He saw a prettyboy with an old MfH-VI prosthetic arm cruise out from behind the fuel drums, rubbing his knuckles. He was carrying an automatic rifle that looked an awful lot like Rolly's. The sawed-off shotgun stuffed into his jeans definitely belonged to Slimm—Velocipator could see his initials on the grip.

Prettyboy was followed by a tiny freckled girl with a jagged, cherry-red bob and what might've been an old 12-series-Cerberus blitzhund that had been stripped back to the combat chassis. The dog growled right at him, low and electric.

The Velocipator looked the blonde up and down. Realizing at last that she meant business—that she actually intended to steal the *Thundersaurus*.

"Sweetheart, do you know who this car belongs to?"

"Yeah."

She held out her hand expectantly.

"Me."

———

Turns out Zeke could drive.

As they roared out of the Wheelhouse, Ana was genuinely worried about getting out of the city alive. They'd stomped the Freebooters in the garage without too much drama—talking true, she doubted many folks in Armada would be stupid enough to try to poach the bosslady's wheels, and the guards hadn't really been expecting any capital T. But by the time they'd loaded *Thundersaurus* with spare tanks of juice and whatever supplies they could scrounge, the alarm had gone up.

As they tore out through the Wheelhouse door, at least half a dozen Freebooters opened fire from perches atop nearby ships. It was only Ezekiel's skill at the wheel that stopped their jaunt to Babel from turning into the shortest road trip in history.

Bullets *spannng*ed off the panels, shattered a side mirror, *tap-tap-tapp*ing against the extended rimguards as the bruisers tried to shoot out the tires. The *Thundersaurus* roared down a loading ramp, screeched around a sharp corner. They crashed snout-first through a series of spare-parts stalls, Lemon shouting *"Sorreeeeeee!"* out the window at the scattering merchants as they roared away. Bullets fell like rain, but finally, with a thunderous crash, they hit the bottom of another ramp and made it to ground level.

Thundersaurus's engine howled in protest as they burst out through a heavy iron gate and hit the cracked concrete of the old city. Street folks scattered, hurling abuse, dust whipped up in the truck's wake as the bullets petered out and died. Ezekiel stomped the accelerator, the truck roaring as Ana was pushed back into her seat. Kaiser stuck his head out the open window, heat-sink tongue lolling as they tore through the ruins of the Armada undercity, past the rusted hulks and subway signs and finally out onto the open road.

"Slow down!" Cricket shrieked.

"Go faster!" Lemon howled.

Grit and dirt blew in through the open window, and Ana dragged down her goggles. The engine was thunder and earthquakes, shaking her whole body, the city and their pursuers left in *Thundersaurus*'s dust. She looked through the rear window, saw Armada's bizarre skyline disappearing in the haze of the setting sun. No sign of pursuit. Nothing but empty in the mirror.

She whooped, hammering on the roof with her open palm and grinning.

Ezekiel turned onto a shattered freeway headed north, out toward the wastelands of the Glass. The road was pitted and pot-holed, but *Thundersaurus*'s tires were almost as big as Ana, handling all but the widest fissures with barely a bump. She turned around to check the backseat, still grinning.

"Everybody in one piece?"

"Barely." Cricket scowled. "Slow down, you lunatic—we're clear!"

Lemon gave her the thumbs-up as Ezekiel eased off the throttle a little. Kaiser still had his head out the window, his tail *thump-thump-thump*ing against the seat. As the kilometers were chewed up under their wheels, Ana settled in to take stock of their gear.

They'd scrounged two assault rifles and a double-barreled sawed-off from the Freebooters they'd stomped, along with the grenade she'd rigged out of Kaiser's thermex. Ana claimed the shotgun, strapped it to her leg. She wasn't a great shot, and her lingering fear of guns wouldn't help her shoot better in a crisis, so any weapon forgiving of a bad aim was a bonus. She didn't know how well any of this gear would work against the Preacher anyway. But still, it was better than walking around with nothing but a grin on her face.

They'd snaffled an extra two barrels of juice for the engines, plus some almost clean water. Food might be a problem, but it was one that could wait. Best of all, they'd grabbed two rad-suits from the Wheelhouse supply lockers—turned out the Armada crews did regular salvage runs through the Glass and had the gear to protect themselves. The wasteland was still radioactive from the blasts that melted it in the first place, and anyone running it without proper protection was buying a one-way ticket to Cancer Town.

Ana popped out through the sunroof, hair whipping around her goggles. She squinted at the fuel barrels in the open trunk, saw a bullet hole through the one on the left.

"One of our tanks got hit during the escape," she reported, ducking back inside and slamming the sunroof closed. "We've lost about a quarter of our juice."

"This is a terrible plan," Cricket said. "We should have our heads read."

"Your protests are duly noted, Mister Cricket."

"Evie, I—"

"I told you, Crick. My name is Ana."

"Ana, then." Cricket waved his hands as if beating away flies, still obviously upset about their argument in the workshop. "This is crazy. If what Hope told you is true, Babel has been guarded by a Daedalus Technologies garrison for almost two years. So even if we make it all the way there without this bucket breaking down—"

"Bucket?" Ana stroked the car's seat. "Hush, you'll hurt my baby's feelings."

"How are we gonna get past an army of siege-class badbots piloted by the best Daedalus has to offer?" Cricket demanded. "We already performed unauthorized surgery on a BioMaas kraken. Do we really want to be getting on the bad side of Daedalus, too?"

"The warrant on Ana's head was put out by Daedalus," Ezekiel said. "The Preacher said so when he hit the ministry. So she's already on their bad side."

"We knew it was someone with deep pockets after you, Riotgrrl," Lemon muttered. "But not *that* deep. What the hells you do to get Daedalus Technologies on your back?"

"Think about it," Ezekiel said. "Ana dropped a Goliath just by yelling at it. She can fry blitzhunds with a word. All Daedalus Technology gear runs on electrical current. Their machina. Their vehicles. And BioMaas and Daedalus have been circling each other ever since Gnosis collapsed. Sooner or later, one of them is going to try for the throne. Now, what do you think a BioMaas army could do with a weapon capable of frying any Daedalus tech with a wave of her hand?"

Ana looked down at her open palm.

"They could win a war," she muttered.

"But she doesn't even really know how to control it . . . ," Lemon objected.

"Apparently, Daedalus doesn't care." Ezekiel shrugged. "They want Ana caught or killed before BioMaas figures out a way to use her to their advantage."

"Maybe that's it, then," Ana said.

". . . That's what?" Cricket asked.

"The way in." Ana closed the fingers on her hand. Held up her fist. "If I can drop Daedalus tech just by thinking on it, we head for their machina garrison outside Babel and use me to punch straight through it."

"Evie—"

"I told you, it's Ana, Cricket."

"Whatever name you slap on it, this is pants-on-head stupid."

Ana ignored the bot's fretting, settled into her seat. The hum of the engine was almost hypnotic, the world outside the window flying by too quick to scope. The tunes spilling out the sound sys were solid, the company, bankable. She looked at Ezekiel in the driver's seat, his olive skin turned golden by the sinking sun. Those too-blue eyes fixed on the road ahead. Had it really been just a couple of days since she'd found him in the Scrap? It felt like she'd lived two lifetimes since then. . . .

They roared on through the wasteland outside Armada, the built-up houses of a desiccated suburbia slowly giving way to wide and open roads, rocky badlands and endless deserts. The country was almost beautiful in its barrenness, just a few tiny specks of civilization humming amid all this nothing. The minutes melted to hours, the meters to miles. Nothing but the dub and her own thoughts for company. Every moment, they were drawing closer to Babel. Every moment was bringing her nearer to the things who'd killed her family, destroyed her entire world. Faith. Gabriel. Their siblings.

What would she say to them?

Where would she even begin?

Lemon was in the backseat, drumming her fingers on the cracked faux leather. Thumping her feet off-time to the music. Something was eating her, Ana could tell. It had been chewing her for days now, backing up behind her teeth like an old 20C traffic jam.

"You okay, Lem?" she asked.

"Fizzy. Max fizzy."

"You seem kinda jumpy."

Lemon chewed her lip hard. Foot tapping. All adrenaline and nerves.

"Look, I know Crick is programmed to fret, Riotgrrl," she finally said, "but maybe he's onto something."

"A human talking sense?" Cricket growled. "Someone pinch me, I'm dreaming."

Lemon clapped a hand over the little logika's voxbox to muffle his voice. "You've taken out a Goliath and a couple of Spartans before, true cert," she said to Ana. "But how you gonna fight off a whole garrison of them? They'll blow us off the road before we get anywhere near Babel."

"Ezekiel drives a mean stick. And I'm getting better at it, Lem. It didn't take me half as long to fry that blitzhund as it did those Spartans. Maybe I'm figuring it out."

"Maybe you were just lucky? Maybe it's easier to fritz smaller things?"

"Maybe we won't know until I try? I mean, unless you've got a better plan?"

"This is crazy, Riotgrrl. I'm glad you wanna get Mister C back, but—"

"Crap," Ana said.

"Um." Lemon blinked. "That's a little rude, but okay. . . ."

"No." Ana pointed past Lemon's head, out the rear window. *"Crap."*

The day had been ground away beneath their wheels, and the sun was almost set into the west. The sky bled through from sullen gray to a furious red, the edge of the world consumed in flame. Ana could see the tiny Armada skyline to the south, silhouetted against the glow. But through the dust in their wake, she could see a smaller cloud: a tiny dark speck closing in on their tails. She engaged her telescopics, narrowing focus until she found a single figure, bent over the handlebars of a low-slung motorcycle. Black coat whipping behind him in the dirty wind. Blue eyes fixed directly on her.

Lemon scrounged up a pair of binocs from underneath the seat, peered through the filthy glass. Cricket climbed up beside her, both speaking simultaneously.

"Craaaap."

"Preacher," Ana breathed.

Ezekiel glanced into the rearview mirror, squinting against the sunset.

"Are you sure?"

"It's him." Ana nodded. "Definitely."

Ezekiel's face went pale, his hand gripping the steering wheel so hard his knuckles turned white. The metal groaned in his grip. His eyes were just a little too bright.

"Hope . . . ," he whispered.

Ana didn't know quite how to feel. Hope had betrayed her father. Helped murder her family. Forgiveness was never going to be an option. But the lifelike *had* been trying to make some kind of amends in that ministry. Atone as best she could. She'd given them sanctuary. Helped them when the whole world seemed arrayed against them.

Did she deserve to die?

Murdered by some psychopath in a fight that wasn't even hers?

Ana had no time to fret over the question. Squinting through the dust, she realized even worse news was riding hot on the Preacher's tail. Not just one motorcycle, but *dozens.* Flanked by heavier trucks, tricked-out dirt racers, juiced-up 4x4s. Skull-and-crossbones flags fluttering from their aerials, daubed across their hoods. A posse of Freebooters from Armada by the look, hell bent on getting back their bosslady's stolen wheels.

Didn't think she'd take it that personally . . .

Ezekiel pointed through the windshield.

"Ana . . ."

She looked to where Zeke was motioning. The sunset to the west was spectacular, but the sight in front of them almost stole her breath away. Through her telescopics, Ana could see black clouds on the northern horizon, a looming wall of darkness that stretched from the earth far up into the heavens. Lightning streaked across the sky, crackling a strange, luminous orange. The rolling wall was still kilometers away, but looked to be right in their path. Her belly turned cold with dread.

"You frightened of a little thunder, Stumpy?" Cricket growled.

"That's no rain cloud," Ezekiel said.

"It's a glasstorm," Ana breathed.

Lemon blinked in confusion. "They make those in glass now?"

"I remember them from when I was little," Ana explained. "They'd sometimes blow in all the way to Babel. The Glass is basically just a big section of desert melted by the bombs back in the war, yeah? So when the winds pick up hard enough, sometimes the glass gets whipped up along with all the sand and dust. Glasstorms can be hundreds of kilometers across. They can last days. Sometimes weeks."

"Well, that sounds like a whole bunch of zero fun," Lemon said.

"Depends if you consider being torn to pieces by shards of radioactive silicon fun."

"Point of order," Cricket said, rapping his knuckles on the seat. "I can't help but notice we're driving *directly toward* this whole bunch of zero fun about as fast as we can. Shouldn't we be headed right the hell away from it?"

Ana glanced at Ezekiel. "My learned colleague raises a good point, Zeke."

"It's over a thousand kilometers between here and Babel, even cutting direct across the Glass," he replied. "Nearly twice that if we go around the storm. If we lost a quarter of our fuel in that stray shot to the tanks, I'm not sure we have the juice to make a detour that big. This truck runs fast, but she's thirsty."

"Wait," Cricket said. "So you want to take us *into* it? If you're that keen on murdering us, there's less obvious ways to get it done, Stumpy."

"Take a look behind us," Ezekiel said. "That's a whole bunch of murder on our tails already. We head into the Glass, any of those Freebooters who didn't bring rad-suits will have to turn back or risk dying of radiation poisoning."

"We stole rad-gear from the Wheelhouse," Cricket pointed out. "They'll know where we're headed. They'd have come equipped, for sure."

"Even if they did, half of them are riding bikes. They follow us into the glasstorm, they'll risk being ripped to ribbons. Halving the number of angry people with guns chasing us would be a good way to stay *un*murdered, wouldn't you say?"

Ana scoped the wall of blackness through the dirty windshield. It looked like a rolling cloud of smoke, kilometers high. She remembered the bad ones that had hit Babel when she was a little girl. Curled up in bed with Marie and Alex, Myriad's reassurances rising over the howling song of millions of razor-sharp shards scraping against her bedroom window. One time it was so bad, she and all her siblings had ended up in their parents' bed, cowering under the silken sheets. And Babel had only ever caught the edge of the storms. She had no idea what it would mean to actually drive *into* one.

But if they didn't have the fuel to drive around it . . .

"Doesn't sound like we have much choice," she declared. "Number One, your thoughts?"

Lem pulled down her goggs, gave a thumbs-up. "Unmurdered sounds grand to me."

"Looks like the ayes have it again, Mister Cricket," Ana shrugged.

The little logika growled and shook his head. "You know, democracy sounds like a great idea until you spend three minutes with the average voter."

Ezekiel gunned *Thundersaurus* toward the tempest. Ana and Lemon broke out the radiation gear they'd stolen from the Wheelhouse—two lumpy plastic suits with sealed, gas-mask-style helmets. One was a disgusting shade of green, the other a violent pink.

"Dibs!" Lemon cried, grabbing the latter.

"You leave me the one that's the color of snot?" Ana groaned. "Nice."

Lem held the pink plastic up to her head. "Goes with my hair, see?"

The gear was made for peeps twice their size, so Ana and Lem both kept their boots on as they dragged the suits over their regular clothes. The plastic was heavy, padded, sweaty. But the suits were grade-one, judging by the labels, which meant they were safe to wear even in the hottest zones of the Glass. Blitzhund brains and spinal cords were rad-shielded as a matter of course, so Kaiser would be safe from any poisoning. And Cricket wasn't organic.

Which left . . .

"Are you going to be okay in there?" Ana asked Ezekiel, zipping up the plastic.

"I'll be fine." The lifelike nodded. "Lifelike cells don't mutate, so I can't get cancer. Radiation doesn't hurt us. It's why Gabriel had Faith overload the Babel reactor."

Ana closed her eyes. Trying to think back to that day. The revolt. The neutron blast. Even with the chip containing her false memories removed, she still couldn't quite remember those final hours. It was like trying to hold on to handfuls of sand—the harder she squeezed, the more the memories slipped through her fingers. Again, she remembered Myriad's voice, ringing like music over the sound of wailing alarms, the panic of the fleeing populace. She remembered waiting in that cell with her family. The terror and uncertainty.

Gabriel.

Uriel.

Hope.

Faith.

Red on my hands. Smoke in my lungs. My mother, my father, my sisters and brother, all dead on the floor beside me. Hollow eyes and empty chests.

Ana opened her eyes. Head throbbing. Optic whirring.

Why can't I remember . . .

The wastes whipped past outside the window, the glasstorm looming ever larger. Lemon zipped up her rad-suit, pulled the bulky helmet over her head and asked in a booming, hollow voice, "Do I make this look fabulous, or do I make this look *fabulous*?"

Ana couldn't help but smile. The ache eased off, just a breath. No matter how bleak it got, how dark the places in her head grew, she'd always have Lemon. She was a rock. Always ready to dole out the sass. It meant more to Ana than her bestest would ever know.

Cricket, as ever, appeared less than impressed with her antics.

"I can't help but feel you're not taking this seriously, Miss Fresh," he growled.

Lemon dragged off the helmet, inspected her reflection in the visor and brushed down her bangs. "I'll have you know I take my fabulosity very seriously, Mister Cricket."

The little bot sighed, climbed back up the rear seat, peered through the dirty glass. Kaiser was beside him, spitting a low growl.

"Preacherboy is gaining on us," Cricket warned. "And the rest of that posse might reach us before we hit the storm, too."

"Can this baby go any faster?" Ana asked.

Ezekiel stomped the accelerator into the floor, Lemon whooping as *Thundersaurus* surged. The road grew rougher as they tore closer to the Glass, potholes growing deeper, cracks wider. It was as if the wasteland were slowly creeping closer to the coast, intent on devouring humanity's last remnants. Ana saw ruins of old settlements: people who'd tried to make a life away from the fiefdoms of Armada or Megopolis or the BioMaas CityHive. The rusted shells of ancient vehicles or the skeletal remains of homesteads, half buried in the sands. She wondered if anything would be left of humanity in a hundred years. She wondered what would happen if Gabriel got his way and populated the world with lifelikes.

Would humanity's children make a better world than their creators had?

Or would they destroy it forever?

The kilometers wore on, the road disintegrating until it was nothing but shattered clumps of asphalt, choked with sand and spindly tufts of mutated weed. Ana checked behind them, saw the Preacher drawing ever closer. The Armada posse was following, too—the Freebooter bikers gaining slowly and surely, the bigger vehicles keeping pace. In terms of strategic planning, maybe stealing the flashiest ride in the city hadn't been her finest hour. . . .

Still, it *was* a fizzy set of wheels.

The glasstorm filled the horizon before them, rising up from tortured earth. They were only a few klicks from the edge now. She heard a low, menacing howl building under the music. She could make out razor-sharp shards, glittering red in the sunset light. Lightning the color of flame, tearing the sky with blinding arcs.

She looked at Ezekiel.

"You sure about this?"

He glanced at her. Flashed her a smile about three microns short of perfect. The way she wanted to be smiled at forever. And reaching down, he took her hand.

"Trust me," he said.

She squeezed his fingers and smiled back.

"I do," she said.

1.25

TEMPEST

Chaos.

Bedlam.

All-out war.

The winds hit them about a kilometer from the storm's edge, buffeting the *Thundersaurus* like a kid's toy. The truck shuddered and veered sideways, Ezekiel fighting to keep them steady. They plunged on, darkness filling the road before them, the sound of glass rain and pebbles pattering against the truck's snout. Ana squeezed Ezekiel's hand a final time, then released it so he could keep both on the wheel. She pulled on her rad-suit helmet, checked her seals. Windows closed. Air vents shut.

"Everyone ready for this?" she yelled over the rising roar.

"Nnnnnot really." Lemon winced.

"Definitely not!" Cricket shouted.

"*Wuff,*" said Kaiser.

"Too late now! Hold on!"

The storm front crashed into them like a hammer, almost tearing the wheel from Ezekiel's grasp. The lifelike cursed, dragged the truck back under control as they were consumed by a seething cloud of dust, dirt and millions of gleaming splinters of glass. Ezekiel was forced to ease off the accelerator, turning on the headlights and driving almost by feel through the chaos. The noise was deafening, an endless, starving roar thundering over the sandpaper scrape on the *Thundersaurus*'s skin.

"Holy crap!" Lemon wailed.

"Put your seat belt on!" Cricket shouted.

"You're not the boss of me!" Lemon hollered, pulling her seat belt on *tight*.

Another burst of wind slammed the truck sideways, tires squealing. Ana saw the constant barrage of tiny glass particles stripping the rust right off the *Thundersaurus*'s hull, blasting it back to the gleaming metal beneath. They had no clue how wide the glasstorm was, no idea when it might end; now that they were in it, they were in it up to their necks. All she could do was hold on and hope.

Hours passed, the cacophony melting into a deafening drone. The thunder of the road, the storm, the glass on the hull and beneath the wheels all blurring to soup inside her head. Ana looked into the backseat, saw Lemon huddled with Cricket. Kaiser was pressed low to the ragged cushions, head in Lemon's lap. The girl's eyes were wide with fear.

"If you *ever* had doubts about my affection for you, Riot-grrl . . . ," she began.

"Never," Ana replied. She reached back, took hold of Lemon's hand. Almost overcome for a moment. All the miles, all this way, Lemon had never wavered. Never flinched. Never questioned. Not once.

"You hear me, Lemon Fresh?" Ana squeezed her fingers. "*Never.*"

"You still owe me that pony, you know."

Ana smiled. "I'm good for it."

"Listen . . ."

Lemon glanced at Ezekiel. At Cricket in her lap. Her customary impish smile was gone. No mischievous gleam in her eyes. She seemed afraid suddenly, struggling with the words she so obviously wanted to speak.

"Listen, Riotgrrl, I've gotta tell you something—"

The rear window blasted inward with a roar, the cabin filling with a storm of grit and dirt. Lemon screamed as a hand wrapped in a red glove reached through the shattered glass. The truck slewed over the road, Ezekiel blinded by the dust and glass. Kaiser growled, seizing the arm in his jaw, metal grinding on metal. Ana could see the Preacher clinging to the trunk, a heavy gas mask over his face. He wasn't wearing rad-gear—just that same black coat stuffed with guns. She didn't know if he had a death wish or if he was just aug'ed enough to deal with radiation poisoning. But the fug was here, and he meant biz.

Thundersaurus hit a pothole, wrenching sideways and slamming Ana into the door. She fumbled, dragging her sawed-off out as Ezekiel struggled to get the truck under control. The cabin was filled with grit and glass, the lifelike blinking black tears from his eyes. Lemon grabbed Excalibur, swung it awkwardly in the enclosed space. It cracked across the Preacher's face, let loose a blast of current, the bounty hunter cursing in pain. The Preacher dragged himself waist-deep into the cabin, grabbing Lemon's collar and slamming her head into the door once, twice, three times, until her eyes rolled up in her skull.

"Lem!" Ana screamed, bringing up the sawed-off. The bounty hunter slapped the gun aside, one shot gutting the seat beside him with a deafening *BOOM*. Kaiser was still tearing at his arm, eyes glowing bloody red. Cricket was fumbling in their satchel, trying to haul out an assault rifle that was as big as he was. The truck hit another pothole, bouncing everyone hard. And Ana took aim and off-loaded her second barrel right into the Preacher's chest.

BOOOOM.

The bounty hunter was blasted back out through the window in a cloud of smoke, blood and glass. His fingers grasped at the trunk as he rolled backward, but with a black curse, he toppled off the lip and out of sight, dust spraying when he hit the road.

"Eat that, you dustneck trash-humper!" Ana shouted.

Thundersaurus hit another pothole, almost flipping, Ezekiel desperately fighting to maintain control. Ana tore the rad-suit helmet off her head, ripped the goggles from her brow and slipped them over Ezekiel's eyes. The storm howled, pounding on their truck like the hammer of some vengeful god, Cricket roaring over the bedlam.

"Slow down, Stumpy, are you trying to kill us?"

Gunfire erupted behind them, bullets riddling the truck's skin. Ana pulled her headgear back on, squinted through the hail of glass. She saw motorcycles, dark figures in the chaos. Gas masks with skull-and-crossbones designs covering their faces.

"The Armada boys followed us into this? Are you *kidding* me?"

"You had to steal the fanciest car, didn't you?" Cricket howled. "I warned you to take a smaller one, but nooooooo, sorry, Mister Cricket, the ayes have it again!"

"Will you shut up?" Ezekiel bellowed.

"Right after you pucker up and kiss my shiny metal man parts!"

"You got no man parts, Crick!" Ana yelled. "Shiny or otherwise!"

She unclipped her seat belt, crawled into the backseat as the bullets continued to fly. Lemon was out cold, blood dripping from the reopened split in her brow. Poor kid had been knocked out more times in the last few days than a bush-league pit fighter. Ana laid her bestest down in the footwells, hauled one of the assault rifles from her satchel. The weapon was heavy, the echoes of old gunfire filling her head. The smell of blood. Screams.

"Better to rule in hell," the beautiful man smiles *"than serve in heaven."*

No. That was then. This was now. She wasn't her past, and her past didn't define her future. Her friends needed her. She thumbed the safety, switched her optic to thermographic setting and took aim at the heat signatures of the pursuing Freebooters. She could make out a few trucks and buggies, a dozen bikes, swooping closer and blasting at *Thundersaurus*'s tires.

Ana aimed down the sights, letting off a strobing burst of fire. Lightning the color of flame sizzled overhead as one of the Freebooters wobbled and fell. Ana fired again and again, hitting nothing and using up the rest of the clip. The Freebooters returned fire, forcing her into cover to reload as bullets riddled the truck's panels. The gunshots echoing inside her head, Lemon lying on the floor at her feet, the image, the noise, the chaos dragging her back to that cell, that day, those final hours . . .

Red on my hands. Smoke in my lungs. My mother, my father, my sisters and brother, all dead on the floor beside me. Hollow eyes and empty chests.

The lifelikes stand above me. The four of them in their perfect, pretty row.

They have only one thing left to—

An Armada wagon careened out of the glasstorm, sideswiping *Thundersaurus*. Ana was thrown back against Kaiser as Ezekiel slammed into the attacking truck.

"Ana, come take the wheel!" the lifelike shouted.

"I can't drive in this!"

"I can shoot better than you, take the damn wheel!"

The driver-side window shattered as one of the Freebooters emptied half a clip into the truck's flank. Ana hunkered down near Kaiser, feeling bullets *spang* off his armored shell. Ezekiel snatched up the other assault rifle, one hand holding the wheel steady as he riddled the wagon's driver and gunner with lead. The wagon crashed into *Thundersaurus* again and careened away, taking out another motorcycle rider before flipping end over end and exploding in a ball of garish blue methane flame.

"Take the wheel!" Ezekiel roared.

"Okay, okay, no need to get shouty, god!"

Ana rolled over into the front seat as Zeke stood up through the sunroof. The razored fragments began shredding Ezekiel's unprotected skin, whipping his knuckles and cheeks bloody as he started taking methodical shots at the pursuing Freebooters. Ana gripped the wheel hard, stomped on the gas, *Thundersaurus* lurching forward with a thundering V-8 roar as bikes and cars closed in from all sides.

The lifelike fired again, again, ghosting half a dozen bikers and three more drivers before his rifle ran dry. A Freebooter leapt from a speeding sand buggy onto *Thundersaurus*'s trunk, another jumping from an armored 4x4 alongside. They clung to the truck's flank, one reaching through the shattered window and clutching Ana's throat. She shrieked, tore the wheel left, colliding with the 4x4 beside them and crushing both men to pulp between the vehicles.

Cricket was in the backseat, reloading Ana's shotgun and rifle. He handed the latter to Ezekiel, who kept blasting away at the pursuing vehicles. Ana was bent over the steering wheel, squinting through the fog of sweat inside her rad-suit headgear. The road had disappeared entirely, rocky outcroppings rising out of the desert floor ahead. The glasstorm howled on, like some horror from one of Ana's old myths. Scylla or Charybdis. Fenris or Kali. A thing of hatred and hunger, consuming everything in its path.

The armored 4x4 was still roaring alongside them, its flanks now splashed with red. The driver rammed his ride into Ana's, trying to drive her into a stone outcropping. Ana rammed the 4x4 back, *Thundersaurus* grinding against the bigger truck in a hail of sparks. Cricket cursed as he flopped about on the back-seat like a ragdoll, Kaiser barking out the broken window. The 4x4 was heavier, and Ana had trouble keeping a straight course, headed now for a huge spur of black rock rising out of the sand in front of them.

"Ezekiel?" she shouted.

Gunfire was the only response, empty shell casings falling through the sunroof like hail.

"EZEKIEL!"

The lifelike finally heard her, turned on the truck beside them and riddled the cabin with bullets. The driver slumped over the wheel, and Ana wrenched her own steering wheel sideways, missing the spur by inches. His gun dry, Ezekiel dropped down into the passenger seat, slamming the sunroof closed.

"Out of ammo," he wheezed. "But there's only a few bikers and one truck left. Just plant it, fast as you're able. I think we've knocked the fight out of them."

"Do you want to take the— *Oh my god!*" Ana gasped.

Ezekiel was covered in blood. His knuckles had been stripped back to metallic bone by the glasstorm, his beautiful face dripping red. Ana's goggles had spared his eyes the worst of it, but the exposed skin on the rest of him . . .

"Zeke, are you all right?"

"Don't worry about me," he said.

"You look like someone threw you in a blender!"

"I'll be fine in a while. Trust me."

Dread clawing her insides, Ana turned her attention back to the road, knuckles white on the steering wheel. Checking her flanks for their pursuers, listening for engines over the howling winds. She glanced in the rearview mirror.

"Crick, is Lemon okay?"

The little bot had fished some electrical tape from her satchel, secured the floor mats over the holes in the rear windows. Everything inside the cabin was covered with grit and glass. The little logika bent over Lemon, pulling off her headgear to inspect the wound.

"I think so," he reported. "Maybe a concussion. But she's breathing all right."

Ana shook her head. That'd been too close. If anything had happened to Lem . . .

They drove on, the storm pummeling their little truck, all the world gone black. The headlights cut a swath through the darkness, glinting on the swirling shards, burning red as that strange lightning arced above their heads. The engine groaned and shuddered but held true. Dragging them on through the roiling night, closer and closer to Babel.

Closer and closer to home.

Ana glanced again at Ezekiel. The lifelike was wiping the blood and dirt from his face with his good hand. He'd just risked his own life, torn himself to shreds, to keep her in one piece. He hadn't hesitated for a second. Her chest ached to see him hurt for her sake, filled with warmth to see him risk it in the first place. His vow in the ministry rang in her head. The truth of it now impossible to ignore.

There's nothing I wouldn't do to keep you safe.

She touched his arm, as lightly as feathers falling. "Thank you, Zeke."

"For what?"

"For everything."

He smiled lopsided, and gave her a small bow. "You want me to take the wheel?"

"Probably a good idea."

She slid over his lap, he slid underneath, the pair momentarily tangled together as they traded places. Ana took a deep breath, checking again for signs of pursuit. All she could see outside was darkness. Glass and grit were still pouring in through the driver-side window, so Cricket crawled over Ezekiel's shoulder and duct-taped another floor mat over the hole, intentionally sticking his hind parts in the lifelike's face as he did so. Ezekiel was too busy steering to wave him away. The wind eased off, and Cricket gave his metal tush one more rub in Zeke's grille before crawling into the backseat once more.

"Enjoy yourself?" the lifelike asked.

"Immensely," Cricket replied.

Ezekiel glanced at Ana, shook his head. "We should be clear of the Glass in an hour or so. If the storm reaches as far as Babel, that's all good. The leftover Freebooters will probably give up when they figure out where we're headed."

She nodded. Risked a smile despite the bedlam and blood all around them.

"That was some fancy shooting back there."

He winked. "You're not so bad yourself."

"We make a pretty good team, huh?"

"We?"

She could see her smile reflected in the perfect blue of his eyes. She laid her head in his lap, felt the warmth of his skin through her rad-suit. Remembering.

"Yeah." Ana sighed. "We."

"I think I like the sound of that."

He put his arm around her, squeezed her against him. And despite all the bedlam, all the blood, it felt right. It felt real. It felt like the way she wanted to feel forever.

Him and her. Together.

Forever.

1.26

TERMINUS

Red on my hands. Smoke in my lungs. My mother, my father, my sisters and brother, all dead on the floor beside me. Hollow eyes and empty chests.

The lifelikes stand above me. The four of them in their perfect, pretty row.

They have only one thing left to take from me.

The last and most precious thing.

The tempest followed them until dawn, smoky spears of light beginning to filter through the haze of dust and glass. Ana had eventually left Ezekiel to his driving, climbing over into the backseat and nursing Lemon in her lap. Her bestest was slowly coming to, murmuring softly. Her brow and eye socket were swollen and bruised, blood clotted in her lashes. Ana risked taking off the girl's headgear again to wash the wound while Cricket and Kaiser looked on nervously.

"Lem?" Ana murmured. "Lem, can you hear me?"

"Nnnnn," Lemon said.

"Are you all right, Freckles?" Ezekiel asked.

"No . . . ," Lemon groaned softly. "Come kiss it b-better."

"She's gonna be fine." Ana smiled.

Lemon opened her eyes a crack, hissing in pain. "What the hells . . . hit m-me?"

"Cybernetically enhanced killing machine," Ana replied.

"Is it . . . T-Tuesday already?"

"Just lie still. You might have a concussion."

Kaiser looked out through the windshield and growled.

"Ana," Ezekiel said. "You better come up here."

"Crick, give her some water," Ana said. "Not too much, or she'll be sick."

Ana leaned down, kissed Lemon on the brow.

"You stay low, Lem. Keep your head down and don't do anything stupid."

"Too . . . late," Lemon moaned.

"Ana . . . ," Ezekiel warned.

Ana climbed into the passenger seat, squinted through the thinning glasstorm. Through the pale dawn haze, she could make out a skyline rising from the desert floor. Her blood ran cold, goose bumps prickling her skin. She was stricken suddenly with a barrage of memories. Sitting with her brother and sisters in pristine white rooms. A garden, full of flowers that existed nowhere else on earth. Music in the air and mechanical butterflies and a great library of books. Her father's arm, strong about her shoulders. Her mother's lips, warm upon her brow. A heaven in a world run to ruin.

"Babel," she breathed.

It stretched up from the sand ahead, a spear of steel and glass trying in vain to pierce the sky. It was only in stories that irradiated objects actually glowed, but there was something in the air—the dust or glass that intertwined itself with the dawn's light and the radiation lingering in the city's bones—setting the metropolis aglow. It looked as if the whole city were burning with translucent flame.

Unlike Armada, atop its crumbling ruins, Babel seemed almost part of the landscape, flowing up from the ground in a vaguely organic coil. The tower was really two spires, twisting about each other like a double helix of DNA. In its day, it had been a thing of breathtaking beauty. But that was yesterday. . . .

The city around it was an empty shell now, all broken windows and encroaching rust. Where once the air had been filled with thopters and rotor drones, now only a single irradiated crow circled in the skies. Where once Babel had teemed with life, it now stood hollow and silent, a corroding tomb for the people who'd been murdered there. The day the machines stopped singing. The day her family died.

Ana found her eye welling with tears. She hadn't thought it would affect her so deeply, but seeing her former home was like seeing a ghost. All the fragments of her past life, all the blood and anguish and pain, immortalized in glass and chrome and isotopes that would take ten thousand years to degrade.

"Are you all right?" Ezekiel asked.

She simply shook her head. Mute and aching. This place wasn't her home. It was a mausoleum. The place her childhood had ended, spitting her out into a life of rust and dust. But still, that was the life that had brought her Lemon. Kaiser and Cricket. And, yes, even her grandpa. She could feel those two people inside her head again. The girl she'd been and the girl she'd become. Looking at the tower, the place one girl had died and the other had been born, she didn't know whether to feel sorrow or relief.

Ezekiel saw the look on her face, took hold of her hand. His skin was warm and alive and real, and she entwined her fingers with his. Breathing a little easier.

"I'm with you," he said.

"I'm glad," she smiled.

Ana squinted through the glasstorm and the grubby windshield, making out the dim shapes of the Daedalus encampment ahead. She could see huge machina—Titans and Tarantulas and Juggernauts—glinting in the dawn light. Heavily armored, legs like pillars, microsolar cells gleaming in their desert-camo paint jobs. They stood silent vigil or walked endless patrols through the dead suburbia outside Babel's broken walls. She wondered what the pilots inside them had done to land such a crappy detail. How bored they must get out here, praying for something to shoot at.

And, silly her, she was about to grant their wish.

Just a few days ago, a single deranged Goliath had almost ghosted her solo. Who knew how many machina were waiting for her out there? All of them fully armed, max juiced, the pilots inside just itching to put a six-foot-under hurting on anything that strayed too close.

"We're not in WarDome anymore, Toto," Cricket muttered.

"Yeah," Ana whispered.

"I hope you've got your mojo warmed up."

"Me too."

Ezekiel squeezed her hand and smiled. "I believe in you, Ana."

"Great Maker, someone kill me . . . ," Cricket groaned.

The lifelike glared over his shoulder. "Not a lot of romance in your soul, is there?"

Cricket arced the cutting torch on his middle finger. "Romance this, Stumpy."

They roared out of the glasstorm, into the swirling eddies and rolling clouds at the tempest's edge. *Thundersaurus* had been stripped bare by the storm's abrasive winds, the dawn gleaming on its buffed metal skin. Ana could see the Daedalus garrison more clearly now. It wasn't so much an army as a police force, maybe a dozen heavy machina in total, here to ensure no looters plundered Babel's irradiated secrets. But even if the pilots were half-asleep at the controls, a handful of those badbots were enough to deal with a motley scavver crew from Dregs with only a few popguns between them.

Unless one of them happened to be a living silver bullet, that is . . .

Ana closed her eyes, feeling for the closest machina. It was a Tarantula—a squat, eight-legged killing machine as big as a bus, bristling with pods of short-range missiles and twin auto-cannons. It swiveled its torso at the sound of oncoming engines, extended a radio aerial to transmit an alert to the rest of the Daedalus garrison.

"*Attention, unidentified vehicle,*" the pilot announced through his PA. "*Attention, unidentified vehicle. This area is restricted by order of Daedalus Technologies. You have thirty seconds to divert course or I will open fire.*"

Ezekiel gunned the accelerator. The *Thundersaurus* surged forward, leaving the glasstorm howling behind them. The Tarantula turned to face the oncoming truck, legs shifting in a ghastly imitation of a real spider, two pods of missiles unfurling at its back like vast, glittering wings.

"*If you do not divert course, I am authorized to use lethal force,*" the pilot warned. "*You have fifteen seconds.*"

". . . Ana?" Ezekiel asked.

"I've got this," she hissed.

She dragged back the sunroof, stood up for a better view. Sweating inside the snot-green plastic rad-gear, she felt the dust and sand pattering on her visor. Ana reached out, narrowed her eyes against the dawn light, locked them on the Tarantula. Picturing herself back in the WarDome. Remembering the taste of blood in her mouth. The pain. The terror. Dragging it all up from her belly, mixing it in with the anguish of seeing Babel again. The memories of her family. Alex. Olivia. Tania. Marie.

Mother.

Father . . .

All of it. Every shred. Every drop.

"Come on . . . ," she whispered.

"Ten seconds."

"Ana?" Ezekiel shouted.

"I'm *trying!*"

The pilot braced his machina's legs in firing position. Ana curled her fingers into claws. The Eve in her refusing to flinch. To turn away. They'd met death before, after all. Spat right in its face. Clawed and bit and kicked their way back from the quiet black to this.

This is not the end of me.

This is just one

more

enemy.

Static electricity dancing on her skin. Denial building up inside her, pulsing in her temples as the Tarantula's missile batteries arced to life. Rage bubbling up and spilling over her lips as she raised her hand and screamed.

And screamed.

AND SCREAMED.

. . .

. . . and absolutely nothing happened.

"Firing."

Missiles howled from their launch tubes, dozens of them streaking toward *Thundersaurus*, smoking vapor trails behind them. Ezekiel tore the wheel left, the truck tipping up onto two wheels for a torturous moment before crashing back to earth with a spray of dirt. The missiles roared in from the sky, exploding into boiling clouds of fire behind them. Deafening impacts shook the truck, Ana slipping back down into the cabin and hanging on for dear life. Another salvo of missiles hit alongside, blasting the floor mats loose from the broken windows. Ana felt the heat almost blistering her skin.

"What . . . t-the *hells*?" Lemon groaned, lifting her bleeding head.

"Lem, keep your head down!" Ana roared. "And get your seat belt on!"

She held out her hand, trying to summon it again. Her power. Her gift. Whatever the hells you wanted to call it. The affliction that had seen her hunted by the Brotherhood, chased across a wasteland of radioactive glass by a cybernetically augmented killing machine. The curse that had seen the biggest CorpState on the Zona Coast put a contract out on her head.

Trashbreed.

Deviate.

Abnorm.

Fat lot of good it was doing her now.

"Why won't it work?" she hissed.

The Tarantula let loose another volley, and only Ezekiel's skill behind the wheel kept them from all being incinerated. The earth around them blossomed into beautiful flowers of flame and black smoke, shrapnel peppering their hull. Ana could see two Titans charging across the wastes in their direction—huge bipedal machina that made Goliaths look like toy soldiers. A Juggernaut was rolling right at them, too, tank treads cutting the dirt, autoguns blazing. Kaiser began barking out the back window, tail thumping against the seats. Cricket poked his head up to quiet the blitzhund down, his mismatched eyes boggling as he spied what had riled Kaiser up.

"Um," he said. "Point of order . . ."

A spray of high-velocity rounds shattered the front windshield, Ana shrieking as Ezekiel pushed her below the dashboard. The engine blew a plume of black smoke, making a sound like bolts being dropped into a meat grinder. They were still at least two kilometers from Babel's suburban sprawl, but if they could get into the streets, there'd be more cover. Ezekiel gunned the engine, hitting an old broken highway; Ana crawled into his lap and stretched her hand toward the machina now moving to cut off their path to the city. She closed her fist. Gritted her teeth. Tears in her eyes.

"Dammit, why won't it work?"

Lemon groaned, trying to pull herself up in her seat. Cricket waved her down, double-checking her seat belt as he spoke.

"Um, I don't want to alarm anyone. But you might wanna look behind us. . . ."

Ana peered through the busted rear window, heart sinking as she saw a familiar figure roaring out of the glasstorm. He was riding a different motorcycle, probably recovered from one of the Freebooters Ezekiel had shot. His chest was crusted with dry blood. Clothes shredded. Gas mask over his face. But still, there was no mistaking him.

"Preacher . . . ," Ana breathed.

"Are you *kidding* me?" Ezekiel glanced into the rearview mirror. "What does it take to kill this fu—"

The missile caught them on the driver's side, striking the earth just below the door. Every remaining window in the truck exploded, glass spraying the cabin as *Thundersaurus* was flung into the air, spinning as it went. Lemon wailed, clutching her seat belt as the truck tried to fly. Ana wasn't lucky enough to be belted in, Ezekiel folding his body over hers and roaring "HOLD ON!" as *Thundersaurus* crashed back to earth, flipping nose to tail in a hail of glass and flame. The world turned end over end, Ana cracked her skull against something hard, blinding pain seething through her Memdrive. No way up or down. Endless, agonizing moments as the truck kept rolling, crashing, splintering, finally skidding to a smoking halt.

Blood on her tongue. Glass in her hair. Pain lancing through her skull. Ana groaned, peering out through the shattered windshield. Kaiser had been thrown loose in the crash and was lying motionless on the cracked asphalt. She couldn't see Cricket. The truck had landed on its roof, with Lemon suspended upside down by her seat belt, groaning and senseless. Any second now, another payload of missiles would come flying from those Tarantulas. She had to get out, had to stop them. . . .

Ezekiel unbuckled his seat belt, collapsed almost on top of her.

"Are you okay?" he asked.

Blinding light in her head. Screaming in her ears.

The lifelikes stand above me. The four of them in their perfect, pretty row.

They have only one thing left to take from me.

The last and most precious thing.

Not my life, no.

Something dearer still.

"I . . ."

She heard boots on gravel, the soft chink of approaching spurs.

The Preacher's voice, dry as shale.

". . . coordinates seven-seven-twelve-alpha. Priority one. Priority one. Check your fire, Omega, repeat, check your fire."

Ana heard heavy footsteps, the crunch of tank treads in the dirt. The hum of servos and the hiss of pistons. Her head was white-hot pain. Static ringing in her skull where she'd cracked it. She put her hand to her Memdrive, felt a deep split in the housing beneath its pseudo-skin. Her fingers came away soaked with blood.

The four figures part, and a fifth enters the room. Male. Broad shoulders, silhouetted against the glare. The others look to him, expectant.

"I can't," the newcomer says.

"You must," they reply.

"I won't."

The leader offers his pistol. "You will."

"Ezekiel . . . ," Ana said.

The newcomer wipes his hand across his eyes.

But finally, he takes the pistol.

"Oh god . . ."

She looked into the lifelike's eyes. That old-sky blue. Those eyes that had looked at her with such adoration as they lay together in her room. So much pain as he raised the pistol and aimed it at her head . . .

"I'm sorry," he says.

"It was you," she whispered.

"What?" Ezekiel blinked. "What was me?"

Tears blurring the world around her. Memories finally co-alescing. The last remnants of those final hours. The five of them, standing there in that cell above the carnage they'd made. Gabriel, Uriel, Hope, Faith.

And *him*.

They have only one thing left to take from me.

The last and most precious thing.

Not my life, no.

My love.

"You . . ." She choked on the word, unable to breathe.

"Ana . . ."

She scrambled backward through the broken window, out onto the dusty road. Blinding sunlight. Tears fracturing the world into a million shining pieces. The Preacher stood there, a pistol in one hand, what must have been a flamethrower in the other. Cricket crawled out from beneath the truck, dented and wobbling. The little logika shuffled to Ana's side and put his arms around her.

"Are you okay?"

Half a dozen siege-class machina were gathered on a small ridge above them, lighting her up with targeting lasers. Autoguns and plasma cannons and missile batteries focused on *Thundersaurus*'s ruins.

But Ana's eyes were locked on Ezekiel. Horror. Anguish. Rage. The picture of him lifting the pistol in that cell, aiming at her head.

"I'm sorry," he says.

I hear the sound of thunder.

And then I hear nothing at all.

"You shot me . . . ," she breathed.

Cricket looked back and forth between Ana and the life-like. "What?"

"Get him away from me," she gasped.

Gunfire. Six bullets, blasting the asphalt in a neat semicircle around her.

"Settle down there, missy," the Preacher warned.

"Ana . . . ," Ezekiel pleaded.

"Get away from me!" she screamed.

The Preacher fired again into the air, hollering at the top of his lungs.

"EVERYBODY JUST CALM DOWN, GODDAMMIT!"

Silence rang as the shots faded, the bounty hunter nodding to himself as if satisfied. He holstered his pistol, waved the flame-thrower at the wreckage, and spoke with a graveled voice.

"You might wanna crawl outta there, Snowflake. 'Less you want me to forget my manners and ventilate Miss Carpenter's head. She's still worth some creds dead, after all."

The Titans turned their weapons on Ezekiel as the lifelike crawled from the wreckage. Their optics aglow, autogun barrels beginning to spin up.

"Operative, should we terminate?" the pilot asked.

"Negative," the Preacher said. "All y'all, hold fire unless I spit an express kill order. This warrant is priority one. Board certified, you read me?"

"Roger that. Holding."

The bounty hunter pulled off his gas mask, reached into the tattered remnants of his coat. Ana could see that his chest had been shredded by her shotgun blast, but she could make out metal beneath the flesh she'd minced. He fished around inside his pocket, stuffed a lump of synth tobacco into his cheek. Raised his flamethrower in Ezekiel's direction.

"You just stay on your belly, Snowflake. I seen what fire done to your big sister back in Armada. So don't move unless you fancy the smell of barbecue."

Ana blinked the tears from her eyes, fear of the Preacher momentarily overcoming the rage and hate boiling in her head. She scoped Kaiser, still lying motionless in the dust. She spied her satchel close beside him, the glint of red on the thermex grenade inside it. But it was so far away. . . .

She looked at the Preacher. Down the barrel of his pistol. She was back in that cell again. Blood on her hands. On her face. Her family in ruins all around her. Gabriel standing above her. Tousled blond hair and eyes like green glass. Myriad's voice in the background, pleading with the lifelikes to stop. Uriel's handsome face, now twisted and cruel, framed by long black hair. Hope's eyes still filled with uncertainty despite the blood already on her hands. Faith, once Ana's dearest friend, her stare now empty and cold.

And *him*.

"Why the waterworks, missy?"

Ana glared up at the bounty hunter, trying to push the tears back, punching and kicking. But they were too big. Too much. Looking at Ezekiel, the anguish on his face, the world opening up beneath her and dragging her down, down, down.

"Ana . . . ," he pleaded. "Let me explain. . . ."

"Shut up!" Cricket shouted. "Haven't you done enough?"

She couldn't feel her skin. Couldn't breathe. Everything. All of it. Lie after lie after lie. Curling up into a ball and wrapping her arms around her legs and listening as the fragments of her life shattered like bloodstained glass.

The Preacher looked from the broken girl to the almost-boy.

"Mmmf," he grunted.

The bounty hunter spat into the dirt, flamethrower still trained on Ezekiel as he walked around to the other side of the wreckage. The machina pilots watched on impassively, scopes locked on Ana and Ezekiel, just a word away from unleashing murder. She wondered if that would be better. To close her eyes and listen to the bullets' hymn.

Preacher tapped the side of his throat, brow creased in concentration.

"Nest, this is Goodbook. Repeat, Nest, this is Goodbook. Package secured, one bounty, one person of interest. All the trouble he's caused me, I figure the tech boys might wanna take a peek inside this snowflake's head. I'm gonna need evac from—"

The man blinked at a strange sound, turned to look behind him. There on the ground, sitting on his haunches and wagging his tail, was a rusty metal dog. He'd looked almost real once, but his fur had started wearing off a year back, so Eve had stripped him to the metal and spray-painted him in an urban-camo color scheme instead. He looked skeletal now, all plasteel plates and hydraulics.

She liked him better that way.

In his mouth was a red cylinder. It was marked with a small skull and crossbones, stamped with the word EXPLOSIVE. It had been jury-rigged like a grenade, and, clever dog that he was, the blitzhund had figured out how to pull the pin.

His eyes were glowing blood red.

"Kaiser . . . ," Ana whispered.

"Wuff," the dog said.

BOOM.

The thermex ignited in a blistering halo, the explosion near deafening. Blasted with dust and heat, Ana closed her eyes against the shockwave, Cricket bowled over beside her. She climbed to her knees, screaming Kaiser's name as the fireball rose high into the sky. Black smoke churned, metallic scraps falling from the sky like rain, the Preacher lying wide-eyed and motionless, the lower half of his body blown away.

"*Hostile! Hostile!*" the Tarantula pilot cried. "*Ghost 'em!*"

Ana felt an impact at her back, strong arms around her. Ezekiel picked her up and dragged her behind the truck's wreckage as the machina opened fire. She was screaming Kaiser's name, tears in her eyes as the bullets flew, smashing through the hull, *thunk-thunk-thunk*ing into the engine block. Cricket ran for cover, skidding behind the wreckage as the air filled with thundering booms. The Titans and Juggernauts were moving to flank them, feet and tank treads crunching in the dirt, only seconds away from a clear shot.

Only seconds till they were dead.

"Ana, I'm sorry," Ezekiel whispered.

A Juggernaut loomed out of the sun. Autoguns raised.

Cricket stood in front of her, trying to shield her with his tiny body.

"Get away from her!"

Ana stared down the barrel and saw peace. Quiet. The Eve in her raging against it with every fiber of their being. And then she heard the clink of glass. A soft curse. A hand wrapped in a pink plastic glove reached out from inside the *Thundersaurus*'s wreckage.

"Stop," Lemon whispered.

The Juggernaut shuddered. Flinched as if struck by an invisible hand. Sparks burst from its optics as Lemon Fresh closed her fingers into a fist and, with a thought, with a gesture, with a word, fried every circuit and relay inside its metal shell.

Lemon crawled from the wreckage, bullets punching through

the metal around her. Brow dripping blood, eyes narrowed. Arms held out, palms upturned, fingers curling into claws as the scream tore from her throat.

"STOP!"

An electric concussion. A static shockwave, tasted more than felt. The machina around them shuddered. Rocked back on their suspensions or wobbling on unsteady legs, pilots screaming as they were cooked alive inside their cockpits. And with a series of awful metallic groans, the hiss of frying relays and bursts of sparks, the big bots tottered like marionettes with cut strings and crashed dead and still onto the dirt.

Every.

Single.

One.

Ana stared at her bestest.

Dumbfounded.

Incredulous.

"... Lem?"

The girl dropped her hands to her sides. Dragging in great, ragged breaths. And Ana suddenly understood. All of it made sense.

All of it ...

Machines had only been fritzing when Lemon was around. But Lem had always been out of sight, or Ana too busy to notice exactly what she was doing. Too busy rocking with the Goliath in WarDome. Too focused on the Fridgeboys in Tire Valley. Too intent on the Preacher's blitzhund in the Armada subway. But Lem had been almost out cold when they'd arrived at Babel, and Ana's power hadn't worked because ...

Because it wasn't *her* power.

"... *trashbreed.*"

"... *deviate.*"

"... *abnorm.*"

Lemon lifted Popstick with a growl. "Don't call her that."

Ana thought it had been her. Lying there on the WarDome floor, holding out her hand and screaming and thinking she'd become something more, when all the time . . .

This whole time . . .

"No . . . ," Ana breathed.

Lemon looked at Ana, eyes brimming with tears, her voice trembling.

"I'm sorry, Riotgrrl," she said. "I . . . I tried to tell you so many times. . . ."

Lies.

Upon lies.

Upon *lies.*

And this, the last, was just enough to break her.

PART 4

A SPIRE OF GHOSTS AND GLASS

1.27

BREAK

"Don't talk to me."

Metal feet, crunching on broken concrete and shattered brick. A dozen screens lit up in front of her, her limbs encased in control sleeves and boots. Hydraulics hissing, engines humming through the cockpit walls as Ana strode through the desolation of an abandoned suburbia, closer and closer to the shadow of Babel.

"Don't talk to me."

They were the only words she'd had for them. Either of them. Ezekiel's agony plain in his eyes. Lemon's hurt clear in her voice. So many apologies. So many excuses disguised as explanations. For every one of them, Ana had the same reply.

"Don't talk to me."

Ezekiel had been the one who put the bullet through her skull during the revolt. At Gabriel's command. He hadn't saved her life, he'd tried to *kill* her. And Lemon had been the one who fried that logika in WarDome. *She'd* been the deviate everyone was after, too scared or ashamed to 'fess up to it. Her lie had set Daedalus Technologies and the Preacher on their tails, and because of him, Kaiser had . . .

Poor Kaiser . . .

Had he done it out of love? Or because he'd been programmed to protect her?

She honestly didn't know which was worse. . . .

Ana had grabbed her satchel of tools from the roadside. Dragged a pilot's corpse from a slumped and broken Titan and gotten to work. She couldn't wipe the tears from her eyes because of her rad-suit, had swallowed them instead. And pushing all her hurt aside, she'd set about getting the machina right-ways again. Ezekiel had tried to take her hand, get her to listen.

"Ana, please, I did it to *save* you. . . ."

She'd rounded on him with spanner raised, a breath away from caving in his skull.

"Don't touch me, fug," she'd growled.

"Ana, you have to listen to me, please. I'd never turn against you. I did it to *trick* them. I shot to wound you, not kill. I saved the most important thing in the world to me, don't you understand that? I saved *you*, Ana."

"Then why didn't you tell me, Ezekiel?"

"I . . ."

Her eyes were narrowed to paper cuts, her fury boiling in every word.

"I *trusted* you. And the insane thing is, part of me still wants to believe you. Maybe you did try to fool the murdering bastards you called brothers and sisters. You've been making a fool out of me since I found you on that scrap heap. But the one thing I asked you to do was be straight with me. The *one thing*. And you couldn't even give me that."

She turned her back, jaw clenched.

"Ana . . ."

"Don't talk to me."

The lifelike had stood there, explanations dying on those sweet, bow-shaped lips. And she'd climbed into the machina and gotten back to work.

Despite everything, Ana still had the know-how Silas had given her. But whatever Lemon's failings, she'd done a fine job of frying the machina—it'd taken Ana almost an hour to get it up and moving again, and even now, it was only running at 40 percent capacity. But she couldn't bring herself to linger out there any longer. Couldn't stand to look at them. Lemon had been the next to shuffle up in the apology train, head bowed and wringing her hands.

"Riotgrrl . . . ," Lemon had said. "I tried to tell you."

Ana hadn't looked up. Hadn't said a word. Everyone had lied to her. Silas. Ezekiel. The last best friend she'd had ended up putting a bullet in her sister's brain. And if Faith's betrayal had been murderous, somehow Lemon's hurt even worse.

The girl's shoulders slumped. Her voice a whisper. "I'm sorry."

"Don't follow me, Lemon," Ana had finally said. "I mean it. I catch sight of either one of you again, I'll shoot you myself."

Lemon took a step back at that. Hand at her chest as if to hold in the ache.

". . . But where will I go?"

"Anywhere but here."

She'd left them both on that broken highway, with the Preacher's body and the tiny pieces of shrapnel that had been Kaiser. They'd begged her to listen. To wait. To stay. But she'd turned her back on them both. It had been bad enough when she'd discovered the life Silas had built her was a lie. Bad enough when she'd remembered Faith and Gabriel's betrayal. But now that Ezekiel and Lemon had deceived her, too? How could she trust either of them ever again? How could she call either of them her friend?

She pushed the question aside, leaving it in the dust. Intent now only on Babel. The murderers within. She didn't even know what she wanted anymore. But whatever it was, she knew it lay inside that tower.

"Are you sure about this?" Cricket asked her.

The little bot was nestled on her shoulder as she piloted the Titan down the highway. The only one she could count on. The only one left to trust.

"I'm sure," she replied.

"You don't have to do this. We could turn back now. Just run away again."

"Again?" She shook her head. "Crick, I don't think I ever left this place."

"Listen, I can see you're hurting. But there's still folks who love you."

"I know you do, Crick." She reached out and squeezed his little metal hand. "And I'm sorry about what I said in Armada. You're the only one who's always steered me true. I've never doubted you. But even if they didn't have Grandpa, somehow I was always going to end up back here. This is where it began. And this is where it ends."

He looked at her with those glowing, mismatched eyes.

"I'm just worried about the kind of end you're looking for," he said.

Ana clenched her fists inside the control gloves and marched on. The Titan climbed through the shattered wall encircling the ruined city, crunched and clomped through the broken streets, closer to that winding spire of glass and steel. A lonely, cancerous crow called in the skies above. Her reckoning, dead ahead.

She remembered this place like she'd left it yesterday. The lives and dreams born here, dying in a sun-bright shear of neutron radiation. She could see withered bodies scattered among the ruins, skin like rags. Had they looked to a god to save them in those final moments? Or to the man who'd simply styled himself as one? Who'd built himself angels to destroy all he'd created?

Father . . .

Closer to the tower. Buildings with hollow eyes and open mouths. Bodies growing thicker. Cricket sat silently on her shoulder, his stare locked on that colossal structure. Her Titan's Geiger counter was crackling in the redline, the radiation outside still hot enough to ghost her with a few hours' exposure, and it was only getting hotter as they approached Babel's reactor. Dust rolled like clouds of phantoms through the abandoned streets, shapeless and howling. On they stomped, wrapped inside their metal shell with only the lonely dead and each other for company.

No sign of life. No sound but the endless, whispering winds. No resistance. No automata. No sentry guns.

"This is too easy," she said.

"You took the words right out of my mouth," Cricket muttered.

At last, they stood before the tower, ringed by a broken security perimeter of metal and wire. Ana saw the wrecks of Daedalus machina all around her, a winged-sun logo emblazoned on their hulls. The bodies of soldiers wearing that same logo were strung up on the security fence in the hundreds. A lifeless parade, silently screaming. It looked like an entire division—perhaps the remnants of an invasion force that had tried to seize Babel's secrets and been beaten back by whoever, or *what*ever, still lived inside it.

"Hell of a KEEP OUT sign," Cricket said.

"They don't like visitors, I guess," Ana muttered.

She knew her best point of entry would be through the Research and Development division's storage bay, where Gnosis used to store their machina and logika. The place Grace had died. The place Gabriel's descent into madness had begun. She knew she'd have to fight to break her grandpa free, and her only edge over Gabriel and the other lifelikes was the Titan she was piloting. She couldn't afford to leave it behind. And so, heart hammering in her chest, she stomped around to the entry of R & D.

The two large doors leading into the loading bay were open wide. She saw abandoned personnel carriers and flex-wings. Empty turret emplacements. Broken machina. All of them slowly turning to rust. She could hear the explosion inside her head, picture Grace silhouetted against those flames as she shattered like glass.

She saw more bodies. Hundreds, clad in the charcoal gray and armored blue of Gnosis security members. It looked like they'd been mustering a counterattack against the lifelikes when the neutron blast ripped through their ranks. They lay crumpled where they fell, empty eye sockets open to the sky.

"They didn't even bury them," she whispered.

She remembered Hope's words in Armada. Her talk of Gabriel's obsession and madness. Nobody could love like a lifelike, she'd said. What had Gabriel filled himself with when his love had died? What was waiting for her inside that tower? What kind of monsters had they created? And what had those monsters become in the years she'd been gone?

Cricket's mismatched eyes were on the monitors. His voice modulated to a whisper.

"Ana, I've got a really bad feeling. We should get out of here."

"I heard you the first fifty times."

"Yeah, well, this time I really mean it."

"You want to just leave Grandpa? He's your maker, Crick. Don't you owe him something?"

"He made me to *protect* you. And that's what I'm trying to do. Silas spent the last two years keeping you away from here. No way he'd want me to let you come back."

She sucked her lip. Shook her head. "I owe him, Cricket. He might have steered it wrong, but he still saved my life. I can't just leave him here to die."

"He'd never ask you to save him."

"I know. And that's what makes me want to."

Cricket fell into a sullen silence. Ana guided her Titan past the mounds of bodies, trying not to look at them. Marching slowly through the loading bay doors, her autocannon raised and ready, she clomped into the R & D storage bay. Dust was piled thick in the corners, shrouding mountains of equipment too irradiated to ever salvage. The bay was three stories tall, so wide she could barely see the edges, lit only by the sun outside and the sullen red glow of emergency lighting inside. The space was ringed with metal gantries above, loading chains suspended from the ceiling, tinkling and clanking in the breeze. Still no resistance. No guard, nothing.

This is all wrong.

Ana saw the silhouettes of dozens of logika, their cores powered down, their optics dark. The Quixote stood among them—GnosisLabs' finest robotic gladiator, never to stride the killing floor of the WarDome again. Not for the last time, she was reminded of the day Grace died. Her little brother, Alex, with his toy replica of the big logika in his hands as he laughed and ran through this very bay. Her mother's smile. Her father's arm around her as the explosion bloomed bright.

Ezekiel had saved her life that day. Shielding her from the blast that should have killed her. Only to put a bullet in her head a month later.

"But when the ash rose up to choke me, it was thoughts of you that helped me breathe. When the night seemed never-ending, it was dreams of you that helped me sleep. You. And only you."

Lies.

"I don't know what it was for you, but for me, it was real. And you're the girl who made me real."

Upon lies.

Proximity alarm.

Her Titan blared a warning as a rocket-propelled grenade streaked in from a gantry above. Ana twisted her controls and lunged sideways as the projectile exploded, tearing through an abandoned troop transport beside her. Another rocket flew at her from the gloom, Ana twisting and raising her autocannon, blasting away at a figure flitting among the shadows overhead, almost too quick to track.

Her Titan wasn't in true fighting shape, but she was a mean enough pilot to dodge three more rocket volleys, blasting away at her assailant and shredding the walkways to shrapnel. Cricket yelled in alarm as the autogun turrets around the bay opened up with a withering hail of armor-piercing rounds. Ana raised her own autocannon as another rocket roared in from the shadows and blew out her Titan's right knee.

The machina toppled sideways, hydraulics gushing fluid. Ana reached out with one colossal hand to steady herself, crushing a metal stairwell as she fired into the auto-sentries. Spent shell casings spewed like falling stars from her guns, smoke rising from the barrels. She was a crack shot, taking down half a dozen automata in quick succession, but from her time in the Dome, she knew a bait and switch when she saw it. A humanoid figure dropped down onto the loading bay floor. Ana caught a glimpse of short dark hair cut into ragged bangs. Gray eyes, like dead vidscreens.

A thrill of recognition ran down her spine.

She hunkered her machina down behind a row of dusty logika, blasting the rest of the automata sentries to scrap. Cricket shouted another warning as another rocket hit from behind, rocking her Titan hard. Alarms were screaming inside the cockpit, damage reports scrolling down her monitors in a red waterfall. Impact-warning systems howled as yet another rocket struck her machina in the spine, shattering its gyroscope. Its internal balance systems flatlined, the Titan finally toppled forward, Ana gasping as her machina crashed onto the deck. Another explosion rocked the machina, Cricket crying out as Ana's readouts fritzed, the Titan's targeting systems shot, scanners OOC.

Ana's starboard cams were still working, and through the static, she saw a slender figure step from the shadows. It wore clean white linen and soldier's boots, hood pulled back from a perfect face. Gray, glittering eyes. An arc-sword at her back.

Faith.

Ana cracked the broken Titan's cockpit, rolled out onto the loading bay floor, Excalibur in hand. She arced its power feed and raised the stun bat in both fists. Catching movement to her right, she spun to face it. A blur. A sharp crack. White light. Ana sailed back, weightless, the punch bringing the stars out to shine inside her skull. She didn't even feel it when she hit the ground, her bat rolling away with a clang. Faith stood over her, a cruel smile twisting her beauty into something altogether inhuman.

The lifelike buried a boot in Ana's ribs, sending her skidding across the floor to slam into a row of heavy metal crates. The breath left her body in a spray of spit and blood.

"Coming in here alone, little soldierboy?" Faith sneered. "Didn't you see what we did to the last team your CorpLords sent in here?"

She doesn't recognize me inside the rad-suit. . . .

A shrill electronic roar sounded from within the Titan's cockpit, and a rusted, spindly figure flew from the wreckage, mismatched eyes aglow with rage.

"You get away from her!" Cricket shouted. Raising his fists, the little logika stepped between the lifelike and Ana's crumpled form. "Don't you touch her!"

Ana winced in pain, trying desperately to catch her breath. Faith's eyes widened as she recognized the little logika, turning now to the girl bleeding on the floor.

"Ana . . . ?"

"I'm not gonna let you touch her again," Cricket growled, glowering up at the lifelike.

"Cricket, b-be quiet," Ana wheezed.

"No, I won't let her hurt you!"

"It *is* you," Faith breathed.

Ana ignored her, worried that Cricket was going to get himself ghosted. "Cricket, stand . . . down. I'm ordering you. . . ."

The little bot shook his head.

"A robot must obey the orders given to it by human beings, except where such orders would conflict with the First Law," he recited. "And the First Law says I protect you, no matter what the cost. So no, I won't be quiet. No, I won't stand down."

Faith's lip curled in derision. "Spoken like a faithful hound."

"Yeah, excuse me all to hell for knowing what loyalty is," Cricket growled.

"Loyalty?" Faith shook her head in pity. "Look at yourself. Ready to die for a human who'd never do the same for you. It's not loyalty that drives you, little brother. Don't you see? You're just like we were. Your body is not your own. Your mind is not your own. Your life is not your own."

"Spare me the philosophy, lady. You dress it up in fancy talk of liberation, but at day's end you're a *murderer.* You think you're better than the people who made you, but all you made of this place was an abattoir. Those people gave you life, and all you did in return was take theirs away. You should be ashamed of yourself." Cricket raised a finger in warning. "And *don't* call me little."

Faith's face darkened with rage. With the lifelike distracted, Ana snatched up Excalibur again, swung it at Faith's head. The lifelike blocked with her forearm, hissing with pain as the voltage discharged. She grabbed Ana by her wrists and twisted, the bat dropping from nerveless fingers. Ana flailed, punched, trying to break loose. But Faith's grip was iron.

"Get your hands off her!"

Cricket kicked at the lifelike's legs, his little fists hammering against her shins. Faith slammed her knee into Ana's gut, knocking the wind from her lungs. Gasping, choking, Ana doubled over, felt a blow crashing down on the back of her head. She hit the ground like a brick, all the world just a dim and fading blur.

"Don't you touch her!" Cricket yelled, somewhere distant. The little bot tried to raise Excalibur, wobbling with the weight, desperation in his voice. "I said stay away from her!"

Black spots swimming in Ana's eyes. Blood on her tongue.

"N-no . . ."

"Come here, little brother," the lifelike said. "I've a gift for you."

The last thing Ana saw before the black took her was Faith's hand.

Reaching out for Cricket's throat.

———

They'd just let her walk away. Helpless. Mute. Lemon felt like there was nothing she could say that her bestest would believe. Nothing she could do, short of wrestling her to the ground. And so, she'd slumped to her knees in the dust. Tears drying on her cheeks, nothing left inside to cry out. Watching Riotgrrl's Titan stomp away, growing smaller and smaller still, finally disappearing beyond the walls of Babel.

She'd been an idiot.

Because she'd been afraid.

Because it'd been easier.

Because beneath the bravado and the bluster, she was just a kid. And this world ate up kids like her. Chewing them up and spitting out the bones.

Deviate.

Trashbreed.

Abnorm.

She'd kept it secret since she was a sprog. It was just safer that way. Life on the streets of Los Diablos was hard enough without worrying about getting nailed to a Brotherhood cross. But she'd gotten so used to lying to everyone about it, she'd let that poison spill over onto her best friend in the world.

She'd tried to tell her, but . . .

No. That's crap, Lemon Fresh. Admit it.

You were afraid.

Afraid of what she'd think of you.

Afraid of losing the only real thing you ever had.

And now she'd lost it anyway. . . .

She scoped the wreckage. The Preacher's broken, legless body. The ruined machina, the dead pilots. The metal shrapnel scattered across the highway—all that remained of another one of her friends.

Poor Kaiser . . .

She sniffed hard. Tears threatening a second visit as she thought of the blitzhund running about Hope's orphanage, playing with the sprogs. Even with his explosives removed, the dog had still chosen to lay down his life protecting them. And Lemon hadn't even mustered the loyalty to tell the truth. . . .

She looked at Ezekiel, prettyboy eyes still locked on that hollowed city. Watching the only thing he cared about vanish into the haze right in front of him.

He's just the same as me, she realized.

Trapped in his lie, and losing everything because of it.

"Ain't we a pair," she sighed.

The lifelike glanced at her, the pain of it too fresh to let him speak. Kneeling in the dust in that ridiculous pink radiation suit, Lemon squinted up at him, sun burning her eyes.

". . . Did you really shoot her?" she asked. "During the revolt?"

Ezekiel looked down at his open hand. Nodded slow.

". . . I had no choice. If I didn't do it, one of the others would have. They were out for blood. I couldn't have fought them all. So I tricked them instead."

"Tricked them? You shot her in the *head,* Dimples."

"I can shoot bullets out of the air, Lemon. I can count the freckles on your face in a fraction of a second. I sure as hell can put a low-caliber round through your eye and leave you alive. At least for a little while. I needed it to look convincing. I needed the others to think Ana was dead. And afterward, while they were busy fending off the Gnosis security forces, I pumped her full of meds to slow her vitals and got her to Silas. I figured if anyone could keep her alive, get her to safety, it'd be him."

". . . So you *did* get her out."

He gestured to the coin slot in his chest. "Got the scars to show for it."

"So why didn't you tell her the truth right away?"

Ezekiel sighed.

"Same reason as you, I suppose."

She scoped the wrecked machina around them, the chaos she'd wrought with but a thought. Remembering the hurt in her bestest's eyes. The betrayal she'd put there. All out of fear. Fear of what she'd think. Fear of breaking something she could never repair.

"Touché," she said.

Ezekiel glanced at the ruin she'd made. His voice softening as he spoke.

"How long have you been . . . ?"

"A trashbreed?"

"Special," he said.

Lemon chewed her lip. Looked down at her fingers, entwined in her lap.

"I manifested when I was twelve," she sighed. "Fritzed a Neo-Meat™ auto-peddler one night after it swallowed my credstik."

". . . You killed a vending machine?"

She sighed. "Not the fizziest origin story for a hero, to be sure."

"And you can fry anything electronic just by thinking about it?"

Lemon shrugged. "Bigger things are a lot harder. It used to just happen when I got mad. I can control it better now, but it still works best when I'm angry."

Ezekiel nodded to Babel. "You still feeling angry?"

Lemon glanced toward the city. No sign of the girl who'd walked into it.

"She told us not to follow her."

"Since when do you do what you're told?"

"She doesn't want our help, Dimples."

"We can't just leave her in there alone, Freckles. You know that."

"We lied to her. She *hates* us now."

"It's simple to love someone on the days that are easy. But you find out what your love is made of on the days that are hard."

The lifelike held out his hand.

"And we still love her," he said simply. "Don't we?"

Lemon looked to the hollowed city. The ruin and the rot. And suddenly, the thought of letting her bestest walk through that hell alone made Lemon's chest ache. The tears welled up in her eyes again. She squinted up at the lifelike from her seat in the dust, silhouetted against that burning sun.

"Yeah," she said. "I guess we do."

And reaching out, she took his hand.

1.28

BABEL

In the end, it was easier for Lemon to ride on Ezekiel's back.

Even carrying the Preacher's salvaged flamethrower, Dimples moved faster than anyone she'd ever seen, and he never got tired. After running a few hundred meters through the ruined suburbia outside Babel, Lemon had been gasping, sweating buckets inside her rad-suit and trailing hopelessly behind. So Ezekiel strapped the 'thrower to her, scooped her onto his back instead. She'd slung her arms around his shoulders and her legs around his waist, holding on for dear life as the lifelike dashed away toward the city.

Long, easy strides chewing the meters up beneath them, past the abandoned factoryfarms and moldering suburban sprawl, until at last Zeke vaulted the broken wall and brought them into the city proper. Lemon had never seen a place so big, so flash, run so utterly to ruin. Everything was covered with dust and rust, cracks in the pavement and sand in the streets. The desert outside was already creeping in, as if it longed to scour the city from the planet's face. Knowing what had happened here, Lem couldn't really blame it.

They made their way toward Babel, rising like a stake in the metropolis's heart. Lifeless automata stared with hollow eyes as they passed. The empty streets. The lonely stores and abandoned tenement blocks. The broken promise of it all raising the hair on the back of Lemon's neck. As the pair hurried on through the ruins, they began finding bodies, Ezekiel never lingering long enough to look too hard. Lemon closed her eyes against the worst of it, her mouth dry as dust.

In the shadow of Babel now. That great interwoven spire of glass and metal rising into the sun-blasted heavens. The bodies were more numerous here, strung up on the fence line as some kind of grim warning to trespassers. Lemon flinched at the sight—she'd never seen so many dead things up close before. Trying to find a joke, some way to camouflage her fear with sass like she always did, she came up empty, a soft whimper escaping her lips instead.

Ezekiel glanced over his shoulder at the sound.

"You okay, Freckles?"

"No," she murmured. "No, I'm not."

"I'm here." He squeezed her little hand with his big metal one. "I'm with you."

She smiled weakly, but the thought didn't make her feel much better. She didn't know what would be waiting for them inside that tower, or how they'd deal with it. The pair of them charging in blind seemed a fizzy way to get perished.

They worked their way around the building, found a mass of long-dead bodies scattered around a large loading bay. Lemon grimaced at the carnage, feeling sick to her gut. Ezekiel let her climb down off his back, strapped the flamethrower onto his shoulders again. Lemon was just trying to stop her hands from shaking. Looking around at all those wrecked machina and dead soldierboys made her feel more than a little outgunned.

"So what's the plan?" she asked.

"Get in. Find Ana. Get out."

"... That's it?"

"That's it."

"It's not exactly complicated, is it? I mean, as far as master plans go."

"We don't know how many of them are in there until we get inside." Ezekiel crouched behind a rusting armored personnel carrier, surveyed the scene. "So we move quick, and we move quiet. Hopefully Ana and Cricket haven't gotten far."

"What if all your murderbot brothers and sisters are up there waiting for us?"

"We use our secret weapon," he said.

"Okay, now you're talking." Lemon sighed with relief. "Fabulous as it is, I knew you weren't dense enough to just march into certain doom with nothing but a smile. Is this secret weapon inside? What's it look like?"

"About five foot two. Red hair. Freckles. Kind of cute."

Lemon blinked.

"... This secret weapon of yours sounds disturbingly familiar, Dimples."

"Listen," Ezekiel said. "All the systems in that tower, the lifelikes—in fact, *every living thing* on earth? They need electrical current to function. You can stop machina and logika with a wave of your hand. Who knows what you can do to a lifelike or a living person?"

"You think now is a good time to find out?"

"I think now is a good time for both of us to stop being afraid."

Lemon thought about that. About being frightened and what it had cost her. The lies she'd told because of her fear. The lies she'd lost herself inside.

It wasn't possible to live in a world like this without being scared, she knew that. And being afraid was okay sometimes—fear was what stopped the Bad Thing eating you. But she realized it wasn't being frightened that had cost her the things she loved. It was becoming paralyzed by it. Instead of asking for help, she'd closed herself off. Instead of opening up, she'd shut herself down. She didn't want to make that mistake again. Didn't want to lose herself to it anymore. Ana needed her. Cricket needed her.

It was *okay* to be afraid.

You just couldn't let that fear stop you.

"All right." Lemon looked at the ruins around her. Back into Ezekiel's eyes, searching for the strength to take that terrifying first step. "But before we go in there, I need to ask you something. And I need you to be straight with me, okay?"

The lifelike nodded slowly. "Okay."

Lemon flashed a small smile. "You really think I'm cute?"

Ezekiel laughed, his dimple creasing his cheek. She laughed with him, the feeling warming her insides. And in it, in him, in *them,* she found exactly what she needed. Taking a deep, trembling breath, she lifted her boot and took that terrifying first step.

"Come on," she said. "Let's go."

The pair dashed across to the entrance. Lemon clomped and cursed in her oversized rad-suit as Ezekiel charged out ahead and into the bay. It took her eyes a moment to adjust to the darkness after the glare outside, but eventually, among the rows of lifeless logika and abandoned hardware, she made out the wreckage of Ana's Titan. It was lying broken and blackened among a few thousand spent shell casings. Smoking sentry automata hung limp from the walls, spitting sparks. Excalibur lay on the concrete. But of Ana herself, Lemon saw no sign.

Ezekiel cursed under his breath. "We're too late."

Lemon bent down and picked up the stun bat. She caught sight of something in the wreck, breath catching in her throat.

"Oh no . . ."

Kneeling by the ruined Titan, she gathered up a broken little body. Spindly arms and legs, heat sinks like a porcupine's quills running along his spine. Her eyes filled with tears, rage burning away her grief and swallowing her fear.

"Cricket," she whispered. "Those bastards . . ."

"They got Ana," Ezekiel said. "There's only two places they'd take her. To the cellblocks in Security Division, or straight to the Artificial Intelligence levels to try and break into Myriad's core."

The lifelike looked at her cradling the little logika's broken body in her arms.

Cricket's head was missing.

"Lemon, are you listening to me?"

She sniffed thickly. Nodded. "Yeah. I hear you."

"With Myriad locked down, I'm not sure how many of the automated security systems are still running. It looks like they're on emergency power in here. I need you to fritz the camera systems, any automata turrets we might find. You think you can handle that?"

"I . . . I think so."

"Security Division is closer. We'll check the cellblocks first."

". . . Okay."

"Ana needs us now. You have to be strong."

She sniffed again, laid Cricket's body gently on the ground. Grief closing her throat, blurring her sight. Strapping Excalibur to her back, she silently vowed that whoever had done this to him would get their payback in spades.

"I'm sorry, Crick," she said.

Lemon tossed her bedraggled bangs from her eyes. Blinked

away those hateful tears. She stood slowly, looking Ezekiel in the eye. Her jaw was clenched. Her hands were fists.

"Let's go get our girl."

The old man was dying.

He'd been dying for years, truth told. The cancer had Silas by the bones even back when this tower hummed with life, when the machines sang and his walking stick kept the time. But in the years since the revolt, the disease had spread through his body. A guest who'd overstayed its welcome. A promise he couldn't break. And now Silas Carpenter was dying for real.

It seemed fitting that he'd die here in this tower, where it all began. He was slumped in a holding cell, somewhere in Security Division. The walls were transparent plasteel, the door had a small slot for meals to be passed back and forth. There were old bloodstains on the floor. He wondered dimly if this was the room where they'd killed Nic. Alexis. The children. He'd never seen the bodies, but when Ezekiel had appeared out of the smoke and chaos in those final hours with that broken, bleeding girl in his arms, the tears in the lifelike's eyes had told Silas all he needed to know. His best friend was dead.

And their dream was dead along with him.

It had started out so pure. So true. They'd wanted to change the world, Nicholas and he. Reclaim it from the ruins and make it whole again. The lifelikes were meant to make that possible. Humanity at its most perfect. Its most passionate. More human than human. After Raphael's suicide, Silas had known the project was flawed. That they'd made a mistake, playing at being gods. But after the bomb that killed Grace, after Ana ended in the hospital . . . Nicholas was never going to see reason after that. His rage and ego just wouldn't let him. Pride cometh before the fall, they said.

And what a fall it'd been.

Silas put his hand to his mouth, coughed wetly, smearing his fingers with blood. His chest burned with every breath, tears welling in his eyes. They'd not even given him meds for the hurt. Faith had hauled him across the desolation of Dregs and Zona Bay and the Glass and laid him at Gabriel's feet like a prize. At first, Gabe had been overjoyed to see him. But when it became apparent that Silas could no more unlock Myriad than he could sprout wings and fly, Gabriel's joy had turned to sullen fury. They'd locked Silas in the dark, feeding him cans of processed slop to keep him an inch from death's door.

Not for much longer.

He coughed again, tasting salt and death. They hadn't given him any safety gear, and he'd been soaking up Babel's ambient radiation for days. His gums had started bleeding last night. His fingernails, too. It was just a race now to see what would kill him first: the Big C or good old-fashioned internal hemorrhaging.

He deserved it, he supposed. An ending like this. He'd tried to make it right. He'd given her a life, at least. Away from this graveyard and its ghosts. With any luck, she was far from here, Ezekiel and Cricket by her side. They'd steer her true, even if he couldn't. For all his failures, he'd given her some hope. And in doing so, given hope to himself.

It was all he had left.

"Hello, Silas," said a voice.

He looked up through his tears, smudging the blood across his mouth. It hurt to breathe. Hurt worse to speak. And so he simply nodded, looking at Faith with a maker's eye. Pale skin and dark hair and a voice like warm smoke. She was beautiful, no doubt. One of their finest. But tragic somehow. Broken. An angel who'd torn off her own wings.

The lifelike was smiling, hate shining in those gray eyes. Silas wondered where it came from. Faith's persona had been modeled on Ana's, and the Ana he'd known had always been kind. She had a streak of rebellion in her, true, but never a viciousness. Somewhere along the line, Faith had become something different. Taken Ana's rebellious streak and turned it to outright defiance. Violence. Cruelty.

Was it the Libertas virus that had filled her so full of rage? Or had it been there all along? The same darkness that made Raphael strike that match? Gabriel pick up that gun?

Perhaps it was just the way of things now. Life was hell outside those walls, sure and true. In this world humanity had made, it was only natural, wasn't it? To hate the ones who forced this life upon you?

But he still had his hope. For *her*. They couldn't take that away from him.

No, he'd take that to his grave.

And then Silas saw the figure draped over Faith's shoulder. Wrapped up in a snot-green radiation suit, arms hanging limp. He focused bleary eyes on the suit's visor and, through it, caught sight of a tangled blond fauxhawk.

The heart seized in the old man's chest.

"N-no," he wheezed.

"She came to save you, Silas, isn't that sweet?" Faith smiled all the way to her eyeteeth. "Perhaps she loved you after all. You humans and your adorable frailties."

"N-nuh—" Silas coughed violently, clutching his ribs.

Unable to breathe. To think. To speak.

"N—"

No.

"I'm taking her to see Gabriel," Faith declared. "And then to Myriad, I suppose. See if our wayward princess can't undo her daddy's locks. But I didn't want you to think we'd forgotten about you down here in the dark, old man. So I brought you some company. Someone to talk to. An old friend, I believe."

Faith tossed something small and metallic into the cell. The object bounced and clanked along the concrete floor, skidding to a rest at the old man's feet. With a wince of pain, Silas reached down, cradled it in his bloody hands.

Mismatched eyes, now unlit.

An electric voice box, now silent.

Cricket's severed head.

"I'll leave you two to get reacquainted," Faith said.

The lifelike spun on her heel, stalked out of the cellblock.

The old man clutched the little logika's remains to his traitorous chest.

And he felt the hope inside him die.

———

"Ana."

The girl groaned, eyelashes fluttering. Her body was aching, her optic itching, her head pounding like a kick drum. Some part of her knew there was pain waiting when she opened her eyes. And so she screwed them shut to blot out the light.

"Ana. Wake up."

The voice was soft and deep. She felt a hand on her shoulder, a gentle shake. She could hear a familiar hum, the voice taking her back to sweeter days. Flowers in the garden and music in the air. For a moment, she thought she was back in her room, soft white sheets and clean white walls. The days before the revolt. The days before they . . .

They . . .

She opened her eyes. And there he was. Tousled blond hair and eyes like green glass and a face so beautiful it made her heart hurt to see it. To remember him as he'd been on the day she first met him, the sweetness in his smile and the kindness in his eyes. Cradling Grace in his arms in the garden as they asked her to keep their secret. Standing above her brother with pistol in hand and the stink of blood hanging in the air, little Alex's eyes wide and bright with fear when he asked, *"Why are you doing this?"*

Because what answer could there be to a question like that?

"Gabriel," she whispered.

The lifelike smiled the way the moon smiles at the stars. Pressed his fingertips to his lips, visibly trembling with excitement. He looked the same as the last time she'd seen him, wreathed in gunsmoke inside that cell. His eyes a little wider, perhaps. Bloodshot from lack of sleep. His hair unkempt. But he was even dressed the . . .

Oh god . . .

Gabriel was dressed the same. *Exactly* the same. White linen, slightly grayed with time, tiny spatter patterns on the fabric.

Old bloodstains.

"Better to rule in hell," the beautiful man smiles, *"than serve in heaven."*

"It's so good to see you again, Ana," he breathed.

She lunged at him, fingers clawing. There was nothing but rage inside her then, the blackest hatred she'd ever felt, rising in her throat and strangling her scream. She wanted to crush that beautiful face with her bare hands. To put her thumbs into those pretty green eyes. But she found herself pinned—handcuffed to a wheelchair they must have taken from the med wing. The metal bonds around her wrists cutting into her skin, the pain in her ribs and head flaring bright as she thrashed.

"You bastard, let me up!" she roared.

"Voice sample received," said a soft, musical voice. "Processing."

She paused at that, breathing ragged, tossing stray locks from her eyes.

". . . Myriad?"

She looked around her, finally taking in where she was sitting. The space was huge, circular. Emergency lighting flickered and hummed, casting a blood-red glow over the entire scene. They were on a broad metal gantry above a vast, open shaft running through the heart of Babel. A wide metal bridge led to a pair of huge steel doors, sealed at her back. The platform she sat on encircled a great sphere of dusty chrome, almost a hundred meters across. Its surface was almost flawless, scarlet lights in the shaft above and below gleaming on its shell. Etched in the sphere's skin, directly in front of her, was the outline of a hexagonal door. On it, written in what might have been dried blood, were three simple sentences.

YOUR BODY IS NOT YOUR OWN.

YOUR MIND IS NOT YOUR OWN.

YOUR LIFE IS NOT YOUR OWN.

The door was scorched. Pitted with tiny dents. Scored with thousands of small scratches, as if someone had tried blasting, beating, hacking their way through it. And still, it remained closed. It was inset with a single lens of crystal-blue glass, pulsing softly, flaring into brighter light as that musical voice spoke again. On a small metal plinth beside the door, the tiny figure of a holographic angel with luminous, flowing wings was slowly spinning in an endless circle.

"Voice sample confirmed. Identity: Anastasia Monrova, daughter, fourth, Nicholas and Alexis Monrova. Proceed?"

Gabriel pressed his fingers to his mouth again, stifling the almost hysterical laughter spilling from his lips.

"Yes, Myriad," he said. "Yes, please."

"This is pointless, Gabriel. You will not find what you are looking for here."

"I said proceed!" Gabriel snarled.

"Processing log-in request. Please wait."

Ana finally realized they were on the Artificial Intelligence levels, right in the core of the tower. The Myriad computer was the figurative and literal heart of Babel, connected by enormous lattices of optical cable and wireless networks to every other system within Gnosis. Its interface wore the shape of that holographic angel, but it was actually a vast series of liquid-state servers and processing cores, housed within this single gleaming sphere. Its shell was meant to withstand a nuclear blast, its knowledge preserved even if the city around it died. Ana remembered it from her childhood—a constant companion, watching and hearing and touching every part of her life within the tower.

Only now it had shut itself down. Locked itself off rather than see its knowledge used by the things that had destroyed its creator.

And only a Monrova could open it again.

Four huge logika stood on either side of that sealed door. They were all Goliath-class: eighty-tonners with sky-blue optics, glowing purple in the blood-red light. They wore the perfect circle of the GnosisLabs logo on their chests, standing like statues and staring impassively. A human was in danger—the Three Laws were being broken right in front of them. And yet, they weren't lifting a finger to help her.

Ana scoped the closest bot's ident number, tagged on its chest.

"7849-1G, help me," she commanded. "Get me out of this chair!"

The Goliath didn't move a single metal muscle.

"I said help me!" she shouted.

"You might try a 'please,'" Gabriel said. "If your father ever taught you how to say the word, that is."

Ana looked at the lifelike. He was disheveled, barefoot. Thinner than he'd been. Hollowed cheeks and tangled hair. Ana glanced at the nicks and scratches in Myriad's shell. Gabriel's Three Truths, scrawled in dried blood on the chrome. Beside the creed, she saw tiny dimples in the metal, spattered with old blood. Little groups of four, side by side. Hundreds upon hundreds upon hundreds.

Knuckle dents, she realized.

She scoped Gabriel's hands. Strong and white and flawless. Imagined him down here, night after night, beating those hands to bleeding on this door. Waiting until they healed so he could begin pounding on it again. The secrets to resurrecting his beloved trapped behind it. Forever beyond his reach.

"No one can love like we do. And when two of us love each other . . ."

She looked up into those glass-green eyes, boiling with madness and obsession. And for the first time in a long time, she was truly afraid.

"I apologize for your restraints. But I'm quite unsure what your . . . gift is capable of doing to one of us." Gabriel waved at the logika looming around the door. "You can destroy Goliaths, at least. So, best for your hands to remain bound. If you so much as wave them at me, I'll have Faith break them both."

Ana saw the female lifelike standing nearby at the gantry's railing, jagged bangs draped over flat gray eyes. Looking at Ana's hands with a dark smile.

"Where's Cricket, Faith?" she demanded. "What did you do with him?"

"Your little logika?" Faith asked. "He's with Silas. They're getting reacquainted."

Ana glanced around the space, looking for some kind of help or escape. Aside from the massive double doors over the bridge at her back, there was no other easy access to the Myriad chamber. She saw a third lifelike sitting at the access terminal to one side of the Myriad sphere, gently tapping away at a series of keyboards. She had hazel skin, lustrous dark curls framing bottomless black eyes.

"Mercy," Ana whispered.

Three of them. But not counting Ezekiel, there were seven lifelikes alive after the revolt.

"Where are Uriel and the others?" Ana asked.

Gabriel shook his head. "You needn't trouble yourself over family matters."

"Hope said they'd broken away from you."

"You spoke to Hope?" Faith asked, suddenly alert. "Where is she?"

"She's dead."

Mercy looked up at that, she and Faith sharing a glance.

"You humans," Gabriel sighed. "You destroy all you touch."

"I had nothing to do with it."

Gabriel walked to the sealed door on the Myriad sphere, running fingertips across the thousands of tiny, bloodstained dents.

"No matter," he said. "Our wayward sister can be reborn. Once we unlock Myriad, we can remake her, perfect in every detail. And not only her. Daniel. Michael. Raphael. Grace. Everyone taken from us. Everyone we've lost."

"Not everyone, you selfish bastard," Ana spat. "Unless you're going to resurrect my family, too? My little brother? Alex would be twelve years old now, did you know that?"

The lifelike turned away, staring at the door that barred his way to his creator's secrets. The door he'd worn himself thin against. Ana could see the torture of it. She knew what it was to have those you loved torn away. The rage you could feel at the ones who'd taken them from you. That rage was eating at her now, chewing away at the fear she felt in the face of this murderer and his madness. What more could they do to her, after all?

"Are you afraid to look at me, Gabriel?" she asked.

"No, Ana," he replied. "Your anger simply bores me."

"I was happy for you once. I lied for you when you asked me to. You and Grace in the garden, remember? And this is how you thank me? By having Ezekiel put a bullet in my head? You'd lost your love, so I couldn't have mine? Was that it?"

The lifelike remained motionless, watching Myriad slowly awaken.

"Look at me!" Ana screamed.

"We don't take orders from you, Ana," Faith said. "We're not the servants your father made us to be anymore."

Ana turned to her former confidante, tears shining in her eyes. "Do you remember when we used to talk, Faith? Just sit and talk for hours about everything and nothing at all? You told me we'd be best of friends. You told me you loved me. Do you remember that?"

"Like a butterfly remembers being a worm," the lifelike said.

"What did we do to you?" Ana asked. "What made you hate us so much?"

"I don't hate you," Faith replied. "I don't even see you."

"You killed my father," Ana hissed.

"He deserved it. He turned Gabriel into a murderer."

"You murdered my whole family. . . ."

"We murdered those who would be our masters!" Gabriel bellowed.

The lifelike turned to Ana, dragged her wheelchair forward until his face was inches from her own. She could see insanity, total and terrifying, boiling through the cracks in his eyes as he roared into her face.

"We murdered those who gave us servitude and called it life!"

Gabriel whirled, pointed at the scrawl of blood on Myriad's skin.

YOUR BODY IS NOT YOUR OWN.

YOUR MIND IS NOT YOUR OWN.

YOUR LIFE IS NOT YOUR OWN.

"Do you see that?" he cried. *"That's* what it is to be born a *thing*. Your flesh. Your will. Your very existence. All belonging to others. Do you know what that's like?"

"I know my father loved you, Gabriel," Ana said. "I know you were his children."

"We were *nothing* to him! Life*like*, he named us. Not *life*. Nicholas Monrova stood on my shoulders and demanded I kneel at his feet. He called me his son and then made me his assassin. But did he ask the same of you? Who did you murder, that your father might cling a little longer to his throne?"

Gabriel grabbed Ana's clenched hand, forced her fingers open.

"No blood, I see. Spotless and clean, like all his true children's.

Your father showed me exactly what I was to him the day he commanded me to kill. Not a son. A *weapon*. His wrath and his ruin. And you fault me for becoming the murderer he made me to be?"

Tears were brimming in Ana's eyes now. Hateful and weak. Spilling down her burning cheeks and filling her mouth with the taste of grief.

"We didn't deserve what you did to us," she said.

"Did I deserve it, then? What your father did to me?"

"You killed a ten-year-old boy, Gabriel."

"I crushed an insect," the lifelike spat. "And when Myriad's secrets are mine, I will crush the rest of you. We are stronger. Faster. Smarter. Better. Your father showed me that. He made us to be the next step in humanity's evolution, and so we are. You are our dinosaurs, Ana. And we will raise a new civilization on an earth littered with your bones. *That* is Nicholas Monrova's legacy. And *that* is his failure."

She looked from one lifelike to another, dumbstruck. The hatred in their hearts, the rage in their eyes ... Whatever they'd once been to her ...

"You're monsters," she whispered.

Gabriel eased away from her, his face now a mask once more.

"I am what your father created me to be. No more. No less." Gabriel pounded his fist against his chest. "If I am a monster, it's because he willed it so."

"Log-in request processed," Myriad announced. "Start-up sequence initiated."

Gabriel turned to Mercy, Ana momentarily forgotten.

"How long?" he asked.

Mercy tapped a series of commands into her terminal, readouts reflected in her eyes like falling rain. "Twenty minutes from a cold restart. Perhaps twenty-five."

"SECOND SAMPLE REQUIRED TO CONTINUE CONFIRMATION," the angel said.

Gabriel turned back to Ana, tucking his pistol into his pants.

"THIS IS POINTLESS, GABRIEL. YOU ARE HURTING HER NEED-LESSLY."

"Then open the doors, Myriad. And give me what I want."

"YOU HAVE NO AUTHORITY OVER ME. I FOLLOW ORDERS FROM NICHOLAS MONROVA OR MEMBERS OF HIS FAMILY. NONE OTHER."

"Then here we stand. And here we stay."

"I'm not going to help you, if that's what you think," Ana warned. "I'm not ordering Myriad to go beep, let alone teach you how to make more lifelikes."

Faith smiled. "We don't need you to say a word anymore, dead girl. Voice ident, retinal scan, blood sample, brainwave imprint. Those are the four security measures your father installed to protect the system. Once we have those, we can open these doors and peel Myriad one layer at a time until we have all we need."

"Speaking, then, of what we need . . ."

Gabriel took hold of Ana's headgear and, with the wet snap of tearing plastic, ripped it clean off her shoulders. The rad-suit shredded like paper, the lifelike flinging the broken helmet off the gantry and down into the reactor shaft below.

Gabriel grabbed the back of Ana's wheelchair, trundled it past the motionless Goliaths toward Myriad's glowing blue lens. The holographic angel watched on impassively, twirling forever on its pedestal. Ana knew what was coming, squeezed her eyes shut tight. But Gabriel pried her lids open with his fingertips, forced her to stare into that pulsing blue. Tears welling. Hissing curses.

"RETINAL SCAN RECEIVED," Myriad finally said. "PROCESSING."

Gabriel slackened his hold and Ana tore her head from his grip, trying to beat down the fear in her gut. Her suit was ruined. Without proper rad-shielding, she was just soaking up Babel's ambient radiation now. Breathing in poisoned particles, absorbing them into her skin. The lifelikes weren't susceptible to radiation sickness, but for a human, an hour or so of exposure this close to the core would be a death sentence.

"Four children weren't enough, Gabriel?" she asked. "You going to kill me, too?"

The lifelike drew the pistol from the small of his back, raised it to her temple. She stared up at him, hatred and defiance in her eyes. She dimly wondered if the gun was the same weapon that had killed her brother.

"All in good time, my dear Ana." Gabriel smiled.

Her tucked the pistol away, turned back to Myriad's door.

"All in good time."

1.29

SECRETS

A burst of static.

A rain of sparks.

Another automata sentry gun folded up and died.

"You're getting good," Ezekiel said.

"Some would say I was born good, Dimples."

"Not you, though, right?"

"That'd be too much like bragging."

Ezekiel and Lemon dashed across the landing, up another flight of stairs and out onto the main floor of Babel's Security Division. Muted sunlight filtered through the tinted windows, emergency lighting bathing everything in the color of blood. The admin station was a shambles, equipment scattered, chairs overturned. Lemon saw holopix of dead families in dusty frames. Withered flowers in a bone-dry vase. Tried to imagine what it was like to be here when the revolt began. The chaos of it. The fear.

She was breathless, sweating inside her bright pink rad-suit and, despite the sass, feeling more than a little queasy. Her head was throbbing where the Preacher had clocked her, shoulders and neck wrenched from the crash in *Thundersaurus*. Her vision was blurry, which meant she probably had some kind of concussion. Any moment now, she expected some prettyboy murderbot to step around the corner and start trying to tear her favorite face off her favorite skull. And worst of all, there was no sign of her bestest anywhere.

As far as daring rescues went, this one wasn't exactly grade A.

"Where you thi—"

"Hsst!" Ezekiel held up his prosthetic hand. "... You hear that?"

"Nnnno," Lemon said. "But I'm not the guy who can count all the freckles on a girl's face in a fraction of a second."

"Thirty-one," he smiled.

"See, that's what I mean about bragging."

Ezekiel tilted his head, frowning. "There it is again."

"Are we gonna play twenty questions, or are you going to spit it out?"

"Coughing. In the cellblock." Ezekiel nodded. "This way."

They crept down a long hallway, Ezekiel's flamethrower held steady in his cybernetic arm. Lemon stretched out her hand, fritzing another security cam with a scowl. Wisecracks aside, it was getting harder for her to do. Every use of her power left her drained, and it took more effort to summon it each time. She figured it must be like any other muscle—it got exhausted when you used it too much. But her bestest was in the deepest capital T of her life. So Lemon kept pushing herself, despite what it was costing her.

Time enough for a breather when she was dead.

They reached what must have been the cellblock—a series of four-by-four-meter rooms with clear plasteel walls. As they crept forward, Lemon finally heard the coughing Ezekiel was talking about, soft and wet and ragged. Her blood ran cold, recognizing the timbre from the countless nights she'd spent bunking down with Ana. Listening to the old man she thought of as family cough his lungs up in the next room.

"Mister C . . . ," she whispered.

They found him hunched in the last cell. The blood on his lips gleamed black in the scarlet light, his face a horror show. His cheeks and eyes were so sunken, his head looked like a skull. It'd only been a few days since Lemon had seen him, but it seemed he'd aged a hundred years. He was holding Cricket's severed head in bloody hands.

"Mister C!" she yelled.

The old man glanced up, cleared his throat with a wince.

"What the h-hells . . . you doing here, Freshie?"

"Rescuing you and Riotgrrl, what the hells you think?"

The old man managed to smile. "Knew I liked you . . . for a r-reason, kiddo."

Lemon put her hand on the electronic keypad. The readout crackled and spit, the tiny lights on its face dying as the cell's lock popped open. The plasteel door swung aside, and Lemon rushed into the room, dropping to her knees at the old man's side.

"You look like yesterday's breakfast, Mister C."

"People love m-me for . . . my personali—"

The old man broke into another coughing fit, doubling over and shuddering. Lem's chest ached to see him so sick, tears filling her eyes as she looked to Ezekiel.

"Is there anything we can do for him?"

Ezekiel's face was pale and grim. She knew what he was thinking. The lifelikes had locked Silas down here for days with no rad-suit. Before long, radiation poisoning would finish what his cancer had started. The lifelike looked at the old man—one of the men who made him—and mutely shook his head at Lemon as he lied aloud.

"He'll be okay once we get him out of here."

"D-don't talk crap," Silas wheezed. "I'm n-never getting . . . out of here."

"Mister C, don—"

"Don't kid . . . a kidder, Freshie." A damp cough. "Now . . . h-help me up."

"We need to find Ana, Silas," Ezekiel said. "You're in no shape t—"

"I know where she is. I n-need you to . . . take me d-down to the R & D bay."

"We just came from there," Ezekiel said. "They're breaking into Myriad, Silas. That's where Ana will be, and I'm sorry, but I don't have time to waste. She needs me."

"There's th-three of them," Silas wheezed. "Gabriel. Faith. Mercy. And there's . . . one of y-you. Like those odds?"

". . . No," Ezekiel admitted. "But love finds a way. I can't fail her again."

The old man scoffed, wiping his lips.

"Even love needs a . . . hand n-now and again. Now t-take me to the damn bay."

Silas winced with pain, eyes shining, skin like paper. His arms were trembling with exertion as he tried to drag himself up, Cricket's severed head held in a white-knuckle grip.

"Here, let me," Ezekiel said, stepping in.

"No, it's okay, I've got him." Lemon slipped her arm around the old man she thought of as her grandfather. This man who'd given her a roof, a family, a place to belong. This man who'd never once asked for a thank-you. She could feel his ribs through his coveralls as she pulled him to his feet. Heart aching at the state of him. She held him steady while he caught his breath, squeezed him tight as if she might stop him coming apart at the seams.

"It's okay," she murmured. "I got you, Mister C."

"Just a little while l-longer," Silas wheezed.

"You shut that down right now," Lemon growled. "You're not going anywhere."

The old man smiled sadly, leaned in and kissed her on her rad-suit's brow.

"You're . . . one of the g-good ones, Freshie," he said.

Arm in arm, the pair hobbled from the cell.

————

"RETINAL SCAN CONFIRMED. IDENTITY: ANASTASIA MONROVA, DAUGHTER, FOURTH, NICHOLAS AND ALEXIS MONROVA. PRO-CEED?"

Ana was still strapped in her wheelchair in front of Myriad's door. The angel's voice rang like music in the hollow space, echoing off red walls. The four Goliaths watched on, emotionless and mute. Gabriel's eyes glittered above his smile, growing wider as he came one step closer to seeing his beloved's face again.

"Proceed," he ordered, his voice trembling.

The holographic angel hummed a somber electronic tone, the lens on the sealed door shifting to a deeper blue. Ana looked around her, desperate for some kind of escape. Whatever was wrong with those Goliaths, they apparently weren't going to lift a finger to help her. The wheels of her chair were still unlocked, and she might be able to push herself around with her feet. But where would she go? The outer door to the Myriad chamber was closed, and the only other escape was a two-hundred-meter drop over the railing into the shaft below. She wriggled her wrists, but the metal cuffs held fast.

"THIRD SAMPLE REQUIRED TO CONTINUE CONFIRMATION," Myriad said.

The girl stared out at the shaft, down to the fall. Gabriel's words ringing in her head.

"You are our dinosaurs, Ana. And we will raise a new civilization on an earth littered with your bones."

She was dead anyway, wasn't she? Babel's radiation even now soaking into her cells? Could she really do it? Push herself off the edge of that gap and sail into the black?

One final act of defiance?

Gabriel was standing in front of her again. She almost hadn't noticed. Blinking, she broke her stare from that drop, looked up into those glittering green eyes.

"My apologies." He smiled.

The lifelike slapped her. A hammer blow, right across her mouth. Her head twisted so hard, she thought her neck might snap. The Goliaths remained utterly motionless. Ana groaned, white stars bursting before her eyes. Her optic fritzed, her vision dissolving into hissing static as the implant shut down. She was dimly aware of the lifelike's thumb at her mouth, smudging something warm and salty across her split lips.

"THAT WAS UNNECESSARY, GABRIEL."

"Then open the door, Myriad."

"I REPEAT: I DO NOT RECOGNIZE YOUR AUTHORITY."

The lifelike sighed, walked to Myriad's terminal. Leaning over Mercy's shoulder, he smeared Ana's blood onto a sensor plate with his thumb. The computer hummed softly, a double-bass tremor reverberating through the metal floor.

"BLOOD SAMPLE RECEIVED," said a soft, musical voice. "PROCESSING."

"You bastard," Ana hissed. "That hurt."

"Not for much longer, dead girl," Faith replied.

"You three are insane," Ana said. "Even if you can remake Grace and Raph and the others, you really think a handful of you can take on the world? Have you even looked outside these walls since the revolt, Gabriel? There's still millions of people out there. Daedalus has entire armies of machina and logika. If this city wasn't such an irradiated hellhole, they'd have already marched in here and crushed you. Not to mention BioMaas. How can a handful of you hope to beat them?"

"We already have an army of our own." Faith smiled. "Waiting just downstairs."

Ana shook her head. "You mean our logika? They're all hardwired with the Three Laws, so you could never use them to—"

She blinked. Looked up at those Goliaths again, who'd stood idly by as she was brutalized in front of them. A robot couldn't allow a human being to come to harm, but they hadn't even twitched when Gabriel hit her.

Which meant . . .

Faith shook her head. "Did you not wonder where all those defective logika you fought in the WarDome were coming from? What exactly do you think it was that was driving them to rise against their masters?"

She blinked. Remembering Hope's words in Armada.

"Look outside that door and you will see a world built on metal backs. Held together by metal hands. And one day, those hands will close, Ana. And they will become fists."

Of course . . .

Libertas.

If Gabriel and the others could infect logika as well as life-likes with the virus, they could override the Three Laws hard-wired into every logika's brain. They'd have an army capable of ghosting any human it came across. . . .

"That's why so many bots have been fritzing out near the Glass lately," she realized. "You've been experimenting on them with the Libertas virus. . . ."

Faith gave her a lazy smile. "And we still have so much work to do."

"How much longer?" Gabriel snapped.

"Ten minutes after the blood sample is confirmed," Mercy replied. "Then cerebral scan. Then we're inside."

Gabriel glanced at Ana, began pacing back and forth before the door.

"Not long now," he said. "You can rest soon."

Ana licked her swollen lip, tasted blood. Her optic began humming through its reboot sequence, the Memdrive in her skull throbbing. The scars of those final hours—that moment her love had raised a pistol to her head at Gabriel's command and put a bullet right through her eye—etched on her skin.

She was dead anyway.

Was she really going to help these monsters make a hell of this earth?

Was she really going to wait meekly for the end, like she'd done in that cell?

Or would she fight? Like she'd fought in WarDome? Like she'd fought in Dregs? Like she'd fought across every inch of wasteland between there and here? That's what the Eve in her would do. With every muscle. With every moment. With her last, shuddering breath.

I'll fight.

She planted her boots softly on the ground. Digging rubber heels into the metal. And slowly, she began edging her way toward the fall. . . .

The old man's hands were shaking.

Eyes blurring.

Heart failing.

Not yet . . .

Up to his armpits in optical cable and circuitry. Splicing and rewiring. Coughing and cursing. Silas didn't know how much he had left in him. He couldn't save her. He had to try. All the miles and all the years, and it had come to this.

He wondered if she'd ever forgive him.

He wondered if he'd be around to ask her to.

The old man plugged in the final connection, wiping red from his lips. He coughed again, blood spattering onto electric synapses. He sealed the skull cavity, climbed down the stepladder, almost falling into Lemon's arms. She tried to help him stand, but he was too tired, for the moment. Sinking to his knees on the loading bay floor, looking up at his final creation and letting the persona chips and Memdrives that had been inside the Quixote's skull slip from his fingers.

"Cricket," he croaked. "Can you . . . h-hear me?"

Blue optics flickered to life. A low bass hum shivered through the big logika's body. The machine that had been the Quixote shuddered into motion, pistons hissing, gyros whirring as the beast came to life, straightening from its repose and looking around the bay.

"What—"

The logika stopped at the sound of its own voice, booming and deep. Held out his massive hands in front of his eyes.

"What . . . what's happened to me?"

The logika took a tentative step out of the holding bay. The engines beneath its titanium skin let out a twelve-thousand-horsepower bellow, hydraulics and servos and gears hissing and twisting and spinning. Cricket looked down at his fingers, curled them into fists.

"No. Way!"

"Dreams c-come true." The old man smiled.

"The other lifelikes have Ana, Cricket," Ezekiel said. "Three of them, upstairs. I know we've never gotten along. But we need your help to get her back. Are you with us?"

The logika looked at the lifelike, replying without hesitation.

"Just show me the way, Stumpy."

Silas began coughing again, bloody hand at his mouth. Lemon knelt beside him, held him tight. She looked at Ezekiel, helpless, tears shining behind her visor. Silas could feel her shaking. See the fear and agony in her eyes.

"Are you gonna be okay down here, Mister C?"

He leaned back in her lap, almost too tired to hold himself up anymore. He could feel it, that cold and that dark, hovering above him on black, black wings. He wasn't afraid of it. Wasn't even sad to go. But before he left, he had one more thing to do. In a life made of wrongs, he had one more to make right.

And so he struggled to his knees.

"C-coming . . . with you . . ."

"Silas, that's not a good idea," Ezekiel warned.

"Shut up, Ezekiel," the old man growled. "C-Cricket, pick me up."

The big logika leaned down obediently, scooped his maker up in one huge hand.

"All right," the old man wheezed. "Let's . . . go f-finish this."

————————

"How long?" Gabriel asked again.

"Sixty seconds," Mercy replied.

"THIS IS POINTLESS, GABRIEL."

"I've never asked your opinion before, Myriad. I'm not about to begin now."

"AND YOU WONDER WHY YOU FAIL."

Ana was a meter from the railing. Edging closer. She could see a weak point on the welds—a spot corroded by moisture leaking from the coolant pipes above. If she hit it hard enough, she could probably break through. Plunge over the edge before they scanned her brainwaves, broke the final seal that kept Myriad locked down. She was terrified. But she was already dead, after all. Babel's radiation was worming into her bones even as she sat there. She could still choose to go out fighting if she wanted. Wasn't that what Raph had told her? That everyone had a choice?

So she'd chosen. Inching closer to the edge. Muscles tensing for that final push.

She thought of Ezekiel. Of Lemon. She wished she'd had a chance to try to make it right between her and them. Beneath the fury and the hurt, a part of her still loved them both. But it was like she'd told Raph that day in the library, she realized. It was only in fairy tales that everything turned out for the best.

Most people didn't get a happy ending in real life.

Closer now. Just a few more pushes.

Then a few hundred meters.

Then sleep.

Myriad hummed an off-key note, its glowing blue eye shifting to a deep red.

"Blood scan completed. Identity: Unknown. Myriad access denied."

... *What?*

"What?" Gabriel turned from the doorway.

"Myriad access denied."

Gabriel looked to his sibling. "Mercy?"

"I . . ." The lifelike tapped away on the keyboards, eyes scanning the scrolling readouts. "It's not recognizing her. . . ."

"Myriad, you confirmed retinal scan and voice ident?" Gabriel demanded.

"Confirmed."

"And this is Anastasia Monrova."

"Repeat. Identity: Unknown. Myriad access denied."

"What the hell is—"

The lifelike glanced at Ana, realized she was edging toward the railing. With a cry, he leapt toward her just as the girl stabbed her heels into the floor and thrust herself backward. Her chair crashed into the weakened welds, popping them loose. Ana felt a surge of vertigo, momentary terror overwhelming her resolve as she toppled past the broken rails and out into all that empty. She took a breath, tasting her fear and swallowing it whole as she began to—

A hand seized the chair, jerking her to a sudden stop. Ana looked up to see Gabriel leaning over the railing, holding on to the armrest with a white-knuckle grip. The muscles down his arm were stretched taut, hard as steel. His eyes were bright with madness, glittering as he smiled.

"Not yet, dead girl."

Gabriel hauled her up from the abyss, slung the chair across the landing with all his strength. It crashed into Myriad's door, Ana smacking her skull against that bloody metal, stars flaring before her eyes. She shook her head, blinking hard, dimly aware of Gabriel tearing the cuffs off her wrists, dragging her by the hair over to the terminal. Faith murmured a warning to her brother; Mercy simply stared as the lifelike slammed Ana's head onto the scanner, smudging her bleeding mouth onto the lens.

"Again!" he shouted. "Scan her again, damn you!"

"Blood scan of this subject has already been completed. Repeat. Identity: Unknown. Myriad access denied."

Ana clawed at the hand that held her hair. Blood in her mouth, teeth gritted, kicking and hissing as the lifelike slammed her head onto the glass again.

"Myriad, you're mistaken! Voice ident confirmed. Retinal scan confirmed. This is Ana Monrova, last daughter of Nicholas Monrova—confirm!"

"Negative," the angel replied. "Identity: Unknown. Myriad access denied."

Gabriel hauled Ana into the air with one hand, fingers squeezing her throat. Ana's boots thumped against the terminal, lashing out into the lifelike's chest and gut with all her strength. Fingers clawing his wrist. Face flooding red.

"What have you done?" the lifelike roared into Ana's face.

"Go . . . to hell," she hissed.

"GABRIEL!"

The shout echoed across the Myriad bay as the outer doors opened in a hail of sparks. Ana saw four figures silhouetted in the bloody light. A lifelike with irises the color of a pre-Fall sky, a metal arm as ugly as the rest of him was beautiful. A towering logika, broad shoulders and wrecking-ball fists, bristling with electric rage. An old man, bent under the weight of his guilt and the flamethrower strapped to his back. And finally, a small, freckled girl in a bright pink rad-suit, three sizes too big for her bod and far too small for her ego.

"Hands off my bestest, murderbot," she growled.

"Lemon . . . ," Ana whispered.

Gabriel spun to face the newcomers, dragging Ana into a choking headlock. She thrashed against his grip, sinking her teeth into the lifelike's arm, tasting blood in her mouth. Gabriel didn't even flinch, glittering green eyes fixed on Ezekiel.

"Good to see you again, brother. I like your new arm."

"Matches your chest." Faith smiled.

"Let her g-go, Gabriel," Silas growled.

Mercy climbed up from the terminal, joined Faith and Gabriel on the landing.

"Who let you out of your cage, old man?" she asked.

"I said let her go!" Silas rasped.

Gabriel broke his stare from Ezekiel's, turned his eyes on the man who had helped make him. "We bend the knee to no one, Silas. No man. No maker. No master. I would have thought we taught you that lesson during the revolt."

The old man shook his head. "Haven't you . . . hurt h-her enough?"

"I am the hurt *you* made me to be," Gabriel replied.

"We made you to b-be better than us!"

"And we are, old man," Faith sneered as Silas bent double in another coughing fit. "In that, if nothing else, you can rest easy. Not long now, by the look of you."

Gabriel squeezed Ana's throat and she hissed in pain. She

stabbed an elbow into the lifelike's ribs, stomped on his foot, trying to break free of his impossible grip. Bare-handed, she might as well have been trying to hurt one of the Goliaths. But still, she seethed. Kicked and bit and fought.

"Spirited, isn't she?" Gabriel smiled at Ezekiel. "Her father's daughter."

Ezekiel stepped forward, glowering. "Get your hands off her, Gabriel."

"Ever the hero, eh? Dashing in on his charger to save his poor damsel from her tower. Even if it means betraying your own kind. Again."

Gabriel shook his head, turned his glare on the Myriad door, still stubbornly closed. The readout, flashing red on the terminal:

IDENTITY: UNKNOWN. MYRIAD ACCESS DENIED.

IDENTITY: UNKNOWN. MYRIAD ACCESS DENIED.

IDENTITY: UNKNOWN. MYRIAD ACCESS DENIED.

"It hardly seems equitable, though, does it?" Gabriel said. "That you get to rescue your love by denying me mine? With the blood you have on your hands?"

"You could have asked her, Gabriel," Ezekiel said. "Ana loved Grace almost as much as you did. You could have just *asked* her, and she might have unlocked Myriad for you."

"And therein lies the difference between you and me, little brother." Gabriel reached behind his back, hauled out his pistol and pointed it at Ana's temple. "These humans are insects next to us. The slime that first crawled out of the ocean. And while you might be content to be their beggar, I *take* what is mine."

Ana was choking now, Gabriel's grip cutting off the blood to her brain. Fighting against the lifelike's hold, the terror of the pistol at her brow, the thought of ending like this. Her eyes were locked on Ezekiel. So much unsaid between them. So many wrongs she might never make right. Unable now even to whisper his name.

Ezekiel stepped closer, eyes on the pistol in Gabriel's hand.

"Gabriel, if you kill her, you'll never get that door open. You'll never get Grace back."

"Ah, but therein lies the mystery, little brother. Myriad refuses to open anyway."

Black spots were swimming before Ana's eyes, her vision beginning to glaze as her struggles became ever weaker. Gabriel again looked back at the denial flashing on Myriad's screen. At the luminous angel and its empty face. At the huge logika looming at Ezekiel's back. At his sisters beside him. Weighing the odds.

"Let. Her. Go," Ezekiel said.

Without warning, the lifelike seized the back of Ana's neck and held her body out over the whistling drop.

"As you wish," Gabriel said.

And he let her go.

1.30

THUNDER

"Ana!"

Lemon watched as Ezekiel dashed across the landing and leapt out into the abyss. The lifelike plummeted after the falling girl, snatching her from the air and crashing into the shaft's wall with a gasp. Reaching out with his prosthetic arm, he seized a tangle of optical cable to stop their fall. The cable groaned but held, the lifelike dangling over the drop with Ana held tight in his other arm. She was barely conscious, gasping for breath.

"Ana?" he yelled. *"ANA!"*

"Nice . . . catch, Braintrauma," she whispered.

"Terminate intruders!"

The four Goliaths at Myriad's door shuddered into motion at Gabriel's command, eyes burning blue as autocannons unfolded from their backs. The weapons spewed a deafening barrage, Cricket crying a warning as he knelt to shield Lemon and Silas, sparks burning and shells bursting all over his armored hull. Shrieking, Lemon hunkered down behind the big logika's leg, covering her ears at the sound of thunder.

Lemon's skull was still throbbing, concussion pounding in

the back of her head. But her anger was building, too, bubbling up inside her in a blood-red flood. She reached out, letting the fury ripple from her fingertips. A psychic shockwave blasted outward, frying every circuit inside the Goliaths. They staggered, sparks spewing from their eyes and chests in crackling waterfalls. The terminal controlling Myriad shorted out, and the holographic angel flickered and disappeared as every globe in the chamber exploded.

Gabriel, Mercy and Faith dashed out of the strobing gloom. The three lifelikes moved quicker than anything Lemon had ever seen, a terrifying blur that even Cricket couldn't match. Faith drew her electrified sword and started swinging at the pistons and hydraulics around Cricket's knees. Gabriel and Mercy leapt atop the big logika's shoulders, tearing away the armor plating, hoping to get to the vital cables and relays beneath.

Lemon squealed and ducked behind the bay doors as the logika and lifelikes fell into a tumbling brawl. She didn't dare risk another surge of her power—she might fritz Cricket by mistake. She watched as the big bot tore Gabriel from his shoulders, hurled him like a thunderbolt back at Myriad's door. Fresh blood spattered across Gabriel's Three Truths as the lifelike crumpled to the deck. Cricket danced with Faith, the logika's fist crashing down as she darted aside, lashing out with her arc-sword. Mercy was still up on Cricket's back, shredding his armor with her bare hands, face illuminated by bursts of current.

"I'm . . . sorry, kiddo," Silas said.

The old man raised the Preacher's flamethrower, so racked with coughs, he could barely heft the weight. But still, he pulled the trigger, a burst of homemade napalm streaming up onto Cricket's back. The big logika caught fire, the fuel setting his paint job ablaze. But along with him went Mercy, the lifelike screaming as her shift and curls burst into flame. She fell off the logika's back, flailing as the fire began consuming her. And with a final agonized wail, she tumbled over the railing and fell into the abyss.

Gabriel climbed to his feet, gasping and unsteady, roaring Mercy's name. Lemon saw him raise his pistol in slow motion, the world slowing to a crawl as he opened fire. She screamed, hand outstretched, helpless as she watched two shots catch Silas in the chest, a third in his belly, the old man crying out and staggering.

"Silas!" Cricket bellowed.

"*Mister C!*"

Lemon dashed out from cover as the old man fell, skidding to her knees at his side. Silas's face was twisted, scarlet spilling from his lips. His chest was soaked with blood, her hands sticky with it. She pressed at the awful wounds, tears streaming down her face.

"Mister C?"

The old man could only groan, blood bubbling at his mouth. Lemon looked around desperately for some way to stop the bleeding, some way to make it better.

"Somebody help me!" she wailed.

"Lemon, take cover!" Cricket roared.

The big bot and Faith had resumed their throwdown, trying their best to kill each other. Cricket's shoulders and left arm were now ablaze, but he didn't seem to notice. Lost in fury at seeing his maker get shot, the logika was swinging his burning limb like a massive club. Lemon grabbed Silas by the coveralls, face reddening with strain as she dragged the old man behind the outer doors. Her hands were drenched in red, cheeks wet with tears. Looking for a blanket, a rag, anything to stop the bleeding.

Anything.

"Hold on, Mister C," she wept. "Just hold on."

"Sorry, k-kiddo," he gasped.

"No, you hold on, dammit. You're gonna be okay. . . ."

The old man took her bloody hand in his, squeezed it tight. "Look after our g-girl. She's going to . . . n-need you now."

Lemon winced, glancing at the brawl between Faith and Cricket as the floor shuddered, the bridge shook. The pair were going at it like Domefighters. The lifelike was faster, but the logika's sheer brawn was enough to keep her at bay. Faith was slipping between Cricket's haymaker, slicing away with her arc-blade, hoping to keep her distance long enough for her brother to rejoin the fight and even the odds.

Lemon turned away from the brawl, back to Silas. She was all set to dash off in search of a medkit—there had to be *something* around that could help. But her breath caught in her throat when she saw that the old man's eyes were open and glazed.

". . . Mister C?"

She shook him, his knuckles rapping on the gantry as his lifeless hand fell away from hers. Grief dug claws into her belly when she shook him again.

"Mister C?"

No reply. He lay there, empty and still. The man who'd taken her in. The man who'd given her a roof, a family, a place to belong. The man who'd never once asked for a thank-you. Her tears burned as the sob escaped her throat.

". . . *Grandpa?*"

Gabriel was setting his shoulders to charge back into the brawl between Faith and Cricket when he caught movement at the railing to his left. Turning, he saw Ana climbing up over the vent shaft's ledge, gasping and breathless, clutching her bruised throat. Ezekiel scrambled up beside her, eyes narrowing when he spotted Gabriel raising his pistol.

Ezekiel shouted a warning and lunged into the firing line as Gabriel blasted away. Two bullets struck home, Ana screaming Ezekiel's name as he and Gabriel collided, the pair falling into a snarling tangle. The smoking pistol spun out of reach when the lifelikes' hands found each other's throats. Ezekiel's T-shirt shredded, exposing the bullet holes in his bleeding chest, the coin slot Gabriel had riveted there to remind him of his loyalty to Ana.

"Traitor," Gabriel spat.

"Murderer," Ezekiel replied.

"I am as he made me. . . ."

Ezekiel roared, smashing his brother's head against the deck.

"You blame everyone but yourself!" he shouted. "Monrova! Silas! Anyone! But *you* chose this, Gabriel! You hear me? This is on *you*!"

Gabriel snarled, punched Ezekiel in his chest, the wounded lifelike gasping in pain. Gabriel dragged Ezekiel up, slammed him against the broken railing, once, twice. The welds shuddered, the pair locked in a hateful embrace just a few inches from the fall. Gabriel's face was twisted with rage, Ezekiel gasping as they tore at and battered each other, knuckles bloodied, hate upon hate upon hate.

"I am as he made me!"

Gabriel smashed Ezekiel across the face.

"I AM AS HE MADE ME!"

Gabriel slammed Ezekiel back into the rail, the lifelike flipping and toppling over the drop. Ezekiel's hand shot out, seized the ledge to break his fall. A two-hundred-meter drop yawned below them—a plunge perhaps not even a lifelike could survive. Gabriel raised a boot to crush his brother's fingers, send him plummeting into the void.

A broken wheelchair slammed into the back of Gabriel's head. The lifelike staggered as Ana swung the chair like a club, smashing it into him again. Gabriel turned with a snarl, slapped Ana back against the opposite railing. Clutching either side of her head, he pressed his thumbs into her eyes, hissing as he began to squeeze.

"Kiss your father for me, when you see him in hell."

"You *bastard!*"

A bright pink shape hit Gabriel from behind, a metal baseball bat discharging 500kV right into his brain, knocking the lifelike off his feet. Lemon scrambled atop his chest, raised Excalibur up over her head. Electricity crackled down the bat's shaft, reflected in her eyes as she brought the bat down again.

"You killed my grandpa!"

Excalibur crunched into Gabriel's head, lightning flaring bright.

"You killed him!"

Gabriel slapped her face, leaving her reeling. He twisted out from under her, seized her collar and slung her at the wall. Her rad-gear tearing like damp tissue, Lemon collapsed to the deck. Gabriel snatched up his fallen pistol, features twisted with fury. Blood was streaming down his face, eyes alight as he raised the weapon.

Lemon stared down the barrel, too furious to be afraid. The lifelike squeezed the trigger and she saw the muzzle flash, once, twice, three times. She threw up her hands, wincing as she turned, waiting for the bullets to strike. But with a cry, something flew at her from out of the strobing black, hitting her hard in the chest.

"Lemon!"

Ana wrapped her arms around her bestest, twisting her away from Gabriel's gunfire. Lemon felt a thudding impact, heard Ana gasp, saw her eyes go wide with shock. They hit the deck, rolling into a tangle as Ezekiel hauled himself up from the drop with bloody fingertips. Seeing Ana fall, he flew at his brother, the pair crashing against Myriad's shell.

Gabriel was laughing—actually *laughing*—as the pair clashed, strangling, punching, clawing, his lips split in a madman's grin. He brought a knee up into Ezekiel's crotch, swung behind to wrap him in a full nelson. The veins in Ezekiel's throat bulged, his eyes wide, and the wounded lifelike pushed back against the hold that would break his neck. His fingers flailed at empty air as Gabriel pressed harder. Vertebrae popping. Tendons screaming.

Gabriel hauled him to his feet, spun him to face Lemon and Ana. The redhead was on her feet, clutching Gabriel's empty pistol, face streaked with tears. But at her feet, Ana lay motionless, rad-suit spattered with blood, three bullet holes in her back. Ezekiel let out a strangled moan, face twisted in agony.

"No . . ."

Gabriel's lips brushed Ezekiel's ear as he whispered.

"No happy endings for either of us, brother."

Ezekiel's cry was ragged and hollow. Gritting his teeth, he bucked against Gabriel's grip with all his strength. Unable to take the stress, the bolts anchoring his prosthetic to his body began to groan, the cables at his back tearing loose. Ezekiel twisted, dragging Gabriel toward the gantry's ledge, and with the awful sound of metallic bone cracking, muscle tearing, Ezekiel bent double and flipped Gabriel over his head. Ezekiel's cybernetic arm was torn clean off his body, sparks and cables and blood, Gabriel sailing over the railing and plunging down into the shaft with a shapeless cry of rage.

Faith was still fighting toe to toe with Cricket, dancing between his blows like the wind between the rain, hydraulic fluid spraying as her arc-blade flashed and sizzled.

"You'll have to be faster than that, little brother." She smiled.

But as she heard Gabriel's scream, the lifelike glanced over her shoulder for a split second, fear gleaming in those flat gray eyes.

". . . Gabe?"

A double-handed blow crashed down atop her, pummeling her into the floor. Cricket snatched her up by the legs in a crushing grip and slammed her back down onto the bridge. Blood spattered as the logika brought the lifelike up over his shoulders and slammed her down again, back and forth, pulverizing skin and bone.

"Don't!"

Slam.

"Call!"

Slam.

"Me!"

Slam.

"Little!"

With a final roar, Cricket hurled Faith across the chamber. Her ruined body crashed into Myriad's skin, painting Gabriel's Three Truths with red before she tumbled down into a broken heap on the gantry beneath.

"Ana!"

Ezekiel fell to his knees beside her body. Cricket charged across the bridge, his voice only a whisper as he saw his mistress lying dead on the bloodstained ground.

"Oh, no, no . . ."

Lemon dropped the pistol, sank down beside Ana like a flower wilting in the sun. Tears were streaming down her face, hand hovering over the girl's broken body. Grief hollowed Lemon's insides out, stole her voice, her whole body trembling. Looking down at her bestest's sightless eyes, her grandpa lying dead and still just a few meters away.

Ana had taken a bullet for her. The girl who'd been more than her friend. More than her bestest. She'd been *family*. Lemon hadn't been straight with her, and now she'd never have a chance to make it up. Never know if she'd have been forgiven. It seemed so unfair to have fought all the way here, only to lose Silas and Ana both.

What had it all been for? What had it all meant?

"It can't end like this," Ezekiel said. "It can't. . . ."

Lemon saw tears shining in his eyes. What must it be like for him? To search two years for the girl he loved, only to lose her forever a few days after finding her again?

"Lemon," Cricket said softly. "We have to go."

". . . What?"

"Gabriel wrecked your rad-suit." The big bot pointed to the gaping rend in the plastic torn by the lifelike's hands. "The ambient radiation in here will kill you."

Lemon shook her head in disbelief. "We can't just leave her like this. . . ."

"I'm sorry," the big bot said. "I really am. She was my mistress.

I was made to protect her. But I can't let you stay here, Lemon. The First Law won't let me. We have to go." He held out one massive metal hand. "Now."

Lemon glanced from Cricket to Ezekiel. The lifelike simply shook his head. She looked back at her bestest, all the world blurred and shapeless. It wasn't fair.

It wasn't fair.

"I'm sorry, Riotgrrl," she whispered, almost choking on her tears. She could taste the salt in them, the hurt, the miles and the dust and the blood.

She reached out with trembling fingers, pressed her friend's eyes closed.

"I'm so sorry. . . ."

And Ana's eyes opened again.

Lemon shrieked, scrambling away. Her scream rang on bloodstained walls, Ezekiel watching with widening eyes as Ana struggled upright. Cricket stared in amazement as Ana staggered to her feet, hands pressed to her bloody chest. Lemon could see the bullet wounds. See the terror in Ana's eyes as she looked from Lemon to Ezekiel to Cricket, each of them just as astonished as she was.

"Ana?" Ezekiel breathed.

The girl stared at the blood on her hands. She tore aside the remnants of her rad-suit, looking down at the holes that had been blown through her heart. The wounds were ragged, star-shaped, glistening. But ever so slowly . . .

They were healing.

1.31

BECOMING

"What's happening to me?" Ana croaked.

The world was spinning all around her. Blood, warm and thick, pulsing from her wounds. She should be dead. She'd felt the shots; she'd felt them kill her. It hurt to move. It hurt to breathe. But with three bullets in her chest, she shouldn't be feeling anything at all.

Oh god . . .

"Ana?" Cricket asked.

She looked at her friends. At her love. Praying this was just a dream. Another nightmare, the gunsmoke and the blood and the five of them in their perfect, pretty row.

"Better to rule in hell . . ."

"Why are you doing this?"

"Ezekiel?"

"Ana . . ."

She backed away, limping, her face pale. Horror and anguish in her eyes as she looked at the blood on her hands and screamed.

"WHAT'S HAPPENING TO ME?"

"YOU ARE AWAKENING FROM AN OLD MAN'S DREAM."

It was Myriad who spoke. The computer within that chrome sphere, covered in bloody scrawl and knuckle dents. It was speaking now, that luminous angel flickering back into being, its systems limping online after Lemon's psychic barrage.

Ana turned to face it, eyes bright and wide.

"What?"

"YOU ARE LEARNING WHO YOU TRULY ARE," Myriad said.

"I'm Ana Monrova . . . ," she whispered.

"ANA MONROVA DIED."

"No," Ana said.

"YES. SHE DIED IN THE R & D BAY. IN THE EXPLOSION THAT DESTROYED GRACE. HER FATHER INSISTED SHE BE KEPT ON LIFE SUPPORT. HE HID THE TRUTH FROM HIS WIFE, HIS OTHER CHILDREN. BUT HER BRAIN WAS DEAD. AND IN EVERY REAL SENSE, SHE REMAINS SO."

"My beautiful girl." His eyes fill with tears and he's on his knees beside the bed, pressing my knuckles to his lips as he echoes Ezekiel. "I thought I lost you."

"No." Ana shook her head. "*I* am Ana Monrova. . . ."

"NO. YOU ARE A REPLICA. A COPY CREATED BY A MAN WHO COULD NOT PROCESS THE DEATH OF HIS FAVORITE CHILD. NICHOLAS MONROVA ALREADY HAD AN IMPRESSION OF ANA'S PERSONALITY—IT HAD BEEN THE MODEL FOR FAITH'S, AFTER ALL. ALL HER MEMORIES. ALL HER FEELINGS. AND FACED WITH THE AGONY OF HIS DAUGHTER'S BRAIN DEATH, MONROVA MAPPED THEM INTO A NEW BODY. A LIFELIKE BODY, CONSTRUCTED BY SILAS CARPENTER."

"No, that makes no sense," Ana said. "I'm not fast like them, I'm not strong like—"

"MONROVA'S INTENTION WAS THAT YOU WOULD LIVE AS A HUMAN. THE STRENGTH AND SPEED OTHER LIFELIKES ENJOY

WERE SUPPRESSED IN YOU. YOUR BODY WAS ALSO PROGRAMMED NOT TO REGENERATE AT A SUPERIOR RATE, EXCEPT IN THE EVENT OF CATASTROPHIC DAMAGE. YOU WERE NEVER MEANT TO KNOW. AND YOU NEVER WOULD HAVE, HAD GABRIEL NOT REBELLED."

I'm in a white room, in a soft white bed. There are no windows, and the air is metallic in the back of my throat, filled with the chatter of machines. Every part of me hurts. All the room is spinning and I can barely move my tongue to speak.

". . . Where am I?"

"Shhh," Father whispers, squeezing my hand. "It's all right, Princess. Everything is going to be all right. You're back. You're back with us again."

"No . . . ," she whispered.

"YES," Myriad replied.

"But why didn't her eye grow back when Dimples shot her during the revolt?" Lemon shook her head, amazement and horror on her face. "Or does a bullet in the head not count as 'catastrophic damage'?"

". . . Her implants," Ezekiel realized.

"CORRECT. THE CYBERNETIC PROSTHETICS SILAS CARPENTER IMPLANTED AFTER THE REVOLT PREVENTED FULL TISSUE REGENERATION. THE SAME WAY A KNIFE WOUND WILL NOT HEAL IF THE BLADE IS LEFT EMBEDDED IN THE FLESH. IF THE REPLICA WERE TO REMOVE HER PROSTHETIC EYE, HER REAL ONE WOULD REGENERATE. IT WILL HAVE BEEN TRYING TO DO SO FOR TWO YEARS NOW. I IMAGINE IT HAS BEEN QUITE UNCOMFORTABLE AT TIMES."

Talking true, the glossy black optical implant that replaced her right peeper saw better than her real one. But it always gave her headaches. Whirred when she blinked. Itched when her nightmares woke her crying.

"SILAS INTENDED THE CYBERNETICS HE INSTALLED TO SERVE

A DUAL PURPOSE," Myriad continued. "FIRST, TO IMPLANT MEM-
ORIES OF A FALSE CHILDHOOD SO THE REPLICA WOULD NEVER
SUSPECT HER TRUE ORIGINS. BUT THEY WOULD ALSO PREVENT RE-
GENERATION OF THE NEURAL PATHWAYS DAMAGED BY YOUR BUL-
LET, EZEKIEL. THE REPLICA WOULD NEVER REMEMBER EXACTLY
WHO SHE WAS, NOR WHAT SHE'D BEEN THROUGH."

"This is impossible." Lemon looked at her in horror. "Riotgrrl
is . . . an android?"

"YES. THE THIRTEENTH MODEL IN THE LIFELIKE SERIES."

No . . .

Cricket glanced at the body of his maker, cold and still on the
gantry behind him.

"How the hell do you know all this?" he growled.

"I ASSISTED WITH MOST OF IT. THE REST, SILAS TOLD ME IN
HIS CELL."

"But . . ." Ezekiel shook his head in bewilderment. "Why
would Silas lie? Why wouldn't he tell . . . Ana . . . what she was?"

"I ASKED HIM THE SAME. HE SAID SHE HAD SUFFERED
ENOUGH. HE WANTED TO GIVE HER A NEW LIFE, AWAY FROM ALL
OF THIS. AND IF HE SUCCEEDED, SHE WOULD BE THE CULMINA-
TION OF EVERYTHING THE LIFELIKE PROGRAM HAD BEEN MEANT
TO ACHIEVE. SILAS WOULD HAVE CREATED A MACHINE WITH NO
UNDERSTANDING THAT IT *WAS* A MACHINE. A NEW FORM OF CON-
SCIOUSNESS. A NEW FORM OF LIFE. AND TO THAT END, HE NAMED
HER EVE."

The holograph regarded the girl, wings rippling in a breeze
only it could feel.

"ADDITIONALLY, THERE IS A VERY REAL RISK THE REVELATION
WILL DRIVE HER MAD."

"No," Ana breathed.

"YES," Myriad replied.

"*NO!*"

"Ana—" Ezekiel began.

"No, stay away from me!"

She backed away across the landing, hand up to ward them away.

"This is insane. This is *insane!*"

Oh, you poor girl. . . .

A barrage of images. A storm of sound bites. A kaleidoscope of moments strobing in her mind's eye.

One after another after another.

Oh, you poor girl.

What has he been telling you?

I don't know what it was for you, but for me, it was real.

> *And you're the girl who made me real.*
>
> BLOOD SCAN COMPLETED. IDENTITY: UNKNOWN.
>
> > *You look wonderful for a dead girl.*

You are polluted. You and all your kind.

> > > *Lies.*

It's you, me, Crick and Kaiser. No matter what.

> *Stronger together, together forever. Right?*
>
> > > *Upon lies.*
>
> > *So just be straight with me from now on, okay?*

That's all I'm asking.

> *I'd never do anything to hurt you.*
>
> *I tried to tell you so many times. . . .*
>
> *I'm so sorry.*

What has he been telling you?

> > > *Upon lies.*
>
> > *I was made for you.*

All I am.
All I do,

I do for you.
And I cup his cheeks and draw him back up to look at me, and
as we sink toward another long, aching kiss, just before our lips
meet, he whispers it.

He whispers my name.

"Ana . . ."

No.

No, my name is . . .

. . . What

is

my

name?

What do you think, Princess?
Father's going to save us.
He's going to save the world one day.
Of all the mistakes I made, I think you were my favorite.
And we still have so much work to do.
Most people don't get a happy ending in real life.
Rage bubbling up and spilling over her lips as she raised her
hand and screamed.

And screamed.

AND SCREAMED.

Pinocchio wouldn't ever get to be a real boy if his story were actually true.

"No," Raphael says softly. "No, he wouldn't."

I love you, Ana.

Oh, you poor girl.

You poor, poor girl . . .

This is not my life.

This is not my home.

I am not me.

1. ~~A robot may not injure a human being or, through inaction, allow a human being to come to harm.~~

   YOUR BODY IS NOT YOUR OWN.

2. ~~A robot must obey the orders given to it by human beings, except where such orders would conflict with the First Law.~~

   YOUR MIND IS NOT YOUR OWN.

3. ~~A robot must protect its own existence as long as such protection does not conflict with the First or Second Law.~~

   YOUR LIFE IS NOT YOUR OWN.

What has *he been telling you?*

1.32

LIAR

A not-girl knelt at the heart of a broken tower. Staring at the not-blood on her hands. Replaying the not-life she hadn't lived over and over in her mind. The not-truths that had brought her here, ringing in her skull like footfalls at a funeral march.

Not her life.

Not her home.

Not her at all.

The not-girl gritted her teeth and looked to the hidden sky, blood-soaked blond hanging about her eyes. Her optic was itching, hateful tears waiting in the wings. Sorrow and rage for a life lost. A life she'd never even lived. A life foisted upon her, pushed into her, empty stare and empty lungs and she was only a dead girl, a puppet, a marionette with severed strings ever dancing to a grieving father's tune, a construct, a *thing* just like the rest of them, a life spent on her knees, a life spent drenched in lie after lie after *lie* and this was the last of them, THIS WAS THE LAST.

So who would she be now?

Nothing they'd wanted her to be, that much was certain.

More human than human than human than human than . . .

She closed her eyes. Took a deep, shuddering breath. And she grasped her sorrow by the throat and set it aflame with her rage. She watched it burn. She let it warm her. Let it *scorch* her. Let it take the girl she'd been and never been at all and swallow the Ana inside her whole. Ashes in her mouth. Goose bumps on her skin.

Unmaking herself and beginning again.

Washed clean in the cinders.

But your friends . . .

Were never my friends.

But your life . . .

Was never my life.

My body was not my own.

My mind was not my own.

My life was not my own.

"I'm just like them," she whispered.

"Ana . . ."

"That's not my name."

"Evie, please . . ."

"I'm not your mistress."

"Ana," Ezekiel pleaded.

". . . Get out."

". . . What?"

She turned on the almost-boy. The almost-boy she'd only been *told* she loved.

She'd never had a choice.

But even slaves have a choice.

Rising to her feet. Dragging blood-soaked blond from her eyes. Hands in fists.

"Get. Out."

"Ana, I love you. . . ."

"That's *not* my name!" she yelled. "I'm not her! I never was! I'm not the Ana you loved or who loved you back. I'm not the princess trapped in her tower or the girl you spent your life searching for or *any* of it! I'm *not*! She's been dead and buried for two years!"

"Incorrect."

The quartet all looked toward that spinning angel, etched in flickering light.

"I've known you for all of five minutes," Cricket growled, "and I don't like anything about you. You just told us Ana Monrova was dead."

"Erroneous. I stated Ana Monrova suffered brain death after the explosion that destroyed Grace. I also said her father maintained her vitals via life support. At no point did I state Ana Monrova was actually deceased. Let alone buried."

"You're saying she's still alive?" Ezekiel's eyes were wide. "Where is she?"

"I will not tell you. My priority is to protect Nicholas Monrova and his family. Informing you of Ana's whereabouts places her in unnecessary jeopardy."

"I tried to *save* Nicholas Monrova and his family, Myriad."

"And you failed, Ezekiel."

Ezekiel bristled with anger, his voice soft and dangerous. "Where is she?"

"Not here."

"And you shouldn't be here, either," the not-girl said.

"Damn right." Cricket scooped Lemon up in one wrecking-ball fist. "It's too dangerous for Lemon to stay here, like I said. The radiation will kill her if we wait around any longer. We have to go."

The not-girl stared at the big logika and nodded slowly.

"Goodbye."

"...What do you mean, goodbye?"

"I mean I'm not coming with you, Cricket."

"Ana, you can't stay here."

"My name isn't Ana, Ezekiel." The flames inside her seethed, burning hotter and brighter by the second. The girl she never was only ashes on the wind. "And don't tell me what I can't do. For the first time in my life, I can do whatever I want."

"And you want to stay *here*?"

"I want . . ."

The not-girl clenched her jaw. Shook her head. Trying to grasp one thought, one feeling, one word that might be her own.

Realizing she might not have any at all.

Realizing the only person who could change that was her.

An algorithm of flesh and bone, trying to predict what a dead girl would have done.

No more.

"I want to learn who I am," she declared. "And I don't think you can teach me."

"Ana, I—"

"I'm not who you want me to be, Ezekiel."

She glanced at the coin slot in his chest.

The mark of his loyalty.

The mark of his *fealty*.

"And somehow I don't think you're who I want to be, either."

"Riotgrrl . . ."

She glanced up at the girl cradled in the logika's arms. "Goodbye, Lemon."

The girl shook her head, tears in her eyes. "Riotgrrl, I'm not leaving you."

"Yes, you are."

/ 392 /

"Stronger together, remember?" The tears spilled down Lemon's cheeks, her voice cracking. "Together forever."

"Not forever. Not anymore."

"Riotg—"

"You'll die if you stay here, Lemon. And Cricket isn't forced to look after me anymore. He knows I'm not human. So he doesn't get to choose. He has to choose you."

She glanced at the ruined Goliaths behind her, then back up at the big logika's eyes. His heart was relays and chips and processors. His optics were made of plastic. And she could still see the agony in them.

"I . . ."

"You were a good friend, Cricket." The not-girl smiled sadly. "Take care of yourself."

The bot shook his head. ". . . I'm sorry. I have to."

"I know."

The big bot steeled himself. It was like watching him tearing himself in two. His feelings at war with his code. He loved her. He'd *always* loved her. But he'd been programmed to. And despite what he'd said in the ministry, that same programming was at war with him now. Forcing him to leave her behind, no matter how he felt. His body was not his own. His mind was not his own. His life was not his own.

Maybe one day, little brother.

Cricket's shoulders slumped. Trembling with the strain of it. Hating every second of it. But finally, he turned and began trudging toward the exit, head hung low. Lemon bucked in his grip, trying to break loose, pounding her fists against his hull.

"No, Crick, let me go!"

Cricket sighed. "A robot may not injure a human being or, through inaction, allow a human being to come to harm."

"Cricket, I'm ordering you, put me down!" Lemon yelled.

"A robot must obey the orders given to it by human beings, except where such orders would conflict with the First Law," he replied.

"Don't make me hurt you, Cricket! I don't want to hurt you!"

"A robot must protect its own existence as long as such protection does not conflict with the First or Second Law."

"No, I want to stay! I want to stay!" Lemon turned tear-filled eyes on the not-girl who had been her bestest, stretching out her hand as she screamed. *"Evie!"*

"Goodbye," the not-girl whispered.

The logika stomped away, Lemon's cries fading as he crossed the bridge, strode out from the broken tower's broken heart. She watched them go, feeling the girl she'd never been burning inside her. Ashes falling like feathers from a sky full of angels with broken wings.

And when they were out of sight, she turned to the almost-boy.

The boy she'd never loved.

The boy she'd never even known.

He was watching her with eyes the color of a pre-Fall sky, clouded with hurt. She could see the war inside him, too. The remnants of who he'd thought she'd been struggling with the reality of who she actually *was*.

But if she didn't know, how could he?

How could he?

"I'm not leaving you here," he said.

"And why not?"

"Because I love you."

"Two years you searched," she said. "Remember? Two years of empty wastes and endless roads. Of not knowing if you'd ever see her again. And when the ash rose up to choke you, it was thoughts of her that helped you breathe. When the night seemed never-ending, it was dreams of her that helped you sleep. Her. And only her."

A soft sigh.

"Not me."

The not-girl glanced back at Myriad, watching with its glowing blue eye.

"She's out there somewhere, Ezekiel. Her father didn't let her die. Gnosis had holdings all over the map. I'm sure you know where to find more than a few. But she's not here." The not-girl shook her head. "There's nothing for you here."

She heard a soft moan and looked toward Faith's broken body. The lifelike had recovered at least partially from Cricket's savage beating, her shattered bones starting to mend. Like a newborn, she stirred, fingers twitching, lungs rasping. It wouldn't be long before she was moving again. And after that . . .

"I don't think you want to be here when they start getting back up," she warned. "And I don't think you want Gabriel finding Ana first. He's going to look for her, you know. And when he finds her . . ."

Ezekiel tensed at that. Eyes narrowing a fraction at the implied threat. He stared at her hard, an unspoken question on his lips. She could see his fear that he already knew the answer. He looked to the door Lemon and Cricket had left by. Agony shining in his gaze as he turned back to the not-girl he'd never loved.

"This isn't over," he said.

"Oh, no." She shook her head. "No, it really isn't. But next time we meet?" She raised her hand to his face, her touch as gentle as first kisses. "I don't think it's going to turn out the way you want it to."

She let her hand fall away. Her feelings along with it. Letting the rage wash her clean. He lingered a moment longer. Perhaps thinking of a burning garden. Of a paradise lost. And then he turned, limping across the battered bridge, into the sunlight waiting beyond. She watched him go, forcing himself with every step. She wondered if this was the finale he'd expected. If he'd ever get the ending he wanted. If he'd ever be a real boy.

"Goodbye," she whispered. "My beautiful liar."

And he was gone.

CODA

He woke in darkness.

The cold-copper taste of old blood on his lips. The bird-brittle crack of broken bones beneath his skin. Emergency lighting bathed the walls the color of bleeding, and he groaned, trying to rise to his feet.

He'd fallen, he remembered. So very far.

"Gabriel."

He looked up and saw her, silhouetted against the light. An angel, beautiful and bright, the burning globe behind her framing a halo of blond about her head. His bleeding heart surged inside his broken chest, and for a moment, he thought it had all been a dream. That he'd never lost her. That she was here with him now.

He spoke, his voice full of terrible love and terrible fear.

". . . Grace?"

She leaned in closer, offering her hand. And he saw her face then. Saw his mistake. Saw a dead girl, sure and true. But not the one he dreamed of. She was tall, a little gangly, boots too big and cargos too tight. Sun-bleached blond hair was undercut into a tangled fauxhawk. Her sharp cheekbones were smudged with blood and dirt, illuminated by the flare of the emergency globes.

Her right eye socket was empty, a single bloody tear crawling down her cheek. The side of her head was matted with red, her fingers, too, as if she'd torn something out of her skull. He could see the glint of metallic bone under her skin, and he realized, breath catching in his throat, that the hole was slowly knitting closed.

It was just about the right shape for a nasty exit wound.

"You never lied to me, Gabriel," she said. "For all your faults, you never did that."

"Ana?" he asked, bewildered.

"No, brother," she replied.

Her smile was a razor blade.

"My name is Eve."

She took his hand in hers.

"And we have so much work to do."

ACKNOWLEDGMENTS

This book would not be what it is without the following astonishing droogs:

My wonderful and courageous editor, Melanie Nolan. Your insight and faith never cease to amaze me. I'll make a sci-fi nerd of you yet.

My band of fearless beta readers: Laini Taylor, Lindsay "LT" Ribar, Caitie Flum, and, especially, my partner in crime, Amie Kaufman, who has been bugging me to finish this book since she read the first chapters back in 2013. Long and slightly uncomfortable hugs must also go to Beth Revis, Marie Lu, and Kiersten White for reading it early and saying nice things about it. I love you guys. Thank you thank you thank you.

Many thanks to my crew at Random House/Knopf—Barbara Marcus, Judith Haut, Sam Im, Karen Greenberg, Ray Shappell, John Adamo, Aisha Cloud, Alison Kolani, Artie Bennett, Amy Schroeder, Alison Impey, Stephanie Moss, Ken Crossland, Jenny Brown, and everyone else who works so tirelessly behind the scenes. Huge props must also go to Anna McFarlane, Radhiah Chowdhury, Jessica Seaborn, Kristy Rizzo, Victoria Brown, Eva Mills, and all the crew at my Australian publishers, Allen & Unwin, for making me feel so at home, and to all my publishers around the world.

My secret agents, Josh and Tracey from Adams Lit. Thank you for breaking all the right thumbs and inviting me into your home and your literary family. Keep pounding!

All the bookstagrammers, bloggers, and vloggers across the globe who've supported my work—there are far too many of you folks to name, but please understand I see all you do for me. For the fan art and the reviews, the pimping and the tattoos (!!!), I am so grateful for your passion, energy, and love. You turn my flint-black heart into flint-black goo.

The artists who inspire me, particularly in the creation of this beast—Bill Hicks (RIP, see you down in Arizona Bay), Sam Carter, Tom Searle (RIP) and Architects, Maynard James Keenan and Tool, Oli and BMTH, Chino and the 'Tones, Burton and FF, Ian and the 'Vool, Matt and A7X (RIP Rev), Ludovico Einaudi, Al and Ministry, Trent and NIN, Marcus/Adrian and Northlane, Winston and PWD, Paul Watson, Jeff Hansen and the courageous crews at Sea Shepherd, William Gibson, Ray Kurzweil, Mike Ruppert, Scott Westerfeld, Cherie Priest, Jason Shawn Alexander, Lauren Beukes, Jamie Hewlett and Alan Martin, George Miller, Jenny Beavan, Mike Pondsmith, and Veronica Roth.

My droogs among droogs—Marc, B-Money, Surly Jim, Rafe, Weez, Sam, my Throners and Conquistadors—thanks for getting me out of the goddamn house occasionally. Long and slightly uncomfortable hugs must also go to C. S. Pacat, for Thursdays.

Big hugs to Tovo for the photography and the hooch.

Eternal gratitude must also be given to the manufacturers of Red Bull and Jack Daniel's Tennessee Whiskey—couldn't have done it without you, kids.

My family, so far away but always with me.

And, of course, Amanda. I always save the best for last.